RIVER OF DESTINY

A historian by training, Barbara Erskine is the author
of twelve bestselling novels and three collections of
short stories that demonstrate her interest in both
history and the supernatural. *Lady of Hay,* her first
novel, has now sold over three million copies world-
wide. She lives with her family in an ancient manor
house near Colchester, and a cottage near Hay-on-Wye.

For more information, visit her website,
www.barbaraerskine.com.

BARBARA ERSKINE

River of Destiny

HARPER

While some of the events and characters are based on historical incidents and figures, this novel is entirely a work of fiction.

Harper
An Imprint of HarperCollins*Publishers*
77–85 Fulham Palace Road,
Hammersmith, London W6 8JB

www.harpercollins.co.uk

This paperback edition 2013

5

A catalogue record for this book
is available from the British Library

ISBN: 9780007302321

Typeset in Meridien by Palimpsest Book Production Limited,
Falkirk, Stirlingshire

Printed and bound in Great Britain by
Clays Ltd, St Ives plc

MIX
Paper from
responsible sources
FSC C007454
www.fsc.org

FSC™ is a non-profit international organisation established to promote
the responsible management of the world's forests.
Products carrying the FSC label are independently certified
to assure consumers that they come from forests that are managed
to meet the social, economic and ecological needs of present and future
generations, and other controlled sources.

Find out more about HarperCollins and the environment at
www.harpercollins.co.uk/green

For Jon, who keeps the wheels on the wagon

. . . rich swords lay . . . eaten with rust, as they had lain buried in the bosom of the earth for a thousand years . . . the princes who placed their treasure there had pronounced a solemn curse on it which was to last until doomsday: that whoever rifled the place should be guilty of sin, shut up in dwelling-places of devils, bound in bonds of hell, and tormented with evil . . .

Beowulf

Prologue

The woman was watching, flattened against the wall of the house, her eye to a knothole. She hardly dared breathe as she watched the scene unfolding inside.

With the kiss of steam wreathing round the blade, her husband raised his hammer and struck sparks from the iron. The forge was hot from the blazing charcoal and sweat dripped into his eyes. Even she, his wife, could sense his power, sense the magic he was creating as he conjured the alchemy of metal and fire.

'Is it ready?' The thegn's reeve, Hrotgar, stood in the doorway, his huge bulk blocking out the light.

'Not until the gods say so,' Eric said curtly.

'The gods!' Hrotgar echoed wryly. 'Maybe the gods see no need to hurry, but everyone in this village sees clearly why Lord Egbert is so anxious for it.'

'Tell him he'll have to wait.' Eric didn't bother to look up. He could picture the shocked anger on the other man's face. He bent back to his task, his tongue between his teeth, a soundless whistle drowned by the hiss of the fire. At his feet the flames reflected in the deep iron-bound yew-wood bucket

1

of water. Like most of the tools in the forge he had made it himself. 'You're blocking my light,' he yelled suddenly. 'Get out of here. When it's ready I'll tell you.'

For a moment Hrotgar hesitated, then with an angry growl he stepped outside and disappeared. The forge was lit by torches thrust into brackets on the wall, by the red glow of the furnace, but even so, the sudden low shaft of sunlight through the doorway illuminated the dark corners and spun reflections off the blade. Eric gave a grunt of satisfaction. The magic was growing stronger.

'Eric?' The voice behind him was tentative. 'It is true, you are making Lord Egbert angry with your delays.'

'Go away, Edith!' Eric spun round furiously. 'Out! Now!' Her very presence was weakening. He could sense the carefully built tension in the blade wavering. He could sense it in the air. Only warriors could come near the sword now, new born as it was, in its birthing pangs of fire and water. He muttered the sacred charms, feeling the vibrating waves of Wyrd settle. He wasn't sure how he knew what to do but the smith's magical art was in his blood, in the memory of his veins and bones, handed down to him by his father and his father's father going back into the mists of time. Through that memory he knew the sorcerer was right. There was no place for a woman in the forge or in his bed while he was creating this particular weapon. He had called it Destiny Maker and it was his greatest challenge.

Outside, Hrotgar was standing staring down towards the river, shading his eyes with his hand against the glare of sunlight on the water. Behind him the villagers went about their business calmly stacking the storehouses against the coming winter.

'Is the Lord Egbert improving?' Edith had come up behind him silently, her shoes making no sound on the scatter of bright autumn leaves. For a moment he didn't answer and she nodded sadly. 'Will he live?'

His jaw tightened fractionally. 'If it is God's will.'

The thegn was a comparatively young man, strong, in his prime, but a month ago he had fallen ill and before the shocked eyes of his followers and his family he had begun to waste away, racked by fever and pain. Hrotgar glanced down at her. She was beautiful, the smith's wife. Her long fair hair, plaited into a rope which hung to her slender waist, had broken free of its binding and blew in soft curls around her temples. He felt a quick surge of desire and sternly dismissed it. This was forbidden territory. He looked away, narrowing his eyes as she scanned the river. The sun was almost gone, the last dazzling rays turning the water red as blood. He shivered as the thought hung for a moment in his mind. Then his expression cleared. A fishing boat was rounding the bend, the slender prow breaking up the crimson ripples, turning the wavelets to gold. He smiled grimly as a breeze swept up the river and threw spray across the men bending to their nets, hauling them up on deck.

'Try and make him hurry,' he said at last. 'The thegn wants, needs, that sword.'

'You know I can't go near him,' she retorted. 'It is forbidden.'

He looked at her quickly and then back at the river. 'I know what is forbidden,' he said quietly.

Neither spoke for a long time, both watching the fishermen with exaggerated concentration. At last she stepped away from him. 'I have to go.'

'To an empty house?'

'To an empty house,' she echoed.

He watched her as she retraced her steps across the hard-baked ground. In another day or so the rain would come. He could smell it in the air, and this place would become a quagmire. Further up the hill the thegn's house and the great mead hall were on quick-draining soil on the edge of the heath. They would stay reasonably dry, at least for the time being. He sighed. For how long would it stay so quiet, so calm? As the thegn's health failed so the restlessness had grown. The warriors were watching, waiting, his brother and his two sons keeping their counsel; the brother, Oswald, was hungry, the sons, Oswy and Alfred, too young yet to do more than hope and strut and dream. He glanced up at a flight of birds heading up from the river, arrow straight towards the thegn's hall. Gulls. White winged. No sinister message there.

In the age of the Anglo-Saxons it is the year AD 865

In the age of Queen Victoria it is AD 1865

And it is today . . .

1

The river was thick with mist. It lay like a soft white muffler on the water between the trees, hiding the mud banks and the lower woods. Above, where the cluster of old barns stood on the edge of the fields, brilliant sunshine touched gold into the autumnal leaves, still holding some of the warmth of summer. Zoë Lloyd was standing at the kitchen sink of the oldest and to her mind the most beautiful of the three barn conversions, gazing out of the window down through the trees towards the river. She shivered. The room had grown suddenly cold in spite of the sunlight. A huge sail had appeared, hazy in the fog, sailing slowly up-river towards Woodbridge. It was curved, cross-rigged, straining before the wind, decorated with some sort of image; she couldn't quite see it behind the trees. She watched it for several seconds. There was no wind, surely; it had to be moving under power. If she were outside she would probably be able to hear the steady purr of an engine. She gazed at the trees, which were motionless, and then back at the sail. The mist was thickening, wrapping itself ever more densely over the river. In a moment the vessel would be out of sight.

'It's there again. The Viking ship. Look, Ken,' she said over her shoulder to her husband.

There was no reply and she turned with a sudden stab of panic. The kitchen was empty. But she had heard him seconds before, felt him, sensed him behind her, sitting at the table in the sunshine. She looked at the empty chair, the unopened newspaper and she groped with shaking hands for her phone. 'Ken? Where are you?'

'Still down here on the boat.' The voice broke up with a crackle. 'Did you want something special?'

'No.' For a moment she wondered if she were going mad. 'Ken? Did you see it? The Viking ship going up-river. It must have gone right past you.'

'I didn't see anything. The fog is thick as porridge down here on the water!'

'OK. Don't worry. See you soon.' She switched off the phone and slowly put it down. Of course he hadn't seen anything. Out on their boat on the mooring, with his head no doubt down in the engine compartment as he tinkered with the motor, he wouldn't have seen or heard the entire Seventh Fleet. Glancing out, she saw that the sail had gone. Rays of sunlight were slowly breaking up the mist. Her momentary panic was subsiding.

It was a couple of minutes later as she hung up the dish-cloth and turned to walk through into the high-beamed living space which formed the greater part of the building that she paused and looked back into the kitchen, which had been constructed in what had once been a side aisle of the barn. The house was empty. There was no one there. If Ken had not been sitting in the chair at the table behind her, who had?

It was barely three months since they had moved into the barn conversion overlooking the River Deben in Suffolk. Part of a group of medieval barns, theirs, somewhat prosaically

8

known as The Old Barn, was the closest to the river. Below them the ground fell away steeply across mown lawns and through a narrow strip of woodland towards the water. Looking through the huge picture window to her left, Zoë watched as a small yacht appeared, moving steadily upstream towards Woodbridge, the morning sunlight reflecting through the trees onto the gently curved sails. The mist had lifted as suddenly as, in the evening, it would probably return. It was moments like this which reassured her that they had done the right thing in moving to the country. The view was utterly beautiful.

It had all happened in such a rush. They had been sitting late over dinner with some friends in London, just after Christmas, discussing their mutual plans for the summer. Both couples were childless and Zoë sometimes wondered if that wasn't one of the main things that held them together. 'We're not having a holiday this year,' John Danvers had announced. He and Ken had been at school together some twenty-five years earlier and there was still an edge of competitiveness between them which their respective wives alternately ignored and gently mocked. 'We're moving out of town. Can't stand the pressure any more. And anyway, why not? What's keeping us? With fast broadband we can work from anywhere. We're going down to Sussex. Just think of it, Ken. Sailing every evening if we want to, no traffic jams, no rushing down at dawn on Saturdays and crawling back into town on Sunday evenings. Just fresh air all the time.'

Sussex. Chichester harbour, where both couples kept their boats, moored near Bosham. Looking at Ken's face, Zoë had felt a sudden sick foreboding deep in her gut. Their base was London. She loved London, she adored their life there. She enjoyed her job. Although they had often sailed together as a foursome and Zoë did enjoy it on a relatively calm day when the others were there, sailing was not her thing.

Zoë's relationship with her husband's passion for sailing

was complex and slightly ambiguous. She enjoyed being in the boat. She loved pottering about at the anchorage and often found herself wishing she had a suitable hobby, sketching perhaps, or bird watching, to employ her while Ken endlessly played with his boat's engine or the rigging or the sails. Her enthusiasm dimmed somewhat, however, once they cast off the mooring and headed out into the open water. It had taken her a long time to realise it but finally on one of their voyages out of the harbour and into the choppy seas of the Solent she had forced herself to acknowledge the fact that she was scared. When the boat was gently heeling before the wind, with the ripple of water creaming under the bow, she was perfectly happy, but the moment something happened – the wind changed, the boom swung over, the sails momentarily thundered and snapped, the speed increased – she began to feel nervous. She didn't like the unpredictability, the sudden veering, the water lapping dangerously close to the rail. And here, on the Deben, there was something else; for all its beauty and comparative calmness in good weather, the river under cloud and rain and mist had a thick opacity which frightened her; inexplicably it seemed deeper and more sinister and far more dangerous than the seas and harbours of the south.

Because of her discomfort it became the usual practice, more often than not, that Ken would sail on his own or with John, or occasionally with someone else as crew, while she and John's wife, Amanda, would take the car and retreat to Chichester and the Sussex hinterland in the quest for antiques and picture galleries and soft country villages out of the reach of the stinging salt air of the coast. She had come to love Sussex, but not as a full-time home, centred on sailing, no.

There was no point in arguing. There never was. In the wake of Ken's enthusiasm and determination she was swept away like some helpless duckling in the wake of a passing speedboat and he had convinced her that she too wanted more than anything to leave London with all its noise and pollution and crowds. It was not as though they hadn't discussed it before. They had. And now, he insisted, was the time to invest in the country.

As it turned out, he agreed with her that they couldn't go south. Not to the same place as John and Amanda. Of course not. That would be too obvious. Nevertheless, their flat was put up for sale, and within weeks was under offer and a decision was made on the strength of the property pages in a couple of Sunday papers. Suffolk was the county Ken favoured. Far enough away from London for the property to be good value, but not so far he couldn't get on a train and be there in less than two hours. Beautiful, unspoiled, far less crowded than Sussex. It was worth some exploratory visits, he told her, nothing for certain, just look, just test the water, and she had agreed, had gone along with it. Why? Why had she given in so easily? It was only now, from time to time, that she asked herself this. Was it that she was too tired to argue, or was she also, at base, tired of London, and therefore, following the axiom of Samuel Johnson, tired of life? They had spent just four weekends house hunting, and viewed the barn conversion in March. He had fallen in love with it on that first viewing.

That had been her chance, the moment she could have said no. She hadn't. Instead, she had felt two emotions, she realised later, one a faint stirring of excitement, the other a strange sense that some unavoidable fate was reeling them in. And there was another reason for coming to Suffolk, a reason Zoë barely acknowledged, wasn't sure about, had never been able to prove. Anya. It would remove Ken from Anya's orbit: 'A wife always knows,' Amanda had said to her once, when Zoë reluctantly had confided her suspicions.

'But I don't know, that's the point,' Zoë had replied, frustrated. 'I don't even know her name for sure. One of his colleagues mentioned someone called Anya once and I remember how shifty Ken looked and I wondered then. But apart from that he's never given me any reason to suspect him. No lipstick on the collar, no panties in the glove box.' She had shuddered. 'No unexplained calls. It's just a feeling.'

Amanda had frowned thoughtfully. 'It wouldn't surprise me. He's a dark horse, your husband. And very sexy.'

Zoë had glanced at her and smiled. 'He is, isn't he.' But if he and Anya had been having an affair, he appeared to have turned his back on it without regret. Unless she had dumped him. Was that part of the reason for leaving so abruptly? Perhaps it was better not to know. The important thing was they would be starting afresh.

The sale was completed in May, clinched by the fact that a mooring on the river was part of the deal, and they moved in at the beginning of July. Ken's job as an IT consultant could, like John's, be done anywhere as long as there was good access to the Internet and to London if necessary. Zoë's as an assistant in a Bond Street art gallery couldn't; didn't count, apparently. 'You'll find something to occupy you,' Ken had said airily, giving her one of his bear hugs. 'There are galleries and antique shops all over the place up here, you saw for yourself. Come on, sweetheart, you're going to love it. It will be absolutely perfect. And when we're settled in we'll ask John and Amanda to come and stay.'

Was that it? Was that the reason for the entire move? To impress, even upstage, John and Amanda? Had she caved in and agreed to her whole life being turned upside down on a whim, to try to compete with their best friends? Drying her hands on a towel Zoë gave a deep sigh and turned back to the window. Of course she had. Did it even matter? Probably not.

The fact remained, though, that try as she might she had not settled in; the faint excitement had worn off, the feeling that some dire fate was winding them round with sticky threads had become stronger than ever. She still thought of the house as a barn, not a home.

It was an exquisite building, with huge, full-height living space, the massive beams cunningly spot-lit for full effect, and a large woodburner as the focal point of the room, as was of course the enormous window looking down towards the river. Above there was a broad galleried landing and off it two large bedrooms, also with incredible views. Ken's office was at the back, at the end of a short passage off the landing, looking down over the fields, a quiet rural outlook which Zoë secretly feared would be unbearably lonely and bleak in the winter. The two other barns in the group were slightly to the side and back, out of her immediate sight from this window. The Threshing Barn was occupied by a retired couple, Stephen and Rosemary Formby, and The Summer Barn, so they had told her, was owned by a large and noisy family which appeared to use it as a holiday home and, as far as they could see so far, weren't there all that often. From her kitchen window she could see part of the communal gardens and the river, always the river, tidal for its first dozen or so miles from the sea, quite narrow here just round the bend from the lovely old town of Woodbridge, where it broadened, then narrowed again as it changed character to meander through the gentle Suffolk countryside. From here they were looking across towards open country and off to the left of the barn towards a fourth house, The Old Forge, much smaller than the barns and the only building of the group with a large private garden which, from what she could see of it behind its neat hedges, was pretty and productive. She gathered it was occupied by a single man, another passionate sailor, so she had been told, but she had yet to set eyes on him. He was, according to her neighbour, Rosemary, her source of all information about the other occupants of the small select community, something of a recluse, which turned him into a mystery.

A loud knock made her jump.

'Zoë, dear?' Rosemary Formby put her head round the

door. She was a small woman, somewhere in her late sixties, her iron-grey hair cut boyishly short, her face, devoid of make-up and weather-beaten, highly coloured, which served to emphasise eyes which were a brilliant Siamese cat blue. 'Steve and I are going into Woodbridge. I wondered if you needed anything?' Coming in, she dropped her shoulder bag and car keys on the table in such a way that Zoë understood she was on the move and wouldn't be stopping, something for which Zoë was secretly pleased. Their new neighbours were friendly and hospitable but perhaps a little too enthusiastic and in your face.

The woman glanced towards the window. 'Is Ken down at the boat again?'

Zoë nodded. She had already put the memory of the mist and her strange attack of panic behind her. 'He's making the most of every moment of this glorious weather.'

'Well,' Rosemary was already scooping up bag and keys again, 'don't let him turn you into a sailing widow. There are enough of them round here already.'

Zoë shuddered. It was just an expression but nevertheless it was an unfortunate turn of phrase.

As Rosemary headed back to the door she paused. 'I see Leo's back.'

'Leo?'

'Our elusive neighbour.' Rosemary inclined her head towards the window. She hesitated. 'He can be a bit touchy, Zoë. Don't go rushing in there. Fools and angels, you know.' And she had gone.

Fools and angels? Zoë stared after her. Then she went to look out of the window again. Sure enough a thin stream of blue smoke was rising from the chimney of The Old Forge. Zoë loved a mystery and as this man was the nearest thing to it in her life at the moment he intrigued her. It was very hard to resist the urge to make a neighbourly call.

*   *   *

Leo Logan was standing in his garden staring down at the river. It was a view of which he never tired. Whatever the light, whatever the state of the tide, the water fascinated him. The sages knew. You can never step in the same river twice. The sunlight was catching the soft cinnamon-red bark of the pine trees, warming them, dancing on the trunks, painting them with ever-changing shadows. He heard the latch on the gate behind him and scowled. He had already guessed who it was. He had seen that they had moved in. He knew someone would eventually buy the place but it had been a blissful few months of peace while it was empty. He took a deep breath, nerving himself for what was to come, and turned round.

It was the woman. She was tall and slim with short wavy blonde hair, artfully streaked to look as though it was sun-bleached. Her eyes were intriguing. Amber. And nicely shaped. But her smile had frozen into place as he knew it would the moment she saw his face.

She swallowed and held out her hand. 'Hi, I'm Zoë Lloyd. Your new neighbour. I just thought I would say hello.'

'Hi, Zoë. Leo Logan.' He grasped her hand momentarily then turned away to give her a moment to compose herself. 'How do you like it here?'

'I'm reserving judgement.'

Her answer surprised him. He had expected her to gush nervously and head for the gate. As it was she held her ground and even more astonishingly she confronted him at once. 'What did you do to your face?'

'Accident in a forge.'

'God!' She came to stand beside him, also looking down across the hedge towards the water. 'What a bugger.'

'An irony, isn't it, considering I'm now living in one!' He gave a bark of laughter. 'And before you ask, I do not wear a mask like the Phantom of the Opera. One day I will prob-ably have plastic surgery but at the moment I can't afford it and the insurance money, if there is any, will probably not come through until I am in my dotage and no longer care. I try and present my best side to strangers. You took me by surprise.'

She smiled. 'I am sorry. Given the option I nearly always manage to do the wrong thing.'

'How refreshing.' He folded his arms. 'So, is there a Mr Lloyd? Lots of little Lloyds? Dogs? Cats? Horses? Boats?'

'Hasn't Rosemary given you our life history yet?'

He shook his head. 'Rosemary and I are not bosom friends. As it happens, I have been away for a while, but also, I value my privacy.'

'I see. And I have barged in, I'm sorry. I'll go.' She turned away, rebuffed. 'For the record,' she added over her shoulder, 'there is a Mr Lloyd and a boat. The other things, no.' Her voice sounded, even to her ears, strangely bleak as she said it.

She half expected him to call her back as she headed towards the gate, but he said nothing. A quick glance as she unlatched it revealed a resolutely uncompromising back view, taut shoulders beneath the denim shirt, an air of concentration as he studied the river.

Fools and angels indeed.

Pushing open the kitchen door she came to an abrupt standstill, staring round. 'Ken? Are you there?'

Again she was aware of the eerie sensation that there was someone around, someone who had just that second left the room. 'Ken?' She knew it couldn't be him. Once he was down on the boat he would be there until lunchtime if not later. She glanced at her mobile, still lying where she had left it on the antique pine table, and shook her head. She was not going to call him again.

'Zoë?' The voice from the doorway behind her made her spin round. It was Leo. He had followed her across the grass. 'Sorry. I was rude. Can't help myself. It wasn't intentional.

Peace offering?' He held out a wooden trug. In it was a selection of vegetables and on top a spray of golden chrysanthemums. He put it on the table and glanced round. 'This has the potential to be a nice place. I'm glad you've got rid of the chichi blinds.'

She smiled, looking round, seeing the kitchen through his eyes. It had been well designed and expensively fitted, a country house kitchen with soft lavender-blue walls, a cream Aga, a refectory table and old chairs which she had found only weeks before in a shop in Long Melford. 'There weren't any blinds when we arrived. They must have gone with the previous owner. They didn't stay here long, did they?' Without her realising it there was a touch of anxiety in her voice.

'No, thank God.' He began to unpack the trug, scattering earth across the table. 'I'll take this back, if you don't mind. There is one thing I will mention while I'm here. You need to kill those damn security lights. They illuminate the whole area like a football stadium when they come on. They destroy the view of the night sky for everyone for miles around. Do that and I would be eternally grateful.'

Zoë was taken aback by his vehemence. She had barely noticed the lights; all the barns had them. When she had, it was to enjoy the shadowed views they cast across the lawns. She decided it was better to ignore the comment for now, say nothing and respond later if he brought it up again.

'This stuff is very welcome,' she said. 'Ken isn't a gardener. It was one of the attractions of this place, that most of the gardens are communal and are mown by someone else.'

'And you?' He scanned her face enquiringly. 'Don't you garden either?'

She shrugged. 'I've never thought about it. We lived in London before.' She was watching his hands. They were strong and well formed; his nails were filthy.

'So why on earth have you come here?'

'Ken wanted to live in the country, and he adored the idea

17

of having a mooring for the boat at the bottom of the garden.' She didn't realise that she hadn't included herself in this statement; that she was distancing herself from the decision.

'And he couldn't find a mooring nearer London? What does he do?'

'IT consultancy.'

'And you?'

'Nothing at the moment.'

'A lady who lunches, eh?' Was there a touch of scorn in his voice?

The colour flared into her face. 'No,' she said defensively. 'Hardly. I don't know anyone round here to have lunch with. And anyway, I shall be looking for a job.'

'Which would be?'

'I worked in an art gallery.'

'I'll bet it was a posh one. Bond Street?' There was no touch of humour in his voice.

She didn't dare look at his face. 'Yes, if you must know.'

His laugh was soft and, she realised, sympathetic. 'Some friends of mine have an antique shop in Woodbridge. I can ask them if you like. They might know of something which would suit you.'

'That would be great.' She risked another glance at him. The scars, now she knew they were there, weren't so bad. There was an area of red, puckered skin and tight silvery marks from his temple down across his left cheek almost to his chin. His eyes, she realised, were blue, not the bright almost harsh blue of Rosemary's, but a deep misty colour. 'Leo –' She paused for a second, then took the plunge. 'Our other neighbours. In The Summer Barn. Do you know them?'

'Indeed.'

'They don't seem to be here much.'

'No, thank God!'

'What happens in the summer?'

18

'Usually they go to Marbella or somewhere like that. Suffolk is too quiet.' Leo gave a throaty chuckle. 'Don't worry. We don't have to contend with that. And if they come down for Christmas at least they keep the doors shut.'

'Is it possible,' again a moment's silence, 'is it possible that one of the children might come in here, and somehow hide, move things around?'

He smiled. The scars affected his smile, gave a strangely quirky twist to his mouth. 'Anything is possible with them. But I think it unlikely. They live somewhere down near Basildon and the kids seem to think coming up here is the next best thing to parental-inspired torture. The youngest, Jade, is almost bearable, she's about eleven, but she would be at school. And there would be all hell to pay if she wasn't, so we can rule her out. One thing Sharon and Jeff are fanatical about is that the girl should get her education. The boys are, I fear, beyond hope.' He put the empty trug down by the door. 'I take it you have had the feeling there has been someone in the house?'

She nodded. 'Stupid. It's just taking time to get used to the place. It's so big after the flat and it's so quiet here.'

He glanced round. 'There's no need to be worried about it. This place has always had a strong feeling that there are things going on. Not the kids next door, not real people. Just echoes.'

For a moment she said nothing. 'Is that why the people before us left?' She walked over to the window, fighting the tightening in her chest. He was going to tell her it was haunted. That was all she needed. 'It's a new conversion,' she went on. 'Hardly anyone has lived here. No one has died here, have they? It can't be ghosts.'

He frowned. 'This building is hundreds of years old. Surely you realise that.'

'But it's a barn. Nobody lived here,' she repeated firmly.

'No. Nobody lived here.' Whatever he had been going to

say, he changed his mind. 'Don't worry about it. These old buildings creak and groan with every change of wind or temperature. You'll get used to it. In the end you won't hear it any more, or if you do you will feel it's like a conversation. My place is the same. I can tell what the weather is like and which way the wind is blowing just by which beam creaks in the morning when I wake up.'

She smiled. 'That sounds positively friendly.'

'It is.'

'I'll keep the security lights in mind,' she said as he stooped and picked up his trug.

'Do that. They desecrate the night.' He turned towards the door. 'Right. I must go. You must introduce me to Mr Lloyd one of these days.' And he had gone.

Zoë clenched her fists. There was no ghost. There could not be a ghost. Just a creaky house with a past as a farm building. She could live with that.

2

The huge barn doors were open to the afternoon sunlight. Several chickens were scratching at the dusty cobbles. They scattered at the approach of the horse.

'Daniel!' The woman leading the elegant mare towards him across the yard was slim and beautifully dressed in a burgundy riding habit with a black hat adorned with a veil. The horse was lame.

'My lady!' Releasing the pump handle with a start, Dan Smith straightened abruptly, letting the water sluice off his broad shoulders as he tossed his hair back out of his eyes. 'I'm sorry, my lady! I didn't hear you coming.' He groped for his shirt, forcing it on over his wet skin.

Emily Crosby smiled. She let her eyes linger a few seconds more on his body as he wrestled with the damp material before turning to the horse beside her. It stood dejected, its head hanging almost to the ground. Her gloved hand touched the animal's neck. 'My mare has cast a shoe and it was easier to bring her straight here than walk her back to the Hall.'

Dan hesitated, then he approached the horse, running an expert hand down its leg and lifting it to inspect the hoof.

'Where was your groom, my lady? Surely Sam or Zeph or one of the stable boys could have brought the horse in.'

'I was riding alone.' Her voice sharpened. 'I am sure there is no harm done. She just needs a new shoe.'

He glanced over his shoulder towards the forge. The fire had died down and his tools were stowed away for the night. 'If you'll leave her here, my lady, I will shoe her in the morning and bring her up to the Hall for you.'

'I don't think that's good enough, Daniel.' Her face set in a petulant scowl. 'How do you expect me to get back?'

He eyed the side saddle and her long-skirted habit. 'Walk, why don't you?' The words hovered on his lips, but he bit them back. 'I can put your saddle on the squire's cob. He's here in the yard.'

Emily stared round, her grey eyes widening. 'The squire is here?'

'No, my lady. His horse.' Daniel suppressed a smile. He pushed his wet hair back from his eyes. 'No one has come down to collect him from the Hall stables yet. It will only take me a minute to put the saddle over for you.'

'Very well.' She handed him the rein. 'Be quick. I need to get back in time for dinner.'

Dan walked the mare across the yard and tied her bridle to a ring in the wall. It took him seconds to release the girth and hump the heavy saddle onto his shoulder.

The squire's cob was not happy. It tossed its head angrily as he reached under its belly to cinch the first buckle tight. 'It doesn't fit him. It will rub. You will have to ride slowly, my lady.'

'You can lead me. I can't ride this great brute without an escort.' She eyed the horse with disfavour. She watched for a moment as he led it towards the mounting block. 'I can't get on it on my own, Daniel,' she said sharply. 'You will have to lift me.' The veil of her hat blew for a moment across her eyes as she looked round at him, her gloves and whip in one hand, the train of her habit in the other. Dan sighed.

22

'She didn't weigh much more than a child,' he said later to his wife, Susan, when at last he was back home in the cottage behind the forge. 'And she behaves like a child at that. One toy broken, so she needs must have another. That poor mare was drenched with sweat. It took me hours to rub her down and bed her for the night. And she's that jumpy. I doubt I'll get near her in the morning to shoe her.'

Susan was standing over the small black iron range, stirring rabbit stew. She straightened, her hands to her back. 'She's a spoiled madam. Just because she's an earl's daughter! She runs the squire ragged, so they say.'

'They?' Dan grinned. 'You mean that blowbroth sister of yours?'

Susan laughed. Her sister Molly was lady's maid at the Hall and there wasn't much gossip around up there that hadn't reached the home farm within the hour. She blew a strand of hair away from her face and wiped her hands on her apron. 'I felt the baby move again today.'

He grinned. 'That's good.'

'It was my turn on the churn. Betsy says it's good luck to feel the baby move in the dairy. Means he'll grow strong and tall.'

Dan nodded. 'As long as you don't exert yourself too much.'

'It's my job, Daniel! If I can't work in the dairy what will I do?' She turned to the dresser and, picking up a jug of cider, poured him some. 'You drink that down you and I'll fetch you some more to have with your dinner. It won't be long till it's ready.' She set down the jug again and stood watching him as he pulled up a stool and sat down at the table. 'Where had she been, do you know?'

'Lady Emily?' He shook his head morosely. 'She just said she was riding alone. And I know for a fact the squire has said she should always have a groom with her, or one of the men. She's fallen off that mare more than once.'

'But she was all right when you took her back?'

'Yes.' He looked at her sharply. 'Why are you asking about her, Susan?'

His wife looked smug. 'Just something Molly said. About her ladyship being sick in the mornings.'

'You mean she's expecting?' Daniel frowned.

'Maybe. And if so,' Susan picked up a cloth to pad her hands against the heat of the pan, 'whose is it, that's the question.' She glanced at him coquettishly.

Dan frowned. 'You shouldn't be spreading gossip like that, Susan. And nor should Molly. She'd be sent off if anyone heard she'd been talking about the folk at the Hall.' He stood up and reached for the cider flagon from the dresser. 'No.' He held up his hand as his wife opened her mouth to continue. 'Enough. I don't want to hear any more.'

He didn't want even to think about the squire's new wife. There had been something deeply unsettling in the way Emily Crosby had looked at him as he had stooped to take her foot in his cupped hands and tossed her up onto the squire's bay cob, and the way she had trailed her fingers across his shoulder and, just for a fraction of a second, across his cheek as she reached down for the rein.

He shod the mare next morning with no trouble, and sent her up to the Hall with one of the farm boys. There was no sign of her ladyship and no word from Molly. Dan straightened his back for a moment, his hands deep in the pocket of his heavy leather apron, eyeing the pair of Suffolk punches awaiting his attention in the yard as two of the men manoeuvred a heavy wagon out of one of the barns. Behind him the boy, Benjamin, was renewing his efforts with the huge pair of bellows. Dan glanced once down at the river where a heavy barge was making its way slowly on the top of the tide towards Woodbridge, then he turned again into the forge and after a moment's consideration chose a new shoe from the pile in the corner.

Ken Lloyd was sitting in the cockpit of the *Lady Grace*, a can of lager in one hand and an oily cloth in the other. He had spent all morning working on the engine. He threw down the cloth, wiped his hands on the knees of his overalls and gave a deep sigh of satisfaction. Over his head the halyards were tapping against the mast; he could feel the pull of the tide jerking the boat gently at her mooring. He glanced down at his mobile, lying on the seat. It was switched off. If Zoë wanted anything she could come down and call from the landing stage or get in the car and go into town herself. He looked lazily across at the neighbouring boat. It had sailed in earlier while he was distracted by the engine and he had paid little attention as its skipper had turned into wind, neatly picked up the mooring, then climbed down into the dinghy and rowed towards the shore. He had vaguely noted a tall, dark-haired man, seen the sail bag tossed onto the boards of the small boat, then seen him tie up at the landing stage and stride up through the woods towards the barns. He studied the boat now. *Curlew.* He saw the name on her stern as she swung to the mooring. A neat, seaworthy little craft with tan sails and, as far as he could see, no engine at all.

Losing interest he scanned the far bank. Slowly the tide was beginning to cover the saltmarsh on the edge of the river. He could see a family walking down the path in the distance, two dogs running ahead of them. It would be perfect for sailing soon. If he could persuade Zoë to come with him they could take the *Lady* down-river, maybe stop for a bite of lunch at a pub. With a satisfied grin he leaned across and picking up the mobile he switched it on and pressed speed dial.

There was no reply.

Emily Crosby was sitting in the library, writing a letter. Or at least she was seated at a table in front of the window, a pen in her hand, but her eyes were fixed on the distant farm buildings beyond the park and the pasture, where the land sloped down towards the river. The group of old barns clustered in a slight hollow of the gentle hillside where oak and birch woodlands, interspersed here and there with great forest pines, lined the river bank. She could see the blue smoke rising from the chimney of the forge and she smiled. She couldn't get the image of Daniel Smith out of her head. She had been transfixed by the beauty of his body, clad only in his leather-patched trousers as he washed at the pump yesterday, the rippling muscles, the tanned skin which betrayed the fact that he was often outside without his shirt and jerkin. She smiled to herself at the memory of his embarrassment at the sight of her as he pulled his shirt from where he had thrown it across the shafts of one of the farm wagons and dragged it on over his head. She could feel her body reacting at the memory and unconsciously her hand strayed to her bodice, stroking the swell of her breasts through the fine muslin of her gown.

'Emily?' The door opened and Henry Crosby walked in. He paused for a moment, a slight man, in his early forties, his face pale, his hair already thinning at his temples, and looked at the table, frowning. 'Who are you writing to?'

She grimaced. 'Mama. Except I haven't started yet. It is such a lovely morning and I was staring out across the fields. Look at the colour of the trees, Henry. They are like fire in the sunshine.'

She turned back towards the desk, as he walked across the room towards her. She could smell the pomade he wore on his hair, and the less pleasant mustiness of his shirt. He paused behind her and she could sense him looking down over her shoulder. She had written, 'Dear Mama, How are you?' That was all. It seemed to satisfy him, however. 'How are you feeling, Emily?' he enquired after a few moments' silence. 'Beaton said you were unwell yesterday.'

Her fingers tightened on her pen. She did not look at him. Was it impossible to keep anything to oneself in this damnable house? Molly had seen her vomiting, carried away the chamber pot, and of course she had to have told Mrs Field, the housekeeper, who had wasted no time in telling Beaton, the butler, who had probably relayed it round the village. By now the news had probably reached Ipswich via the carrier and by tomorrow it would be in London. 'I am well enough today, thank you, Henry. I think I must have eaten something disagreeable. Mrs Davy's oyster pie has made me sick before.'

'So, you're not –' He paused, unable to proceed or hide the disappointment in his tone.

'No, I'm not, Henry. I'm sorry.'

He reached out and almost timidly touched her shoulder. 'So am I,' he said.

She tensed. There was something in his tone which was unsettling. She turned and looked up at him. 'It will happen, Henry.'

He nodded. 'Do you think,' again he paused, 'do you think you ride too much, my dear?'

'Ride too much?' She pushed her chair back abruptly and stood up. Standing as they were, side by side, she was a good two inches taller than he. 'What do you mean?'

'I mean, maybe it is bad for you to go thundering around the countryside every day the way you do. And yet again yesterday you went out unescorted in spite of my express instructions –'

'Instructions!' she echoed, her voice rising. 'You do not instruct me what I may and may not do, Henry.'

'But I am your husband, Emily. It is my duty to look after you and make sure you are not too headstrong. Your father said you needed a firm hand.' He looked unhappy as he stared past her, unable to meet her eye.

'My father may have used a firm hand,' she retorted. 'You may not. If I wish to ride alone, I shall.' She threw down her pen and swept past him towards the door. 'In fact I shall go and ride this morning.'

'But my dear –' he protested.

She did not choose to hear him. Pulling open the library door she swept out into the hall.

'– we have company for luncheon,' he went on softly, his voice lost in the empty room. He moved closer to the window and stood staring out. The tide was high. In spite of the sunlight up here illuminating the fields and woods, a hazy mist was forming over the water and he could see what looked uncommonly like a Viking longship forging slowly through it, heading up-river towards Woodbridge. He frowned for a moment, puzzled and strangely uneasy as he studied the single short mast, the broad curved sail, the banks of oars, then he smiled, nodding, pleased at the distraction. It must be some new vessel belonging to one of his neighbours. He stared at it until the fog closed in and swallowed the image as though it had never been.

'Where the hell were you?' Ken strode into the kitchen and confronted Zoë as she put the last of Leo's vegetables into the bottom of the fridge.

'I walked over to see our new neighbour. He came back this morning.'

Ken swung to stare out of the window, following her pointing finger. 'The Old Forge?'

She nodded. 'Nice man. He gave me those flowers from his garden.' She pointed to the vase on the centre of the table.

'I wanted us to go sailing.' Ken had already lost interest.

28

'We still can. It will only take me a minute to change.' She manfully ignored the sinking feeling in her stomach. It had developed into a quiet day with mellow sunlight playing on the water. It would be lovely on the boat.

'It's too late now.'

'Why?'

'If you'd come when I rang we would have had time to get down-river and back.' Ken was a small wiry man, still handsome, with sandy hair and grey-green eyes. His face, cheeks windblown and threaded with small red veins, was a picture of discontent.

'We still have.' Zoë watched as he washed his oily hands at the sink. 'Give me two minutes, then I'll throw a baguette and some brie and salad into a basket and we can be down on the boat in less than half an hour and have a picnic.' She was already opening the door of the fridge, taking out the cheese. She changed the subject, her voice deliberately casual, trying to diffuse his irritation. 'Did you see the Viking ship go up-river? It was incredibly beautiful. With a huge billowing sail. They must be having some sort of regatta in Woodbridge.'

'If they are I haven't heard about it.' He was drying his hands now. He was going to let her persuade him but he was going to make her work at it. 'You can't have seen a boat go up-river though. There isn't enough water for anything with any draught to it. The tide has only just turned.'

She didn't argue. Having thrown the picnic together, she ran upstairs to grab a jacket and pull on her sailing shoes.

It was lovely on the river, she had to admit it. The gentle breeze was against them and Ken didn't bother to raise the sails as the engine purred smoothly into action and they made their way slowly down the main fairway, past the saltings, past deserted anchored yachts, past the crowds on the terrace outside the pub at Waldringfield, the tables shaded by blue and white umbrellas, then on down round the bend.

'What was he like?' Ken said at last. He was sitting back, his arm over the tiller, squinting at the glare on the water.

'Who?'

'Our neighbour.' He glanced at her.

'Nice enough. A bit prickly to start with.' She described him.

'I remember Steve telling me about him. He was messing about with some sort of metal working and he wasn't wearing a face guard. Something exploded.' Ken leaned forward and helped himself to another crusty sandwich. Zoë had made a pile of them in the cabin as they'd headed down-river.

'Rosemary didn't say.'

'Stupid woman.' It seemed a general comment rather than a criticism of her capacity to gossip. 'You know what she's doing?' He threw a piece of crust overboard. 'She's involved with some group of walkers, taking on the local farmer about rights of way. Steve says it's a nightmare. He loves walking but it's anything for a quiet life with him; she's the one. She wants the path to take some short cut across a field and all the locals are up in arms. Stupid woman!' He repeated the phrase with some gusto. 'If you're going for a walk from nowhere to nowhere, for the sake of just going for a walk, why would you want to take a short cut, for heaven's sake?' He narrowed his eyes, adjusting the course slightly to pass another boat coming upstream under sail.

'She strikes me as being a bit of an obsessive,' Zoë said. She climbed out of the cabin and sat down opposite him.

'Typical childless woman!' Ken snorted. 'Needs something to keep her occupied.'

'Does that go for me too, then?' Zoë didn't look at him. 'My need for a job to keep me occupied.'

Ken looked startled. For a moment he didn't reply. 'We agreed we didn't want kids, Zoë,' he said at last, his tone heavy with reproach. 'It was a joint decision.'

'Was it?'

He didn't reply.

The water slid by gently, smoothly, an opaque green-brown beneath the blue of the sky. The saltmarsh at this stage of the tide was indented with narrow creeks and channels in the mud. On the bank opposite she could see the trees coming down to the water's edge, the leaves beginning to turn to red and gold. Seagulls were diving into the tide edge, their screaming the only interruption to the peace save for the gentle ringing of the wind in the halyards and stays. She squinted up at the burgee flying at the top of the mast. In a moment of devotion when they were first married she had made it for Ken, stitching the little flag with her own hands. He threw another piece of crust overboard and Zoë saw with some alarm that something invisible seized it almost at once and dragged it down beneath the water. A stronger gust of wind sent ripples all around them and she shivered.

'My lady, your husband said one of us should go with you.' Pip, the boy who had saddled Bella for her, did his best. 'What if you should fall?'

'I won't fall.' She gathered the reins and gestured at him to help her mount.

The boy shrugged. It wasn't his job to argue with her lady-ship. He watched as she settled into the saddle, let go of the rein and leaned back against the wall, whistling, as she trotted through the arch and out onto the long drive which led down to the main gates of the estate. Halfway down she took the broad fork in the track which led towards the home farm.

The barnyard was empty as she rode in and reined the mare to a standstill. She stood for a moment staring round. Wisps of hay blew round the horse's hooves. From somewhere she could hear the contented grunting of pigs and the sharp grate of a hoof on cobbles but there was no sign of anyone there. The working horses were out in the fields with the men, bringing in cartloads of turnips to store for the winter.

The dairy was neat and scrubbed, the huge pans of cream covered by muslin cloths, the churns waiting for the evening milking. Her gaze turned thoughtfully to the forge. There was no smoke coming from the chimney but the door was open and she heard sounds coming from inside. Clicking her tongue she urged the mare into a walk.

'Is anyone there?' she called.

Dan appeared after a few moments. He had taken off his heavy apron, but his sleeves were rolled to the elbow. 'My lady?'

'There is something wrong with the shoe you put on,' she called down. 'I'd like you to look at it.'

She saw his eyebrow move and smiled to herself. So, she had insulted his workmanship. Good. That would put him on his metal. 'Help me down, Daniel.'

He stepped forward and after a moment's hesitation he held up his arms. She lifted her leg clear of the pummel and slid towards him, trusting him to catch her. Just for a moment she felt his strong hands on her waist and smelled his sweat as she fell towards him, then he released her and took a step backwards. 'I'll look at the horse, my lady.'

He seemed angry as he led the mare to the wall and tied the rein. Then he bent, running his strong hand down the animal's foreleg. Emily smiled to herself. 'Could it be loose, do you think?'

'No. It's fine and solid.'

'How strange. Perhaps it is one of the others.'

'I don't think so, my lady. I checked them all this morning. They were all right and she was sound.'

'How odd.' She stepped closer to him. 'Could she be going lame, do you think?'

'Dan!' The voice came from close behind them. Lady Emily straightened and took a step back. Susan's face was white as she stared at them. 'I am sorry, my lady, I didn't know you were here.'

Dan winked at her, his hand gently stroking the horse's nose. 'Lady Emily is having trouble with Bella's feet, Susan. I was just taking a look for her.'

'Indeed.' Susan gave Lady Emily a cold smile. 'Please don't let me interrupt, my lady. I can wait.'

Emily stared at her, her eyes hard as flint, then she nodded. 'I was wrong. I must have imagined it. If Daniel says the horse is all right, then of course it must be. Perhaps, if he could just help me up,' she turned and smiled at him, 'then I can be on my way. I am already late for luncheon.'

'Dan!' Susan caught at his hand as Bella turned out of the yard and disappeared with her rider. 'You have to be careful. You know what she's like.' She looked up at him pleadingly, aware as never before of the contrast between her swollen body, her greasy hair covered by a stitched cap, and her rough strong hands, and the beautiful slim creature who had ridden out of the yard with her chestnut curls and elegant features beneath the riding hat and veil.

Dan laughed and threw his arms round her, planting a kiss on the end of her nose. 'Don't you fret, missus,' he said with a grin. 'She's doesn't hold a candle to my Susan. Silly primping female who can't control a horse properly and can't even get herself with child.'

'Maybe it's the squire's at fault.' Susan followed him into the forge. 'It took long enough for him to get Mistress Elizabeth with child. And then for it to kill her in the birthing, poor soul, and the baby dead too.' They were both silent for a moment. The squire's first wife had been highly popular in the village and on the farm. It was barely two years since they had all followed her coffin to the church, and only four months after that, to the shock of everyone for miles around, Henry Crosby had brought home a new wife after marrying her in London. Susan put down her basket. In it her husband's lunch of bread and cheese was wrapped in a chequered cloth; with it were a couple of new season's apples and a flagon of

33

cider. He drew the cork with his teeth and took a swig. 'That is good, Susan. Thank you.'

Outside on the river the mist was drifting slowly in with the tide. Barely visible in the shadows beneath the trees the square sail of the Viking ship hung swollen with an imperceptible breeze.

It was nearly dark when they tied up at last at the mooring below the barns and began to tidy the boat. They had sailed for a while in the end, so the sails had to be neatly furled and covered, the cabin left immaculate, the basket, empty now of food, lowered into the dinghy. The tide had turned again, exposing pebbles and green weed and dark shining mud at the edge of the water. The wind had dropped. Already the mist was coming back.

'Hurry, Ken. Let's get home.' Zoë was conscious suddenly that her skin had started to prickle. She glanced round uncomfortably, aware of a chill off the water which hadn't been there before, and the incredible loneliness of the silence around them as the night drew in. She watched in an agony of impatience as, remembering a book he wanted to take back with him, Ken ducked once more into the cabin and began to search through a locker.

'I'll only have to come back tomorrow if I don't find the wretched thing now,' he retorted as she protested. 'It'll get damp.' He was rummaging amongst a heap of papers and charts and magazines. 'I should clear all this out before winter. Zoë?' He turned. She was still in the cockpit staring into the mist.

'There is someone out there,' she said as he climbed the steps out of the cabin and joined her. He was feeling in his pocket for the key to the doors.

'Someone going up to the town quay.' He frowned, trying another pocket. 'They'll have to hurry. The water is dropping fast.'

34

'Listen.' Zoë held up her hand. 'You can hear the boat.' Instead of being reassuring the sound was somehow disturbing.

Ken paused. She was right. He could hear the rush of the tide against a bow, the creak of rigging. It sounded very close. The sudden thunder of canvas made them both reach for the rail, staring out into the mist. It had thickened until it was a dense wall hanging round them. 'That was close; too close.' Ken's voice was indignant. 'Are they crazy, sailing at that speed when the visibility is so low? They've broached, by the sound of it. Where the hell are they? I can't see anything.'

Nearby Leo's boat was a faint shadow against the whiteness of the mist. Groping in the bag lying on the bottom boards ready to be thrown down into the dinghy with the basket, Ken found the torch and switched it on, shining it out across the water. All it showed was white swirling fog.

'Listen,' Zoë was whispering. 'Oars.'

The creak of wood on metal was unmistakable.

'Ahoy!' Ken shouted out across the water. 'You're too close to the bank! You'll run aground.' His voice was swallowed and dulled by the fog. They looked at each other. The sound of the oars had stopped. There was nothing to hear at all now save for the gentle gurgle of ripples against the hull of the *Lady Grace*. A breath of wind stirred the mist for a moment, lifting it, showing the river, empty of movement.

'Where are they?' Zoë gave an uncomfortable little laugh. 'Did we imagine it?' She waited for Ken to laugh too. He didn't. He was still staring across the water. He had pulled the key to the cabin door out of his pocket and was standing holding it as if mesmerised. Zoë glanced down at the small dinghy, tugging at its painter alongside, suddenly terrified at the thought of climbing down into it and setting off across the narrow strip of water towards the landing stage. Only half an hour before there had appeared to be plenty of light to see what they were doing as they picked up the mooring; now they were enveloped in mist, and total darkness had crept up the river. She felt frightened and vulnerable and alone.

Ken had switched off the torch. 'We had better save the battery,' he said softly. She could hear the tension in his voice; he was feeling it as well. He put the key in the lock and turned it, then he moved towards the stern and reached for the painter. The rope was covered in droplets of moisture. 'Ready?' He sounded uncertain.

'Perhaps they got stuck on a mud bank?' she murmured.

'Must have.' He managed to smile but his attempt at a jovial tone didn't quite come off. 'Come on. Let's go home.' He pulled the dinghy alongside and held it steady for her. She climbed down and sat in the stern, glancing over her shoulder into the dark. The water gleamed dully only inches from her, gently moving as if it were breathing. Already the reeds were poking above the water. Somewhere close by there was a splash. The dinghy bobbed up and down as Ken let himself down into it and sat carefully amidships, reaching for the oars. 'Only a minute or two and we will be there.'

He pulled strongly, spinning the small craft round and headed for the little jetty. Zoë was clutching the torch, still switched off. She could just see the short wooden landing stage jutting out into the river in the faint reflected light off the water. Her sense of panic was increasing at every stroke of the oars. She fixed her eyes on Ken's face. He could see behind them. He was watching, staring out into the darkness.

'Slow now,' she murmured. 'We're nearly there. OK, ship your oars.' She had the painter in her hand. As they came alongside she reached out for the wet weed-covered wood of the jetty and pulled them towards it, slipping the rope around one of the stanchions with a sigh of relief. 'Made it.'

Ken sat still. His eyes were still fixed on the river. 'They are still there. I saw a glimpse of the sail.'

'I don't care. Let's get out of here.' She heaved the basket and bag up onto the boards of the landing stage. 'Come on, Ken. What are you waiting for?'

'The sail was still up. Filled with wind.' There wasn't a breath of wind now, the mist hanging round them in damp folds.

She shook her head. 'It must be the re-enactors. Perhaps they are filming or something. Perhaps it is a pretend sail. They are probably motoring.'

'Can you hear a motor?'

She shook her head. Unsteadily climbing to her feet in the small boat she hauled herself up and scrambled onto the landing stage. 'Come on, Ken. Get out of the boat. I want to go home.'

He turned, following her, checking the dinghy was firmly tied up and heading for the path up through the trees. 'Where's the torch?'

'Here. I've got it. I just don't want to put it on.' She was still whispering.

'Why on earth not?'

'In case they see us.'

For a moment he stopped, staring after her, then he turned and surveyed the river. He could see nothing in the mist and all was silence.

Leo could see the moorings from the window of his living room. He had watched his new neighbours make a neat job of picking up the buoy and stowing sail in the dusk. She was an attractive woman, Zoë. Her husband was older, competent, an experienced sailor, by the look of it. Leo turned his attention to his own boat, the *Curlew*, lying some twenty-four boat lengths further up-river. She was swinging easily to the mooring, neat, poised, as always reminding him of an animal, asleep, but ready for instant wakefulness.

Behind him a door banged in the small house. He ignored

it. The Old Forge was full of strange noises, as he had told Zoë. Creaking beams, rattling windows, they were to be expected. But the other sounds: the echo of a woman crying, the screams which might just be an owl, though he never heard them outside, those were less predictable, less easy to ignore. Unsettling, he acknowledged wryly, but not frightening, not yet. He jumped as the phone rang close beside him and smiled bitterly. A cause for far more terror, the unexpected ringing of the phone.

It took twenty minutes to pack a bag, lock up and head out in his old Saab, up the mile-long communal drive to the narrow country road. If he was lucky he could catch the fast train from Ipswich with time to spare.

3

'What does Leo do for a living, do you know?'

Rosemary had cornered Zoë in the garden next morning and reluctantly Zoë had allowed herself to be talked into going next door for a coffee. The Threshing Barn was slightly larger than theirs, and stood at a rough right angle to it. The buildings had been erected centuries apart and with no regard to the congruity of the group. The largest of the three, The Summer Barn, belonging to Sharon and Jeff Watts, formed the third side of the inverted C. That too was medieval, though not much of the original building had survived and it had retained fewer barn-like characteristics in its layout. The shutters were closed and it looked faintly bedraggled. Following Zoë's gaze Rosemary sniffed. 'They will be up for half-term, like as not.' She reached down a biscuit tin from the cupboard.

Each building had a small enclosed back garden, barely more than a terrace, and a front area, slightly larger and more informal. The Watts's was gravelled and bare, Rosemary and Stephen's was of neatly mown grass with a narrow flowerbed and a low hedge around it, and Zoë and Ken's was paved. Lately Zoë had begun to think in terms of terracotta pots and flowing pink and grey foliage. Gardening had never been her thing, but she had begun to dream of something pretty to set off the starkness of the renovated barn behind it. Only The Old Forge had a proper garden, partly enclosed by an ancient wall and partly with a hedge. That area, according to the ever-helpful Rosemary, was where the horses had waited for their turn to be shod, tied to iron rings which were still there in the wall.

'As for Leo, I've never asked him what he does now and he's never volunteered so I haven't a clue. Nothing much, as far as I can see. Obviously he was once a blacksmith of some kind. I expect someone paid him millions in compensation for those awful scars. If I were him I would have sued the socks off them.' She shuddered ostentatiously.

Zoë felt a twinge of distaste at the woman's lack of charity. Hadn't he said he was still waiting for an insurance payout? She changed the subject quickly. 'Is he married?' Leo intrigued her.

Rosemary glanced sharply at her. 'Not that I've heard. He never seems to have any visitors at all.' She was laying a tray with a neat lace cloth and silver sugar bowl. 'He sails,' she added as an afterthought. 'As do the Watts. Theirs is the bright red boat.' She sniffed. 'Typical!' There was another pause as she stood staring at the kettle, as though trying to will it to boil more quickly. 'They will take it away soon. I think it gets hauled out of the water over in one of the marinas. It is a hideous thing. No sails. Just a great big noisy engine.'

Zoë hid a smile. She agreed with Rosemary there. She didn't like noisy motor boats either. She hadn't noticed a large red boat down at the moorings, so perhaps it had already been hauled out for the winter. The only other boat riding on the tide at the moorings this morning was the small brown sailing boat she had noticed the day before, which presumably was Leo's.

'Someone told me you're a keen walker,' she said as the silence drew out between them and threatened to become awkward.

Rosemary nodded vigorously. 'You must come and join us, dear. It's a wonderful way to meet people and to get to know the countryside.'

'Maybe.' Zoë shook her head enthusiastically, belying the hesitation implied in the word. She couldn't think of anything worse than going for prearranged walks with a group of people she didn't know, like small children two by two following their teacher round the pavements of London. She had seen groups of walkers like that round Woodbridge and as far as she could see they never seemed to be enjoying themselves. 'I like exploring on my own, if I'm honest, and I love running.' Not that she had done a lot of running since they had moved, which was odd as there was so much beautiful country to run in, but she wasn't going to admit that to Rosemary.

She followed her hostess into a room which Rosemary called the snug. It was anything but, in Zoë's eyes, but it had the benefit of a view across country towards the distant woods. Beyond she could see the roofs and upper storey of neighbouring Timperton Hall, beautiful on the hilltop in the emerging sunlight. Their barns had been part of the home farm when the Timperton estate still existed.

Glancing round as she sat down, she noted the beams overhead, not so large as theirs or so gracefully arched, but still beautiful. 'Does your barn make a lot of noise in the wind?' she asked suddenly. 'Creaks and groans?'

Rosemary shook her head. 'Not really.' She passed Zoë a cup and then stared at her anxiously. 'Oh, no. Don't tell me you're hearing things over there already.'

Zoë felt a cold draught whisper across her shoulder blades. 'I know our predecessors heard strange noises. Leo told me.'

'Sarah was a bit of a silly woman,' Rosemary sniffed again

– it was her version of a punctuation mark, Zoë realised –
'but I have to say she did have a point. It's because your
place is so old – much older than either of the other buildings. I think someone told me it was fifteenth century or
something like that. It is bound to move. You take no notice,
dear. I'm sure you are a sensible person. She was hysterical,
that one. Completely unstable. I'm surprised they stayed as
long as they did.'

'You never heard anything?'

'Good Lord, no. And if I thought there were any ghosts
here I would soon have them chased out. They are nonsense
anyway. People with too much imagination see ghosts.'

Zoë stifled a smile. Privately she doubted if any ghost would
have the courage to shack up with Rosemary.

'What about ghost ships?'

The question was out of her mouth almost before she had
thought of it.

'Ah.' Rosemary hesitated and then topped up Zoë's cup.
She hadn't taken a sip yet, and the unnecessary gesture made
the liquid slop over into the saucer. Rosemary didn't look up
and Zoë realised suddenly that her hand had started to shake.
She put down the pot and finally glanced up with a hesitant
smile. 'I don't believe it, of course, but there are plenty of
people round here who would tell you about it.'

'A ghost ship?'

Rosemary nodded.

'A Viking ship?' It was a whisper.

Rosemary's eyes widened. 'You haven't seen it?'

'I've seen a Viking ship. Twice. Yesterday morning, I could
see it through the window. Then last night when we came
back from sailing, we heard it. Ken saw it through the
mist, or at least he saw something.' She paused for several
seconds. Rosemary said nothing. 'I thought maybe it was
people coming for a regatta or something – re-enactors, you
know . . .' Zoë's voice trailed away.

Rosemary was staring at her, her blue eyes intent on her neighbour's face, concentrating as though trying to decide whether or not to believe her. She shook her head. 'I've never seen it. Nor has Steve. There's an old legend about it. Pete, the man who comes to mow our grass, told us about it. You should ask him. Loads of people have seen it over the years.'

Zoë stared down at her cup. The coffee in the saucer looked disgusting; there were several drops on the table as well, a splatter trail leading to Rosemary, who had her hand still on the handle of the coffee pot. Neither woman said anything for several seconds, then Rosemary released the pot and stood up, and went back into the kitchen with Zoë's cup. She poured the contents down the sink, hunted for a cloth to wipe the table and returned with a clean cup and saucer.

'It's all superstitious nonsense, of course,' she said at last. 'The river can be quite sinister sometimes in the dark and when it's foggy like it has been these last few nights.' She poured the coffee once more, this time with a steady hand, and then put the pot down with a sharp bang. 'What did you see?'

'A sail. A huge sail, bellied out in the wind, though there was no wind. We went out under power. There wasn't enough to sail.'

Rosemary sat forward, her eyes still fixed on Zoë's face. 'Leo has a book which has a picture of the sail. It is some old book about Suffolk he found. You should ask him to show you.'

Zoë nodded. She wasn't at all sure she wanted to see it.

'It was a sketch made by one of the farmhands who worked here, in these barns in Victorian times. Very rough, but it showed the pattern on the sail. He saw it a hundred or so years ago, but Noddy Pelham at the golf club told us lots of people have seen it over the years. He reckons that to see it is a portent of doom.' She laughed and then covered her mouth with her hand, looking stricken. 'Not that I believe any of it. Steve says it's probably the shadows of the pine trees falling on the mist. Or a mirage, like in the desert, reflecting sailboats out at sea somewhere.' Her voice trailed away. 'Are you all right, dear?'

Zoë nodded. 'I think Steve is probably right. But it did feel,' she hunted for the right word and found one which was totally inadequate for the weird, panicky sensation she had felt, 'odd.' She thought back suddenly to the night before, the creak and squeak of the oars, the sense of a huge vessel so close to them that even Ken was frightened for a moment, and she felt once more the prickle of fear across her shoulder blades. 'It's weird, isn't it?' she went on weakly. 'But a bit intriguing. As long as the guys on the boat don't come ashore.'

Both women laughed a little uncomfortably and both almost involuntarily glanced towards the window. There was no view of the river from here. All they could see was the spread of the lawns, some distant trees and a hedge beyond which the fields rose gently up towards the crest of the hill where the eighteenth-century Hall, now converted into flats, sat in elegant repose in the sunlight.

U

Mr Henry Crosby sent for Daniel the following morning. 'My wife has complained that you were insolent to her,' he said. They were standing in the study at the Hall. Dan had his cap twisted between his hands.

'I'm sorry to hear her ladyship had reason for complaint, Mr Crosby.' Daniel felt a surge of anger which he was careful to hide. 'If I gave offence it was unintentional, sir. Did she say in what way I was insolent?'

'She brought her horse to you and you told her there was nothing wrong with it.'

Daniel was speechless for a moment. 'But there was nothing wrong, sir. She said the mare was lame.'

'Because of your incompetent shoeing.'

'There was nothing wrong with my shoeing, sir. Nor with the horse's feet either. I checked carefully.' He could feel the heat rising up his neck.

'Are you calling my wife a liar?' Henry Crosby's voice dropped dangerously.

'No, sir. Of course not, sir.' Daniel looked down at his boots, biting his tongue.

'I'm glad to hear it.' Crosby walked across to stand behind his desk. He leaned on it, his hands flat on the blotter, fixing Daniel with an angry glare. 'Take the mare back with you and see to her. Make sure there are no more mistakes if you want to keep your job, is that understood?'

'Yes, sir.' Daniel hesitated for a moment, then he turned away. 'Thank you, sir.'

Outside the door he stood still for a moment and closed his eyes, trying to keep his temper under control. Then he began to walk slowly down the passage. There was no one in the kitchen or the servants' hall. He made his way out to the yard and round to the stable block where Bella was tied in her stall. He walked to her head, making crooning noises, and was surprised when she backed away from him, her eyes rolling. She was sweating profusely. Glancing down as he ran his hand down her shoulder, his eyes widened at what he saw and he swore viciously under his breath. Her front legs were a mass of cuts and bruises; blood was pooling on the straw.

It took him a long time to walk the mare down to the barnyard. She was very lame, and he would have preferred to leave her where she was, but a short consultation with Sam, the head groom, whom Dan had found in the harness room, convinced him otherwise. 'She brought the mare home in that state,' the older man said quietly. 'Forbad me to touch the poor animal. Said she had been to you and you had said there was naught wrong and that she was to ride her home.'

Dan was too angry to speak for several seconds. 'Then she told her husband?'

Sam nodded. 'She called you all sorts, she did.'

'That mare was fine when she brought her to me.'

'I thought she probably was. What did you say to upset her ladyship then?'

Dan shook his head. 'Lord knows.'

Sam gave him a quizzical stare. 'Well, let's hope the Lord will tell you because otherwise you are in big trouble, Daniel, my friend. You keep out of that woman's way, that's my advice to you.'

Dan put the mare in one of the line of loose boxes which had been built in one of the bays of the old barn. He washed and poulticed her legs, and Susan made her a bucket of bran mash. They both stood watching the horse listlessly sniff at the food. She didn't touch it.

'You'd best keep out of her ladyship's sight,' Susan said softly. She leaned back against the wall, her arms crossed over her belly. 'That woman is trouble.'

'But why?'

Susan gave a fond smile. 'Because you are a handsome man and she expected you to show you like her.'

'But I don't like her.'

'Oh, Dan, you duzzy old thing, don't you see?' She reached up and ruffled his hair. 'There's a certain type of woman who wants every man she sees to fall at her feet.'

'But I'm just the blacksmith.'

'You're a man!'

'And if I laid a finger on her she would run screaming to her husband.'

'Probably. That's the way such folk are.'

'And I love you, Mrs Smith. I'd never look at another woman.'

'I know.' Susan glanced over her shoulder into the shadows of the great barn and shivered. Several other horses stood quietly in their stalls, their great haunches shadowy in the fading light. There was no one else there, but somehow she had felt a breath of cold air touch her face.

There was a small stone church on the hill near the great hall of the thegn. The priest was a good man of some seventy summers; the people of the village liked him and so did the Lady Hilda. She was with him now, sitting on a stool in the cool shadows of the nave. 'My husband is dying, father, we both know it,' she said, speaking quietly even in the privacy of the empty building. 'I need you to bring him the sacrament.'

'I can't do that, my lady.' Father Wulfric shook his head sadly. 'He has refused baptism yet again.' He sighed. 'His father was a good Christian and so is his brother, but the Lord Egbert is adamant in his apostasy. He cleaves to the old gods in his despair.'

'My husband is a superstitious fool!' she retorted with spirit. 'He has found himself a sorcerer from the forest and reveres him as though he were a priest! The man gabbles spells and charms, and scatters runes like spring seed, and promises him a place at the side of Woden and Thunor. And,' she added bitterly, 'Egbert keeps on calling for the swordsmith. All that matters to him is that that wretched sword is finished before he dies.'

'And his brother? What says he to that?' Father Wulfric tightened his lips in disapproval. He was holding a small beautifully illuminated book of Gospels in his hand. It was the church's most treasured possession, presented by Lord Egbert's mother. Kissing it reverently he laid it on the altar.

'He is preoccupied with raising men for the fyrd. King Edmund is calling warriors to his standard at Thetford. They are expecting more attacks from the Danish host.'

'So we will soon be left unprotected.' Father Wulfric turned back to her and sighed again.

She glanced at him, alarmed. 'The Danes won't come near us, surely? What would they want with a small settlement like ours?'

Father Wulfric didn't answer for several breaths. They both knew what befell any settlement in the path of the Viking horde. 'Please God they will not even know we are here,' he said at last.

He stood and watched Lady Hilda walking slowly back towards the Hall, her blue cloak clutched closely round her against the sharp autumn wind. Her shoulders were slumped, her whole stance defeated. He shook his head sadly as he turned towards his own house, then he stopped. The sword-smith was standing watching him from the door of the smithy, his arms folded, his face thoughtful. For a moment Father Wulfric considered walking over to join him, but already the other man was turning away into the darkness of his work-shop. The door slammed and the old priest heard the bar fall into its slot.

At first she thought Leo wasn't going to ask her in, but after a moment's hesitation he stood back and ushered her into a small cluttered living room. Zoë glanced at once towards the window. Yes, he too had the ubiquitous view of the river; his hedge had been trimmed low so he could just see the moorings below the trees. She could see his boat and the *Lady Grace* tugging gently at their buoys, swinging with the tide. The fire was unlit and she could see an old rubbed leather Gladstone bag on the floor just inside the door. 'I am sorry. Were you just going out?'

'I just came back.' He folded his arms. 'How can I help you?' There was no smile to alleviate the slightly irritated tone and she felt an instant reciprocal bristling of irritation.

'I have come at an inconvenient moment. I'll come again when it is a better time.'

'I doubt there will be a better time,' he said. 'Please, spit it out. Whatever you came to say was presumably important, or are you merely here to pass the time of day?'

She reined in a flash of temper. Had she given him a reason to be so rude? 'I wanted to ask you about the ghosts, if you must know. The house is getting to me. But I will phone first next time and make an appointment.'

'What makes you think I know anything about them, beyond the fact that they scared your predecessors away? At least, they scared her; he was an insensitive clod who wouldn't have noticed if the entire angelic host had descended on his house.'

She found herself biting back a smile. 'I wasn't actually here to talk about the barn. Rosemary said you had a book with a picture of the ship.'

He stared at her thoughtfully for a moment and she saw the tension in his jawline. It accentuated the scars slightly. 'You've seen the ship?'

She nodded. 'I think so. Twice.'

'Ah.'

He continued to study her face for several seconds, then he turned towards the bookshelves which lined the wall opposite the window. In front of them there was a long shabby sofa, covered by an old tartan rug. The room was nice, Zoë decided in the silence that ensued. Scented with an all-pervasive smell of woodsmoke, it was furnished with some decent antiques, and some attractive paintings, both modern and old. It felt lived in and comfortable and far more homely than the huge space which they called the great room at home.

He stood in front of the shelves, his eyes ranging left to right; his books were not arranged in order then. She watched silently, folding her arms as she shifted her weight, aware that she was not going to be asked to sit down. 'Here,' he said at last. He pulled out a small volume with a rubbed red cloth cover. 'It's in here.' He handed it to her. 'I'm in no hurry to have it back, but look after it. I will want it eventually.'

'Thank you.' Taking it she moved towards the door. She reached out for the latch, then she turned. 'Have you seen it?'

'The ship? Yes.'

'What does it mean?'

'Mean?'

'Yes. Is it a sign of some sort?'

'That one is barking mad, for instance?'

'No, that there is something wrong. Is it a portent of evil?'

He smiled. 'Who knows? Read the book.' He moved towards her and reached past her for the door, pulling it open and waiting for her to leave. 'Are you a religious woman, Zoë Lloyd?' he said as she stepped out into the porch.

'No.'

'So evil is for you a philosophical concept rather than a religious one?'

'I suppose so, yes.'

'And what you really meant to say is, is it a sign of bad luck? Impending doom.'

'I meant what I said,' she retorted coldly. 'Thank you for the book. I shall take care of it.'

She was tempted to hurl it at him.

Back at home, she made her way through the kitchen into the living area which she and Ken had by common consent come to call the great room. It had seemed appropriate in every sense on the first day they moved in and the term had stuck. She went to stand by the huge window, staring out towards the river. It was deserted, the sunlight glittering on the water. From here all she could see of the two boats were their masts. She listened. The room was silent. There was no feeling today that there was anyone else there in the house with her.

Curling up in one of the chairs she had placed so that

there was a clear view of the river, she looked down at the book in her hands and turned it over so she could read the title on the spine. *Tales and Legends of Bygone Suffolk, collected and retold by Samuel Weston*. The page she was looking for was marked by a discoloured cutting from a newspaper. She unfolded it carefully. Dated 1954, it related the sighting of a ghost ship in the river: *The great sail was set and the ship seemed to move before a steady wind, but there was no wind. The vessel has been seen in the past and on this occasion its passing was witnessed by two fishermen lying below Kyson Point. The men watched as it came close and both described the air as growing icy cold. It passed them round the corner and when they scrambled ashore and ran to look from higher ground the ship had disappeared. There was no sign of life on board and no sound other than the usual lap of the river water. When asked, both men agreed it had been a frightening experience.*

She refolded the cutting and tucked it into the back of the book, then she began to read the chapter. It more or less repeated the description of the fishermen, adding details of several more documented sightings in the eighteenth and nineteenth centuries. She turned the page and there it was, a woodcut said to be taken from the sketch made by one of the farm workers on the Timperton Hall estate. It showed the ship exactly as she had seen it, with a curved sail and on it the design which she had not been able to make out clearly in the mist but which the unnamed farmhand had shown as an animal head with a long ornate tongue protruding from its open mouth. She scrutinised it thoughtfully and decided it might be a boar or perhaps a dragon. He had also shown the animal on the prow of the ship, a kind of figurehead high above the level of the water. He was obviously a man of no little talent – the sketch was detailed and had a pleasing sense of perspective. There was no comment with it, though, no record of what the man had felt. She skipped through the succeeding pages, but there seemed to be no further reference to it. Resting the book on her knee, she stared out of the window again. The sun was lower in the sky now, and the river looked like a sheet of silver metal. There were no boats in sight, real or ghostly. She listened. The room was quiet. How strange to think that the man who had sketched the Viking ship had probably worked in this very barn, perhaps stood with a hay fork in his hand on this very spot where she was sitting. She shivered and glanced round in spite of herself. The roof of the room was lost in shadow without the lights on, the great beams slumbering, hinting at the ancient oaks from which they came.

The door to the kitchen opened revealing the light she had left on over the worktop. 'Ken? You're back! I didn't hear the car.' She turned to greet him. There was no reply. 'Ken?' She stood up uneasily. 'Are you there?'

The house was silent. There were no sounds of anyone moving around in the kitchen. Putting down the book, she walked across to the door, aware that her mouth had gone dry. 'Ken?' She pushed the door back against the wall and stood staring round the room. 'Who's there?' Her voice sounded oddly flat; without resonance as though she was speaking in a padded recording studio. The sun shone obliquely in at the window; in minutes it would start to slide down below the fields on the opposite side of the river. She had to force herself to move forward towards the work island in the centre of the floor. 'OK, enough is enough,' she said firmly. 'I don't like this. Who are you? What do you want?' She clenched her fists, suddenly angry. 'If you are not going to show yourself, I want you to just bugger off!' She wasn't sure if she was addressing the neighbours' wayward children or some ghostly presence. Either way she acknowledged that she was scared.

Her heart was thudding in her chest. The feeling that there was someone listening intensified; behind her she heard something roll across the table and it fell to the floor with a rattle. She spun round and stared. A bent corroded nail lay beside the table leg. She stared at it and then looked up. Had it fallen from the ceiling? In here there were fewer beams, the ceiling between them smoothly plastered. There was nowhere it could have appeared from. Hesitantly she stooped and picked it up. It was rusty, squarish, with a small head, cold as it lay in her palm.

She dropped it hastily on the table. 'Is that yours?' she called. She was addressing the ghost. 'Are you trying to tell me something?'

There was no reply.

Seconds later she heard the crunch of car tyres on the gravel outside and, glancing through the window, she saw Ken's car sweep round the side of the building.

She scooped up the nail and put it into a small bowl on the dresser; minutes later Ken had opened the door and walked in, bringing with him a blast of cold air. He piled some paper carriers on the worktop. 'I missed the blasted post again! Here, do you want some sausages? From the farm shop. I thought it might be nice for supper.' He pushed a packet towards her. 'The forecast is good; shall we go out early tomorrow? See if we can get down the river and over the bar?'

'Out to sea?' Zoë picked up the sausages with a slight grimace and went over to the fridge.

He laughed. 'Yes, out to sea, with waves.' There was an edge of hardness to his voice.

'Why not?' She forced herself to look pleased. Even sailing seemed better suddenly than staying alone in the house with – her thought processes stalled. She thought of it – the ghost, if there was a ghost – as him.

It occurred to her that Ken was watching her and she gave him a forced grin. 'We could cook the sausages tonight to take with us tomorrow.'

He nodded. 'That would be nice.'

'OK. How early do you call early?'

He smiled, all charm now he had got his way. 'We need to go out so that there is enough depth going over the bar.'

'And come back when the tide turns?'

He nodded.

'Great.' She managed to sound enthusiastic. 'I'll make the picnic up tonight.'

He nodded. 'I'll just go and send out a couple of emails then I'll wash up for supper.'

That's me sorted for the evening; cook supper and pack the picnic. Zoë suppressed a surge of irritation. It wasn't as if she had anything else pressing to do, or that she didn't enjoy cooking.

Ken was heading for the door when she heard him give an exclamation of annoyance. He stooped. 'Bloody nail on the floor! Look, I've scratched the boards.' He threw something into the rubbish bin and walked out. It didn't seem to occur to him to wonder where it had come from.

For a moment Zoë didn't move. She stared at the bin then slowly moved towards it. She pushed open the lid and looked inside. There, at the bottom of the empty white rubbish bag, lay another rusty nail identical to the first.

She reached down and picked it out and put it with the first one in the bowl, then stood for several moments looking down at them before putting the bowl back on the very top shelf of the dresser.

Leo watched them leave next morning with a sardonic grin. Obviously they hadn't listened to the forecast. Walking away from the window, a bowl of cereal in his hand, he went into his studio and stood looking at the work in progress. It was proceeding well and he had to admit, albeit grudgingly, he was pleased with himself. There was a rattling noise from the kitchen door.

'Come in!' he called. 'I saw you there.'

The door opened and a face peered in. 'Hi, Leo.'

'When did you come down?' He hadn't looked round.

'Yesterday.' The face was heavily freckled beneath a thatch of fiercely red hair. 'Mum drove me and the boys down. It's half-term, in case you didn't know.'

'I didn't.' It meant the Watts family, occupants of The Summer Barn, would put an end to the reasonably civilised peace of the area for at least a week. He sighed.

'What are you doing?'

'Working.'

'Boring.'

'No. Exciting. As you would know if your father had anything like a decent work ethic.' He often wondered where the family got their not inconsiderable pots of money from. Better not to know, maybe.

'What's an ethic?'

The child moved into the room and stood staring down at Leo's work. She had a can of Coke in one hand and a wire led from some hidden pocket to the small earphones which dangled round her neck. Otherwise her wardrobe consisted of shabby jeans and a Simpsons T-shirt, probably a castoff from one of her brothers. It seemed inadequate for the chill of the morning but she didn't seem to notice.

'Drop a millilitre of that stuff anywhere in this house and you are toast,' he said equably.

'You're more likely to spill that stuff you're eating. What is it? It looks gross.'

'Muesli.'

'What's that?'

'Bit like an ethic.' He turned to face her. 'Have you come for a reason or are you just here to annoy me?'

She shrugged. 'Bored.'

'Is your mother not taking you shopping?'

'There's no decent shops.'

'Ah. I see the problem.' He didn't bother to ask what decent shops consisted of in her opinion.

'And your brothers won't play with you?'

She stared at him. 'Play?' She seemed shocked at the word.

'I know. I am sorry. It's not a concept you are acquainted with. What are they doing? Should I be barring the windows and calling the police?'

She giggled. 'Probly.'

He frowned. 'Jade, do me a favour, love. Tell those vile pigs who are your siblings to keep away from the new people in The Old Barn. OK? They are nice people and we don't want them being chased away like the last lot.'

She grinned. 'That was good. They was real scared!'

'Jade!'

'I know.' She sat down on the couch and took a swig from her can. 'This is shabby. My mum thinks you must be very poor.' She was fingering the torn throw which covered the worst holes and frayed edges in the upholstery.

It was his turn to laugh. 'Your mum is a wise woman. But fortunately I don't mind being either poor or shabby.'

She looked at him thoughtfully. 'You've got a boat, though. Can I come out on her?'

'Have you learned to swim?'

She shook her head.

'Then you know what the answer is.'

'My dad says sailors never learned to swim 'cos if the boat sank, then they drowned quickly and there wasn't time to get eaten by sharks.'

Leo nodded, trying to hide a smile. 'Sounds good logic to me. OK, if I go out I will take you, but only if one of your parents signs something to say I have their permission to drown their child. And I want no brothers.'

'Nor do I.' She beamed at him. 'Can we go today?'

'No. The wind is going to get too strong.'

'They've gone.' She nodded vaguely behind her. Leo took her to mean Zoë and Ken.

'I know. But I think they are experienced sailors. You are not.' He folded his arms. 'Right; this visit is concluded. Can you go home, please, Jade. I am busy.'

'OK.' She stood up, seemingly happy with the cursory dismissal. 'Can we go tomorrow then?'

'We'll see! Out!' He jerked his thumb towards the door.

He watched her as she wandered back through his garden, through the gate, leaving it wide open, and up the grass towards The Summer Barn. He couldn't see it from here, but he could imagine the scene. From peaceful emptiness it would have changed to noisy chaos. The huge people carrier would be parked as closely as possible to the front door, which would be open. Noise, lurchers and general mess would have spread exponentially across the front garden and into the communal grounds, and his peace would be shattered for the next however many days they stayed. He gave a wry grin. He liked Jade, and her parents were decent enough, if congenitally noisy and untidy, but her brothers were the pits! He gave a deep sigh. The first thing he had to do was go out and close his gate against those damn dogs.

Rosemary was standing in the field below the barns, a carefully folded Ordnance Survey map in her hand, turning it round first one way then the other, her eyes narrowed against the wind. It was cold and her hands were turning blue but she had forgotten her gloves. She looked round again, carefully noting the lie of the land. There was no footpath marked, but there had been one on the old map she was looking at this morning in the library. The field lay diagonally to the river; almost at its centre there was a roughly circular area of scrub, which was fenced off from the rest of the field with rusting barbed wire. On the map the footpath would have gone through the middle of this patch, followed on down the slight hill and debouched onto the lane below the hedge. When you thought about it, it was the logical place for a path to go, otherwise it was necessary to veer left up quite a steep slope towards the gate in the top corner of the field and then walk down the far side of the hedge to join the lane several hundred yards further on. She reached into her pocket for her notebook and folded it open, fighting the increasing wind as the pages flapped wildly for a moment until she smoothed them flat. She drew a quick sketch and began carefully to pace the line of a possible path down towards the scrub. When she reached the barbed wire she paused, staring into the undergrowth. Why had it been fenced off? Squinting, she tried to see if there was a pond or feed bins or maybe a sign that there were pheasant-rearing cages in there. That was always reckoned to be a good enough reason for farmers to close off access. There was nothing that she could see, just a substantial mound of earth, brambles, nettles and several small skimpy trees. She began to circle the wire, sure there would be some means of access on the far side. There wasn't. After getting badly scratched by brambles and mauled by the wire she gave up and stood, frustrated, staring down towards the river. The wind was rising. She could hear it roaring through the trees and, out of sight, on the moorings she could hear the clap of metal halyards against a metal mast. Briefly she wondered if Zoë and Ken had come back yet. She had seen them walking across the grass early this morning laden with a sail bag and basket, and each with a serviceable-looking day sack on their back.

Turning with her back to the water, she stared up the line of the missing path and saw through her whipping hair that someone was approaching her down the field. It was the farmer, Bill Turtill. She had always found him polite and, if not overfriendly, at least approachable, and she walked towards him with a smile. 'Bill, how are you?'

'All right, Mrs Formby. And yourself?'

'I am well, thank you. Cold in this wind.' She gave a theatrical shiver to illustrate the point.

'I'll be ploughing this field in the next week or two,' he said after a moment. 'You would find it easier walking if you stayed on the footpaths.'

'Oh, I know.' Her smile froze on her lips. 'I was just wondering, Bill, why the footpath doesn't come straight down across the field any more. You do know that it used to come across here?'

He shook his head. 'The footpath follows the hedge up to the lane.'

'It does now, yes. But originally it came directly across the field.'

'I don't think so. Not in my time or my father's. It is clearly way-marked, Mrs Formby, and on all the maps, as I'm sure you've seen.' He looked pointedly at her Ordnance Survey map.

She sighed. There was always trouble when anyone suggested to these yokels that a right of way needed to be reinstated. Still, there was no point in putting his back up prematurely. She smiled again. 'I'm sure you're right, it just seems strange when it is such an obvious route. Well, never mind. Once you have ploughed the field it will be impassable anyway.' She sighed as she shoved the map into the pocket of her jacket and tightened her scarf. 'It was nice to see you, Bill. Do give my love to Penny.'

She set off up the field with the wind behind her, conscious of his eyes on her back as she walked, determined not to hurry or divert from her route. It took her once more up to the wired-off area and once more she paused to gaze into the undergrowth. After a moment she walked on, skirting it as before. Why had he left that area of scrub in the field? It was a complete waste of space, not something the average man of the soil, who round here would plough up every extra centimetre if given the chance, would tolerate for a moment, in her experience.

The mound of earth in the centre could easily be bulldozed. She huddled more deeply into her jacket. There were several things to find out before she took her findings to Arthur, who chaired the local walking group's committee. She considered talking to Leo. He had taken an interest in local history since he had arrived, but then again he had told her that she and her walking group were a load of interfering bored trouble-makers. She hadn't spoken to him since, and he had never apologised; so not the man to turn to for information. She had to find someone else to ask. But research was what she was good at and confronting Bill Turtill would, she suddenly decided, be an enjoyable experience. It might make him a bit less cocky. She shivered, for real this time, imagining his eyes, still cold and antagonistic, watching her as she made her way across his field.

4

'Oh my God, we've hit something!' Zoë heard her voice screaming above the roar of the waves and the wind.

'Don't panic.' Ken was fighting the tiller with all his strength. 'We touched the shingle bank for a moment, that's all.' His words were carried away on the wind. 'Come on, you stupid woman, use some strength. If we tear the bottom out of the boat, it will be your fault! Hold on!'

Desperately Zoë hung on to the slippery rope in her hand, aware of the tightly reefed sail, the proximity of the beach as they turned into the river, feeling the enormous strength of the wind, fighting it, terrified that at any moment she would lose her grip. Ken was swearing at the helm. She couldn't hear the words, but as she glanced across at him she saw the gleeful exhilaration in his face, the bulging muscles in his neck and arms. He was putting every ounce of strength he had into the battle, and he was enjoying it.

Then suddenly the boat came round a few degrees and the power of the sail slackened. 'Yes!' Ken let out an exultant yell. 'That's it. We're in. We've done it, we've crossed the bar. That's fine. Let the sheet out a bit. There, what did I tell you?' With uncanny suddenness the water calmed and the boat righted herself, heading meekly into the river mouth. 'Phew!' He smiled again and she heard a note of relief in his voice in spite of his glee. 'I was a bit worried there. I don't know where that squall came from. I'm sure they forecast good weather for today.'

'Well, they were wrong.' Zoë had been holding the wet main sheet so hard her knuckles were locked, her hands white, the skin of her fingers wrinkled. There had been no time to put on gloves. The cockpit was awash with water and she was soaked to the skin, aware of people standing on the seawall watching them as they passed the shingle banks at Bawdsey and threaded their way between the moorings at Felixstowe Ferry and the quiet wooded stretch of shore on the far side.

'That's something like it!' Ken went on, his voice gaining in confidence again with every second. 'Exciting. Listen to those waves crashing over the shingle. I timed it a bit early, that's all. We should have waited, but with the storm coming . . .' His voice trailed away as he saw Zoë's face. 'Were you scared? There was no need. I was in control.'

'Yes, I bloody was scared!' she said with some force. 'I was terrified. God, I hate this boat!'

'My fault. I was an idiot,' he conceded unexpectedly. He screwed up his eyes against the glare, passing the red marker buoy and heading up the channel. 'You don't really hate it. You know you don't. I always forget you're not as experienced as I am. But you are very good. You are learning.' He grinned again.

It was dark before, under power and with the sails tightly furled, they nosed up to their mooring and made fast to the buoy. Zoë was still shaking with cold as she gathered their stuff together. The wind was still strong, the trees thrashing, the water choppy as Ken released the dinghy and pulled it alongside.

'Can you find the torch?' He was exhausted too, she could hear it in his voice as he lowered the first of their bags over the side. She passed the empty food basket across to him, then suddenly she froze. Over the noise of wind and water she could hear the sound of oars. 'Ken!' Not again. Please, let it not happen again.

He stopped scrabbling amongst their bags and looked up. 'What?'

'Listen.'

He couldn't see her face but he could hear the tone of her voice. He straightened and stared out across the river. For a moment both of them were silent. The squeak and pull of the oars was close by; several oars; the sound of a sail flapping and the thud of metal on wood. Ken scrabbled for the switch on the torch and, turning it on, shone it out across the water. The powerful beam lit up the empty river. Carefully he swept it first one way and then the other. The sound had stopped. All they could hear as the wind died for a moment was the lapping of the waves against the side of the *Lady Grace*. 'Where is it?' he whispered.

'There's nothing there.'

'There has to be.' He swept the torch round again then he stood up. 'Ahoy!' he shouted. 'Who is out there? You are too close to the shore.'

There was silence. No oars. No sail. She could feel the emptiness. Whatever, whoever had been there before, had gone. Zoë sat down on the thwart. 'It's a ghost ship.'

'Oh, yes,' he scoffed. 'Or men from Mars. More likely someone bringing illegal immigrants up-river.'

'No. It is a ghost ship. People have seen it before.' She hadn't told him about Leo's story or the picture. What was the point? He wouldn't have believed it last night any more than he believed it now.

The mare was very lame the next morning, her legs swollen her head hanging listlessly. She had ignored her feed. Dan ran a hand down her near fetlock and shook his head grimly. He doubted she would recover.

'How is she, Daniel?' The soft voice at his elbow made him jump. He stood up too quickly and put out a hand to reassure the horse, but it wasn't necessary; the animal had hardly moved.

'Likely she'll have to be shot,' he said harshly. 'Whoever did this has a lot to answer for.' He turned to face Lady Emily.

'It was your fault, Daniel. You didn't see the injuries when I brought her to you.'

He clenched his jaw, keeping his temper with difficulty. 'No, my lady, you are right. I was very remiss.'

'It's a shame. She was a nice horse.' Her voice was light and careless. 'Do whatever has to be done.' She turned and walked back towards the large barn doors which stood open to the sunlight. Outside, a sprightly breeze tossed wisps of hay around the yard. The working horses had gone out early into the fields and the yard was deserted save for the roan pony tied to a ring by the forge. 'I will need help to mount, Daniel,' she called over her shoulder.

He gritted his teeth. 'Of course, my lady.' He walked out after her. 'You have a new horse, my lady. I haven't seen her before.' He waited as she gathered the reins.

'I'm thinking of getting my husband to buy her for me. I would have asked your opinion, but I see now you know nothing of horses.' She glanced at him, her mouth curved with disdain.

'I am a smith, my lady, not a groom,' he said calmly.

She smiled. 'Of course. I must remember that.'

He stooped to take her foot in his hands and tossed her up into the saddle; this time she was wearing a habit of Lincoln green with a lace jabot. The horse braced itself and shook its head as she looked down at him. 'Tell me, was that your wife who was here before?'

'It was, my lady.'

'She's expecting your child.'

'She is, my lady.'

She raised an eyebrow haughtily. 'Then she should take care not to overexert herself. It would be sad if she were to lose her job in the dairy. She does work in the dairy, I assume?'

'Yes, my lady, she does.' Daniel stood away from the horse and folded his arms. He looked up and met her eye.

She smiled. 'I will see you soon, Daniel.' She tapped the horse with her whip and trotted past him, pulling the animal so close he had to leap back out of her way.

For several minutes he stood still, looking after her, a deep frown on his face, then he turned and walked out of the yard. He followed the path across the field towards the woods; there, out of sight of the barns, he stopped and leaned back against one of the tall ancient pines in the lee of the oak woods and, taking a deep breath to stop himself shaking with anger, let the soft scent of the needles envelop him. Below him the river, swollen with the tide, glittered like silver, criss-crossed with ripples in the sunlight.

'Did you enjoy your bath?' Ken looked up at Zoë as she walked into his study. He had been standing behind his desk contemplating the darkness outside.

'Yes, thank you.' She was wearing a towelling wrap and her hair was still wet, standing on end as she rubbed at it with a towel.

'I am sorry if you were frightened, darling. There wasn't any real danger, I knew what I was doing out there.'

'Did you?'

The heaviness of her voice startled him. 'You know I did.' He sounded wounded. He turned his back on the window and looked at her. 'What are we having for supper?'

'I don't know.'

'Are you feeling all right?'

65

It was a moment before she replied. 'Tired.'

'Shall I make you something?' He put his head on one side and gave her a small hopeful smile. 'To cheer you up? Boiled egg and soldiers?'

'I'm not a child, Ken,' she snapped.

For a moment she wondered if she was going to hit him but somehow she managed to restrain herself. 'Sorry, I'm still feeling a bit frazzled,' she went on at last. 'An egg would be nice,' and she headed back onto the landing. Below her in the shadows of the living room something moved and just for a second she thought she heard the chink of a horse's harness and the scrape of a hoof on cobbles.

'Ken!' It was a whisper. 'Ken, come out here.'

He didn't hear her. Already he had become immersed in the screens on his desk. He had probably completely forgotten her. She stood leaning on the balcony's wood and glass balustrade, looking down. There were horses down there, and with them a man; shadows, imprints in time. She could see them, sense them, hear them, then they were gone.

Edith threw down her spindle with a groan and walked across to the door of the cottage. She ought to be waiting on the Lady Hilda in the weaving house with the other women, but she had dawdled at home, hoping and praying that her husband might appear even if for only a short time. She had made him a new leather jerkin, stitched with waxed thread; it hung from a peg even now, catching her eye as it swung to and fro in the draught. She missed him desperately; his voice, his humour, his company, and above all his strong agile body in her bed. But he had decided suddenly, and as far as she could understand completely arbitrarily, that while he made a sword for the lord of their village he must abstain from his wife's embraces and keep himself pure. Even thinking about it made her eyes fill with tears. As if she were impure. Something unclean. This was some heretical belief of the thegn's. He had denounced the Christian beliefs of his family and his wife and begun praying to the gods of his forefathers.

As had Eric.

The knowledge had been there all along, buried deep inside her, and she had tried to ignore it, but why else had he turned away from her bed? Why did he make excuses not to go to church? Why had he agreed to make this sword a pagan sword; how else would he have known the spells and the charms to be recited over the blade as he forged it in the fire?

She sighed. The gods of their ancestors had been powerful gods. She found herself thinking suddenly about Frige, the goddess her great-grandmother had worshipped, the goddess who made marriages fruitful, whilst now, she bit her lip thoughtfully, though she prayed often and fervently to the Blessed Virgin, her own marriage to Eric was still childless.

'Edith?'

Lost in her dreams she hadn't seen the figure appear in the doorway. Eric stooped and came in, pushing the door closed behind him, shutting out the light. 'Eric!' She threw herself at him and for a moment they clung together. She nuzzled his neck, and pulled his face to hers, seeking his lips with something approaching hunger. 'Have you finished the sword?' she whispered. 'Have you come home?'

For a moment longer he held her close against him then slowly he pushed her away. 'I'm sorry. Not yet. But it won't be long, sweetheart, I promise.'

Bereft, she stood for a moment, her eyes closed, fighting her tears, then she straightened her shoulders. 'Why are you here then?'

He didn't answer for a moment, then gave her a sheepish grin in the twilight shadow of the small house. 'I thought you would be in the weaving house with Lady Hilda.'

'Which is where I should be.' She waited but he said

nothing more. For a moment he seemed to hesitate, then he turned to the door and lifted the latch. 'It won't be long, I promise, my darling.' However long it took to engrave the magical runes, the special symbols, the words of power which would make this sword unique.

She watched as he strode away towards the edge of the village where the tithe barn hid his forge and workshop from her view, then she turned back to the fire. Overhead the drying herbs hanging from the ceiling rustled gently, disturbed by Eric's passing.

'I'm sorry. I was rude again, wasn't I?' Leo was standing on the back doorstep. He was empty-handed this time, his hair blowing in the stiff breeze, dressed in a heavy blue Guernsey and faded jeans. 'Can I apologise?'

Zoë stood back and nodded towards the kitchen. 'Five minutes. It's my turn to be busy. I am just going into Woodbridge.' Now that she was used to the scars on his face she could see what a good-looking man he must have been. She led the way into the kitchen where her handbag and shopping basket were sitting side by side on the worktop with her car keys.

He grimaced. 'Bad timing. My trademark. Just like you.' He followed her in and stood by the table. 'I just thought a word might be timely about our mutual neighbours. I dare say you've noticed that they are here for half-term.'

'I noticed but I haven't spoken to them yet.'

'The youngest kid, Jade, she's a good mate of mine. Something she said rang alarm bells. I think there might after all be a plan to try and scare you both. Playing ghosts. Weird noises in the night, you know the sort of thing. They are a malicious bunch and their idea of a joke might not be yours. Or mine, for that matter.'

'So the whole ghost thing is a scam?' She heard her voice

rise at the tightness in her throat. She exhaled sharply. 'It's all a joke?'

'Not all of it, no,' he said quietly. He glanced at her face then looked away again. 'Sorry. But as they are here, and they appear to be in malicious mode, you might be in for an escalation of events for a few days.'

'They weren't here, though, when the noises started, were they?' Her moment of relief disappeared as soon as it had come.

'No they weren't.'

'So all the door banging was real.'

'Might have been the wind.'

'And last night,' she was silent for a moment, trying to make up her mind whether to tell him or not, 'we came back tired after the most god-awful sail I have ever had and I was upstairs, looking down over the balcony and I thought I saw, heard, horses, quietly munching their hay, scraping their hooves. Maybe I didn't actually see or hear them. I just sort of sensed it.' She shook her head, embarrassed, sorry she had mentioned it as soon as the words were out of her mouth. 'Don't laugh at me. I expect I was hallucinating. I was so tired.'

'I'm not laughing. I am sure horses have lived in here on and off over the centuries. Buildings hold memories. You were tired; your mind was relaxed, open.' He hitched up to sit on the corner of the work station, one leg swinging. 'So, what was so awful about the sail? I got the impression you were seasoned mariners.'

'Ken is. He loved it. We were out in the sea, it was a bit rough, I suppose, and he decided to come back and we touched the bottom and suddenly I realised I was scared. Really scared, more scared than I have ever been in my life.' She put her hands to her face for a moment.

'We all get scared from time to time.' He spoke with an unexpected gentleness. 'That's what gives the adrenaline.'

She shook her head violently. 'No. Not like this. It is supposed to be fun. And yes, exciting, but not so deeply, deeply frightening.' She looked at him for a second and then shook her head again.

'Why did you let him drag you up here if you hate it?' he asked after a moment. 'The move wasn't for your benefit at all, was it?'

There was a long pause. 'I don't hate it. I thought it would work. It was a challenge.' She held his gaze defiantly.

'And sailing, is that a challenge too?'

She walked across to the window and stared out. 'I can't live my whole life afraid.'

'It strikes me that you would be afraid of very little,' he said thoughtfully.

She grimaced. 'But then you don't know me very well. Perhaps afraid is the wrong word. In a rut, then. London was comfortable and safe.'

'And sailing isn't safe.'

'We sailed before.' She hunched her shoulders defiantly. 'It was fine. It is fine.'

In the distance the river water was dull, sluggish, creeping in, creeping up between the banks. She could feel the cold tiptoe across her shoulders and deliberately fought the reflexive shiver. The kitchen was warm.

'It was partly because of his enthusiasm that we came here, of course it was. Our life together has always been like that. He's the match, and I smoulder into flame.' She broke off and it was a moment before she laughed. 'But this time the flame hasn't caught. Or not the way I expected. I thought I would like it here. I did – do – love it here. But something is wrong.' Why was she confiding in him like this?

'Does Ken know how you feel about all this?' he said after a long pause. He had been watching her while she spoke.

She nodded.

How could she explain the complexity of their

70

relationship? It was Ken's enthusiasm, his drive, his passion which attracted her, his wiry single-mindedness. But it was that same single-mindedness which excluded her, blanked the parts of her personality which did not fit his template. Once she had thought she could change him, but the change, if there was to be change, would have to be hers, and that admission, that she had judged him wrongly, and that she must change herself or be for ever sidelined had been too hard to make.

'You love the river,' she said, turning back to face Leo.

'Yes.'

'And you love sailing.'

He nodded.

'Are you never afraid?'

'Everyone is afraid sometimes, Zoë.'

'Yes, but in Ken's case he's hooked on the adrenaline. He's competitive. He is always testing himself against something. Fear excites him.'

He made no comment and she turned back to the window. 'Ironically it was the river that drew me to this house. It fascinates me. But now we are here for some strange reason it –' she hunted for the right word – 'it repels me as well. I find it as sinister as it is beautiful.'

'I saw you sketching it.'

She glanced at him, startled. 'When?'

'You were down on the boat.'

She shook her head. 'I can't draw. I can't do anything. I was trying to find something to occupy me while he tinkers with the boat. Sketching will not be it.'

'I'm sure you will find something.' He grinned. 'Do you have to go down on the boat to keep him company?'

'I don't think he even notices I'm there half the time.'

'There you are then. You need a land-based hobby.'

'I jog, but that is hardly a hobby. Not for me, anyway. I need to sort out my life, my relationship, my whole *raison*

71

d'être.' She shrugged. 'No. Forget I said that. That is part of something I have to sort with Ken.'

He gave a half-nod. 'Fair enough. It's forgotten.' He stood up. 'My five minutes is up. Just keep a wary eye out for the kids from hell, OK?'

She gave a faint smile. 'So, apart from your mate, Jade, how many did you say there are?'

'Three boys. Darren, Jamie and Jackson. Jackson doesn't feature much, thank goodness,' he grinned. 'He's left school and is for all I know collecting ASBOs; I doubt he has any other qualifications. Which is a shame. Jeff and Sharon are decent people, chaotic and noisy and sometimes irritating to a grumpy codger like me, but still salt of the earth.'

Zoë put her head on one side. 'In my experience when people are described as salt of the earth it usually means they are just the opposite.'

'Then your experience is unfortunate. I meant it.' His voice had hardened.

'Sorry.' She felt a surge of irritation at the rebuke. 'So, the two I have to watch out for are Darren and Jamie.'

'That's right.'

'Thanks for the warning.'

'Just being neighbourly.' He headed towards the door.

She stayed where she was, watching as he walked past the window and across the grass towards his house.

'Was that our new neighbour?' Ken had appeared in the doorway and she turned with a start.

'Why didn't you come and say hello?'

'He seemed to be in a hurry. What a dreadful state his face is in. Why on earth doesn't he get it fixed?'

'Money.' She reached for her car keys off the counter. 'I was going to pick up some stuff in Woodbridge. Do you want to come?'

He shook his head. 'I thought I would go down to the *Lady* for an hour or two. Unless you want me for anything else?'

72

'No.' She managed to restrain the sigh. 'Do you want lunch later or shall I leave you to do your own thing when you come in?'

'Why not do that? I lose track of time a bit down there.' He gave her his boyish smile.

She smiled back. Don't you just, she thought.

She hadn't planned on visiting the library after the supermarket but suddenly it seemed a good idea. She found her way to the local history section and located one book which looked as if it might enlighten her about the area. She thumbed through the index, looking for Timperton Hall, smiling as she rooted around in her bag for a pen and paper. Did people, she wondered, always start a ghost hunt like this?

In the event there wasn't much information to be had. The Hall had Tudor origins but had burned down and been rebuilt in the late seventeenth century by the Crosby family, who had lived there for nearly two hundred years. Nearby was the home farm. There was no village as such, apart from the site of an early church which had long since disappeared. That suggested that at some point there had been at least some sort of hamlet in the area. Now there was nothing to suggest that – apart from the barns, which clearly had been part of the estate – there had ever been any kind of settlement on the edge of the river nearby. The nearest church now was St Edmund's at Hanley Heath, two miles away, and it was there, apparently, that the last members of the Crosby family, which died out in 1873, were buried.

Zoë leaned back thoughtfully against the bookshelves. A small country estate with no particular history. A microcosm of English history. She smiled. Rosemary had made friends with someone who lived in the Hall and had offered to take her up there. It would be nice to go inside, but she suspected that, as had happened with the barns, most traces of its previous history would have been eradicated by the developers. How sad.

She glanced down at a map of the estate at the end of the book, which showed the cluster of barns, the tracks through the woods, an old landing stage, several small houses, which she hadn't noticed and were probably long gone, and found herself wondering whether she would ever begin to feel at home there.

Putting down roots was a mysterious business which had never happened to her. Her parents had moved often when she was a child and she felt that at base she had never really called anywhere home. She stared unseeing at the map. She had gone from boarding school to Durham University to read English and had then found a job in London where she had shared various flats with a motley selection of people until she and Ken had married ten years before. They had moved twice, both times within a fairly small area, always aware that they would move again. This launch into the country was a change of pattern, an uneasy step, as she had told Leo, out of her comfort zone. Once she had got used to the idea it had seemed exciting and a bit zany. Her friends thought they were stark staring mad, and she had laughed at them, jeering at their lack of sense of adventure, but now she was beginning to realise they were right. She and Ken didn't fit. No one in the barn complex fitted. They weren't local. They didn't belong. They had all been plonked as though from outer space into a pretty piece of countryside and the safety net had been whisked away. And the real locals, the real inhabitants, be they alive or long dead, resented them. Especially the long dead. She looked up, mulling over the disturbing thought. They were still there, still doing their thing as though nothing had changed. And they resented the newcomers bitterly.

'Excuse me, we're closing in five minutes.' The librarian was standing beside her with an apologetic smile. Deep in her reverie Zoë hadn't noticed her.

She glanced at her watch. 'I was dreaming. I had no idea I had been here so long.' Flustered, she pushed the book back onto its space and tucked her notes into her bag then she went to find a coffee shop. She already had a favourite. Surely that meant something.

Lesley Inworth had the ground-floor flat on the right-hand side of the front door of Timperton Hall. She led Zoë and Rosemary into the sitting room and gestured round. 'Isn't it a lovely room? I think it's the nicest in the house. We have this marvellous view down across the river in the distance. The rest of the flat is small. It's been divided so everybody gets one or two nice rooms and then one or two of the smaller ones at the back. My bedroom was the squire's study. The stables have been turned into another flat at the back and there are two more upstairs.' She was a wispy woman, thin and wiry, in her late forties, widowed, according to Rosemary, who had given Zoë a quick update on her background as they walked up the hill, with two daughters who both lived in London. Her passion was gardening and she was employed by the residents' committee to supervise the grounds and to look after the Victorian gardens, which had miraculously survived and which were very beautiful.

Zoë had been wrong about the Hall losing its character. It had been converted with great care to conserve its architecture and make use of its features. They sat down round the fire, which burned in a beautiful Regency fireplace, while Lesley poured coffee and produced some homemade cake.

'The history of the house was very sad at the end,' she said in answer to Zoë's query. 'The Crosby family had lived here for generations, then the last squire had no children so the estate passed to some distant cousin who never actually came here. Then his son was killed in the First World War and there was no one else. It was sold up. I expect that happened to so many families.'

'And after that it was converted into flats?'

Lesley shook her head. 'It was sold to the farm. Bill Turtill's dad or granddad. It is an extraordinary turnaround of fate. The Turtills were farm managers to the estate in the nineteenth century, but somehow they ended up buying the farm and a lot of the land, then in the fifties they bought the Hall and the rest of the estate for a song. They showed themselves to be pretty astute. They resold the Hall and kept the land and the barns; then much later they sold the barns for development. They had trouble getting planning permission because they were so old and listed but they managed it in the end.'

'And so, here we all are.' Rosemary beamed at them both. 'And it's Bill I need to talk to again about the footpaths. He has closed one of them off; changed its route completely.'

Lesley gave her a close look. 'I hardly think the route matters in the great scheme of things. As long as people can still walk the fields.'

'Ah, but there you are wrong.' Rosemary set down her cup purposefully and sat forward on the edge of her chair. 'These are ancient highways, rights of way. They have to be protected.'

Lesley sighed. 'My dear, that path you keep going on about, across Dead Man's Field, it doesn't exist. I have looked at all sorts of maps and plans. It's just not there. And there is a lovely walk along a pretty lane down the edge of the field.' She glanced at Zoë. 'Has Rosemary signed you up to her footpath mafia yet?'

Zoë shook her head, embarrassed. 'No, not me. I jog. I don't like walking. At least not with lots of people.'

'No more do I.' Lesley gave a sudden snort of laughter. 'Ghastly thought! I am sorry, Rosemary dear, but you know it's true. I've seen them. Your friends don't look at the country-side, they are not interested in flowers or birds or even the views of the river. They won't let anyone take a dog with them, for heaven's sake! All they want to do is criticise, compare it to some approximation of a town park, measure that the grass is the right length and if the poor farmers haven't cut it, they want to know why not; as though these guys haven't got better things to do. Bill should put a socking great bull in that field. That's what I say!'

Zoë hid a smile. 'Why is it called Dead Man's Field? That sounds a bit spooky.'

'And rightly so. There is a tumulus in the field. Now that is on a lot of the maps, as I'm sure you've noticed, Rosemary, though you've chosen to ignore it. The field has long had a reputation for being haunted. Another reason the locals wouldn't walk there if you paid them and why there wouldn't be a footpath across it. Why is it, Rosemary, it is always newcomers who stir these things up? Why don't you ask the locals if there was ever a path there? And listen to their answers.'

'Because the locals aren't interested.' Rosemary sniffed. 'They don't care about the countryside half the time.' She wasn't going to admit that she had at the beginning overlooked the fact that the silly little pile of earth she had contemplated bulldozing was a tumulus. Most of the maps didn't show it any more anyway. 'All they are interested in is if they can stuff the latest plasma telly into their front rooms.'

'Oh, my dear, that is so wrong.' Lesley shook her head. 'Read the history, the proper history of the estate, not your little maps which were probably drawn up by retired clergymen in the thirties who never set foot in the fields themselves.' She was looking agitated. 'I've read a lot about this area; it's my job as part of restoring the gardens.'

'Well, the farm was never part of the gardens,' Rosemary said stiffly. 'The local people wanted access to the river. It is the obvious route if you look at the maps.'

'The local people have the lane, Rosemary. That is why it is there. That is where it goes. To the river.'

'They'll thank me in the end.' Rosemary helped herself to a piece of cake. 'They don't know anything about rights of way and they are too lazy to bother, but they will use the path once it's there, you'll see.'

Zoë stared at her. 'That sounds awfully snobby and

patronising, Rosemary, if you don't mind my saying so. Are there any farm workers' cottages belonging to the estate?' She changed the subject hastily, looking at Lesley. 'I was looking at a map in the library and it didn't seem to show any that are still there.'

'No. There aren't any left now.' Lesley stood up and reached for the coffee pot. Tight-lipped, she topped up Rosemary's cup and then Zoë's. 'The Old Forge next to you is the only one left, as far as I know. I am sure there were cottages; there must have been on the estate, when the farm was in its heyday, but I expect they collapsed over the years. They were probably fairly basic, and once the family had gone who would care? They were not part of a village, after all. Bill might know.' She glanced at Rosemary. 'Come on, don't sulk, old thing. Hurry up and drink that and we'll show Zoë round the gardens.'

Straightening up for a few moments to rest his back after bending over the engine housing, Ken saw Steve Formby strolling down the path towards him. He groaned inwardly, but managed a cheery wave. 'The girls have gone up to the Hall for coffee, I gather,' he called.

Steve nodded. He lowered himself carefully onto the edge of the landing stage and sat with his legs dangling over the water. 'It is so lovely here,' he said. 'Peaceful.'

Ken contemplated a response and decided to say nothing. He was not a fan of Steve's wife. She was noisy and bossy and far too aggressive for his liking. He leaned back against the cabin door. 'I hear the Watts family are down. We haven't met them yet.'

Steve blew gustily through pursed lips. 'I wouldn't bother. They are a nightmare.'

'Noisy?' There had been a never-ending blast of sound from The Summer Barn this morning. Music, shouting and revving engines, to say nothing of dogs barking.

'Noisy,' Steve confirmed. 'The blessing is that they don't

stay long. The kids will have to go back to school at some point.'

Both men were silent for a while. Ken reached for an oily rag and began slowly to wipe his fingers on it. 'Odd thing happened the other night when we came home after dark,' he said thoughtfully. 'Did Zoë mention it to Rosemary? Strange noises out here on the river.'

Steve laughed. 'Yes, she told me. I've never heard them.'

'But you know about them.'

'Load of crap, in my view.' Steve was rhythmically kicking the seaweed-covered post beneath him 'Sound carries over water, we all know that. There was probably someone messing round upstream somewhere. They could have been a long way away so you wouldn't have been able to see them.'

Ken grinned 'You're right. That could well have been it. Or I did wonder if it could have been smugglers bringing contraband up-river, drugs or illegal immigrants. It was a bit odd.'

'The little woman scared?' Steve laughed again.

'Something like that.'

'I reckon you're more likely to be right than the girls' theory that it is a ghostly visitor.' With another snort of laughter Steve drummed a further tattoo with his heels on the wooden piles beneath him. 'Don't let her talk to Leo about it,' he went on. 'He's a bit fey, in my opinion. Probably something to do with that ghastly accident the poor chap had. He reckons it is a Viking longship.'

Ken nodded sagely. 'I haven't met him yet. He always pops in when I'm not there.' He sensed rather than saw Steve glance at him sharply.

'I wouldn't worry.' Steve thought for a minute. 'I doubt if he's a lady's man. Not looking like that. He would stir up compassion in a stone wall, but I don't get the feeling he's a danger to our women.' Ken refrained from pointing out that Steve's wife was a weather-beaten battle-axe, while his was still young and attractive. It seemed unnecessarily unkind.

'He's not gay?'

'No. In fact I think he's married. But separated. Our cleaning lady, Annie, mentioned it; said she walked out on him after the accident. What a bitch.'

Ken noticed Steve pat his pockets speculatively for the third time and he gave a knowing grin. 'Am I right in thinking you've given up smoking?'

Steve nodded. 'Can't get used to not having any on me.'

'Would you like to come aboard for a lager? Then you can tell me about this Viking ship.'

Ten minutes later the men were seated in the cockpit of the *Lady Grace*. 'You know we're only a few miles from Sutton Hoo, the Anglo-Saxon site where they found the great ship burial,' Steve said as he made himself comfortable and pulled the tab on the can.

'We haven't been there yet.' Ken leaned back into the corner and rested his arm companionably over the tiller. 'Is it worth seeing?'

'I enjoyed it. There is a museum and a café and a shop, and then you walk out to these burial mounds. Nothing much to see there, just grass, and nice walks overlooking the river, a bit like this actually, but round where they found the ship it all feels a bit special, even I have to admit that.'

'And this ship is the same as the one Zoë and Leo are talking about?'

Steve frowned. 'I assume so. Is Viking the same as Anglo-Saxon?' Both men shook their heads. 'History is not my thing,' Ken said after a moment. His attention was caught by a movement over Steve's shoulder. Out in the river a cormorant flew low over the water, its dark iridescent wings and sharp head and beak a black arrow against the green of the rising tide.

5

Eric shaded his eyes from the glare with a raised hand and watched as the bird skimmed low over the river. It came to rest on a tree stump and shook its wings, almost at once staring around at the water, ready to dive if it spotted a fish. He gave a grim smile. Observant bird. Cunning. Not missing a thing. He hooked his thumbs into his broad leather belt, feeling the cold working its way into his bones. He had spent too long indoors, too long with the furnace and hammer. Not enough time with his wife.

'Is the sword ready?'

The voice behind him was persistent, always there.

'I will tell you when it is ready!' he yelled, and he spun round furiously, his fist raised. There was no one there. He stared left and right incredulously. There was no one in sight; the village was deserted, the women indoors at the loom or spinning, the men out in the fields making all ready before the first of the autumn storms.

He took a deep breath to steady himself and turned back to the river. He was imagining things again.

Beware of elf-shot. He heard his mother's voice in his head and smiled fondly.

What would the priest say to her warnings; unexplained illness and injuries caused by insidious small arrows fired by unseen spirits? Oh, Wulfric believed in the spirits too. They all believed in the spirits, but he would have a different weapon against them. Cross yourself, man. Ward off the evil eye. Guard your woman with Christian prayers. Eric shook his head slowly. No, he had tried Christian prayers. They did not work; they did not bring him fine sons. Working for a man who had turned back to the old ways and the old gods had made him realise their potency. And yet. He closed his eyes for a moment. Whose voice was it he thought he had heard? Hrotgar, the thegn's reeve. The man was a devout Christian like the Lady Hilda. As was his own wife, Edith. He sighed. He was spending too long on the sword; there were other things to make, other people waiting, including a weapon for the ealdorman at Rendlesham, who was a kinsman of King Edmund, but this sword was special; it was his masterpiece; it would be carried into war against the Viking host, if not by Lord Egbert, then by his successor, and it would bring safety and blessing and renown to their village.

His eyes narrowed as he saw a movement in the distance; beyond the palisade someone was walking across the beaten earth, heading up towards the hall; a man, and there, in front, he could see the soft green of his wife's tunic and cloak. He saw Edith hesitate and he saw her turn to wait for the second figure. The two converged, their shadows merging in the bright sunlight. He clenched his fists as he watched. They had stopped walking. They were talking. They were standing very close staring into each other's faces and then as he stood helplessly, the length of a field away, he saw them turn from the path and disappear between the houses. His cry of anguish echoed out across the cold water. At the sound the cormorant stretched out its wings and launched itself upriver and out of sight.

He was spending too much time with Bella. Dan was well aware of it, but he blamed himself for the horse's state, and she was responding. She greeted him now with a soft whinny of recognition when he approached her stall, and she had begun to eat. The swelling was going down on her legs, but nothing could be done about the terrible scars which remained as ugly gashes over her fetlocks. How had the woman done it, he wondered, and how could she, how could anyone, have brought themselves to injure such a gentle, willing creature?

The barns were full of grain and hay and straw against the long winter, the stalls for the horses empty now except for Bella's as the animals were out working on the farm, bringing in heavy wagons of turnips, tumbrils full of cider apples, collecting the last of the potatoes for the clamps in the yard. Dan was busy in the forge. As farrier and blacksmith to the estate he was in constant demand, shoeing all the horses on the farm and up at the Hall, and making a constant stream of iron goods; at present he was forging sets of gate hinges and railings for the park. He rubbed Bella's nose. 'I must get on, my lovely,' he whispered. 'I'll be back to see you later.' He froze as he heard the tap of heels in the doorway.

'Daniel!'

He hadn't seen Emily Crosby for several days and the sound of her voice filled him with resentment. He saw the mare's ears flatten against her head and he held his breath. Did the woman know he was there? Silently he tiptoed out of the stall, instinctively knowing she mustn't catch him near the horse. Keeping to the shadows of a pile of straw bales he edged his way towards a side door.

'Daniel!' The voice was closer now, sharp. She was walking towards Bella's stall, the heels of her riding boots noisy on the cobbles. 'Drat it! Where is the man?'

He did not want her near Bella; he had to distract her.

Ducking round the far side of the bales, he walked towards her as though he had just come in from the yard. 'My lady? Were you looking for me?'

'Isn't it obvious? I was calling your name.' Her tone was sarcastic. She was as usual dressed for riding. 'I need you to check my horse.'

'Of course, my lady.' Meekly he followed her outside. The roan pony was tied up near the forge, tossing her head up and down irritably. Something was obviously distressing her. It took him only minutes to find the burrs beneath the saddle-cloth. 'That must have been vexing her badly, my lady,' he said as he extracted them. 'It would be very sore. They are a bother at this time of year. I've found them under the harness of the working horses as well. Shall I help you into the saddle, my lady?' He knew very well she had put them there herself; no one saddling the horse could have failed to see them.

'If you please, Daniel.' She narrowed her eyes at him like a cat, holding out her hand. As he stooped to take her foot she put her arm round his neck. 'You could lift me off my feet so easily, Daniel, a great strong man like you,' she murmured. She turned towards him. 'You find me attractive, don't you, Daniel?' Her voice was low and seductive. 'You would like to kiss me, I'll be bound!'

He took a step back, repelled. 'No, my lady. I know my place.'

'But your place is to do as I tell you, Daniel.' She moved closer to him. 'I trust your wife is not going to make a habit of appearing suddenly. She might find it hard to understand how tempted you are by my beauty.'

'Dan, where are you, my friend?' The voice came so suddenly from the far side of the yard that for a moment neither of them moved. Not Susan. It was a man's voice. Leaping backwards, Daniel looked round and saw to his immense relief the sight of Jem, one of the horseboys with two of the Suffolks. He was riding astride one and leading the other, the harness hitched on both of them. 'We're done for the day so I brought these two back, Dan,' he called. He seemed to notice Lady Emily for the first time. 'My lady!' The young man touched his forelock as he drew to a halt in the yard and slid off the great horse.

Daniel saw the flash of fury in her eyes as she turned back to her own mount. He stooped again for her foot and threw her none too gently into the saddle. 'Is there anything else I can do for you, my lady?'

For a moment she stared down at him. 'There is, Daniel, and you would do well to remember it. You were shirking your duties. If I find you avoiding me in future you might well find yourself in need of a job.' She paused. 'It wouldn't do to be put off, would it now, Daniel, and you and your wife with a baby on the way?' She brought her whip down on the pony's rump, sitting the saddle remarkably well as it gave a small buck of resentment.

'Phew!' Jem winked at him as she rode out of the yard. 'George and me, we reckoned you needed rescuing. George saw her heading down here from the Hall.' The head horseman had appeared behind them leading three more of the working horses into the yard.

Dan grinned. 'Pity the squire can't rein her in.'

'You don't fancy yourself fathering the heir then?' Jem guffawed.

'No, I don't!' Dan threw a mock punch at him, then he sobered, all humour gone. 'It's no joke, though. She's threatening to have me and Susan thrown off.'

'You'll have to do what you're told then, boy!' Jem clicked his tongue at the horses and walked them over towards the water trough to drink. 'I wonder where you'll get the strength.' He was still grinning as he dodged out of reach a second time.

'A word to the wise.' Leo saw Zoë walking towards the landing stage and hurried down the path to catch up with her. 'Our friend Rosemary has upset Bill Turtill in a big way.'

Zoë put down her basket, pleased to see him. In spite of his occasional brusqueness he was, she realised, one of the few people in her new life who interested her and whose company she enjoyed. He kept her on her toes. 'Who is Bill Turtill?' She frowned. 'Yes, I do know, he's our neighbouring farmer, right?'

'Right.' Leo nodded. 'She's had a go at him about the footpath.'

'But surely everyone knew she was going to do that.' She sighed. 'I'm not even sure where this path is supposed to be.'

'It's over there.' He turned and pointed. 'You can see where it would go from here. There's a ten-acre field on the slope going down towards the river; in the centre there is a copse with a tumulus in it and she wants the path to go right through the copse and presumably over the tumulus.'

'Dead Man's Field,' she said thoughtfully

'Ah, you've been doing your homework.' He gave her an approving grin.

'Lesley Inworth told us.'

'Nice woman. Knows her stuff.'

She nodded, pleased he was confiding in her. 'Why is it that Rosemary is so keen on this? It seems so obsessive.'

'Why indeed. Bill was nearly apoplectic. He says the fact that there is an earthwork there proves there has never been a path there, and she told him there was, because she had seen it on some hand-drawn map in a little booklet she bought in Woodbridge about nice walks and she didn't care about the earthwork; she said it isn't marked on most maps, and that anyway highways and byways take precedence.'

'Highways?'

He laughed. 'The woman is mad. Please, have a word with her if you've any influence. I haven't. She's no time for me, but I've seen this sort of thing before. It could escalate and we are a very small community and we do want to stay friends with Bill. He's a nice guy.'

'But surely you've told him we have nothing to do with her.'

'We all live at the barns, Zoë. In his eyes that makes us all part of the same gang. His dad may have sold off the barns and probably made a packet on the development, but that doesn't stop Bill, and everyone else in Hanley for that matter, from resenting us. You must have noticed. You and I and your husband are townies. We don't fit. However friendly they are, we will never be part of the community. Not really. And this sort of nonsense will make them close ranks. He thinks we are all in it. Especially you.' He glanced at her. 'He heard that you and Rosemary went up to see Lesley at the Hall.'

'Yes, we did. And we did mention the path – or Rosemary did, but I didn't say anything to support her.'

'Well, Lesley must have said something to him to give him the impression that you did.'

Zoë looked round with an air of bewilderment. 'I'm sorry. I didn't mean to. I really don't support her. I've made it clear to her I don't want to join her walks.' She sighed then frowned as she saw Ken emerging from the shadows of the trees. As he strode towards them she sensed Leo withdrawing into himself. She put her hand on his arm before he had a chance to turn away. 'You haven't met my husband, Leo. Wait. Let me introduce you.'

The two men shook hands. She could see Ken giving Leo's face a quick glance then turning away, pretending not to have noticed. 'You've met Bill Turtill, haven't you, Ken? What was he like?' she said after moment's awkward silence.

'He seemed a decent enough bloke. Why?'

Her explanation elicited a snort of derision. 'I hope he takes no notice of that woman. She's a complete pain. Always round our house!'

Zoë hid a smile. 'Not always, Ken,' she said gently. 'But more than I would like, I must admit. Please, Leo, if you see Bill again can you tell him we have nothing to do with her paths?'

'Weird guy,' Ken said after a few seconds as they watched Leo retrace his steps across the grass. 'Not very sociable, is he?'

'I don't think he likes people looking at his face.'

'I didn't.' Ken was indignant. 'I came to find you. I was getting hungry.'

They spent the afternoon on the boat and, without actually saying so, made sure they packed up to return to the house before it grew dark.

Hurrying up the path between the pines they came to a halt at the edge of the communal lawn. Someone had set up a huge gas-fired barbecue on the grass with, round it, two or three tables surrounded by chairs. 'Oh God! Our neighbours are going to have a party,' Zoë whispered.

Ken grimaced. 'I hope they don't invite us.'

They did. Barely had they walked in through the door of The Old Barn when a large florid woman in tight jeans and a T-shirt embellished with the words *Daddy's girl* across a bust which must have been heading towards size twenty, hurried after them. She introduced herself as Sharon Watts 'just like *EastEnders*,' she added so automatically that Zoë realised she must always say it, assuming everyone would know who she meant. 'You must come,' Sharon went on. 'We've asked Rosie and Steve and old ugly mug from The Old Forge. They are all coming. A barn get-together for half-term. Don't worry about booze. We've got enough. Just bring yourselves!'

'Christ!' Ken murmured once she had gone. 'What have we done, moving here? We don't seem to have a single normal neighbour.'

Zoë shook her head, suppressing a smile. 'We'll have to go.'

'Can't I have flu?'

'No you can't. She saw you. Besides, it would be good to meet them all. Better the devil you know, and all that.'

'Did I hear right – she called Leo an ugly mug?'

'Vile woman.' Zoë shook her head. 'I think he's quite attractive once you get used to his face.'

*   *   *

'Have you seen the ghosts yet?' Jamie Watts was a redhead like his sister; whereas in her it contributed to her gamine attractiveness, in him, combined with a receding chin and a thick crop of acne it looked thoroughly unwholesome. He sneered at Zoë as he swigged from a bottle of lager.

'I have.' She smiled at him with an attempt at graciousness. 'I gather you are quite the expert on our ghosts.'

He looked taken aback for a moment, unsure how to take her remark. 'They're scary,' he said after a pause.

'They are,' she agreed. 'So, tell me, don't you have ghosts in your house? I would have thought all these barns would be haunted. They are prime examples of paranormal habitat.'

He narrowed his eyes. 'Are you taking the mickey?'

'No. Are you?' She held his gaze, fending off an inquisitive lurcher looking for titbits.

They were interrupted by Leo, who had arrived carrying a bottle of wine which he gave to Sharon. In exchange he was handed a glass of Pimm's, containing more fruit than seemed possible. 'So, young Jamie, how are you? Any GCSEs under your belt yet?'

The boy flushed. 'No. I take them next year.'

'Your mother will be proud of you.' Leo spoke deadpan though Zoë presumed there was some kind of subtext there. She wondered how old Jamie was. Sixteen, she would have thought, though perhaps more. She saw a flash of something like hatred cross the boy's face and winced for Leo. She wondered why he had come.

The party, once it got going, was passable. Jeff seemed a master of his barbecue and turned out a succession of wonderfully grilled meats and sausages, much coveted by the two slavering dogs, while Sharon had made several mouthwatering salads, which, Zoë noticed, her children appeared to boycott, preferring their ketchup and mayonnaise unadulterated. As far as she could see, Sharon and Jeff were going out of their way to be nice; the two boys the opposite. The girl sat close to Leo but said little. Of the eldest boy, Jackson, there was no sign at all.

By the end of the evening Zoë was convinced they were in for trouble. As they wandered back across the cold, dew-soaked grass under a hazy moon she said as much to Ken. Leo was walking with them. 'I think you're right. The little buggers will be planning something. They were doing their best to put the wind up you.'

Ken snorted. 'We'll be ready for them.'

Leo gave him a sideways glance. 'Don't underestimate them. They may look thick. They are actually quite bright, as I know to my cost.'

'Besides which,' Zoë added, 'some of the ghosts are real, aren't they?'

Both men looked at her.

Leo said nothing.

Ken gave a muffled snort.

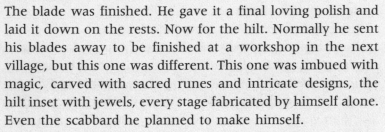

The blade was finished. He gave it a final loving polish and laid it down on the rests. Now for the hilt. Normally he sent his blades away to be finished at a workshop in the next village, but this one was different. This one was imbued with magic, carved with sacred runes and intricate designs, the hilt inset with jewels, every stage fabricated by himself alone. Even the scabbard he planned to make himself.

He glanced up from the work table. Was that a footstep outside? He threw a cloth over the table, hiding the blade from view, and walked over to stand listening behind the door. He could hear nothing but the whine of the wind in the crannies of the workshop, the rustle as the ash bed stirred in the furnace. Grabbing the latch he pulled the door open and looked round. It was growing dark; the sun had set stormily into a bank of black cloud. He could hear the trees thrashing down in the woods. He took a step outside and looked round again. The village seemed deserted. He could see no one but there was someone there, he could sense it. He stared round again, feeling the hairs on the back of his neck stir. 'Hello?' His voice was lost in the sound of the wind. 'Who's there?' There was no reply.

He retreated into the workshop and pulled the door closed, barring it against the night, then he lit another lantern and, pulling off the cloth, drew a stool up to the table. Even in the poor light he could make a start.

In their house in the village his wife, Edith, was listening to the same wind. She shivered, drawing her cloak around her shoulders. She should be up at the hall even now. All the women would be there, her neighbours, her sister, her cousins, her friends, joining in the evening's entertainment. They had been there from early morning, cooking then eventually serving the food, clearing the tables and benches, and by now settling down to listen to the singers and the travelling bard who had arrived in the village just that day. Any newcomer was an excitement, a treat not to be missed. Lord Egbert would not be there; he was still confined to his sickbed, but his brother, Oswald, led the men now. He would lift the great drinking horn to give the toast and invite the scop to recite, and lead the singers far into the night. At his side, his brother's reeve, Hrotgar – the man who had told Eric that his lord had need of a very special sword, the man who had threatened Eric if it were not finished on time, the man whose eyes followed her as she walked to the spring, or to the bake house, or the workshop or to and from the hall – would be waiting and watching every person in the hall.

She sighed. She had not joined the others because she had been feeling sick again this morning. It had taken her a long time to rise from her bed. She stood looking down at the hearth thoughtfully and on impulse stooped to pick up one of the statues of the goddess Frige Eric had made for the Lady Hilda. Pagan. And powerful. She bit her lip, then slowly

91

leaned down and let it fall back in the basket. Could it be that after all this time she was pregnant? She rested her hand lightly on her flat belly, trying to remember when she had last bled. Surely, two full moons had passed.

There it was again, the sound of scratching at the door. She moved across the floor, straining her ears. Behind her an extra gust of wind sent sparks and ashes blowing across the room from the fire and she turned, stamping them out, clutching her cloak to her. There were shutters over the windows and the door was firmly barred. She was safe, but she couldn't help the tremors of fear which were running up and down her spine. Someone was out there, she knew it.

'Eric?' It was a whisper. 'Is that you?'

He wouldn't be able to hear her against the storm and she didn't dare call out loud. Whoever it was knew she was in there. They would be able to see the light from her candles through the chinks in the shutters, but if she made no sound, then maybe they would go away.

The scratching sound came again, louder this time, then a soft knock. Three times in rapid succession, softly, near the bottom of the door. It was their secret sign. With a whimper of relief she grappled with the bar and lifted it from its socket, pulling the door open, filling the room with the scent of the river and dust and pine needles and a fresh blast of wind to stir the fire. It wasn't Eric. Hrotgar stepped inside, wrestled the door shut and slammed the bar back in place. All but one of the candles had blown out and the room was nearly dark.

'Get out!' she cried. 'How did you know our knock?'

He gave a low laugh. 'I have heard him do it often enough. It is hardly secret. The whole village knows.'

'I don't want you here.'

'Oh, but you do. I've seen you watch me, lust after me. I've heard no complaints when I have come to visit you and keep you company.' He made no move towards her now that he was inside. He folded his arms, staring at her, shadowed as she was in the small room. 'Your husband is in the service of Lord Egbert. While he slaves over this precious sword it is for me to make sure that his wife is content.'

'No.' She shook her head, backing away from him. She placed herself behind the table and leaned forward, her arms braced. 'You get out of here, Hrotgar. I need no visits from you. I have never needed visits from you. I am a faithful wife.'

'You are an obedient wife.' He smiled at her. 'One he can be proud of. But, you see, he needs to know that you are not missing him. He needs to know that he has as much time as he needs. If he hurries in his work because he worries about you, then all is lost.'

'But he told me the Lord Egbert needs him to hurry.'

'The Lord Egbert has all the time in the world, my dear.' He paused.

'What do you mean?' She was studying his face, trying to understand his expression. 'Is something wrong? Is he worse?'

'Your husband needs a hair from your head to put in with the molten metal of the sword.' He spoke slowly, almost dreamily, ignoring her questions. 'Unbind your hair, Edith.'

She shook her head. 'If he needed something from me he would come home and tell me.'

'But he cannot come home. That is part of the magic.'

'No. This is all wrong. It makes no sense. The sword is nearly finished.'

'Magic is not bound by reason, my dear. Nor is it to be spoken of. He trusted me with the message and me alone as go-between, between him and the Lord Egbert.'

She hesitated. 'And you have given me the message.'

'So you need to unbind your hair.'

She was watching his face in the half-light of the single candle flame and she saw him run his tongue across his lips, a quick feral movement which frightened her even more than his words had done. She could feel the deep frozen terror of the rabbit confronted by a weasel. 'If my hair is needed Eric can take a strand with his own hands,' she said at last.

'It is Eric who has demanded it. At the forge. And he has forbidden you to set foot there. It is for me to take it to him.'

She shook her head uncomfortably. 'Then I will pull one out myself, and tie it to the doorpost of the forge and he can come out and pick it up when I have gone.'

'That is foolish. And not what he asked.' He was getting angry now. He took a step towards her. 'Unbind your hair, woman.'

'Edith!' The sudden call at the door was accompanied by the thudding of a fist on the thick wood. 'What are you doing in there? Why have you barred the door?' The latch rattled up and down. 'Edith?' It was a woman's voice.

'Open it.' Edith whispered. 'Open it now.'

Hrotgar looked taken aback. With a scowl he turned on his heel and walked towards it, pulling the bar free and throwing it on the ground, then pulling open the door to let the fresh air and wind sweep in. 'Come in, goodwife. What is all the noise about?' he growled. 'What I discuss with the smith's woman is nothing to do with anyone else.' He swept past her out into the darkness.

Edith's neighbour, Gudrun, the wheelwright's wife, stood staring after him, then she ducked in through the doorway and pushed the door shut behind her. 'What was he doing here, with the door barred?' she said suspiciously. 'I don't trust that man.'

'No more do I.' Suddenly Edith was shivering. She moved closer to the fire. 'He came with a message from my husband.'

Gudrun bustled about lighting the lanterns and the candle which stood on the table. 'Why aren't you up at the hall?'

'I didn't feel well.'

'And he came to find out why?'

Edith shook her head. 'No.' But of course he had noticed her absence. Why else had he come here?

'So, what is wrong with you? You're not breeding at last?'

Edith gave a wry smile. 'I'm not sure. I wondered if it was possible. I feel sick. But perhaps it is just that my head hurts. I have been working on Eric's jerkin after the light has gone for too many evenings. I just wanted to sit quietly and rest my eyes. There will be noise and celebration enough when he has finished the sword and we take it up to the hall for the Lord Edbert.'

Gudrun was looking at her closely. She gave a knowing smile. 'I think there will be reason for noise and celebration in this house if I read your signs right, neighbour mine.' She smiled. 'But we'll say nothing yet. Not till you are sure. Eric will be so pleased. As for the celebrations up at the hall, I doubt if that day will happen.' She shook her head.

'Why? It will be the best sword he ever made!' Edith bridled with indignation.

'No, no, I'm not doubting his skill, it is the Lord Egbert I'm thinking of.' The older woman sighed sadly. 'He hasn't been seen for weeks now and rumours fly round the hall that he is dying, if he isn't dead already. His sons and his brother wrangle and fight like dogs over a bone, and the warriors are taking sides ready to jump this way or that. They say the ealdorman will ride over from Rendlesham and the king's reeve might come himself. Lady Hilda is white as a sheet and looks exhausted, and that man,' she ducked her head towards the door, 'is in the thick of all the gossip.'

'And I have been missing it all.' Edith grimaced.

'Do you know how long it will be before the sword is finished?' Gudrun pulled up a stool and sat down close to the fire, holding her hands out to the embers.

Edith gave a wry smile. 'He wouldn't tell me, even if I had seen him,' she said.

Gudrun looked up at her, then back towards the fire. A log slipped and a flame lit up the lazy spiral of smoke rising towards the blackened underside of the thatch, before making its way out into the night. 'I know he's been home. I saw him.'

'Then you should mind your spying eyes, madam,' Edith scolded good-humouredly. 'He didn't come, you understand, and anyone who says different is a liar. He told me nothing anyway.'

'And the message Hrotgar brought?'

'Is not your business.' Edith shook her head with mock exasperation. 'Fetch that jug of ale from the sideboard, and we'll have a sup to wet our whistles. I'm feeling better, thanks to you.'

It was a great deal later that Edith, wrapped in a dark cloak, let herself out into the night. Gudrun had long gone and the village was silent. She crept towards the forge, stopping dead for a moment as a dog barked from somewhere behind the church, then she moved on. Under the hood of her cloak her hair was loose.

The forge was in darkness, the smokeholes cold. She paused, wondering what to do, then she crept closer. Eric often slept there; he had been doing so for the last month or more. Even the thought of him so close, lying, perhaps naked, wrapped in one of the furs she had seen stacked in the corner of the workshop, made her body tense with longing. She waited, her ear to the oak door slats, listening. There was no sound from inside. Cautiously she put her hand to the latch and silently began to slide it up. The hinges creaked and she stopped, her heart thudding, gazing round in the darkness. It wasn't her husband she feared, it was the other man, the lord's reeve, with his lustful eyes and his leering face and his power to intercede between Eric and the warriors for whom he worked.

The door wasn't barred. After another protesting squeak it eased open and she peered in. 'Eric?' she whispered. She could smell the charcoal, the leather, the very scent of the iron, the oil with which he worked and then, suddenly she could smell him, his skin, the rough smokiness of his hair. 'Where are you?'

'I thought I forbade you to come here, Edith.' She still couldn't see him, but his voice was close. She imagined him waiting, poised to see who was trying to gain entry to the forge in the dark of the night, and for a moment she pictured the knife he probably held in his hand. The thought frightened her even as it gave her a strange frisson of excitement.

'Hrotgar came to the house; he said you needed a hair from my head for your sword magic,' she whispered. She was still poised on the threshold, knowing better than to try to set foot over it without invitation. 'I wouldn't give it to him. He frightens me. But if it's what you need you can have every hair on my head.' She pushed back the hood and shook her head gently, feeling the weight of her long hair on her shoulders, wondering if he could see her against the starlight.

She heard a smothered groan. 'Edith! Sweet wife, but I miss you!'

'Then why do you stay away from me?'

'I have to. You know I have to. Lord Egbert directed every stage in the making of this sword according to the ancient rule. I knew nothing about when it was first spoken of, but he was right. It was a true memory of past traditions. I sensed that here.' He thumped his chest with his fist. 'Something which should never be forgotten. It is too important. And part of that tradition is that I forbid you my bed until it is finished.'

She narrowed her eyes, trying to see him, overwhelmed with a sudden suspicion. 'Was it Lord Egbert himself who told you all this, or his reeve?'

The silence which greeted her question might have been answer enough, but suddenly he was at her side. 'It was Hrotgar. You are right. I never discussed this with the thegn himself. He has been too ill for too long. All I was told has come from his reeve. But it was right, Edith –'

'And did you ask for a hair from my head?'

'No.'

There was a long silence.

'It may be that the magic is real, Eric. I wouldn't want to profane your work, but outside under the stars, can there be weakness for the sword in that?'

He was so close to her now she could see his bulk. But still he hadn't touched her.

'The blade is finished,' he said huskily. 'It needs no hair from anyone's head. It is tempered and polished and gleams like silver. It is the best I have ever made, ready for the king's service against the enemy host. All it needs is the crosspiece and hilt.' He glanced behind him at the work table where the beginnings of the hilt lay beneath a linen cloth.

'Then can we celebrate together?' At last she reached out towards him, touching him lightly on the chest. He was fully clothed, but she felt the spark between them.

'Not here, but you're right; I think we can celebrate under the stars.' She heard the smile without being able to see it.

Still in total darkness he took her hand and they tiptoed away from the forge towards the woods which bordered the river. He put his arm round her and pulled her close and at last, as she looked up at him, he paused to stoop over her and kiss her long and hard.

In the shadows nearby the small movement behind the house of the harness maker showed that they were being observed and in the woods an owl cried warning.

6

'Ken.' Zoë's whisper sounded loud in the silence of the darkened bedroom. She had been awake for hours listening to the owls in the wood. 'Listen. There's someone downstairs.'

For a moment Ken lay, paralysed with sleep, then slowly he opened his eyes and she felt his body tense beside hers in the big bed. 'What did you hear?' He sat up.

'I'm not sure. Footsteps? The creak of floorboards?'

'We locked the doors. I double-checked. Is it those bastard kids next door?' He was pulling on his dressing gown.

'It might be.' She slid out of bed too. 'There! Listen!'

There was a definite sound from downstairs, a creak and then a long dragging noise as though someone was moving a piece of furniture. 'It might be burglars,' she whispered. 'Be careful.'

'Get your phone. Be ready to call the police if necessary.' He had his slippers on now and was heading for the door. Pulling it open, he reached out to the wall and flicked the bank of switches there, flooding the landing, the staircase and the huge room below with light. Nothing happened. There was total silence.

'Who's there?' he shouted from the top of the stairs. 'Come out. There is no point in hiding, you're on CCTV.'

Silence. Zoë had followed him onto the landing, the phone in her hand. She leaned over the rail and stared down into the brightly lit room below. 'The chairs have moved,' she whispered. 'Look.' The semicircle of comfortable armchairs, which were placed to take advantage of the view from the great window overlooking the river, were now sitting in a straight line.

'OK, you stupid kids. You've had your fun. That is enough!' Ken roared. He headed for the staircase. 'We are calling the police!'

Zoë looked at him. 'For real?' she whispered. He shook his head and put his finger to his lips. 'Wait. Let's see where they are,' he whispered back. 'I don't want to make trouble with the neighbours if we can sort this.' He began to walk down the stairs.

She followed him, staring nervously round the room. She had no sense that there was anyone there. It was almost starkly empty.

They found nothing. The doors were locked, the security lights outside didn't seem to have been triggered, the kitchen was exactly as they had left it when they came in from the barbecue.

'I love this window in the daytime,' Zoë said quietly when at last Ken had repositioned the chairs and they were both standing near it, looking round, 'but it makes one feel so exposed at night. Anyone could be out there in the dark watching us now, at this very moment.'

'And enjoying every minute of it. We'll have to get curtains or blinds,' he agreed. He walked over to the window and stared out. All he could see was his own reflection. 'They could have keys, of course. It's quite possible. Why don't you have a quiet word with Sharon tomorrow? It's less threatening if you do it.' He had rammed his hands down into the pockets of his dressing gown. 'I don't think they've done any damage, but that's not to say that they might not. The fun of merely re-arranging the furniture might pall quite quickly.'

Zoë lay awake for a long time, listening. Beside her, Ken was breathing deeply and steadily, his head buried in a pillow, but beyond the distant hoot of an owl from the trees on the far side of the lawns she heard nothing. Slowly the darkness of the room began to lessen. She could see the square outline of the window, then the mirror, then slowly the other details of the room began to appear. Eventually she gave up trying to sleep. She crept out of bed and, quietly dragging on her bathrobe, she let herself out onto the landing. They had left the lights on and she peered over the banisters at the room below. The chairs were as they had left them, the room quiet as the cold light of dawn filtered through the huge window. She tiptoed down the stairs and stood for a moment frowning. It was very cold.

In the kitchen the back door was wide open; on the work surface in the centre of the room lay three rusty nails.

'Horseshoe.' Leo looked at them for only a second. 'Quite old. Maybe fifty, hundred years. Where were they?'

He led her into his kitchen and reached for the kettle with a huge yawn.

'On the worktop. With the kitchen door open.'

'And you think the kids put them there?'

She gave him a long thoughtful look, then she shook her head. 'No. I think they moved the furniture around, but I don't think they brought the nails. It's not the first time we've found nails like this and last time there wasn't anyone there. There couldn't have been.'

'Ah.' He was dressed, in jeans and shirt with an old torn fleece over it; he was unshaven and his face looked crumpled and sleepy. She wondered if that was how he dressed for bed. She couldn't quite imagine him in pyjamas and smart dressing gown like her husband, and suddenly she found herself visualising him with no shirt at all.

'What?' He was watching her.

She felt herself blush. 'Sorry. Lack of sleep is catching up with me. I'm not going to let this rattle me, Leo. I'm just not sure what to do. Do you think I should go and speak to Sharon? Ken thinks I should.'

'No.' He shook his head. 'She'll go off like a demented firecracker and tear the kids to shreds, which will make them ten times worse, in my experience.' He paused for a moment and she saw a strange expression flit across his face. A mixture of pain and wry amusement. It wasn't the first time he had hinted that they had at some time made his life a misery as well as that of their predecessors. 'Leave it, is my advice. Don't do anything or say anything. Just wait and see what happens. They are only down here for ten days at most. Keep quiet, watch and listen. If nothing happens they will be disappointed. They will want to know why. They will wonder if you noticed what they did.'

'And they will come back.' Zoë scowled.

'Well, the key thing is easily solved. A good old-fashioned bolt on the inside of your doors. Get Ken to fix them, quietly. Today.'

She nodded. 'Good advice. Is that what you did?'

He nodded. 'I have an ally. Young Jade is a good kid. She's afraid of nothing and will make some man the most terrifying wife one day.' He reached for a jar of instant coffee and made them each a mug full. He added neither milk nor sugar as he handed one to Zoë.

'And if it still happens, even with a bolt?'

'Ah, then,' he smiled, 'then you have a problem.' There was a long pause as they both stared out of the window. A great spotted woodpecker was clinging to a container of peanuts a few feet from the front of the house. 'Did you tell your husband you don't want to go sailing again?' he asked. He was still studying the bird.

'Not yet.' She had wrapped her hands around the mug. The instant coffee, strong and thick, smelled disgusting.

'Are you going to?'

'I was rather hoping the season would end and the boat get put away before I had to say anything, then I can get round to it slowly over the winter months.'

'Isn't it a bit unfair not to tell him straight away? You have come down here under false pretences.'

'I have not!' She turned to face him, indignant.

'Didn't you tell me that you moved here to be near the sailing?'

'I suppose so.'

'And sailing is his whole life outside work.'

'Pretty much.'

'And you hate sailing and you haven't told him.'

'I don't hate it.'

'That's not what you said before.'

'I like it in the river where it's calm. I was frightened before, but that might not happen again.' She was beginning to resent his persistence.

'Believe me, it will.'

'I am getting to love this place, I am pleased to be out of London, I genuinely am. You leave me to decide when I speak to Ken, Leo, please.' She spoke so sharply he moved back a step.

'Sorry.'

'These nails,' she pointed to his draining board where they lay in the saucer amongst some biscuit crumbs, 'are they rare?'

'No. If you take a metal detector you will find them all over the fields. And this was the forge. I expect the generations of chaps who worked here were both the estate blacksmith and the farrier; they would probably have made them.'

'And Sharon's boys could have collected them?'

'Easily.'

'So they aren't necessarily some sort of supernatural thing that has appeared out of thin air.'

'Quite possibly not. Chuck that down the sink if you don't

like it.' He had noticed her only half-concealed grimace of distaste at the coffee.

'Sorry.' She tipped it away. 'Too early in the morning for black coffee for me.'

'You should have said. I do have milk.'

'That's OK, I'm sure you do.' She gathered up the nails and held them in the palm of her hand. 'I'm glad to hear they are quite ordinary. I felt there was something a bit spooky about them before. Cold and otherworldly.'

He laughed.

'Did you make things like this?'

'No.' He looked faintly amused. 'I wasn't a farrier.'

'And a farrier is . . .?'

'Someone who shoes horses.'

'I thought that was a blacksmith.'

'Sometimes it's the same thing, it was in the past, but not me. I did fancy wrought-iron gates, things like that.'

'But you don't any more.'

'No.'

'So what do you do now, if you don't mind my asking?'

'A bit of this and that.' He folded his arms.

'But you aren't going to tell me?' She felt strangely hurt.

'You wouldn't be interested if I tried.'

She inclined her head in defeat. 'OK.' She wasn't going to let him see that she cared.

'And now you're going to run back to the barn to have a boiled egg with hubby.'

'I am?'

'You are. I'm busy. I don't get up this early for the state of my health. I have to go out for the day.'

'I'm sorry. You should have said.' She slipped the nails into her pocket and turned towards the door.

'Stay safe, Zoë,' he called after her, but he was already walking through into the other half of the house and she didn't hear him.

He held the horseshoe nails between his lips as he hauled the hoof of the heavy horse off the ground and positioned it between his knees. The animal blew through its nose and shook its head up and down, but it stood placidly, balancing on three legs with ease as he set the new shoe in place. He could sense her watching him, had been conscious of her ever since she had appeared at the door of the smithy with her high-crowned hat and veil, and the slender whip provocatively tapping against her thigh. He removed the shoe, pushed it back in the fire, waited for it to glow red before hitting it several times with the hammer, then he plunged it into the bucket of water and waited for the rush of steam to disperse before he fitted it again to the horse's hoof. This time he was happy with the snugness and set one of the nails in the first hole, ready to hammer it home.

'And will you polish her ladyship's nails as well?' The voice was coldly amused as he set the foot down and watched the great Suffolk horse stamp on it experimentally.

He smiled. 'She'd like me to. I sometimes give them a wisp of oil and a quick go with a rag.'

'And how is Bella?' Emily's voice took on a hardness he didn't like.

'She does well enough.' The horse was still lame. Secretly he doubted she would ever be fit to work again.

It was as if she read his thoughts. 'If the animal will not recover have her destroyed. It is not worth keeping her.'

He could feel her eyes on his face; they were bright with triumph. He forced himself to remain impassive as he turned back to the great horse beside him and slapped it on the rump. 'That's your decision to make, my lady, but I wouldn't give up yet. It would be a waste of a fine animal. Mr Crosby paid a lot for her, I believe.'

Subtle, but he saw her eyes narrow slightly.

'I will allow her a few more days. Have the boy take that great brute away. I need to talk to you.'

He turned away, hoping to hide his lack of enthusiasm. 'Ben,' he called. 'Take him back to his stall.'

The boy, who had been strenuously pumping the bellows, had slipped outside as Emily appeared. 'He's needed back out in the field, Dan.' Ben took the horse's bridle and turned him, leading him out towards the gate. 'Jem's waiting for him. There's work to do yet up at Coppins Wood.'

Dan stood and watched them go, then he turned back to Lady Emily. 'So, what else can I do for you, my lady?'

She reached out and took his wrist, and holding him at arm's length led him into the forge. There she pushed the door closed with her shoulder and stood, her back against it, looking at him. It was dark after the sunlight outdoors, but he could read the look in her eyes even through her veil. 'My lady –'

'Don't speak, Daniel. Don't say anything. I don't need you for your conversation.' She pulled off her hat and threw it down in the corner, then she began to pull open the buttons on her riding jacket. 'Don't just stand there, man, help me!'

He hesitated, half wanting to turn away and run, half fascinated by the sight of her body, emerging from the stiff fabric of her habit. Under it she wore a tightly laced corset out of which her bosom, white and full, rose with a voluptuousness her clothes had hidden. She pulled off her skirt and was left standing in her corset and boots. He closed his eyes for a moment, praying, knowing he was not going to be able to resist. She paused in her disrobing to look at him. 'For pity's sake, man, what is the matter with you?' She moved forward and took hold of his belt, wrenching the buckle open, revealing all too easily the fact that he was finally and massively aroused.

Dragging him into the corner where there were some old sacks folded on some hay bales, she pulled him against her with a gasp of excitement. He thrust at her again and again, his lust goaded by his self-loathing and shame into a frenzy of angry violence. It was a long time before he fell back on the cobbled floor, panting, leaving her lying spread-eagled on the sacks, her hair tangled, her nails broken where they had raked the flesh of his back, both of them exhausted.

He sat up at last and crawled over to where his shirt and trousers lay in a tangled heap. Pulling them on, he climbed to his feet, amazed to find he was shaking. She smiled up at him, dazed. 'You had better help me dress.'

When at last he dragged open the door and looked out the yard was deserted. He walked over to her waiting horse and stood for a moment stroking the animal's nose until she appeared at the door of the forge, fully clothed and, at least at a first glance, neat and well groomed. She began to walk towards him. Only her high colour showed that anything out of the ordinary had occurred. He threw her up into the saddle and stood looking up at her for a moment. She stared down, her face once more the cold arrogant mask of earlier in the day. 'Remember, Daniel. This is between us. One word and your wife hears of your betrayal.' She raised the whip and in spite of himself he ducked. She smiled. 'No, Daniel, not for you, not this time.' Bringing the crop down smartly on the horse's rump, she turned out of the yard and put the animal up the track towards the Hall at a canter.

'No. I don't want to sail. Not today.' Zoë was sitting in the cockpit of the boat, sketching the river bank. She had made a complete mess of the drawing and tore it out of the sketchbook angrily, screwing it up and tucking it into the sail bag lying at her feet.

Ken was squatting on the foredeck, coiling down some ropes into neat perfect circles. He had looked up suddenly and pointed out that the tide was perfect and it was a glorious day with a brisk wind. He looked taken aback. 'Why on earth not?'

'Because I told you last time I didn't like it. I was terrified. We nearly sank!'

'Oh, what rubbish! It was the most glorious day.' He looked genuinely bewildered. 'Oh, come on, Zoë, you've always loved sailing.'

'No.' She put down her pencil and pad and stood up, feeling the boat move restlessly under her feet. 'I haven't loved it. I have enjoyed it from time to time when it was calm, and I love it like this, on the mooring, sketching or reading my book, but I do not like it when it is rough, and when the wind is tearing out my hair, when my ears ache and I've got salt in my eyes and my hands are numb and wrinkled with the sea water and my clothes are sticky and you are screaming orders at me which I can't hear because of the wind and I am expecting to die at any moment. I don't find that exciting! I don't find it a challenge!'

'But Zo –'

'No. If you want to sail, fine. Go without me on your own, or find someone to crew with you. What about Leo? Or Steve or Jeff?'

He had dropped the length of rope and was making his way back along the side deck. Jumping lightly into the cockpit he sat down. 'I thought you loved it here.'

'I do love it here. I love everything about it. Just not the possibility of drowning. For goodness' sake, Ken, it is almost the end of the season anyway.'

'Would you come if we just motor?'

'Maybe. But not today. I've got a headache and I can't bear the stink of fumes from the engine.' She stood up. 'Look, Ken, I'm sorry, I really am. I should have said it before, but I have never been so frightened. Row me ashore now, and then go on your own. You often went by yourself when we sailed in Sussex.'

He looked crestfallen. 'I don't like being on my own.'

'Then you'll have to find someone else to sail with. It would be much more fun for you. You could find someone who is experienced and knows this river and the bar and the sea outside, and you could go off for real adventures.' She gave him a small smile. 'Please, don't be angry.'

'I'm not angry.' He was, though. She could see by the white patches under his cheekbones as he clenched his jaw.

He rowed her towards the landing stage, held the boat steady while she climbed up, and had already pushed off back towards the boat as she reached the top of the short ladder and stood for a moment looking back at him. As he rowed he was facing her, but he looked over his shoulder towards the *Lady Grace* until he had come alongside and climbed up into the boat again. Once there he disappeared down the companionway into the cabin. Zoë gave a deep sigh and turned to make her way back to the house.

'I take it that was your defining moment?' Leo was standing on the river bank in the shadow of the trees. She jumped at the sound of his voice, then shook her head sadly. 'You were right. I should have told him years ago.'

'What did he say?' He leaned back against the trunk of one of the pines; she could see the feathery shadows from the branches playing across his face.

'Nothing much. He was pretty upset.'

'That's tough. Maybe I'll offer to sail with him some time. Do you think he would like that?'

'I'm sure he would.'

They walked together up the track and over the lawn towards the houses. Where the path divided, right to Leo's and left to Zoë and Ken's, she paused. Suddenly she didn't want him to go. 'Do you want to come up for a drink or something?'

He hesitated. 'Do you think that is a good idea?' He held her gaze.

'Why not?' She looked away.

He shrugged. 'OK, I'd like to.'

'If Ken comes after me you can suggest sailing with him. I'm sure he would be pleased.'

They were halfway across the lawn when Leo stopped suddenly. 'Did you leave your front door open?'

'What? No.' She followed his pointing finger. 'Oh God!'

'Wait.' As they walked into the hall he put his hand on her arm to hold her back. 'Is there anyone there?' His voice was surprisingly powerful in the silent house. They waited.

There was no reply.

Zoë pushed past him and stood in the doorway to the large living room, peering in. The armchairs were back in a straight line.

'Someone has been in and rearranged the furniture.'

'You'd better check if there is anything missing.'

She glanced round. 'There are things down here a burglar would have taken – sound system, TV. I don't think anything has been touched. The kids wouldn't steal, would they? Wait here and I'll check upstairs.'

She ran up to their bedroom and stared round. On the dressing table lay the gold chain and pendant which she had been wearing the night before. On Ken's cabinet there was a wad of notes he had taken out of his wallet to pay for fuel for the boat and for some reason put down before transferring it to his pocket. She shook her head. Anyone who had come to raid the house would have taken it. She ran back downstairs.

'I don't think there is anything missing.'

'Look.' He had moved across to the coffee table and bent to pick something up. A handful of horseshoe nails, lying a-midst a scattering of rust and dirt.

Zoë stared down at his palm. 'You still think it's the kids?'

'Hmm.' He was still looking down at his hand. He sniffed the nails cautiously then dropped them back on the table. 'Did you mention putting bolts on the doors to Ken?'

'Yes. He thinks it's a good idea. He hasn't got round to it yet. And perhaps we should change the locks as well.'

'Leave me to talk to Jeff. I think I will bypass Sharon

– she's too volatile – but he might have an idea of what the boys are up to.' He smiled at her. 'Don't let this scare you. No harm has been done and nothing is missing. It's a prank, that's all.'

'And if it isn't the kids?'

'It is.' He walked towards the window. 'Do you want a hand with putting the chairs back? You had them in a sort of semi-circle, didn't you?' He moved across and heaved one of the chairs into place. Under it there were half a dozen more nails. For a moment neither of them moved.

'I wonder where they're getting them,' Zoë said hoarsely.

'Metal detector. Or they might have just found a stash of them around the grounds somewhere. Unlikely, though. They have been used. If they were new I would say someone has found a pot of them lying around – though that would most likely have been at my place as that was the forge.'

'How long was it a forge, do you know?'

He shook his head. 'No idea. The forge and the smith's cottage have been converted into one dwelling now, of course, but I sense the forge itself is far older. On an old estate, it is probably as old as the estate itself. It's in an ideal position for the farm and not too far from the Hall and the stables up there.'

'Did you buy it because it was an old forge?'

'No. In fact that almost put me off.' He grabbed the next chair and swung it into position.

'No nails.'

'There can't be an infinite supply of them.' The last chair back in place, he straightened and headed for the door. 'I'll pop over to the Watts's now, I think, and see if Jeff would be up for wandering over to my place for a bevvy. Perhaps it would be better if you didn't come.'

'Why?' she said indignantly. 'It is my house that has the problem.'

'Exactly. I don't want to put him on the back foot. Leave it to me, OK? I'll let you know what happens.'

'What is it, Dan?' Susan was standing watching him. She had been stirring the pan on the stove and he hadn't noticed her stop and straighten her back, letting the spoon drip on the floor for a moment while she studied him as he sat at the table staring straight ahead of him at the wall.

He jumped. 'What did you say?'

'I said, what is wrong?'

He shook his head. 'Just tired, I reckon. One of the Suffolks came down today for a new shoe and I pulled my back a bit.' He shook his head. 'I'll have to watch it; I must be getting old.' He forced a smile as he looked up at her.

She wasn't fooled. 'I've never known a horse get the better of you, Daniel Smith, not once in all our years together. Are you sure that's it?'

'Of course that's it, woman!' He pushed back the chair and stood up angrily, swearing as a twinge of pain hit him afresh.

She turned back to the pan and stood with her back to him. 'If you say so,' she murmured.

He went over to her and put his arms round her. 'Sorry, Mrs Smith! You're right, it never happened before. It's a frightening moment, like a cold wind down one's neck. Father Time is watching me.'

She reached up and gave him a kiss on the lips. 'Father Time will have to fight me for you, Dan,' she smiled. 'And this little one too.' She patted her belly. 'Now you sit down and get some broth inside you.'

Going back to the stove, she reached for the bowls, trying hard to push down her increasing sense of unease. Normally when he came in from the horses he went into the back yard to the pump and swilled the cold clean water over his head before he came in for his meal; this time he had already done it at the pump in the yard, and even the wetness of his hair and the smell of carbolic from the soap they kept in a box near the pump for when they needed to scrub up before performing surgery on one of the horses, couldn't hide the smell of scent – exotic, foreign, musky – the smell she associated with Lady Emily, clinging to his hair, his skin, even his hands.

She set the bowl in front of him and pushed the bread board over. 'I'll get cheese and ham from the pantry.'

He didn't react. Once more he was in a world of his own. She walked across to the pantry door and went in. Only there, in the privacy of her own cold, well-stocked shelves, did she let her tears fall where he couldn't see her.

'Susan?' He had followed her at last. 'What is it? Are you in pain?'

She shook her head, rubbing her eyes with her sleeve.

'Then, my love, tell me. What is it?' She heard the fear in his voice.

'You think I can't smell her on you, Dan?' She turned at last to face him, her eyes glistening with tears. 'She's been all over you!'

He didn't even try to deny it. He stood there in front of her, paralysed.

She waited for him to say something, but he just shook his head. He backed out of the small room and headed for the door, grabbing his coat and striding out without a backward glance. His food lay untouched on the table.

She lay awake a long time that night, conscious every second of the empty half of the bed beside her. She had been too proud to go after him, or ask any of the men if they had seen him. Before she went to bed she had heard the horses come in late from the field, going straight into the old barn to their stalls next to the lame mare, Bella. She pictured them reaching up to tug at the hay racks and searching the mangers for chaff and oats. Once she thought she heard one of the men calling Dan's name, but maybe it had been her imagination. The yard grew quiet and dark, and at last she had gone up the narrow box staircase to their bedroom. Tired of watching the lazy shadows licking across the rafters of their bedroom ceiling she put out the lamp at last and lay under the covers shivering until at last she dozed off, her hand on the swell of her stomach where she felt, as she lay there alone, the comforting, fluttering signs of the new life inside her. He never came.

'You think it was my kids?' Jeff was leaning on the garden wall next to Leo, a glass of Adnams in his hand. Both men were pleasantly mellow.

'Yup. It would be just like them.' Leo was laughing. 'Go on, deny it.'

'Well. I can and I can't.' Jeff took another deep swig of beer. 'On the one hand it would be just like the boys, you're right. Right buggers, both of them, but on the other hand, if it happened today they weren't here.'

Leo felt a sudden shiver of unease. 'What do you mean, they weren't here. Where were they?'

'They went off last night after the barbecue with a mate who lives in Leiston. I made sure he was sober, then we slung them into his van. They'll all have a lot more fun together than they would loitering round here, and I know they got there because their mother phoned this morning. Sharon doesn't seem to appreciate what a couple of losers we've spawned.'

Leo looked pained. 'You don't mean that.'

'Oh, but I do, mate. I'm sure they'll be decent enough young men one day, but just now I've had it with both of them.' He took another lingering sip and sighed with pleasure. 'I love all my kids, Leo, but really they can be a right pain most of the time. You haven't got kids, have you?'

Leo hesitated, then shook his head.

'Lucky man.' Jeff paused. 'Look at Rosemary and Steve. I don't think that woman has spoken to her daughter in twenty years.'

'I didn't know she had a daughter.'

'Oh, yes, and grandkids. Sharon wormed the story out of her. She has never seen her own grandchildren! Can you credit that? Her daughter loathes her so much they won't even ring her.'

Leo raised an eyebrow. 'She is not exactly the cuddly nan one might wish for.'

Jeff gave a snort of laughter. 'Good point.' He took another sip of ale.

'Which leaves us with the puzzle,' Leo steered the conversation onto safer ground, 'of who broke into The Old Barn and tried to scare Zoë and Ken by rearranging their furniture.'

Both men were silent for a while, contemplating the view.

'Have you seen the ghost ship?' Leo asked after several minutes.

'Excuse me?' Jeff looked at him, shook his head, and buried his face once more in his glass. 'Did you say, ghost ship?'

'A Viking longship which every so often drifts up-river here. Loads of people claim to have seen it over the years.'

'Including you?'

'Yes.'

'And Zoë and Ken?'

'Yes.'

Jeff put his empty glass down on the wall. 'Have you ever thought, mate, that it might be something in the water, or ergot in the bread, or something?'

Leo laughed out loud. He picked up the glasses and headed for the kitchen. 'Hang on while I get us a refill.' He reappeared moments later with both glasses filled to overflowing. 'You don't ever get ghosts in The Summer Barn, then?'

Jeff laughed. 'My kids would scare termites. You think ghosts would stand a chance?'

'I'll take that as a no.'

'Too bloody right it's a no.'

'And you haven't seen anything like this lying round your house?' He reached into his pocket and produced half a dozen of the twisted misshapen nails.

Jeff frowned. 'No, I don't think so.'

'OK, interrogation over.' Leo leaned forward, his elbows on the warm moss-covered brick, staring down at the river. The sun had gone in and the shadows in the woods were darkening as he watched. He wondered for a brief moment if Ken had come back to the barns or if he was still alone on the *Lady Grace*, down there on the river. And if he was alone, Zoë too was alone, save for whoever or whatever was moving her chairs around.

Jeff downed the last of his beer. 'I'd best be getting back. I promised Sharon and Jade we'd go to the cinema tonight.'

Leo took his glass off him. 'Well, thanks for the company.'

'You'll be all right alone?' For a moment Jeff sounded genuinely concerned. 'We don't want the Vicious Vikings to get you, do we?' He let out a roar of laughter.

Leo gave a good-natured grin. 'Nothing is going to happen that a ready meal and an evening in front of the telly can't cure.'

'Poor bastard. How sad is that!' Jeff walked unsteadily up the path and headed for the gate.

For Jeff's sake Leo hoped that Sharon would be driving when they went out.

U

Lady Emily kept Susan waiting for over an hour in the morning room at the Hall. When at last she came in her face was flushed, and there was mud on her riding habit. She gave Susan a cold stare. 'So, why do you want to see me?'

'I want to know what is going on with my husband.' Susan had been so angry she could barely speak when she had first reached the Hall that morning, but now, after waiting alone in the cold room, with an unlit fire lying in the grate, she had calmed down. She held the other woman's gaze challengingly.

'I can't imagine what you are talking about.' Emily took off her gloves and threw them down on the table. 'Your husband is the blacksmith, is he not?'

Susan narrowed her eyes. 'You know full well who he is.'

'And why would I want anything from my husband's blacksmith?' Emily managed to put so much scorn in the words that Susan blanched.

'I wouldn't know. All I do know is he is my husband and the father of my child, and we are happy, and I will fight for him.'

Emily didn't say anything for a moment. Her look became calculated. 'Poor man. What has he done to deserve such a harridan?' She began to take off her hat and that joined the gloves on the table. 'You work, I believe, in the dairy, on the estate. Clearly the job is too much for you. I will tell the farm manager that he is to lay you off from today so you may take life more easily.'

Susan felt her stomach lurch uncomfortably. 'You can't do that.'

'I can. Please leave now.'

'You can't dismiss me!'

'I can do what I like, Susan. That is the joy of being the lady of the manor.' Emily smiled acidly. 'Besides, I am not dismissing you, I am thinking of your condition.' She looked pointedly at Susan's stomach. 'Surely you wouldn't want to endanger your child's welfare.' With that she walked towards the door, leaving hat and gloves where she had dropped them. At the door she turned. 'I want no more of these ridiculous accusations, Susan. As if I would let a common farrier touch me!' She turned back and stalked out of the room.

Susan stood staring after her, stunned, listening to the sound of the woman's heeled boots on the polished boards slowly recede into the distance. It was several minutes before she began to walk to the door and pulled it open. The corridor outside was empty. 'Hello?' Her voice was shaking. Surely there was someone there? No one came. Ignoring the servants' side passage and the way to the back door she turned the wrong way, headed blindly through the green baize door and along the main corridor to the front hall. There was no sign of any servants; the house was completely silent.

Pulling open the front door she descended the broad flight of steps which led down to the carriage sweep, leaving the door open behind her, and began to walk unsteadily down the long drive. Her mind had gone blank. It was all she could do to put one foot in front of the other. She had crossed her arms in front of her as she walked, hugging herself for comfort, but she didn't see or hear anything around her. When she came to the place where the farm track led off the main drive just before it reached the park gates, she turned automatically towards the farm, dragging her boots in the dust.

She was nearly back at the forge cottage when she heard a shout behind her.

'Susan! I saw you from the window!' Molly was panting hard, her face perspiring as she ran. She had grabbed a shawl and thrown it over her shoulders, but she was still wearing her apron and cap. 'Oh my, what a to-do! What did you say to Lady Emily?'

Susan stopped. She was tired and overwrought, and suddenly she couldn't hold back the tears. 'I told her to keep her nasty thieving hands off my husband!'

Molly was speechless. For several long seconds she stared at her sister. The breeze was strengthening and snatched at the women's hair from beneath their caps as they stood in the middle of the track. 'You said that?' Molly whispered at last.

'More or less. I can't remember what I said.' Susan brushed away the tears. 'She said she would have me sent off from the dairy.'

'Oh, Susan.'

'He came in last night, Molly, and he reeked of her. She had been all over him.' The tears were streaming down her face again. 'With her silks and her satins and her perfumes.'

'Did she admit it?'

'No, of course she didn't. She said she wouldn't let a common farrier touch her.'

'Oh, Susan,' Molly repeated.

'What you said, about her maybe being pregnant. Was that true?'

Molly shook her head. 'I don't know. I reckon she would be more careful if she was.'

'Unless it's not the squire's and she wants to lose it.'

Molly looked shocked.

'How did you know I'd been talking to Lady Emily?' Susan said at last. She rubbed her face miserably.

'Half the house were listening. Mrs Field and Beaton, and William, who's been acting as Mr Henry's valet.'

'Will he tell Mr Henry?'

Molly considered for a moment. 'I don't think so. But you never can tell, can you? Oh, Susan. What possessed you?'

'He's my husband, Molly.'

'But he'd never –' There was a long silence.

Susan turned away and stared across the fields. 'He'd never what? Kiss her? Betray me? Fall in love with her?'

'He'd never do that, Sue. He might kiss; he might do more if she asked him.' Molly looked distraught, but she ploughed on. 'But fall in love? No. He adores you.'

Susan was still standing with her back to her sister. 'He went out last night, after I accused him, and he didn't come back. John the cowman said Dan didn't feed the mare last night, nor this morning. He had to do it himself.'

'He'll come back, Sue. You know he will.'

Susan shook her head. 'I've chased him away. I was a shrew.'

'With reason.' Molly went over and put her arm round Susan's shoulders. 'It'll be all right, my love, I promise. Look how proud he is about the baby.'

Both women turned as below them on the driveway a smart gig trotted past. Just for a second Susan caught sight of the woman at the reins. It was Lady Emily and once again she was alone without a footman or a groom.

The room was dark and filled with the sound of the storm. Lord Egbert lay propped up on his pillows staring intently at the flickering light of the torch in its bracket in the corner. His wife had come in and she had sat with him for a while, holding his hand. Her fingers were warm and soft and soothing. Then she had asked again if he would like to see Father Wulfric and he had shaken his head and summoned the strength to roar at her to go. His eyes were not so dim that he did not see her tears. He ignored them. Now was not the time for sentiment. Now he was preparing to meet his gods. The pattern of his life was run and the Wyrd sisters were waiting for his spirit. The old one from the forest had been two nights before under cover of darkness to make rune magic to guard the walls of the room and bless the exits with sacred herbs. All was ready save one thing. The sword.

The wind blew suddenly harder, whistling in the cracks in the walls and lifting the hangings on their black forged hooks. He shivered. He was cold all the time now, in spite of the great roaring fire with its glittering sparks and the warm furs on his bed. The spirits were coming closer. He could sense them.

Zoë was sitting at the kitchen table, an untouched glass of wine before her as Ken walked in at last.

'There was dirt in the diesel so I had to change the fuel filter and bleed the injector lines,' he said, walking over to the sink and reaching for the Swarfega. She could smell the oil on him – and sweat. 'She's going as smoothly as a baby's pram now.'

She frowned, wondering idly why he should use such a strange simile.

'Do you want to go for a spin in the morning to try her? No sails.' It had finally dawned on him that sailing in the river made her nervous.

'Does it never occur to you, Ken, to ask me where I've been and what I've been doing?' She didn't even bother to look at him.

He went on washing his hands, meticulously massaging the oily soapy mess up and down each finger. 'So, where have you been?' he asked after a minute.

'I had a job interview in Ipswich this afternoon.'

His hands were motionless for a moment under the running water. 'And?'

'And they said no.'

'That's a shame.' He reached for a tea towel.

'Can you please not use those, Ken!' she snapped. 'They are meant for dishes.'

'Sorry.' He looked round for a hand towel, couldn't see one, stood still, defeated for a moment, and then shook the water all over the floor. 'You didn't tell me you had an interview. So of course we couldn't have gone sailing.' He hesitated. 'You will get something,' he said after a minute. 'No hurry. It's not as though we need the money.'

'No, we don't need the money,' she said with exaggerated patience, ignoring the spatter of water drops on the floor tiles. 'But I need the job. I am going insane in this house with nothing to do.'

There was a long awkward silence.

'You need a hobby, love. I told you –' he said at last.

'I don't want a hobby! I loved my job! I was good at it. They wanted me to stay. I wanted to stay!' It was a cry of real anguish.

He looked away uncomfortably and turned towards the door. 'You never said,' he said helplessly. 'But there is still loads to do in the house. Decorating it and buying furniture. You said you would enjoy that,' he added over his shoulder.

Then he shook his head. 'Sorry,' he repeated. He disappeared, leaving her helpless with fury. He would go into his office now, and he would work probably into the early hours. If she took him something – coffee, a sandwich – he would grunt his thanks, barely noticing, his eyes riveted to the screens in front of him, and she would retreat to the huge living room to sit in front of the TV or read or listen to music or wait, her eyes on the shadows between the beams, for the noises to begin.

Ken walked thoughtfully through to his office and sat down in front of his desk. There were times when Zoë was a complete mystery to him. He had given her everything she could possibly want: a glorious house, beautiful countryside, a yacht, for goodness' sake, but she still wasn't happy. He sighed. Perhaps he could help her to find a job if she was so bored. He stood up and went over to the window, staring past his reflection out into the darkness. If he confronted the facts he was probably a bit bored himself. He missed certain aspects of their previous life more than he had expected.

Part of the reason he had decided that a move out of London was expedient was his relationship with Anya Craig-Watkins. What had started as an amusing dalliance, the latest of quite a few, if he were honest, which Zoë, thank God, had never discovered, had threatened to become too intense. Anya had started asking when he planned to get a divorce and talking about moving in together; when instinctively he backed away he had the feeling she was going to turn nasty. Which, all said and done, surprised him. He usually judged his women better than that. He enjoyed the game, the hunt, the hide and seek, the cheating on the husband and the risk always there that Zoë might find out. But it was just that, a game. In his own way he loved Zoë. She was part of his life, and his life-style. He was not about to let Anya ruin the life plan he had so painstakingly put in place.

It was only when she heard the tap of the hammer from the forge that Susan realised Dan had come back. She stood at the door of the cottage and watched the smoke rising from the chimney. There were no horses in the yard. He must be making something for the estate. There was always a pile of things needing to be done. Gate hinges, pump handles, tools, nails, ploughshares. There were two tubs of old rivets standing by the door. The kids picked them out of the soil up Sutton way. The rivets came from the planking of old ships buried beneath the earth, the old men of the village said, which seemed more than a bit odd to her, but Dan bought them for pennies. Melted down they made good horseshoes. For a long time she stood without moving, listening to his hammer, then at last she reached for her shawl and made her way across to the doorway and looked in. He was standing with his back to her, hammer in hand, a piece of metal on the anvil. She couldn't see what it was. Ben was at the bellows by the fire. The forge was very hot. She waited a few moments, then as Dan paused and adjusted the position of the piece of iron she called his name. He started hammering again without looking up. 'Dan?' she repeated, louder.

He threw down the hammer and turned to face her. His face was drawn and there were streaks from the charcoal across his forehead. He was wearing his shoeing apron over his trousers and his shirtsleeves were rolled up to the elbow. He said nothing, staring at her.

'I'm sorry, Dan,' she said.

'So am I.'

'I know you wouldn't –' She groped for a word and gave up looking for it. 'We must hold together, Dan.' She could feel the tears welling up in her eyes and she sniffed, angry with herself. 'Whatever happens, we must hold together,' she repeated. Biting her lip she turned away and retraced her steps towards the cottage. She didn't turn back to see his face but seconds later she heard the sound of the hammer again.

Later she took him down some lunch. Bread and cheese and a pasty wrapped in a fresh cloth, and a jug of her special cider. The forge was empty. She put it down on the work table and left it for him.

Hesitating as she crossed the yard, she turned and walked towards the big old barn. The great doors hung open and there was no sign of any of the farm workers. John the cowman was probably out in the fields with the milkmaids; George, the head horseman, and Robert and Jem were working with the horses down at the far end of the estate, clearing a fallen oak which had come down across the fence and smashed a water trough. There would be plenty of logs there to bring in; they would be occupied for several days more, she reckoned. She walked into the huge dark space and looked round, smelling the warm stacked hay, the sacks of flour, back from the mill, one of the wagons and a tumbril pulled over into a corner. Up in the high rafters an owl peered down at her from the shadows and from the far side of the threshing floor she heard the gentle whicker of a horse. She made her way over to the stall where Bella stood patiently, favouring her foreleg, her warm brown eyes curious to see who had walked into the barn. 'How are you, my lovely?' Susan stroked her neck. 'Haven't you eaten, then?' There was still chaff in her manger. 'You poor creature. Dan reckons she did this to you on purpose. How could she, the witch!'

She cupped her hand round the velvet nose and petted the horse for several minutes, then slowly she turned away and walked back to the house. She should be in the dairy. She didn't know what to do. Had Lady Emily spoken to Mr Turtill, the farm manager? Had she meant it when she threatened Susan with dismissal? Dan had said nothing. Did he know of her impetuous visit to the Hall and what had happened there? If he didn't he must be the only person on the farm not to. With a sigh she reached for her clean apron, tied it round her ever-expanding middle and turned towards the dairy. Betsy would be in there already, cursing her for being late. Betsy would know what had happened and if anyone had spoken to Fred Turtill. Betsy always knew everything that went on round the farm, just as Molly knew what happened up at the Hall.

Zoë went to bed early in the end. She had propped herself up against the pillows, her book against her knees, when she heard a strange sound from downstairs. She froze, listening. It was Ken. It must be. She had turned off all the lights when she came upstairs and he must have finally come out of his study and he was probably groping his way round looking for the switches in the dark. Dropping the book on the bedcover, she slid out of bed and reached for her dressing gown. It was stormy outside and she could hear the moan of the wind in the eaves. It was an eerie sound, cold and lonely. Tiptoeing across the room she pulled open the door and stared out onto the landing. From downstairs there was another sound – something dragging and then a stifled giggle. Everything down there was still in darkness.

At the end of the short corridor she could see the line of light under Ken's office door. She crept down the passage and quietly reached for the handle, pushing it open. He was standing in front of his desk staring at one of the screens, the window in front of him a blank reflective sheet of glass. He never pulled the blind in here, never seemed to sense the awful emptiness outside or to wonder if anyone out there was staring in at him. He turned at the sound of the door opening and she put her finger to her lips. 'There is someone downstairs,' she whispered.

'Not another bloody ghost!' he retorted.

She shrugged. 'I heard someone laugh.'

He sighed. Shaking his head, he came towards the door. They retraced their steps quietly and stood for a moment at the top of the stairs, then Ken reached out for the bank of light switches, flooding the whole area with light.

Two figures were standing on either side of one of the armchairs, in the act of pulling it round. 'OK,' Ken roared, 'stop that right now!'

The boys dropped the chair and fled, racing across the floor towards the kitchen.

'Let them go,' Zoë said. She stood where she was and subsided into a sitting position on the top step as Ken ran down the stairs. She was cross to find that she was shaking.

'Little buggers!' Ken swore as he followed them out into the kitchen. 'Straight out of the back door. I take it that they are those two little bastards from next door?' She heard the door slam and moments later he reappeared.

Zoë nodded. 'It was Darren and Jamie.'

'Right. I'm ringing their father.'

'Why not leave it till morning?' She was amazed to find that instead of being relieved that they had been caught in the act, she was oddly disappointed. 'What time is it?'

'Eleven.' He glanced at his watch. 'Not even late!'

'They could see the lights were off. We should have done as Leo suggested and put bolts on the doors. I asked you, Ken!'

Ken walked over to the sideboard and reached for the phone. He carried it across to the window and stood staring out into the darkness. 'What is their number?'

'I don't know. I've never phoned them.'

He gave an exaggerated sigh and threw the phone down on the table. 'I'll go over there.'

'No, Ken, don't. They are probably asleep.'

'I doubt it! They don't look the types for early nights.' He strode back towards the kitchen and reached for his jacket from the back of the door.

'I'm coming with you,' Zoë called. She stood up.

'Don't worry, I'll deal with it! And don't bother to say I told you so. I forgot about the bolts, OK? And, yes, we ought to change the locks as well. I'll do it tomorrow. We can't all be perfect!' He didn't pause to wait for her. Dragging open the door he disappeared out into the night.

She followed him.

The Summer Barn was ablaze with light; the huge ground-floor windows were uncurtained and showed inside several members of the family clustered round an enormous TV screen. As far as Zoë could see, as she followed Ken towards the front door, Darren and Jamie were there, on one of the large leather sofas; there was no sign of either parent. With them was a motley selection of other young men, some older, some younger; there was no sign of Jade. As they headed across the damp grass the floodlights came on, adding to the daylight effect as Ken reached the door and began to hammer on it.

It was several seconds before it opened. A young man who appeared to be in his late teens or early twenties stood before them. 'Yeah?' The flaming hair and freckles identified him as Jade's missing brother, Jackson.

'I need to speak to your father.'

'He's not here.' Behind him the others appeared in the hallway. Zoë felt a frisson of fear at the sight of them. They did not look friendly.

'Then I will wait for him.' Ken stepped forward. Zoë was impressed in spite of herself. It took courage to face up to this bunch. As it happened he was not required to prove his point any further. Jeff appeared in the hall with, behind him, Sharon. Both were fully dressed. Zoë pulled her dressing gown more tightly round her. She was shivering.

'I am sorry to come this late,' Ken said angrily, 'but we caught two of your boys in our house, messing about with the furniture, pretending to be ghosts. As they assumed we were in bed and the lights were out I think we can assume they broke in. I understand it is possible they have keys to our house.'

For a moment no one said anything, then Sharon turned to face the boys. 'Jamie! Darren! You bleeding little tykes! They only came back this evening,' she yelled. She pounced. Darren managed to dodge out of the way but she caught Jamie by the ear. 'What did I tell you? What? You thieving no-good scumbags!' Her voice had reached a screech. 'That's it. You are going home! I will never ever bring you down here again.'

'I'm sorry,' Jeff said to Ken. 'I really thought we had fixed this.'

'Fixed it?' Ken said incredulously. 'You mean they have done this before?'

'I'm afraid so.' He paused. Sharon had pursued her sons out of sight into the back of the house and they could hear each other more clearly. The other boys sheepishly retreated back into the large living room and reassembled on the sofa. Now, in the relative quiet Zoë noticed that Jade had appeared. She was wearing a T-shirt and knickers, which was presumably her sleeping attire. Her hair was standing on end and her eyes were dazed with sleep.

'Did they do any damage?' Jeff asked wearily. He reached into the hip pocket of his jeans and produced a wallet. 'If it's too much I might have to get some cash tomorrow.'

'No. No, no. I don't want any money.' Ken shook his head. 'I just want to make sure they don't do it again. They have been terrifying Zoë. She thought the house was haunted.'

There was a long silence, broken only by a snigger from the sofa. Jeff looked up. He turned his gaze on Zoë, who was standing immediately behind Ken there in the entrance hall.

He's going to say it is haunted, she thought suddenly, and she felt a wave of panic run through her. She was cold and very aware of her state of undress. He is going to say it always has been.

The sound of Sharon's voice had died away and the house

seemed unnaturally quiet now. 'I am really sorry. Yes, they did do it before, to the poor blighters who lived there before you. I made them give back the keys. They must have kept a set. I will personally see to it that they apologise and that they don't do it again.'

Ken shook his head. 'Just the keys will do, mate. Please don't worry about the apology.'

'I insist.' Jeff glared at them. 'Now, come in and have a drink. To show there are no hard feelings.'

It was Zoë who shook her head this time. 'I won't, Jeff, thank you. I was in bed, and I am freezing and I just want to go home.' She turned and walked away, aware almost at once that Ken had stayed. He had gone in after Jeff and the door had closed behind him, leaving her on her own.

She stood still for a moment, staring round the darkened lawns. She was just out of reach of the light sensors now and the great illuminating spots had gone out, leaving glowing bulbs, fading into the dark. The garden seemed very black and cold. The wind was still strong and she could feel it tugging at her dressing gown and her hair. There was no moon. The cloud was heavy, tinged to a strange muddy red as it streamed overhead. The branches of the pine trees were thrashing up and down and the wind in the wood sounded like the roaring of a train. She could see the gleam of water from the river. There were no lights down there, no lights on in Rosemary and Steve's house, nor in The Old Forge. She wondered for a minute how they had managed to sleep through all the noise, but the barns were quite some distance apart and in the roar of the wind they would have heard nothing of the commotion.

Setting her face into the wind she began to walk home, feeling the chill damp of the grass striking up through her slippers as she headed back towards their own house. There too the lights were blazing; she could see the great room, empty of life. There was no TV on here, no kids, however badly behaved, ranged on the sofas. The place was deserted.

129

Letting herself in she closed the door behind her and walked through towards the stairs. The chairs by the window were still in disarray but she didn't try to straighten them. All she wanted was to go upstairs and run herself a deep warm bath.

Halfway up the flight she paused and turned to look down at the room behind her. The shadows were there again, the echoes from the past; nothing the boys had done had caused this frisson in the air, the sound of a horse's hoof scraping on the cobbles, the smell of dusty straw and the feeling that somehow in this great barn there was unfinished business awaiting its moment for resolution.

No one had stopped her working in the dairy. As she and Betsy worked, skimming the cream off the great flat bowls of milk they had talked easily about the coming baby, about the forthcoming wedding of Betsy and George's daughter, Freda, to Sam the head groom's son, Walter. Susan was making a lace collar for the girl, and Betsy was stitching baby clothes for Susan's baby. The women were comfortable in their gossip. There was no mention of Dan or of Emily Crosby. They heard the skid and grate of hooves as two of the great shire horses hauled the cart down loaded with logs into the barnyard, and they heard the shouts of the men as they began to unload. All was as it should be and peaceful in the cold dairy.

The first yell went almost unnoticed by the two women as they worked. At the second Betsy looked up. She was a short, grey-haired woman, her complexion reddened by wind and weather, but still possessed of the startlingly beautiful eyes which had charmed and won George Roper all those years before. 'Someone is calling for Dan.'

Susan straightened, her hand to her back. 'If he's not in the forge he'll be with the mare in the old barn.' There was a sinking feeling deep in her stomach.

Moments later she heard footsteps outside and George put

his head round the door. A small wiry man, muscular, with a red neckerchief over his heavy brown work shirt, he had far-seeing clear grey eyes which missed little as he greeted his wife with a fond grin, then turned to Susan. 'Do you know where Dan is? We've broken some chain on the trace harness out there. It needs to be welded soon as possible.'

Susan swallowed. 'Did you look in the old barn?'

'We did. He's nowhere in the yard.' There was a pause.

Susan saw man and wife exchange glances, and she groped for the stool near the butter churns and sat down heavily. 'I don't know where he is,' she whispered.

'All right. Don't you worry yourself,' George said. His voice was full of sympathy. 'We'll leave it till later.'

As he ducked out of the doorway Susan felt Betsy's gaze on her. 'Don't worry, my dear,' she said at last. 'You're the one he loves.'

'Does everyone know?' Susan's voice was husky.

'I dare say.'

'She said she would see to it that I couldn't work in the dairy any more.' Susan didn't need to say who she was talking about.

'That's up to Mr Turtill, not her. And he takes his orders from Mr Crosby and she's hardly likely to tell him all this, is she?' Betsy picked up her skimmer. 'You take no notice of that, Susan. And don't think about the other.' She shook her head. 'Whatever she makes Daniel do, he is still yours.'

It was after two a.m. when Ken came back. He smelled of alcohol and crawled into bed beside her without taking a shower. Zoë had been lying awake waiting, not for him, she realised, but for the sounds she might hear from downstairs. Not the Watts boys moving furniture, but the echoes of a working farm. Horses, wagon wheels creaking over cobbles, the scraping of hooves.

131

Downstairs, in the great room, near the hearth, the developers had left some of the herringbone bricks of the original threshing floor, preserved under a plate-glass panel in the floor. It was beautiful, intricate, worn. Was that where the sounds were coming from? She remembered reading an article once about the sounds of a former bar and its customers being accidentally recorded onto the wall of a pub in Wales. It was something to do with the silica content of the bricks. If she remembered she would try and look it up on Google. She turned her back on her husband with a sigh and closed her eyes.

The telephone woke her next morning. She glanced at her watch and saw to her surprise that it was after nine. There was no sign of Ken.

'Zoë?' Rosemary's voice boomed in her ear. 'What a night you had! My goodness, and we heard nothing! Those wretched children! Well, Jeff and Sharon have packed them into the car and gone back home with the dogs. Half-term was just about over anyway. That's the good news. The bad news is that they've left the other two kids here.' Zoë climbed out of bed and walked over to the window, the phone to her ear. 'Jade is at private school,' Rosemary's voice in her ear rattled on without pause. 'Would you believe it? But she's a bright kid and they've got the money – but it means her half-term is longer than the boys'. She's no bother, she's a strange child, but quite quiet, but the eldest, Jackson, is almost as much of a nightmare as the younger boys. He doesn't seem to have a job and I doubt if he's doing any further education. Perhaps he's on a gap year.' She laughed dryly. 'I suppose they didn't want to spoil half-term for the girl and they couldn't leave her on her own.' It was raining. The wind was still strong and the lawns were bleak and wet. The walnut tree out on the lawns was shedding its leaves, black and wilting across the grass. 'Now,' Rosemary went on, suddenly changing the subject. Zoë brought her attention back to the phone call. 'I am having a few people over this evening for a drink at six and I want you and Ken to come. It is important.'

Ken was standing in the ironmonger's looking at a selection of bolts. It was strange how flaky he felt about putting them on. He should have done it days ago, and changed the locks too, but to do so was to admit that they were afraid of a bunch of unruly kids. On the other hand, Zoë was genuinely scared of the boys and her imagination was beginning to go into overdrive.

He reached out towards the display at the same moment as someone who was standing beside him and their hands converged. He pulled back. 'I'm sorry!' He glanced up. The woman standing beside him was an attractive blonde, perhaps in her mid-thirties. He felt an automatic stirring of interest. She wore dark glasses pushed up onto her forehead and an expression of confused concentration. She gave him a distracted smile.

'Does it matter what a bolt is made of?' she asked. Her attention was focused on the array in front of her.

He grinned. 'It depends what you want it for.'

'Garden gate. Kids keep opening it.'

'Ah, we have a similar problem, it seems.' He hesitated. Surely he recognised her. 'We've met before, haven't we?'

She looked up at him properly for the first time. 'Ken Lloyd?'

He nodded. 'You've a better memory for names than I have, I'm afraid.'

'Sylvia Sands.'

He and Zoë had met her at a social evening at the sailing club a few weeks earlier, he remembered now. She was some kind of journalist and had her own boat at the marina. He smiled to himself. He had recognised the sudden flicker of interest in her eyes as she met his gaze and the excitement of exchanging looks for just a second or two longer than necessary.

133

He bought her a coffee and then offered to put on her bolt for her. She lived in a terraced Victorian cottage behind the Thoroughfare and by the time they reached it he already knew she was available and that he was going to sleep with her.

Rosemary met Zoë and Ken at the door and caught Zoë's arm. 'You need to charm Leo,' she whispered. 'He's looking like a wild beast and I need him onside.'

Ken had arrived back late from Woodbridge with an assortment of bolts for the kitchen and front doors and had left them in a bag on the worktop in the utility room. Showering and changing swiftly while Zoë waited, he was ready in ten minutes but they were still late for the drinks.

The people already there turned out to be Leo, Bill Turtill from the home farm and his wife, Penny, Lesley Inworth from the Hall and a couple who lived in Woodbridge called Jim and Dottie Salcombe.

Leo was standing alone by the window, a glass in his hand. The others were seated in a loose semicircle round the fire, chatting. The introductions were made and Ken sat down in the circle. Zoë felt her husband's eyes on her speculatively for a moment and she found herself wondering where he had been to make him so late.

Obediently she followed Rosemary over to the window and stood beside Leo. She gave him a conspiratorial smile. 'What's going on, is this a council of war?'

'That is exactly what it is,' he replied. 'Stupid woman!'

Zoë wondered briefly which woman he was talking about and concluded that it must be their hostess. Bill Turtill, she knew, farmed the land around the barn conversions. It had been his father who had sold the land off for the development. The other couple, Jim and Dottie, were friends of Rosemary's, who belonged to the same walking group.

'I thought if I explained, Bill, why it is necessary to restore the footpath to its original route, we can make all the arrangements to get it signposted without any fuss.' Rosemary had taken up a stance with her back to the fire and was addressing the room as if it were a meeting. 'It can't make any difference to you where it goes.' She had, it appeared, handed out photocopies of a map. Jim and Dottie were nodding. Lesley looked angry and Bill and Penny seemed confused.

'As I've told you before, all the footpaths on my farm are waymarked,' Bill said after a pause. 'I don't see what this is about.' He was a large man in his fifties, fresh-faced with curly blond hair, greying at the temples. 'And if I might ask, who cares about this path apart from you? Where are all these people in such a hurry to queue to cross my field?'

'Oh, they are there, I promise you.' Rosemary gave him a saccharine smile. 'You are very good about your paths on the whole, I give you that. Unlike some. But this is a path which seems to have got lost.' She fixed her gaze on him intently. 'Look at the map.'

'There is no footpath there, Rosemary,' Lesley put in patiently. 'There never has been. I told you. I've checked the records.'

'Obviously not the right ones.' Rosemary shook her head. 'The path across the lower field is vital to the footpath circuit if one wants to get down to the quay.'

'That's right,' Jim and Dottie chimed in as one. 'It's an ancient path. We've seen it marked on the map as well.'

'Which map?' Bill put in. 'I've never seen it.'

'And why would people want to get down to the quay, Rosemary? If by the quay you mean our landing stage, it is private property.' Leo's voice cut in suddenly. 'Can't you just leave this alone? The paths are fine as they are. The one at the top of the field leads people naturally into the lane and from there they can go on with your precious circuit up through the woods.'

Rosemary shook her head vigorously. 'No, Leo. That's the point. There has to be access to the quay. Traditionally walkers have always used it.'

'No,' Bill put in at last. 'They haven't. That jetty was sold with the barns. It was part of the home farm and we let it go with the development. Access to it is private. And always has been.'

'And I think you'll find that is in our deeds,' Ken added suddenly. 'It was the private landing and mooring which attracted us here in the first place.'

'Why don't we have a top-up,' Steve said abruptly. He had been so quiet, sitting slightly apart from the others, that Zoë had forgotten he was there. He stood up and reached for Lesley's glass. 'Same again?'

Lesley gave an absent-minded frown, which he took to be a nod.

'There has never been a path across Dead Man's Field,' Penny said suddenly. She was sitting forward on the sofa anxiously, next to her husband. 'My family, the Bartles, have lived in these parts as long as Bill's or longer. The middle of that field, where the copse is, that was reckoned to be unlucky. Cursed. Dead Man's Spinney, they called that. No one would go there, not if their life depended on it.'

There was a moment's silence in the room. Steve returned Lesley's glass and picked up Bill's. 'Is that right, Bill?' he asked.

Bill nodded. 'In the old days they used to say the horses would refuse to pull the plough past that copse. People wouldn't go for little country strolls in that field, believe me, Mrs Formby. Not that they did anyway. No one had time in those days for little country strolls.' He took the replenished glass from Steve and drank it down in one. Then he stood up. 'I'm sorry, but Penny and I have to go.' He turned to Ken. 'It's been good to meet you and your wife.' He gave Zoë a cursory nod. Behind him Penny stood up hastily. She was as tall as her husband and almost as muscular. The pair made a formidable team, Zoë thought with a wry grin, as they headed for the door.

Steve saw them out. For a moment the silence continued, then Rosemary grimaced, turning back to face them. 'He's wrong. There was nothing unlucky about that field. I've walked it myself. And I have already started to put in place the legal steps to have the path reopened. I only asked them out of courtesy to explain what was happening. Now, it's up to the council.'

'Stupid woman!' Leo's *sotto voce* remark was clearly audible through the room. If Rosemary heard it, however, she chose to ignore it. Ken cleared his throat and made a comment about the Watts boys next door. It seemed a good way of changing the subject. For an uneasy half-hour they chatted, then he and Zoë rose to leave.

'Doesn't that bloody woman realise it is her own privacy she will be spoiling if she allows all and sundry to walk down to the landing stage?' he said as they strolled back towards The Old Barn.

'It's not her privacy,' Zoë put in. 'She doesn't sail. I've never seen her down there. She raised the footpath subject before when she took me up to meet Lesley the other day. Lesley was really cross.'

'I could see that. Well, Rosemary doesn't have a leg to stand on. If it's all written down in our deeds then it must be done and dusted. These people!'

Zoë glanced round. Leo had left with them but he had taken the lower path across the lawns towards his cottage, raising a hand in farewell as he turned away. 'Leo has some old books about the barns,' she said. 'He might lend me one to help fill in the history of this place.'

'You seem to have spoken to him a lot.' Ken's voice was sharp.

'Only occasionally, across the fence.' She was careful to keep her voice even. 'He was the one who warned me about the Watts children.'

Ken sighed. 'Jeff gave me the key they've been using. It looks new. I wouldn't be surprised if they didn't have it cut when they were told to give them back before, the little devils.

So, it's just as well,' he added casually, 'I bought a couple of bolts for the doors when I went into Woodbridge earlier. Just in case.'

'Thank goodness they've gone. I hate the idea that they could have been poking round the house when we were out. Touching things.' Zoë shook her head unhappily. 'Please, can we change the locks, Ken? Just to be sure. We can't bolt it when we go out. It makes me nervous to think there have been extra keys floating around.'

He grunted. 'Maybe it makes sense. I might go back into Woodbridge tomorrow and take a look at some.'

They paused outside the house while Ken felt in his pocket for their own key.

Inside, the great room was full of shadows, thrown by the floodlights outside on the lawn. In the silence the scrape and stamp of a hoof echoed off the walls, and the rattle of a chain against a wooden manger faded eerily into the darkness. As the door opened and the lights came on the room was quiet again.

7

'You can tell Lord Egbert that his sword is finished.' Eric turned from his work bench as Hrotgar appeared in the doorway. The sword lay covered with a newly woven cloth and was out of sight.

Hrotgar stepped inside. 'May I see it?' The room was cold, the charcoal fire extinguished.

'It is for the lord's eyes alone.'

'But that is crazy. He will show it to everyone.'

'That is for him to decide.'

'You did all the extra things he demanded?'

'I did everything just as instructed.'

'The runes and charms and magic?'

'I did everything he asked.'

Both men were silent for a moment, staring at the table.

'I will bring it up to the hall,' Eric said at last, 'and give it to him.'

'He is asleep. You will have to wait until evening.'

Eric frowned and shook his head. 'My instructions were to bring it the moment it was finished. If he is asleep then I will wake him.'

'And the scabbard?'

'The scabbard, it appears, is none of my business after all. It is to be decorated with runes and magical sigils by the sorcerer himself. He did not want Edith nearby as she is Christian and I cannot ask her to stay away any longer.'

Hrotgar gave a cynical sneer. 'The last time I looked it seemed to me that you called yourself Christian, my friend, as we all are. He is being over-sensitive if he objects to your wife but not to you. Or is the rumour true, that you worship the old gods now too?'

Eric shook his head. 'I follow the orders of the Lord Egbert,' he sighed. 'Tonight the sword will be gone and,' he held Hrotgar's gaze a fraction of a second longer than necessary, 'Edith returns to my bed.' He paused for a moment, but still the other man showed no sign that he cared one way or the other. 'It seems to me that this is all a storm over nothing,' Eric went on, 'as it will be his brother or one of his sons, when they are grown, who takes the sword to blood it in battle. Lord Egbert is not likely to see the field of action again.'

Hrotgar frowned uneasily. 'Come when you wish, then. No doubt he has given orders that you be admitted to his bedside whether one of his men is there by his side, or the Lady Hilda. Christ protect you, my friend.'

He turned and strode out of the workshop. Eric watched him go. He leaned against the wall and stroked his chin. Something had made Hrotgar uncomfortable in his presence; his usual swagger and antagonism were missing. He pulled the covering off the sword and stroked the blade with his finger. 'So, my beauty, already there is mystery surrounding you, as well as magic.' He gave a wry smile. Destiny Maker was the finest sword he had ever forged and probably would be the best of his career. It had been from its very inception a special commission, beyond the norm. He shook his head again. Strange, as Lord Edgar had never been a warlike man. He had fought when called to do so, and had displayed his prowess well, but he did not glory in war as some of his friends and relations did. He had not been well, in all probability, for a long time, but he had hidden it behind a brave façade.

Making up his mind, he picked up the cloth and wrapped the sword once more, then carrying it over his shoulder he turned towards the door. The sooner he had delivered it to its destination, the sooner he could go home and into bed with his wife.

Zoë woke with a start and lay staring up at the ceiling in the dark, her heart thudding uncomfortably. She glanced at her side. Ken wasn't there. Sitting up she looked towards the bathroom but the door was ajar and the light off. She was alone.

Wrapping her dressing gown round her, she tiptoed out onto the landing and stared over the edge of the banister down into the darkness, holding her breath. 'Hello?' Her voice sounded reedy in the silence. Scared. 'Come out. I can see you!' she tried again, louder this time. 'Jackson? Jade? I know you're there.'

Nothing. She reached out for the light switches and flooded the place with light. Nothing. The chairs were all as she and Ken had left them. The doors were locked. So where was Ken? She padded through to his study. It was empty. He was nowhere in the house. The boat? Surely not, in the dark. For the first time in weeks her thoughts turned to Anya, but as quickly she dismissed them. Anya was long gone. She glanced towards the windows again, not for the first time wishing that they had done something about blinds or curtains, and then she looked at her watch. It would soon be morning. Turning out the lights she went to stand at the windows, looking out. There was a slight greyness in the east, a lifting of the night. The Old Forge was in darkness.

She shuddered. So, where was Ken? She felt terribly alone. Miserably she crept back to bed. In minutes she had fallen asleep.

U

Emily had found a deserted shepherd's hut at the far side of the estate. Someone, Dan didn't like to speculate as to who, had brought blankets and pillows there. She didn't talk to him. Pulling off her hat and veil, she threw them down on a floor littered with dead leaves and sticks and wisps of hay. She tore his shirt back from his shoulders and raked her nails down his chest, reaching up hungrily for his mouth as she groped for his heavy leather belt. 'Help me, you dolt!' she snapped as the buckle proved too stiff for her. Her rudeness and his anger combined to have the desired effect. He tore open his trousers and wrenched up her skirts, throwing her to the ground as he pulled off her drawers. They wrestled until he had pinned her down. It was over in seconds.

With a gasp he collapsed across her, exhausted. She lay still, staring up at the roof of the hut, a half-smile on her face as he rolled away from her. 'Will that do, your ladyship?' He lay beside her, his arm across his eyes, the chill of sweat cooling on his chest. He heard the quiet whinny from her horse outside.

'I suppose it will have to.' She gave a brittle laugh. 'Though your technique leaves something to be desired.'

'If I'm not good enough for you −'

'All you need is practice.' She sat up and reached for him again. He dodged backwards.

'I think it's time I saw what I'm getting for my side of the bargain. Take that dress off.'

'I don't think so.'

'No dress, no more action from me, my lady.'

'It's not a dress. It's a habit.'

'Then take off your habit.' He folded his arms.

142

Her face tightened with anger, her eyes flashing dislike. 'I have no intention of undressing.'

He laughed wryly. 'It is a little late to worry about your modesty, my lady.' He kept emphasising the title, not bothering to keep the scorn out of his voice. 'Go on. Take it off.'

She was like an animal on heat. He had not satisfied her yet and she wanted him so badly he could smell the lust on her. He reached across and ran his hand up her naked thigh, hearing the sharp gasp she gave at his touch. 'All or nothing, my lady.'

'I can't undress without my maid.' Her voice was tight with resentment.

'So shall we send for her? Molly, is it not?'

She bared her teeth at him. 'Don't be stupid.'

'I wasn't being stupid, my lady. I was endeavouring to make a joke.' He gave a humourless laugh. 'Perhaps I should be the one to undress you, though why you can't undo buttons which run in plain view down your front I cannot imagine.' He reached forward. She slapped his hand away.

'Happen I'll tear off those buttons if I try,' he said quietly. He did not try to keep the threat out of his voice.

'If you lay a finger on me I will tell my husband that you raped me.'

He laughed out loud. 'I think not. All right, have it as you will. Enough. I have horses to shoe.' He scrambled to his feet.

'No!' The anguish in her cry was real. 'No, wait. You can't go.'

'I can't?'

'No.' She rose to her knees and began unbuttoning the jacket of her habit. Standing over her he watched as she pulled it off. Under it she was wearing a white blouse trimmed with a lace jabot at the neck. She tore it off. Beneath it a chemise, and then a short-waisted corset which took what seemed like an age to unfasten, her hands behind her trying to loosen the lacings. He waited, not offering to help, and as it fell away at last, she looked at him defiantly. She had small breasts and a narrow childlike waist. 'Skirt off, and boots.' He kept himself under tight control. 'I want you naked, my lady.'

She gave a loud sigh, but otherwise obeyed him until at last she was standing before him with nothing on. He reached out and stroked her breast. She drew in her breath sharply. 'That's better,' he said quietly. 'Like training a wild filly.' He grinned. 'Perhaps that is enough for the first session. Next time you will be more obedient.' He turned away and reached for his shirt.

'Stop! You can't go!' she let out a shriek. 'I want you now, you oaf!'

'Oh, is that so.' He glanced back at her. 'Well, next time –'

He did not get a chance to finish. She flew at him, grabbing his hair, wrenching his face towards hers, seizing one of his hands and clamping it over her breast.

He could not contain himself any longer. 'Since you ask so nicely . . .' He pushed her back on the rugs and threw himself over her. She let out a scream, clawing his back and shoulders. He felt her draw blood. 'Stop it, you bitch,' he drove into her again and again, hearing her exultant panting as she clamped her thighs around him. At last, spent, he rolled away again and lay staring up at the roof of the hut. There was a hole in the corner where the ivy had torn its way in and he could see the blue of the sky. He glanced sideways at her. She was lying still, her eyes closed, breathing hard.

Slowly he sat up and started to reach for his clothes. She didn't move and he realised at last that she had drifted into sleep. He gave a wry smile. Fully dressed, he tiptoed towards the door. Just this once madam was going to have to dress herself and find a way to scramble back on her horse without his aid.

As he strode across the field he was filled with self-loathing.

Zoë woke with a start. She had been dreaming, the most erotic, frightening dream of a man and a woman making love. They were violent, angry with each other, fuelling their lust with hatred. She lay back on the pillows, realising her own body was aroused, excited in a way she had not felt for years. When Ken and she made love these days it was a dutiful, affectionate, almost automatic response to some unspoken need which occurred less and less frequently. She hugged her arms around herself wistfully as she realised that Ken was still not there and wondered, this time with mounting concern, where he had been all night.

She was in the shower, feeling the water pounding down on her shoulders, streaming down her face, when she realised she could see in her mind's eye the face of the woman she had dreamed about as clearly as if it was in front of her. The woman had fine-boned delicate features with large grey eyes and curling chestnut hair, which was slipping from its combs as she threw back her head, exposing her throat and breasts to the man who was standing before her. She was angry, arrogant, her eyes hard as stone as she pulled him towards her. Shocked at the power of the sudden vision, Zoë reached out for the tap and turned the water off, standing for a moment dripping, incapable of stepping out of the shower and reaching for her towel. She was astonished to find she was shaking. She could feel the woman's lust, her greed for the man's body, her fury that she needed him at all, her shame.

God! Where had that all come from? Groping at last for the towel she wrapped herself in it and walked back into her bedroom, shivering.

She knew what it was, of course. Sex. She needed sex. She could barely remember when she and Ken had last made love; she wasn't sure if she had wanted him even then. She picked up her hairbrush and stared at herself in the mirror.

Did she fancy him any more? No. She wasn't sure she ever had, not with the intensity of desire that woman had shown. But that woman wasn't displaying love – if anything it was loathing she felt for the man standing over her. She had been needy, but not for love. Bending over, Zoë began to brush her hair forward over her face, feeling the hard, scratchy strokes of the hairbrush on her head with grim satisfaction. Finished, she reached for her tracksuit and running shoes. A hard pound round the lanes would do her good, stop her thinking.

It didn't, of course. Somewhere near the top of the river-edge woods she stopped, panting, and leaned for several moments against one of the ancient pines, staring upwards into the lofty branches, her back towards the river.

She had stopped fancying Ken after he had the vasectomy. Up until then there had always been the faint excitement of the possibility that one day she might forget to take the pill and that somehow she might get pregnant.

From the very first moment they had started to get serious about their relationship and discuss the possibility of marriage Ken had made it clear he never wanted a family, and she, to a certain extent swept away by his other enthusiasms, had agreed. She was not naturally maternal, she had decided. She had been brought up an only child and, without nephews and nieces to coo over, had never felt the need to contemplate having a baby. When her friends produced children she viewed them with a completely dispassionate and slightly distasteful polite interest, and had realised without regret that the friendships concerned may well end up on a back burner for years, if not for ever. Room for friendship dwindled anyway, in the all-consuming flurry of bottles and nappies, leaving the non-maternal half of the relationship, in her experience anyway, feeling cheated and excluded.

She closed her eyes, trying to get her breath back. She had let herself go, these last few months, not running nearly as much as she used to, pounding round the streets of London. To start with after the move, there was just too much to do, getting the house straight and organising their new life and job hunting. She opened her eyes, staring up into the branches again. Job hunting. She had thought it would be so easy – Ken had told her it would be so easy. She had assumed that the local shops and galleries would be crying out for someone with her experience and fighting to employ her. No chance. The shops and galleries concerned were all very happy with the staff they had, staff who had probably been there for years. They all politely said they would keep a note of her phone number and call her if an opening came along or if they heard of anyone looking for help, but she knew they wouldn't. They weren't interested in a newcomer from London who anyway might not stay. She sighed. Leo had said he knew someone. Perhaps she could remind him of his offer of an introduction.

With a pang of regret she remembered that Leo seemed to have gone away again. She had glanced towards The Old Forge as she always did when she set out for her run, and his car was missing from its accustomed parking place. He must have left very early. She felt bereft, she realised suddenly, without him there. For all his irascibility his presence was reassuring in what seemed to be an increasingly unsettling world.

Unlike Ken. She gave a wry grimace. She had come out for her run without checking where Ken actually was. She hadn't given his whereabouts another thought after her strange experience in the shower. All she had wanted to do was get out of that house and run and run with the wind in her hair and the cleansing sunlight all around her.

She went home by the lower route through the oak woods, feeling the crunch of acorns beneath her running shoes, following a footpath along the river which brought her pretty much near the bottom of the grounds and allowed her to divert down to the landing stage. Their dinghy was moored there at the foot of the steps next to Leo's. So Ken wasn't out with the boat. That was strange. Unconsciously she had assumed all along that that was where he was; sometimes in the summer when he hadn't been able to sleep he had gone out to the boat and slept in the cabin there, claiming it was cool and soothing after the unaccustomed dry dusty atmosphere of the heatwave which had greeted them after their move.

Her shoulders slumped as she sat down on the boards, her feet dangling over the edge above the water. He must have taken the car. That was the obvious thing and she hadn't checked the range of old cartsheds where they all garaged their cars. But where had he gone in the middle of the night, and why?

Uneasily she scrambled to her feet and turned back towards the house. Both cars were still there parked side by side, her little Audi and his Defender – he had bought it as soon as they moved, enthusiastically saying they would need the great heavy thing once they were living in the deep countryside. She had found it embarrassing – hardly environmentally sound – but she had to admit that a great many people seemed to drive them or cars like them in the countryside, and once it was covered in mud and dust it did begin to look more authentically rural.

She turned and went back to the house. There she reached for the phone. Ken's was switched off. She tried Steve. He answered at once. 'Steve, you haven't seen Ken, have you?' She tried to keep her voice casual. He hadn't. There was no answer from the Watts's phone, somewhat to her relief, nor as she expected, from The Old Forge.

She sat by the phone defeated, not sure what to do next. Could he have gone for a walk and had a fall? Surely he couldn't have tripped as he was getting into the dinghy and fallen in the river. She felt a tremor of panic starting up somewhere under her breastbone. If he hadn't left the property in a car or in the boat, he must still be there somewhere. Standing up she made her way back to his study and stood looking down at his desk, wondering what he had been doing last, and if there was some sort of clue lurking there amongst the neatly stacked papers. She reached for his computer mouse and saw one of the screens flicker back into life. Normally his work involved screens of graphs and figures and diagrams. But this was a website. He had been looking up nightmares.

Zoë stared at the screen, shocked. She ran the cursor down the page. Why had he been checking nightmares, somnambulism, sleep paralysis – for a new client? Somehow she doubted it. Had he been having nightmares and not told her? She glanced round his office but there was nothing else there to give her any idea where he was. Somnambulism – sleepwalking.

She felt a chill of fear settle over her. She wasn't aware that he had ever sleepwalked, he had never mentioned the subject, but was that it? Had he climbed out of bed in the night and wandered off somewhere and if so, where?

Ken lay looking up at the sky frowning. He had no idea where he was or how he had got there. He had thought it was a dream, but it was beginning to feel more and more real. He was cold, unbearably, achingly cold, and his clothes were damp. With a groan he sat up and stared round, for a moment wondering if he had been with Sylvia. Their afternoon together had been passionate and amusing, and he planned to repeat the experience. His conscience had pricked him a little when he had seen Zoë so soon afterwards, but he had ignored it. The guilt would go away. It always had before.

There was, however, no sign of Sylvia now; he was alone. He was in some sort of ruin in the corner of a field. Behind him the remains of a collapsed flint and rubble wall seemed to be giving him some sort of shelter from the wind; he had been lying in a bed of nettles and wild grasses. He scowled ruefully as he felt the sting on his ankles and realised suddenly that he was wearing his pyjamas and that his feet were bare. 'Oh Christ!' It was a sob. It had happened again.

On the three previous occasions he had woken up at home. In his sleep he had ended up once in his study and twice he had gone downstairs and awoke in the great room, just standing there, at the foot of the stairs. He had said nothing to Zoë. The weird feeling of dislocation had terrified him, but it seemed to have a logical explanation. He remembered what it said on the site he had found on the net. Something like a house move could have triggered this. It was nothing to be afraid of. It was a sign of stress, nothing more sinister than that. 'Christ!' he said again. But this was sinister. Where the hell was he?

There was no sign of any other buildings. He was in a landscape of fields and hedges; no view of the river to give him a clue. He couldn't be very far from home, surely. Not even in his sleep could he have walked barefoot for any distance. Could he? Painfully he staggered out of the nettles, feeling his feet jarring on stones and thorns, until he was at last standing on the grass of the field proper. He was shaking with cold and there was blood, he could see now, on his pyjama trousers where the brambles had torn their way through the cotton. He gave a sudden snort of humourless laughter. He often slept nude. At least he could be thankful that with the onset of the cold nights lately he had decided to put something on.

Zoë. He wondered suddenly what time it was. Had she missed him. If so she would be worried sick.

Rosemary and Steve were standing in the kitchen at The Old Barn looking at Zoë with some concern. 'I don't know what to do,' she had said to them. 'Do you think I should call the police?'

As the door opened all three turned.

'Ken!' Zoë let out a cry of horror as he staggered into the kitchen. 'Oh my God, Ken, what happened?'

An hour later he and Zoë were sitting at the kitchen counter over breakfast. Rosemary and Steve had left almost at once after he arrived, and Ken had disappeared upstairs to lie in a warm bath to thaw out. Only when he had returned downstairs and they were side by side drinking coffee and eating scrambled eggs and toast did Ken feel like talking.

'It wasn't all that far away in the end, but I was completely disorientated. I found my way back by sheer luck. I followed the sun and the lie of the land and intuition.' He shook his head. 'I still don't know how I got there, Zo! I was so frightened when I woke up.' He had never before admitted to her that he had been scared about anything.

'It's happened before, hasn't it?' she said gently. 'I saw, on your computer.'

He nodded. 'A couple of times I woke up downstairs. It freaked me out a bit so I thought I would check what it was all about last night when I couldn't sleep. I felt tired in the end,' he gave a hollow laugh, 'so I crept into bed so as not to wake you, and that was the last thing I remembered until I woke up. This time I must have been over a mile away.' He rubbed his face with the palms of his hands and looked at her in despair. 'What's wrong with me, Zo?'

'Perhaps you should see a doctor?' she said after a moment. 'Just for a checkup.'

'Why? It's not the sort of thing you go to a doctor for! I haven't got a headache. I'm not covered in spots.' He sounded petulant and childish suddenly. 'And if you think I am going to see a shrink, you've got another think coming.'

'No, but you are not sleeping well.' Zoë tried to keep the impatience out of her voice. His aversion to doctors was legendary. 'There is obviously something wrong and if it isn't something obvious, like worry about work or the move or us –' she paused. 'It isn't about any of those things, is it?' He shook his head miserably. 'Then you need to find out what is going on. For goodness' sake, Ken, don't be such a wimp! You have to get this sorted. Supposing you sleepwalked over the side of the boat one day when you were sleeping down there?'

There was a long pause.

'It wouldn't happen on the boat,' he said at last.

'How do you know?'

'Because it has something to do with this house.'

She stared at him. 'What?' she whispered.

'I don't know.' He shook his head suddenly, violently, and clapped his hands to his ears, as if trying to rid himself of something whispering close beside him. 'There is someone, something here, Zo, and it wants me to do something.' He stood up suddenly, pushing the stool back hard so that it screeched on the tiles. He half-staggered towards the window and stood staring down towards the river. 'Don't you feel it?' he wailed suddenly.

'Yes, I do,' she said after a long moment. 'You are talking about our ghosts.'

'No!' He shook his head. 'I don't believe in ghosts.'

'You don't believe in them, Ken. But you can sense them as much as I can,' Zoë said thoughtfully. 'Maybe if you acknowledged the fact you would stop sleepwalking.'

U

Emily was sitting on the horse, waiting for him in the accustomed spot. He was deliberately late and was surprised to see her still in the saddle. Walking across the field with long even strides he came to a halt beside her and put his hand on the bridle. She knocked it away with her whip. 'You can go. I don't need you any more.'

152

He stared up at her in astonishment. 'So, you've found someone more to your taste at last, have you?' he said quietly. He stepped back, his hand falling to his side.

She gazed at him for several seconds. 'Your job is done, Daniel.' She hardly ever called him by his name; it sounded somehow insincere coming from her lips. She hauled on the horse's reins, turning its head away.

He stepped forward and grabbed at the bridle. 'Don't I get any more explanation than that, after all you have put me through?

She raised an eyebrow. 'After all I have put you through,' she echoed. 'I would have thought it was more the other way round. After what you have put me through. After all, you raped me. You put your hands round my throat.'

He froze. 'It wasn't like that and you know it.'

She smiled. 'But who are they going to believe, Daniel?' She leaned forward and poked his hand away a second time with the tip of her whip. 'We are going to forget what happened, both of us, and it will never be mentioned again under any circumstances. If it is, you will regret it for the rest of your life.'

Dragging the cob's head round she brought the whip down on his rump and set off at a trot. Daniel was left standing staring after her, his mouth open.

He found Susan lying on their bed. Her face was pale in the dim light from the window in the eaves of their small bedroom and he could see she had been crying. He sat down on the edge of the bed and took her hand. 'It's over, love,' he said softly.

'Really?' She didn't need to ask what he meant.

He nodded. He leaned forward and kissed her gently on the forehead. 'Just you and me now, girl. And the little 'un.' He put his hand gently on her belly. 'I will never ever go away from you again, sweetheart, I swear it. Not ever.'

She smiled, then suddenly she grabbed him. She threw

her arms round his neck and this time she was sobbing in earnest. 'I couldn't bear it, Dan, I've been so unhappy.'

'I know, my love.'

'She had no right.'

'I know that too. I had no choice.'

He held her close, his face pressed into her neck. They lay together on top of the bed for a long time as it grew slowly dark outside. Once they heard Benjamin calling Dan, and later, George. Dan didn't answer. He dozed, then he woke to find that she was at last asleep in his arms. He kissed her gently and smiled to himself, easing his arm from beneath her. He would never give her cause to be unhappy again. Gently he put his hand again on her belly and he felt the baby kick. Susan let out a little moan of protest and Dan smiled. Quietly he got up. There was just time to go and see Bella before he started work.

8

Eric stood looking down at the man's face. The shadows of the flickering lights played over his craggy features, turning his head into a gaunt skull. The woman by his bedside, one of Lady Hilda's attendants, quietly withdrew behind the curtain which hung across the door and he heard the latch clatter as it swung shut behind her.

'I have your sword,' he said quietly. 'As you commanded.' He laid it on the bed covers, his gaze on the man's face. Between them the flickering flame of a candle ran up and down the blade, which threw off blue and silver sparks as it lay on the dark rich fur.

Egbert did not move for a moment, then his hand, lying inert on the fur covers, reached out feebly. Eric hesitated, then he took the man's hand in his own – it was cold and dry and clawlike, the hand of a man prematurely old – and he guided it to the sword. Only then as he touched the blade did the eyes flicker open and a strange smile played for a moment over his lips. 'Thank you,' he whispered. He moved his fingers gently down the blade then up again over the neck and crosspiece until his hand fitted around the hilt. For a moment Eric thought he was going to try to lift the weapon but he merely held it lightly. 'You obeyed all my instructions in the making of her?' he whispered.

Eric nodded, then, noticing that the sick man's eyes were closed once more, said, 'Yes, I followed your instructions, my lord. All is as you wished.'

There was a slight nod of satisfaction from the bed. 'Go now, with my thanks. Your payment is waiting.' He gestured feebly towards the table beside him.

Eric stepped forward and picked up the leather bag which lay there. 'Thank you, my lord.'

'Go now.'

Eric was going to offer to move the sword, to slot it into the ornate scabbard he had spotted lying on a stool by the wall, but the old man's hands were linked around the hilt and he showed no sign of wanting to give it up. For a moment Eric hesitated. He felt a strangely sharp pang of regret as he saw his masterpiece lying there on a sick man's bed. The blade was not yet blooded. It should go into battle with a young robust warrior to earn its reputation as a hero's weapon. He wanted to know what was its destiny, his Destiny Maker.

He heard a click behind him and then the rattle of the curtain rings. The woman had come back into the room. He frowned. This was no place for her; she had come too soon. This was a place for men, a sacred moment when a man was introduced to his weapon, and formed a bond as sacred as marriage. He turned, a frown on his face, and found himself looking at the Lady Hilda.

She smiled at him, coldly, he saw, even angrily. 'You must leave now, Eric. We thank you for your hard work. I trust you are satisfied with your payment.'

'I am sure the payment is fair,' he retorted. 'I have no need to check.' He did not even try to hide the anger in his voice. He saw the answering spark of rage in her eyes and it surprised him. 'It was an honour to be selected to make such a sword,' he added more gently. 'This was my greatest work, the one in which I will always have the most pride.'

He gave a small bow, turned to give one last glance at the sword, lying loosely grasped in an old man's hands, and he turned towards the doorway, ducking through the curtain into the dark.

Susan was lying awake staring up at the ceiling of their small bedroom, listening to the snores of the man beside her. She reached across and rested her hand lightly on his shoulder. It was hard not to picture him with that woman. Whatever he said to the contrary, the differences between them, Lady Emily and her, were so great, so fundamental that she could not but be terribly afraid. He had kissed her and hugged her last night and several times he had rested his hand on the hump of her belly with every appearance of affection and relief, but what had he really been thinking? She bit her lip in the dark. She lay staring at the window watching as the darkness became less dark, as the faintest shapes began to show in the room. Dawn was on its way and with it a new day which for the first time in several weeks should be without fear and resentment and misery. It was several seconds before she noticed the figure in the corner of the room. She held her breath, not daring to move. A woman was standing there, watching them. For one desperate, frantic moment she thought it was Lady Emily but as she turned her head slightly, she saw it was a taller woman, with long fair hair, and almost as she took in those details the woman vanished and she realised that all she had seen was the elongated shadow of something outside the window thrown against the wall. She let out a little sob of relief, her hand closing without her realising it on Dan's shoulder. He turned towards her and reached out for her in his sleep and she snuggled up against him with relief.

When she woke again the bed was empty and she could hear already the sounds of the farm awakening around the cottage, the heavy clatter of a horse's hooves, the shouted commands of George and Robert and young Jem as they harnessed the Suffolks and the great shires and backed them between the shafts of the farm wagons and the plough. Betsy must be feeding the hens, she could hear the frenzied excited clucking, and somewhere one of the dogs was barking. By now Benjamin would have lit the forge furnace and Dan would be out there with him sorting through his tools, glancing out of the open forge door into the sunlit yard. She sat up with a groan and swung her legs out of the bed. She had to wash and get dressed and go out to the dairy. She was late.

As she stood a sharp pain gripped her back. She gave another groan, louder this time and put her hand to her stomach. Surely it was too soon? She stood for a moment waiting to see if the pain came again. It didn't. After a moment she straightened and took a couple of uncertain steps towards the ewer and basin on the chest, and it was as she reached for the washcloth that she saw the figure again in the corner. She swung to face it. The woman was standing where she had the night before, tall, willowy, with long fair hair hanging in a plait over her shoulder. For a moment they looked at each other, then as Susan opened her mouth to scream the woman vanished.

Dan dropped everything and ran at the sound of his wife's cry. 'What is it, girl? Is it the baby?' He had his arm round her shoulder in seconds and helped her to the bed.

She shook her head, sobbing blindly. 'She was there.' She pointed with a wavering hand at the corner of the room. 'The woman. The woman who foretells a death!'

Dan froze. He glanced up at the corner of the room. He knew what she meant; the story was an old one. The ghost would appear only when there was to be a death on the farm, the wraith of a woman, dressed in black, her blonde hair hanging to her waist. He glanced at the doorway and saw a trio of faces peering in, Robbie, George and between them young Jem. He waved them away silently and they vanished, but he knew they had heard her. He knew that the words of her frantic cry would be round the farm in minutes. His father had lived and died in this forge cottage as had his father before him. That was why they were called Smith. As long as time itself his family had lived here and been blacksmiths and farriers on the farm. And for as long as that, as far as he knew, the family legend had been that when one of them was going to die the woman appeared, a harbinger of death.

'It's all right, sweetheart,' he murmured. 'It's because you are nervous about the baby. You've imagined it. It is easy to do with the shadows in here.' He cradled her head against his chest, rocking slightly as they sat together on the edge of the bed. 'You mustn't be frightened. There is nothing to be frightened of, I promise.'

She was clinging to him, sobbing quietly, not daring to look up in case she saw it again. There was a slight movement by the door and Betsy appeared. 'It's all right, Dan. You get back to the forge,' she said, bustling in. 'George told me. I'll deal with this.'

For a moment Susan clung to Dan, then reluctantly she let him go and pushed him away. 'Go on, love. I'll be all right.'

The two women watched as he stood up and waited for a moment, watching her, his face twisted with pain, then he turned and walked outside.

Betsy took his place beside Susan on the bed. 'Tell me what you think you saw,' she said firmly. 'Let's get to the bottom of this.'

Susan shook her head, her face stained with tears. 'I know what I saw,' she whispered. 'It was the ghost. And I felt a pain.' She touched her stomach lightly. 'A terrible pain and it's too soon.'

Betsy shook her head. 'We all get pains, my love, ahead of time. That's part of what happens, getting your body used to the feel of what's to come. I've had six so I ought to know. Don't think anything of that. There is nothing wrong with your little 'un. Nothing at all. It's your own fear that made you imagine things. You can see that. You're a sensible woman. A shadow here, a shimmer of light there and you think you see a figure. You know that is superstition, Susan. You know what the parson would say to that.' She smiled comfortably. 'Come on, my duck. Get you up and wash your face, then we must get to the dairy.' With a combination of bustling and bullying and sturdy common sense Betsy eventually got Susan out of the bedroom and out of the cottage into the sunshine. For a moment both women stopped and glanced towards the forge. From inside they could hear the reassuring sound of a hammer, steady and firm. They looked at each other and Betsy smiled comfortingly. 'Nothing to fear, my dear. Everything is back where it should be.' She reached out and squeezed Susan's fingers, then she turned and headed towards the dairy. For a moment Susan hesitated, staring towards the forge doorway, then she too turned away and followed Betsy across the yard.

Ken was asleep. For several seconds Zoë stood looking down at him as he lay on the bed, fully clothed, his shoes lying where he had kicked them on the rug beside him. She felt a wave of compassion as she studied his face. He looked exhausted and upset, even with his face relaxed in sleep.

She tiptoed out of the room and ran down the stairs. Grabbing her jacket, she let herself out of the kitchen door and headed across the lawns towards The Old Forge. She desperately needed to speak to Leo, to tell him what had happened and to ask his advice. There was no answer when she knocked on his door as she had guessed there wouldn't be. He was still away. With a curse she wandered round the cottage, shading her eyes so she could look in at the windows as though there might be some clue as to where he was. She hadn't walked round the building before. It was long and thin, originally two separate structures, the forge and the smith's cottage, at some point linked by a third building between them. Studying them she could see The Old Forge itself now formed the kitchen and the study. Beyond was the living room and behind it another room which appeared to be some kind of workshop. In the corner a narrow staircase led upstairs out of sight, presumably to the bedrooms. She stared through the glass. The cottage was dark and felt strangely unlived in though he could not have been gone for more than a couple of days. With a sigh she walked on round the building, through pretty gardens which circled the property, round to the river side where there was a French door leading into the central room. She tried the handle and to her surprise it opened. She hesitated, then she pulled it open and looked in. 'Leo?' she called. 'Are you there?'

There was no reply. Again she hesitated, fighting her curiosity. He obviously wasn't there, but supposing he had had a fall or something? He might have been taken ill. No one would go away leaving their door unlocked. She owed it to him to check the place was all right. Stepping inside she pulled the door to behind her and tiptoed across the floor. She was in the long living room. She hadn't noticed the small grand piano on her previous visit. She tiptoed between the armchairs and ran her fingers over the polished wood, wondering if he played.

Still on tiptoe she crept through to the room behind it and found that, as she had suspected, it was some kind of workshop or studio, with a huge table in the centre, littered with pencils and rulers and set squares and Stanley knives. Was this a clue to his profession now he was no longer a black-smith? A craftsman of some kind, obviously. Or a painter. She looked at the portfolios stacked away against the wall, the sketches pinned to the beams. In the corner there was a spare bed, but it wasn't made up. It was heaped with more portfolios and sketchbooks. She crept towards the staircase. 'Leo?' Her voice sounded thin and scared. 'Are you there?' She set her foot on the bottom step and looked up. It was a narrow boxed stair with a sharp right-angle bend halfway up. Holding her breath she made her way upstairs.

There was just the one good-sized bedroom, overlooking the river, and a bathroom, also large, which had presumably been created from a second bedroom. A quick glance showed her the usual selection of male cosmetics, aftershave, garden soap, hairbrush, toothbrush charger, but no brush – of course, he was away. She retreated back to the bedroom, low-ceilinged and heavily beamed like the bathroom, with two small dormer windows. She could smell his aftershave in here, sense him very close. The room was hung with dozens of paintings, the curtains and the bedspread were a strange exotic patchwork of purples and reds. She stared round in delight. This was not the bedroom she would have expected of a single man. She found herself wondering suddenly if he was gay and dismissed the thought at once. Being artistic did not mean someone was gay. So, did he have a girlfriend? She crept across to the chest of drawers between the two windows and looked at the top: photographs but of an older couple – perhaps his parents – and an aged spaniel. And a younger pretty woman with two children.

'What are you doing up here?' The voice from the stairs made her jump out of her skin. She spun round and confronted the figure of Jade in the doorway.

'Jade!' She put her hand on her chest, feeling the thumping of her heart. 'You gave me such a fright. I was looking for Leo, you must have heard me calling him.' She felt shockingly embarrassed and guilty at being caught prying into his things.

'He's not here.'

'I can see that now. I was worried when I found the door open.'

'I opened it. He gave me a key.' Jade looked at Zoë with extreme hostility.

Another member of the Watts family with a duplicate key. She wondered if Leo knew the child had it. 'So, do you know where he is?'

'No. I keep an eye on the house for him when he's away.'

'Well, you certainly do that well.' Zoë tried a friendly smile. 'Do you know how long he will be away?'

'No.' The girl stared at her. 'Why did you come here?'

'I wanted to ask him something.' Zoë paused for a moment, eyeing the girl cautiously. 'About the ghosts. The ones which aren't your brothers.'

Jade looked even more suspicious. 'Here? There is only one here.'

Zoë stared at her. 'There is one here? In this house, you mean?'

Jade nodded.

'And you're not scared?'

She shook her head.

'And Leo isn't scared?'

'He ain't seen her.'

'Why?'

She stared at Zoë challengingly. 'She doesn't like men.'

'In that case, could I see her, do you think?' Zoë sat down on the edge of the bed. Still embarrassed and uncomfortable, she found herself hoping profoundly that Jade would be sufficiently distracted from her hostility to talk about the ghost, and at the same time wanting desperately for the girl to say no.

Jade regarded her solemnly for several seconds. 'Don't see

163

why not. You see the ghosts in your house. Mrs Turtill saw this one, she told me.'

'Really?'

Jade nodded. 'She and farmer Bill stayed here before Leo bought the house. They were mending their farmhouse. I heard her tell Mum and I asked her about it. It's an old legend. When someone sees her it means someone is going to die.'

Zoë looked at her, appalled. The girl was astonishingly articulate, but at the same time the lasciviousness on her face as she said this was somehow shocking.

'And you have seen her?'

'Yeah.'

'And you're not frightened?'

Jade shrugged. 'It's not me that's going to die, is it? I'm a kid. Only old people die.'

Zoë paused to mull over this confident piece of logic for a second. 'And did anyone die after Mrs Turtill saw her?' She knew she shouldn't ask. She shouldn't be encouraging this line of conversation at all.

The girl nodded. She grinned. 'One of Mr Turtill's workers was killed by a chainsaw.'

'And who told you that?'

'No one. They thought I shouldn't know, but I was listening when my mum was talking on the phone.'

'So, I don't want to see this ghost, do I? Because it would mean someone I know is going to die?' She shouldn't go on talking about this, but somehow it was important to know.

'Suppose.' Jade grinned again. 'Scary, innit?'

'Yes, it is.' She slipped off the bed and stood up. 'Look, Jade, I think I should be going home. I came to find Leo but if he's away I will have to wait to talk to him till he gets back. Will you lock up carefully?'

'I always do.' The girl looked indignant.

'Good.'

164

Zoë made her way downstairs, conscious of the small form slipping down after her. Jade followed her to the door and showed her out. Then she closed it behind her and Zoë heard the lock click. Whatever the child was doing there, she was not intending for anyone to walk in on her again.

∪

Emily Crosby was standing staring out of her bedroom window. In the distance she could see the sweep of the river catching the sunlight in a cold blue streak between the trees. She cupped her hands over her belly gently and a slow smile dawned across her face. She was now two weeks late, but it was more than that. She knew. For the last ten days she had known, counting the days, listening to her body, waiting, breathlessly hoping, then beginning to dare to believe it. And now she was sure. Always in the past there had been false alarms but she had never been more than a week late before. Never. And now she could feel the burgeoning life inside her at last. It felt different. Special. A strange internal knowing.

There was a tap at the door and she turned as Molly came in. 'You sent for me, my lady?' Molly's sharp eyes had seen that protective, triumphant gesture.

'Yes, Molly. I won't be riding today. Will you tell them in the stables.'

'Yes, my lady. Of course, my lady.' Molly kept her face impassive. Lady Emily was not the type to share her news with a mere maid. But that would not stop her running downstairs and spreading the word. This was the best piece of gossip she had heard for ages.

Emily made her way downstairs, carefully holding the banister, and walked sedately into the morning room where her husband was sitting in his high-backed chair reading the previous day's papers which had just been brought up from Ipswich on the wagonette. He glanced up as Emily appeared in the doorway and watched her close the door behind her.

Every inch of her betrayed her excitement. 'Emily?' He dropped the paper and stood up. 'What is it, my dear?'

She smiled and, suddenly unable to contain herself, spun in a tight pirouette. 'It has happened, Henry. At last!'

'What has happened, dear?' He was by now thoroughly alarmed.

'I am with child!'

For a long moment he stared at her, his incredulity plain on his face, then at last a slow smile began to spread across his features. 'Are you sure?'

'Of course I'm sure.' She pushed aside the last lingering doubt. 'It has happened, Henry. We are going to have a baby!'

Neither noticed the slight scuffle outside the door as the girl who had been about to come in and tend the fire, dropped her bucket and fled down the backstairs to the servants' hall. But the news had already arrived. Molly, her eyes sparkling, had moments before told Mrs Field and Beaton and William Mayhew, Mr Henry's valet. They were all gathered round the large central table full of suppressed excitement. The girl's confirmation convinced them all except Mrs Field, who still shook her head. 'If that flibbertigibbet is pregnant, I'll eat my hat,' she commented sourly. 'You mark my words.'

'Can you believe it, at last?' Molly found time to run down to the forge later that morning with the news. 'Oh, Susan, you must be so relieved. That means she will have no more time to go riding. In fact she told Sam she wouldn't be riding today and I expect she won't ride again for quite a while. She won't dare risk anything happening, will she?' Riding was the euphemism the two sisters used for the suspicion neither would discuss openly.

Susan gave a grim smile. 'And whose baby is it, do you suppose?'

Molly stared at her, shocked. It was no more than they had said in the servants' hall but for Susan to come out with it so openly shook her deeply.

'Sue –'

Susan was standing by the window looking out into the yard, one hand pressed into her back, finding it uncomfortable to stand or sit. There was a long silence.

'Does it matter, that much?' Molly said at last, her voice gentle. 'Think of Dan's child being brought up to inherit the Hall.' She put her hand to her mouth and giggled. 'It is the squire that's the cuckold, Susie, not you.'

Rosemary's huge kitchen table was covered in maps and notebooks. Zoë glanced at them with distaste. She did not have to ask to know this was all part of Rosemary's footpath crusade. 'I wanted to ask you the name of your doctor,' she said to Rosemary as she followed her in. 'We haven't needed one – neither of us is particularly doctor-minded – but this sleepwalking thing has scared me a bit and I would feel better if I at least had the number of someone to ring if anything happened.'

Rosemary walked over to the counter where their landline sat on its charger and reached for a neat loose-leaf address book. 'I'll write it down for you, Zoë. He's a good chap. Pleasant. Will listen.' She gave a rueful grin. 'So, how is Ken?'

'He's still asleep.'

'Goodness, he must have been tired.' Rosemary glanced at her wristwatch. 'Listen, my dear, I don't want to hurry you, but Jim and Dottie are coming over in a minute. To talk about this path across the field. We want to try and find a way of persuading Turtill to give in without turning this into a fuss.'

'But what is so important about that particular path? Why does it have to be a fuss at all? I still don't get it.' Zoë spoke before she could stop herself. She shook her head. 'No, forget I said that. I know it's important to you.'

'It is. It is a matter of precedent; of national policy.'

Rosemary gave her a small tight smile. 'I know you don't understand. That is why it is better left to those of us who do.'

Zoë opened her mouth to make a retort, then changed the subject instead. 'One thing I wanted to ask you – I went over to see Leo but he's not there and the child Jade was there in his house. Apparently she has a key. Is that OK, do you think?'

Rosemary sighed impatiently. 'I don't understand that man at all. But I know he's fond of Jade and I suppose if he thinks he can trust her, then that's up to him.'

'She was telling me a ghost story. About a woman with long white hair who appears before someone is going to die. Have you heard that one?'

Rosemary hesitated. 'I have, yes.'

'Is it some ancient legend?'

'My dear, you must have realised by now that this place is full of stories and legends and history. There is a ghost at every corner. Ignore it. I expect Jade was trying to scare you off.'

There was a knock from the front door. 'Forgive me, dear, but that will be the Salcombes. Can you find your own way out?'

Zoë gave a wry smile. As she was standing less than six feet from the back door it was hardly likely that she would get lost.

A couple of days later Leo reappeared. He knocked on the door while Ken was in Woodbridge. 'I hear you have had a run-in with my security company.' He grinned.

Zoë felt a wave of embarrassment sweep over her. 'I am afraid she caught me inside. I was worried when I found the door unlocked.'

He gave her a quizzical glance. 'I trust Jade. She's a good girl.'

168

A good girl who had told him that she had found Zoë in his bedroom. She could feel a blush spreading up her neck. 'I am sorry. I will leave it to her in future.'

'She told me she had scared you with her story of the ghostly blonde.' He chuckled. 'She is a little devil!'

'But is it true?'

'True?' He shook his head. 'I should be so lucky! It's a story. One of those tales that gets embroidered and improves with every telling. Don't give it a thought. I don't.'

She led the way into the great room and went to stand by the window. 'Did you hear about Ken sleepwalking?'

He nodded. 'Rosemary told me this morning. I met her as I was driving in. I swear that woman has this place staked out.'

Zoë was staring down at the river. 'Ken really scared me. We still don't know where exactly he went. Somewhere up in the fields.'

'But he hasn't done it again?'

She shook her head.

'Well, perhaps he won't. Perhaps whatever he's worrying about has been resolved.'

'I don't know what it is he is worrying about. He won't tell me. Or at least he says there is nothing, he loves it here and he enjoys his work.

He studied her back, noting the tenseness in her shoulders. 'He's not worried about your ghostly visitations or the kids next door, I trust.'

'I doubt it. He doesn't want to believe in the ghosts. It's far simpler to blame the kids and they would hardly drive him to sleepwalking. Anyway, they have gone.'

'All except Jackson and Jade.'

'Yes, Jade,' she echoed. She turned to face him. 'I'm the one who is frightened of the ghosts.'

'Don't be. They do no harm.'

'Except your beautiful blonde lady who foretells a death.'

169

'My Anglo-Saxon beautiful blonde lady, judging by her costume.' He smiled at her. 'She is my problem. She comes with the forge.'

'But you haven't seen her yourself.'

He hesitated.

'Oh, Leo! When? I thought Jade said she only appears to women.'

He shook his head. 'She's no sexist. But I don't believe in omens and I don't believe in her. I tell myself she's just a trick of the light, no more, and I can see why people think she is a woman. The sun shines in obliquely into my bedroom. The windows are at a strange angle. Perhaps you noticed.' He gave a mischievous smile. 'And the reflection on the wall can look like a woman's figure. I greet her and we go our separate ways.'

'And you're not afraid?' She refused to rise to the dig about being in his bedroom.

'I have already looked death in the face, Zoë.' He touched his scars briefly. 'I'm not afraid of anything any more.'

She shuddered. 'You are a brave man then. I am.' She shook her head. She was afraid of so much, but it was none of his business why she was afraid and of what apart from the ghostly noises in the house.

It was ten o'clock next morning that Ken came into the kitchen looking furious. 'You won't believe what that bloody woman is doing.'

'What bloody woman?' Zoë rinsed her hands and hung up the dishcloth.

She's only got an army of her walking mates out there, ready to trespass on Bill's field.' He went across to the phone. 'I'm going to call him. I bet he doesn't know.'

'Ken! Should you interfere?'

'Probably not, but she irritates the hell out of me with her smug self-righteousness, and this is the poor guy's living. He has to make money out of that farm. Having those people trotting up and down his fields telling him where and why he can't plough his own land is not on.'

Zoë went to the window but whatever was happening outside Rosemary's house was invisible from there. She heard Ken explaining what was happening to Penny Turtill and she heard Penny's voice rising in anger. Ken put the phone down looking satisfied. 'She's going to call Bill on his mobile. He will go straight down there.'

'Are you going too?'

He shook his head. 'Best not.'

'How many people are there?'

'A couple of dozen. Let's go down to the boat. We can see the field from there.'

'Ken!'

'I know. I'm being suburban. But I would love to see her trounced!'

The river was dark green and sluggish beneath the mist but the fields on the south-facing side were slowly emerging into golden sunlight as the party of figures began slowly to walk across the stubble towards the centre of the field. Ken passed Zoë his binoculars. 'Look. She's in front.'

Zoë focused on the group. 'They look very fierce. They've got sticks.'

'Walking poles,' Ken said. 'I don't suppose they are planning to hit anyone. I doubt any of them is aged under sixty-five!' He took the glasses from her and swept the shore again. 'Here's Bill. And there are several people with him. Including,' he twisted the focus knob, 'yes, including our Jade and her big brother. They are shaking their fists.' He grinned and handed back the glasses to his wife.

Zoë watched the scene for a moment. 'I don't understand it. I really don't. Why on earth would she want to make such a fuss about this path? Why is it so special? Oh, look. There is Lesley from the Hall. She is confronting Rosemary.'

Beside her Ken shivered. It was strange sitting on the boat in the cold mist while above them the action was taking place in the spotlight of a patch of autumn sunshine. He glanced over his shoulder into the mist. And heard himself give a gasp of fear.

'Zo.'

She was riveted by the scene playing out in the field and didn't hear him.

'Zo!' This time his voice registered.

'What is it?' She lowered the glasses and turned towards him. 'Oh my God!'

In the distance, barely visible in the fog above the river she could see the sail, the gentle swell of the fabric, the grinning face of the great animal which was painted on it, the curved shape of the prow silently cutting through the water. The glasses fell from her hands into the bottom of the boat with a clatter. 'Ken!' she whispered. She was paralysed with terror. Had they heard the noise of the glasses falling on the bottom boards. 'Can they see us?'

'I hope not.' His whisper was so quiet she barely heard it. 'Don't move.'

'Can you see anyone?'

He shook his head. Slowly, hardly moving, he bent to retrieve the binoculars and trained them on the ship. He swore silently and lowered them, wiping the lenses. 'I can't see anything.' He tried again. 'No. Nothing. You look.' He passed them to her. Zoë ignored him. She was too scared to move, to breathe. Her eyes were straining against the mist, but the shape of the great ship was fading. In seconds it had gone.

They looked at each other. 'We didn't imagine that, did we?'

Ken shook his head. 'It's almost like a projection on the mist. Is it possible, do you think? Is someone on the shore doing this, as a joke?'

He turned and looked back up through the trees towards

172

the field but the mist had thickened there as well and he could see nothing.

Zoë shook her head. 'No, it's not a joke. How could it be when people have been seeing it for years – for centuries? Can't you feel it? It is there, from the past.' She shuddered violently. 'Let's get off the boat, Ken. I want to go home.' She couldn't stop her hands from shaking.

He didn't argue. It took no time at all to pull the dinghy alongside and slip silently into it, both of them watching over their shoulders. Zoë's knuckles were white as she clutched the gunwale, feeling the cold water splashing off the oars. She was listening for that other ship but she could hear nothing but the slop of water against the landing stage as Ken pulled against it and grabbed at one of the rope fenders. 'Go on,' he whispered. 'Climb up.' He was staring out into the fairway. 'Hurry.'

She stood up shakily and reached up, her whole body trembling with fear. Somewhere out of sight a gull began to call, its loud laughing cry echoing in amongst the trees.

Side by side on the landing stage they stood for a moment staring back at the river. The mist was getting thicker.

'I don't like it here, Ken,' Zoë said suddenly. 'I want to move.'

'Move?' He stared at her.

She nodded. 'I want to move. Back to London. I hate this place.'

'Nonsense. You said you loved it. You did love it. It's just now, in the fog. Wait till the sun comes out.'

'No, Ken it's not just now. There are ghosts everywhere. It is lonely and inconvenient and it scares me. It all scares me. I don't want to stay here a moment longer.'

Turning, she began to run up the path.

U

Dan had taken Bella out to the orchard behind the barns and left her there for the morning to enjoy the sunlight and find herself a few leftover windfalls. He spent a few moments rubbing her soft nose and murmuring to her before taking off her head collar and turning her loose. He walked slowly back towards the farmyard and on impulse diverted slightly towards the top of the woods to stand for a few moments and look down towards the river. The warm autumn sunshine beat down on his face as he stood there gazing at the water. It was misty down there, a slight haze drifting between the trees, and he could see the faint outline of a sail coming up-river on the tide. He watched it idly for a few minutes, then he took a few steps forward, screwing up his eyes to see better. The craft had a strange cross-rigged sail and on it he could see the outline of a huge animal head. He moved forward some more, slithering on the soft loam of needles beneath the pines, and paused again, leaning against the trunk of one of the trees, staring at the ship. He watched it for what seemed like a long time, then it headed again into a patch of mist. The sail grew hazy, and after a few seconds it disappeared. He waited for it to reappear as it went round the point and headed up into the reach below the farm. The water there was sparkling in a patch of sunlight. It never came. A breeze got up after a while and the mist disappeared. There was no sign of the ship.

Puzzled, Dan walked back towards the yard. He told George what he had seen and the older man shook his head. 'My God! Don't you tell my missus about that, boy,' he said. 'Don't you know what that is?'

Dan stared at him, puzzled.

'That's the ghost ship, that is.'

Dan's eyes widened. 'You're having me on.'

George shook his head. 'No,' he said. 'You must know about it. Your family has been here as long as time! You ask Fred Turtill. His grandfather saw it that time before they had that outbreak of sickness in the village. Five people died and it was said the ship brought the death with it. Don't you go blathering about this to Susan, now. She's distressed enough as it is what with the ghost in the cottage and all.' Shaking his head he walked away towards the hay barn. Dan stood staring after him, then he glanced at the cottage. Why hadn't he heard the story before? He shuddered. His ma, that was why. She forbad talk of that kind of thing in the house.

Susan was in the dairy with Betsy. Making up his mind, he walked into their cottage and, rummaging around on the sideboard he found a notebook which one of Susan's aunts had given her. She had laboriously copied a few recipes in the front but most of it was empty. Carefully Dan tore out a page from the back. He sat down at the table and began to draw. Good to get it down on paper while the memory was fresh. As to the ship of death story, that was a load of rubbish. He was not a superstitious man.

9

Edith had swept the house, and hung their bedding out to air. Her pots and pans were scrubbed and shining, and Eric's clothes had been brushed and mended. She was waiting for him when he returned from the hall, her long hair hanging loose down her back, combed and scented with the herbs that hung in bunches from the rafters. Tonight she would tell him that she was with child.

When he came at last he was full of excitement and desire. He fell on her with a mock growl, his arms embracing her, his mouth on hers, his happiness overwhelming. He had thrown the leather bag of coins on the table. Later they would count them but for now all he wanted was to make love to his beautiful wife.

Outside, the village was in a state of excitement. The Lord Egbert was to hold a feast. People were running to and fro, meat was cooking on the spits, the women from the village were helping with the baking, the men practising for a tournament of sword play and mock fighting. The lord's brother, Oswald, was coming back from King Edmund's court and it was to celebrate his arrival that Egbert had decreed that it was time for feasting and fun. Winter would soon be upon the land, and in the spring the village would be denuded of its men as the call went out that the fyrd was to prepare for war.

Deep in their pillows Eric and Edith snuggled together, oblivious of the bustle outside. Only one man knew where they were and was watching their door. Hrotgar had walked down from the hall to seek out the swordsmith, but the closed door which greeted him made him fall back. He scowled. He would wait.

It was long dark by the time the door opened again. Eric walked out stretching and whistling, reached for the water scoop beside the barrel outside their door. He was the happiest man alive. Edith had told him that he was to be a father at last. After all these years of waiting. As he poured some water over his head Hrotgar came forward.

'You are to go back to the hall.'

'Why?' Eric started. He had not seen the man arrive. 'My job is done. The sword is finished.'

Hrotgar shrugged. 'Perhaps to acknowledge the plaudits of the company. The Lord Egbert has sent for you. I've waited here for you long enough, my friend. We should go now. Put on some clothes and follow me.'

Edith waited until they were out of sight, then, following them, she too made her way up the hill. The air was rich with the smell of roasting meat, thick with the blue smoke from the fat as it splattered onto the cooking fires. The sound of music and merriment could be heard clear down to the river.

The hall was packed, the long tables buckling under the weight of great platters of food. As Eric and Hrotgar went in a singer was picking up his lyre. Almost at once the noise began to die away and as soon as he started his song there was silence in the great room. Edith made her way in amongst the women who were helping to serve the food and peered

177

round. There was no sign of the Lord Egbert. In his place in the seat of honour was a younger man, his brother. So where were his two sons? Had they stayed in Thetford with the king? She felt the sting of smoke in her eyes and turned back towards the door as Hrotgar threaded his way towards the high table with Eric behind him.

She was hesitating, not knowing whether to wait or go, when suddenly she found herself facing a stranger. She knew without being told this was the heathen sorcerer, Anlaf, from the forest. A space was opening round him in the crowd, people falling back on every side to get away from him as he stood in the entrance to the hall, but she found herself unable to move. He was staring at her, holding her gaze with fierce brown eyes, his wild hair blowing in the wind which was tearing into the hall through the open doors. Two servants rushed forward to push them shut and drop the heavy bar in place to hold them closed. They saw him, stopped and backed away. He gave a humourless smile, ignoring them. 'Come.' He beckoned Edith. 'Follow me.'

She was frozen to the spot with fear, her hands protectively folded over her belly but somehow she couldn't disobey him. As he turned and made his way through the hall she followed, as if mesmerised.

They were halfway up to the high table when the singer finished his song and bowed to the tumultuous applause. As he sat down Oswald, the Lord Egbert's brother, stood up and banged his knife hilt on the table, calling for silence.

'As many of you know, this is a special day. Today Eric our champion swordsmith completed the great new sword which my brother had commanded of him. The sword is called Destiny Maker and it will be the greatest sword in the whole of the Kingdom of the Angles.' He paused as cheers erupted from all around. Edith searched for Eric, who was standing with Hrotgar near the speaker. He met her eye and the two exchanged a secret smile.

'As you all know, my brother is grievously sick,' Oswald went on, 'and so he has asked me to take the sword when we go to battle in the spring and blood it honourably in the defence of this land.' He reached under the table and produced the sword, waving it in the air above his head. The reflections from a hundred candles seemed to catch its blade as it swung back and forth.

There was another great roar of approval. Someone slapped Eric on the back and he raised his right arm in salute to the sword.

Oswald beckoned a serving man over and held out his drinking horn. 'Fill it, my friend, so I can drink health and success to this great weapon, to the man who made it, and to everyone here!'

He was raising the horn to his lips when the sorcerer at last reached the top table, a clear path almost miraculously appearing before him. He raised his hand and turned to face the assembly. 'That is not going to be possible,' he shouted. 'This night the Lord Egbert has gone to meet Woden in the place of heroes.'

A sudden shocked silence fell on the hall, followed by cries of denial.

'Go and see for yourselves,' the man went on. 'At this moment the harbingers of death sit on the roof of this hall. The Lord Egbert's corpse is lying in the arms of his wife, who sobs over his body.'

Oswald had subsided into his chair, his face white with shock as he stared at the wild-eyed man standing in front of him. Eric seemed to have been turned to stone.

Anlaf stepped forward and seized the sword hilt. With almost superhuman strength for such a slightly built man he raised it in his turn, but now it was in total silence. 'This sword will not be blooded in battle. It was made for one purpose alone. It will be buried with the Lord Egbert and go with him into the Otherworld,' he shouted.

'No!' Eric was finally galvanised into life. 'No, this sword was made to do battle!'

'And so it shall.' Oswald hauled himself out of his chair. 'I will not hear such pagan nonsense! My brother can't be dead. I saw him just a short while ago. How does this man know he is dead? He lies!' He thumped the table again. 'We will ask Lord Egbert himself!' He turned towards the curtained doorway behind him. Then he paused and turned back. 'My brother will tell you this sword was made for fighting. And when the time comes for him to die, when it is God's will, we must remember that Christians are not buried with their swords. This sword will be passed on to Egbert's sons, my nephews, when they are old enough, and until they are ready to carry it into battle it will be blooded by me!'

The shocked silence in the hall was once more broken by cheers, but again the sorcerer raised his hand.

'Death, my friend, has visited this place tonight. It is easy to prove, and you are forgetting,' the man's voice was silky suddenly, carrying like a snake's hiss through the hall, 'that the Lord Egbert was not a Christian. He was a follower of the ancient faith of his fathers and as such he is already on his way to the land of heroes. Listen! Do you not hear the sisters of Wyrd?'

In the silence that followed his words they all heard the scream of the wind.

There was a sudden commotion behind the high table. People turned to see what was happening, standing on their toes to get a better view. The curtain over the door had been pushed aside and the Lady Hilda was standing there, her face ravaged by tears. 'My lord and husband has died,' she cried. 'He has gone.'

Edith suddenly realised she was standing almost alone beside the sorcerer and she stepped back, quickly. She was feeling sick. The man was quiet now, waiting and watching for the tumult to die down, but she could feel the power coming off him in waves. At the far end of the hall there was another stirring and fidgeting amongst the people as the men struggled to lift the bar and the great doors were pulled open. She turned. Father Wulfric had appeared. He was standing in the entrance staring up across the tables towards the sorcerer. There was a crucifix in his hand.

'You have no place here,' he called. His old voice did not carry well and it sounded feeble in the huge space beneath the crossbeams of the roof. He moved forward, however, steadfastly holding the man's gaze, holding the crucifix before him. Perhaps only Edith could see that the man's hand was shaking.

The sorcerer did not flinch. His face was hard as flint. 'Do not dare to challenge me!'

'I dare.' Father Wulfric began to walk towards him. The crowds drew away, flattening themselves against the walls, leaving the centre of the hall empty. 'This is a Christian hall and the men and women here are Christians. The soul of the Lord Egbert is crying out in pain because of your evil hold on it. But the Lord Jesus will prevail.'

Edith glanced from the old priest to the sorcerer, who was now standing with his back to the high table. He had not wavered. The Lady Hilda was sobbing quietly, clutching at the arm of her brother-in-law, who had gone white with fury.

It was Hrotgar who stepped forward and raised his hand. Wulfric stopped in his tracks. 'I am as good a Christian as any man here,' Hrotgar called out, 'but I am, I was, the thegn's reeve and my duty is still to him. It was his wish that this sword be commissioned especially for this eventuality. It was made so that in all its perfection and its purity it would accompany the thegn wherever he goes in the next world. I have his orders as to his burial and the ceremony which will be conducted, and that will be attended not by you, Father Wulfric, but by this man here.' He pointed at the sorcerer, whose expression did not change. 'That was Lord Egbert's wish and I gave him my solemn promise that it would be obeyed.' Seizing the sword, he turned and disappeared through the door behind the high table and into the night.

There was total silence in the room. It was the Lady Hilda who broke it at last. With a cry of pain she turned and fled back through the curtain. No one else moved. After a second Edith quietly backed away from the table and made her way round behind it. After a moment's hesitation she followed Lady Hilda out of the hall, through the wind and rain towards the lord's house. Even in the dark her nervous glance up towards the roofline showed the black silhouettes of two large birds perched there. Everyone knew that ravens were the heralds of death. With a whimper of fear she made for the door and let herself in.

There in the bed chamber Lord Egbert lay inert upon the bed.

'Hrotgar is right.' Lady Hilda's voice was broken. 'Those were his orders. He made me swear the oath as well.' She walked towards the bed and stood looking down at the white, still face of her husband. Hrotgar was standing beside the bed. Quietly he stepped forward and, laying the sword on the fur coverlet, gently clasped the dead man's hands around the hilt.

'We can't stay here, Ken. Surely you can understand that?' Zoë was standing with her back to the huge window in the great room. Ken was sprawled in one of the armchairs.

He threw his newspaper down on the floor with an exasperated sigh. 'Calm down, Zo. For goodness' sake.' He shook his head. 'I know it hasn't been all good for you, this move, but you have to give it time. It is wonderful here. Truly wonderful. It has taken me a bit of time to settle in too, but I'm getting there and you will as well. We can't jack it in after only a few months. You've got to give it a chance.'

'So all these bloody ghosts and the neighbours from hell don't worry you at all?'

'Wherever one goes there are going to be difficult neighbours. One just has to get to know them. And we know what the ghosts are now. Kids playing tricks. Look, I bought the bolts and I've fitted them to both the outside doors. They can't get in at night. And anyway, their mother has bollocked them enough to put them off crime for ever and she's taken them away, for goodness' sake! And I'll change the locks if you really think it's necessary.'

'And the ship?'

'The ship –' he paused. 'I reckon my theory about some kind of trick of the light is the right one.'

'A back projection? And what was it in Victorian times when that farm worker guy drew the sketch?'

'Maybe this person today knew about the farm worker guy.'

'And before that?'

Ken shook his head.

'And what about this blonde female in Leo's house who foretells a death? And what about Rosemary alienating everyone for miles around? And what about you sleepwalking?'

'Oh, that's not fair. Don't bring that up,' he retorted. 'It's not my fault. None of this is my fault. Most of it is that bloody man Leo. Has it ever occurred to you that he is trying to scare us away? Scare you away, that is. The man is an antisocial freak. He hated it when we moved in here; he is probably the one who scared away the last owners. Him and that peculiar child of the Watts. My God, he is probably some kind of paedophile!'

Zoë stared at him. 'How could you say such a thing! Even as a joke!'

'I'm not joking. He can't get a woman with all those scars, so he has turned to a child who doesn't know any better –'

He stopped as Zoë dealt him a stinging slap across the face.

There was a long silence. Zoë turned and walked away, running up the staircase and into their bedroom where she slammed the door with every ounce of strength she could muster.

When she came downstairs a long time later there was no sign of Ken.

Emily was standing in her bedroom with tears pouring down her face. She was shaking like a leaf. Her dreams of pregnancy had ended with the arrival at last of the sudden and heavy blood flow which had driven her from her bed as the first light began to peep through the curtains. After several restless nights beside her Henry had taken to sleeping in his dressing room and he slept on, unaware of his wife's despair, of her ringing the bell, the arrival of Molly and Mrs Field, of the bloodied sheets being stripped from the bed and taken away. When he finally awoke and was told what had happened by a sober-voiced Mr Beaton, he went to her room. She was lying on the fresh white sheets, her face almost as white as the linen beneath her, fast asleep. He stood looking down at her, his expression blank, his hopes of an heir yet again destroyed, then silently he turned away.

She found him later in the morning room. 'Henry –'

He looked up at her from the letter he was writing. 'Should you be up, my dear?' His voice was level.

'I'm so sorry.'

'Indeed. So am I.' He hadn't risen to his feet as was his custom when she entered the room and she felt his rejection like a cold wall between them.

'There will be other babies, Henry.'

'As I understand it, there was no baby,' he replied.

'There was,' she cried. 'There was.'

He looked at her thoughtfully. 'Do you wish for me to

send for the doctor, Emily? It may be that you will require a tonic of some sort.'

She shook her head. 'There is no need.' She took a few steps towards him and then stopped uncertainly. She was clutching a shawl tightly round her shoulders. 'Mrs Field says we will be able to try again almost immediately, Henry,' she said. 'She has had children herself. She knows about these things.'

She saw him draw back slightly as though repulsed. 'I am sure it will be better to allow you to recover, my dear.' He stood up at last. 'And now if you will excuse me, I have to go out.' He picked up the letter he had been writing and folded it.

She stared at his back, recognising the implacable angle of his shoulders and after a moment she trailed back towards the door. 'We will talk later, Henry,' she said with as much spirit as she could muster.

He did not reply.

Zoë took herself to Sutton Hoo that afternoon. Pausing beside the kiosk at the entrance to the car park she scrabbled in her bag for a long-unused National Trust card and found it at last, handing it to the young man before parking. The sprawl of modern buildings took her aback; she wasn't sure what she had expected, but not this. As she locked the car and headed for the museum she glanced round curiously. The place didn't seem to be crowded, for which she was grateful. She was in no mood for other people at the moment.

Following the signposts she walked across grass lawns, through a small stretch of woodland towards a field where the famous burial mounds lay clustered above the river. They were smaller than she'd expected, and bare. Somehow she had pictured them surrounded by woodland; the woods were there as a backdrop running down to the river, but here the grassland was grazed by sheep. She walked slowly round the mounds, staring at them, feeling the strange atmosphere of the place, pleased there was nothing there to sensationalise or detract from their stark beauty. On the far side there was a discreet viewing platform, and only there was there a notice describing the various locations.

She moved on, feeling a slight prickle on her skin. This was a very special place, but was it making any sense of her mixed emotions about living here, as she had hoped? She wasn't sure.

The track brought her back to the museum and she stood looking up at the entrance, over which hung a huge mask. No, it was a replica of a helmet. For a moment she stood still, gazing up at it, her heart thudding, then she went in.

In the centre of the exhibition hall was a full-scale replica of the famous ship burial, discovered under one of those mounds outside, first excavated just before the Second World War. It had, she gathered, been reconstructed in faithful and minute detail.

Picking up a spray of bay leaves from a container by the door to what looked like a broad-beamed, upturned boat, she ducked into a low doorway and stopped short in the almost-darkness of the intimate space in which she found herself. She was alone. The body of the warrior king lay at her feet, lit by candles – electric admittedly, but she was prepared to overlook that – the tiny glass flames so weak it took a moment for her eyes to accustom themselves to the flickering light. The king lay on his side beneath a rug. He was wearing a leather jerkin and sported a moustache and beard. His sword and helmet lay behind him, huge drinking horns at his feet.

She stood for a long time, looking at the tableau, taking it all in. There was a huge cauldron once suspended by elaborate chains, beautifully crafted buckets, drinking horns and cups, board games, a lyre with an exquisitely made beaver skin carrying case, and above all weapons, spears, an iron axe, a coat of mail, a shield and the splendid helmet, and by his hand his jewel-hilted sword, all replicas of the treasure they had found in the original burial site.

She was captivated by the atmosphere of the place. It was hushed, respectful, astonishingly moving. The bay leaves were there to leave as an offering. Gently she laid them down, reluctant to move on, aware that this was all pretend, but also aware of the power of the scene before her.

The silence was abruptly shattered as the curtain was pulled back and a group of school children suddenly appeared through the doorway. Her moment of isolation had passed. They pushed around her and the peace and atmosphere in the space had gone. She stooped to make her way out the way she had come and straightened, blinking in the brightness of the museum hall for a moment before starting to wander around the display cases around the edge of the room, stunned by the craftsmanship and beauty of the items which had been rescued from the excavations.

They still could not be sure who this was in the grave, but it seemed almost certain that he was the great East Anglian King Rædwald, who had died around AD 625. This was a man who straddled the pagan and early Christian worlds and who built his Anglo-Saxon kingdom into a rich and powerful entity which would last unchallenged until a hundred or so years later. Then the Viking raids, targeting the rich communities of the eastern seaboard from across the cold North Sea with slaughter, rape and pillage, began systematically to destroy their world.

Zoë stood in front of an image of the Anglo-Saxon burial ship as it would have been before it was dragged up through the woods from the river, with its long body, short mast and huge square sail. Was this the ghost ship which drifted up their stretch of the river, or was the ship, with its sinister cold menace, a Viking raider? She wasn't sure how one could tell.

She crept into the dark of a viewing room and sat on a bench to watch a film loop about the Anglo-Saxon world. As the sonorous beauty of the Anglo-Saxon poetry and the eerie music of the lyre echoed round the room she found herself shivering. This all belonged to the world she now lived in; this past was the past of the coast they now called home, a past which resonated still in the cry of the wind and the wailing of the gulls.

It was some time before Emily called again for the cob and rode down towards the farm. No one came as she rode into the yard and she sat there on the horse for a long time waiting to be helped from her saddle. She did not want to have to shout for help and in the end she lifted her leg across the pummel alone and slid from the horse by herself. She tied it to one of the rings in the wall and walked towards the forge. Daniel was shaping a piece of metal, the furnace behind him roaring as Benjamin pumped the bellows. A heavy hammer in his hand, Daniel was striking sparks from the red-hot metal, his face gleaming with sweat in the firelight. For a moment she stood in the doorway unnoticed, then Benjamin looked up. 'Dan,' he called. Daniel didn't hear him. He stopped pumping. 'Dan!'

At last Daniel stopped hammering and straightened. He picked up the metal with a pair of tongs and plunged it into the bucket beside the anvil. There was a loud hiss of steam. He laid down his tools and, following Benjamin's pointing finger, he turned at last to the doorway.

If she saw the look of fury and impatience which crossed his face she ignored it. 'Daniel, I need you to come and look at my horse.'

'If it needs shoeing, perhaps you would leave it where it is, my lady,' he said curtly. 'I will look at it later.'

'Now, Daniel!' Her voice sharpened.

For a moment he held her gaze then he sighed. He rubbed his hands on his leather apron and strode towards the door, leaving the boy standing wide-eyed behind him.

She watched for several minutes as he examined the cob, running his hands down each leg in turn and lifting it to examine the shoes. When he had finished he straightened.

'I need for us to resume our meetings,' she said before he could say anything. 'Tomorrow. At midday.'

'I don't think so, my lady.' He walked round to the horse's head and examined the bridle, checking the straps one by one.

'You have to.' Her voice rose slightly.

He looked at her across the back of the animal and held her gaze. 'I said no, my lady. That is finished. What we had, what we did was wrong. I have promised Susan that it will not happen again.'

'You told her?' She glared at him, horrified.

'I didn't have to, my lady.'

'What do you mean, you didn't have to?' Her face was white, her lips compressed.

'Everybody knew what was happening.'

She shook her head. 'No. You must have told someone. You fool!'

'I told no one, my lady. I of all people did not want it noised about. It seems you were not as careful as you could have been. You instructed men to take your blankets out to the shelter. What did you expect them to think they were for?' The colour rose slightly in his face. 'Do you despise your servants so much you don't give them credit for having eyes and ears and being able to use them? I have been a laughing stock, my lady, and so have you.'

She was silent. Almost at once he regretted saying what he had, but it was out now, and there had to be an end to it. Everyone had heard of her miscarriage, if indeed that was what it was. And everyone had speculated whose baby it might have been. Molly had said that Mrs Field had said there never was no baby, but whatever happened he was not going to help her get pregnant, a bull to her cow to give the squire an heir.

Her face had grown hard. 'You will regret those words, Daniel.'

'I spoke no more than the truth. Now, you need to go home, my lady. Shall I help you mount?'

'I will send you a message and you will come.' She moved forward and gathered up the reins. 'Do you hear me? You will come!'

He said nothing. He went up to her and, lifting her up, sat her on the saddle. He fitted her foot to the stirrup and waited while she arranged herself and pulled the skirt of her habit into place, then he untied the horse. He turned it and stood back without a word. She looked down at him. 'You will come, Daniel,' she repeated. She lifted her whip threateningly and for a moment he thought that this time she was going to strike him with it, but she brought it down on the horse's rump. The animal jumped sideways. She pulled its head round with a vicious jerk and trotted out of the yard.

Dan turned away and found George standing watching from just inside the old barn door. 'You want to watch that one,' George said quietly. 'I reckon she could turn vicious.'

'She wants a child.' Daniel nodded.

'And doesn't care who she hurts in the process.' George shook his head. 'Mr Mayhew says that Mr Henry has written to his solicitor about the inheritance. The estate is to go to one of his nephews if he has no children.'

'These things have to be taken care of, I suppose,' Dan said grimly.

'Of course she doesn't want that. The whole estate and her dowry going to a stranger. But she's a young woman. She should be healthy enough.' George winked.

'So presumably is the squire,' Dan said acidly. 'His first

wife, God bless her, managed to produce an heir even if the poor mite did kill her.'

George frowned. 'This one's desperate. A cow always goes for the younger bull.'

Dan shook his head. 'I want none of it.' He turned back to the forge where Benjamin, who had been watching with avid curiosity, ducked inside to reach for the bellows again, leaving George shaking his head.

'Oh my days!' Jackson Watts stared at his little sister in horror. 'What is wrong with you?'

Her face was covered in spots.

'Chicken pox,' she said cheerfully. 'It means I can't go back to school. You will have to look after me for the rest of the term. Do you want to ring Mum or will I?'

He subsided onto the low blue couch in front of the TV and for several minutes seemed incapable of speech. When at last he had thought it through he dragged his eyes away from the screen. 'That doesn't mean we have to stay here?'

'Yes it does. I will be in quarantine and you will have to look after me.' She sat down next to him and folded her arms. She was smiling at him triumphantly.

'How come you know so much about it?'

'I caught it from Holly. She was really ill and she missed weeks of school before half-term.'

'So how did you catch it?'

'I went to see her.'

'Did Mum know?'

Jade shook her head. 'It's better to get these things when one is young.' She tried to look solemn.

'Do you feel ill?'

She shook her head. 'It itches a bit. You will have to get me something from the chemist to put on the rash.'

'You'll have to go to the doctor.'

'No way!' She held out her arm to him. 'They are real spots, look. I'm not scamming. Have you had it?'

He thought for a moment. 'Can't remember.'

'Well, if you haven't then you'll get it too and we'll be here even longer. It's great! Go on. Ring Mum.' She hesitated for a moment, then she put her hand to her brow dramatically. 'I think I'll go and lie down while you talk to her.' She paused in the doorway and turned. 'Don't let her come back. Tell her you can cope.'

He watched as she trailed upstairs with her mobile in her hand. Lie down indeed! He could hear her voice echoing down the passage as she headed towards her room. 'Hi, Holly! It worked! I've got it!'

He grinned. As it happened he was quite happy to spend a bit more time in Suffolk. It would give one or two of the scams he was involved in at home time to quieten down. Out of sight, out of mind, as their nan used to say.

He glanced out of the window and narrowed his eyes. Rosemary was standing outside her front door with one of her friends. They were both wearing small backpacks and Rosemary was carrying her walking pole. They were deep in conversation. He reached for his phone. He could call their mother later. This was far more urgent. He waited impatiently for the line to connect. 'Mike? Just to warn you. It looks like the old bag is getting ready to walk it again.' He listened for a minute then he nodded. 'OK. Plan B. See you there.' He tucked the phone into his jeans pocket and went to the foot of the stairs. 'Jade?' he yelled. 'Will you be OK if I go out for a bit?' He waited for an answer, shrugged and headed towards the back door, pulling on his jacket.

He was supposed to keep his gun in a locked cabinet. His dad had one upstairs specially installed for the purpose of keeping their guns and ammunition safe and legal, but it took too long to put it away up there and he couldn't be bothered anyway, so he had stashed his .22 rifle under a pile of old blankets in the utility room. He pulled it out and stuffed a box of cartridges into the pocket of his jacket, then he pulled the door open a crack and put his eye to it. Rosemary and Dottie were heading across the grass towards the fields. He glanced at his watch. Twenty minutes, Mike Turtill had said, and they would meet up to take a few shots at some pigeons down at Dead Man's Copse. Jackson grinned. Mike's dad was off the farm today so no one was going to interfere with their plan.

With the gun safely broken and tucked under his arm Jackson loped silently down behind the house and cut across the grass towards the back lane which led to the line of garages which served the barns. From there he could climb over the stile into the top wood and follow round towards the footpath. His eyes were gleaming. The more he thought about it the more his sister's affliction seemed like a blessing. He had no intention of taking her to the doctor, although he wouldn't tell his mother that. Suddenly half-term was extended by however long this disease took to run its course and he would have to volunteer to stay to look after her. It was the right thing to do. And it seemed to suit them both. She hadn't looked ill. Chicken pox was one of those diseases kids got, wasn't it? Apart from the spots they didn't feel ill, so she could enjoy herself as well. He wondered briefly if the freak next door had had it. It would hardly matter if he got any more scars. Who would notice? He grinned to himself again.

As he neared the woods above Dead Man's Field he slowed down and began to walk more cautiously, keeping his eyes open for Rosemary, who had been wearing a scarlet jacket, stupid cow, and scanning the hedges for Mike, who would be wearing camouflage gear.

'Here, Jacko,' Mike's call came from behind him. Jackson spun round and the two boys did a high five. 'Where is she? Any sign?'

Jackson shook his head. 'She's wearing red so you can't miss her. If you get my meaning.' He sniggered.

Mike Turtill and Jackson had hit it off the first time they had met several years before, and got together every time the Watts came up to the barn. Like Jackson, Mike was eighteen. He was supposed to be in college but with his father away for the day, and his mother preoccupied with some meeting she was going to later, today was one of the days he had decided to skive off. He had been about to phone Jacko when Jacko had called him first. His gun was slung across his shoulders. He glanced up at the sun and shivered. 'It's going to get foggy later. Let's get down to the copse before she arrives.'

They walked side by side down the hedge, keeping close to it, and keeping their eyes skinned. 'My dad is going to plough all this,' Mike said as they headed for the gate. 'That will spoil their fun.'

Jackson was about to make a witty riposte when he stopped. He put a warning hand on his mate's arm. 'Look. There,' he whispered.

The two women were standing by the hedge only about fifty metres ahead of them, staring out across the field.

'They're going to climb through the hedge,' Mike murmured. 'They can't even be bothered to go up to the farm gate on the lane!'

'Muppets,' Jackson commented. 'It's full of brambles. I suppose they will want those cut back too, and notices warning their frigging friends the countryside might be prickly.' He gave a snort of derision.

The young men waited, watching as the two women seemed to confer about where the best place was to force their way into the field through the hedge. 'She's got bleeding secateurs,' Mike said after a moment. And then, indignantly, 'She's cutting a hole through our hedge! She's making an entrance as though there already is a footpath there across the field!'

'Go and challenge her,' Jackson suggested.

Mike shook his head. 'Far better to scare them away. Come on, this way. We'll cut down and get to the copse from the other side. We'll be waiting for them. Wait, though. I can take a picture of them damaging our property. There's a good zoom on this.' He groped in the pocket of his jacket for his phone.

Zoë was perched on one of the high stools in the kitchen with the local paper open on the worktop in front of her. She had a felt-tip in her hand and was scanning the situations vacant. One had caught her eye. 'Part-time help wanted in popular local gallery.' Someone wanted help in a gallery and no one, not one single person had told her, in spite of her pleas and messages and research. She squinted at the sketch of the shop. Did she recognise it? If so, she was going to go there now, today, and talk her way into that job no matter what. She might not want to stay in Suffolk, but as long as they were there she might as well go on looking.

She glanced round for her car keys and slid off the stool to collect them from the work surface near the sink. As she did so she saw Jade running across the grass towards The Old Forge. Even at that distance she could tell something was wrong. She watched as the child reached Leo's door and started beating on it with her fists.

'He's not there, Jade,' she murmured. 'I checked.' She hesitated for a moment then turned towards the door. She doubted she could help with whatever crisis was happening, but at least she could offer.

She walked quickly over the grass towards the forge, aware that Jade had disappeared. She had probably gone round to the back door with her key. Then she saw the child had subsided onto the doorstep. She began to run.

'Jade? What is it? Can I help? Leo is away –' She broke off as Jade looked up.

Her face was blotchy and covered in a rash and she was sobbing bitterly. 'You've got to do something!' Jade cried hysterically. 'Jackson has gone mad! He's taken a gun and he's going to shoot Mrs Formby and I don't know what to do!' She was hugging her knees now, rocking backwards and forwards.

Zoë stared at her for a moment, trying to take in what she had said. 'Where are they?' she asked at last.

Jade shook her head. 'That place she's going on about. The path in the field. She's gone there and Jackson went and took his gun –'

'What sort of gun?' Zoë asked sharply. Not that she knew anything about guns.

'It's a rifle.' Jade sniffed. She stopped rocking.

'Then we should call the police. Now.' Zoë groped in her pocket for her phone. It wasn't there and she remembered suddenly that it was lying on her bedside table plugged in to charge. 'Oh God, have you got Leo's key?'

Jade shook her head. 'You can't call the police.'

'Why not? Have you got your mobile?'

Again the shake of the head. 'The Watts don't do cops.' It was obviously some sort of quote. She sniffed loudly. 'Will he go to prison?'

'He will if he hurts her. I have to get the police, Jade. I don't know what else to do.'

'Go after them. Stop him.' The child stood up. Zoë was suddenly aware that the rash was all over her arms as well, and she was dressed only in a thin T-shirt. 'Are you ill, Jade?'

Jade scowled. 'It's chicken pox.'

'Then you should be in bed. Go home now and go to bed and stay there. I will go down to the field. I know where it is. And, Jade, please, please, ring the police.'

She didn't wait to see what the girl did. She turned and began to run across the grass towards the hedge which ran between the Turtills' farm and their grounds. Halfway down the field there was a gate onto the farm track which ran down towards the river.

She was on the track when she heard a shot ring out, followed almost immediately by another. She stopped dead. 'Oh my God!' It was hard to tell where it had come from. Close.

She set off again, more slowly this time, unable to see much through the thick hedgerow on both sides of the track. She stopped again abruptly. A gap had been cut in the hedge on the left-hand side. It hadn't been there last time she had come down the lane. 'Oh, Rosemary!' she murmured. She examined it quickly – it had been done very recently, the leaves on the clippings lying on the lane had barely started to wilt – then she ducked through the opening and stood on the edge of the field looking down the slope towards the copse in the centre. She could see no one. The whole area was very quiet.

Oh God, what should she do?

'Zoë?' The voice behind her made her jump.

'Leo!' Her delight and relief at seeing him was overwhelming.

'I was just behind you. Jade told me what's happened. Have you seen anything?'

'No.' She wanted to reach out and touch him to convince herself he was really there. 'I heard a couple of shots, but I can't believe Jackson is threatening anyone.'

'No, of course not. She's got the wrong end of the stick, I'm sure she has. Come on.'

He started to stride out across the field towards the copse. The sound of another shot brought them both to a sudden halt. Zoë fought the urge to hide behind him. 'Can you see anything?'

He shook his head. Then they heard a woman's shout. 'I warn you, I've called the police! You get out of here now!'

'Rosemary,' Zoë called. She felt a wave of overwhelming relief.

'Rosemary?' Leo shouted. 'Can you hear me? It's Leo.'

Two figures appeared at the edge of the copse and waved. 'Thank God!' Rosemary called as they approached. 'We were terrified.'

'What happened?' Leo was scanning the undergrowth round them. There was no sign of anyone.

'We were shot at!' Zoë saw that her hands were shaking. 'I don't know who it was, but it was so close. He was aiming at us. He only just missed.'

'Any idea who it was?'

She shook her head. 'I never saw.'

Dottie shook her head too. 'I was too busy lying on the ground.' Zoë realised that both women were covered in dried leaves and earth.

'I'm sure it was just someone doing a bit of rough shooting. I doubt if he was aiming at you,' Leo said after a moment. 'He wouldn't have expected there to be anyone here, not on private property.'

There was a moment's silence. 'Point taken,' Rosemary said. 'All the more reason to make sure this path is made official.'

'What are you two doing here?' Dottie asked after a moment.

Leo gave Zoë a warning look. 'We were walking down the track,' he said. 'To go and look at *Curlew*. My boat,' he added as the woman looked puzzled. 'We heard the shots and then you calling out.' He glanced round, then he strode a few paces away from them into the edge of the copse. It was surrounded by an old rusty length of barbed wire, held up with broken posts. He stepped over the wire and took a few steps into the shadow of the trees. 'Hello?' he called. 'Is anyone there?' There was no answer. The undergrowth was thick with brambles, bracken and holly, with a couple of small oak trees, and as he stared into the shadows he saw the mound at its centre, covered with ivy and nettles.

198

With a squawk of alarm a pheasant blundered past him, leaving a scattering of dead leaves to settle in its wake.

He realised Zoë had followed him. 'No sign of anyone,' he murmured.

'I'm sure he's long gone,' she whispered back. 'My guess is he wanted to scare them.'

Leo nodded. 'Risky.' He turned and made his way back towards the wire. 'I don't think there is anyone here now,' he said as they climbed out into the field. 'But I wouldn't come here any more, Rosemary, I really wouldn't. People do walk around with guns in the country. Although they shouldn't shoot if there isn't a clear line of sight, it happens. This is at the moment private ground and you are putting yourselves at risk forcing your way into it like this.'

'What do you mean, forcing our way?' Rosemary was bristling with indignation.

'You cut the hedge, right?'

'They had blocked the path from the lane.'

'I think you will find that the law sees what you are doing, damaging Bill's property, as illegal,' Leo said calmly. 'You have to do this legally.'

'She's right, Rosemary,' Dottie said with a sigh. 'I don't think we can say people have been walking here recently. You'll have to go through the council and get them to look for ancient rights of way. Truly there isn't anything here now.'

Rosemary shook her head wearily. 'You're wrong.' She saw Leo's expression and pointed at him. 'I don't expect you to understand. This is vital.'

'If you say so.' He looked pained. 'Well, I suggest we leave you to it. You obviously don't need rescuing, and Zoë and I are on our way down to the boat.'

'She won't be told.' Zoë followed him back towards the lane. 'I saw them,' she added quietly. 'When you went into the copse. Two of them. Jackson and another boy, both with guns. They ran out and got away while you were distracted.'

'I'll have a word with Jeff. Poor guy. His kids are a handful.'

She followed him through the newly cut gap in the hedge, feeling the brambles and thorns catching at her jacket. 'Which reminds me. Jade looked really ill. Did she tell you, she said she had chicken pox?'

He nodded. 'I told her to go home. We ought to go and check on her, I suppose, and make sure they've told her mother.' He sighed. 'Do you want to come down to the landing stage first? To establish our alibi, as it were.' He gave her a sidelong glance and then looked away.

The boats were lying quietly to their buoys. There wasn't a breath of wind. Golden leaves were scattered over the water, drifting gently under the overhanging trees. 'Is Ken at home?' Leo asked as they stood side by side looking out across the river.

She shook her head. 'He had to go to a meeting with someone in Woodbridge.'

'So, you're not in a hurry?'

'No.' Somehow the job vacancy didn't seem important any more.

'Do you want to come out to *Curlew*? Just to check her over.' He stooped and picked up the mooring rope to bring his dinghy close. 'I should have pulled this one up on the shore before I went away. There's a lot of water in the bottom.'

She smiled. 'I don't mind.' She realised suddenly that she wanted more than anything in the world to be close to him.

'So you'll come?'

'Why not?'

His hand on her arm was strong as he helped her into the small boat and clambered in after her. He settled himself at the oars and pulled strongly out into the river. The *Curlew* was a smaller boat than the *Lady Grace*, and had a low graceful profile, and she was moored to a buoy further out in the main channel. She was wooden, Zoë saw, while their boat was more modern and made of fibreglass. Climbing aboard after Leo, she sat down in the corner of the cockpit as he pushed open the door to the cabin. It wasn't locked. 'I can offer you tea, without milk,' he said as he ducked inside. 'I have the minimum of supplies, I'm afraid.'

'Tea would be lovely,' she said. 'It has been a rather stressful few hours. I've never run so fast. I was convinced we would find bodies.'

'Jade has always been a drama queen,' he said with a fond smile. 'But I think she was genuinely scared. I wonder who the other boy was.' He was rooting about in the cabin. 'I'll find out,' he added a little grimly. He unscrewed a water carrier and poured some into the kettle he retrieved from a shelf over one of the bunks, then he put it on a gas ring in the small galley compartment, and reached first to turn on the gas bottle, then into his pocket for some matches. 'Are you OK?' He had been watching her surreptitiously from inside the cabin as she sat out in the cockpit.

She was gripping the gunwale with white knuckles. She nodded. 'It's the Deben effect.'

'As long as it's not me.'

She shook her head. 'No, it's not you.' For a moment they looked at each other, then she turned away to study the river bank. 'I never used to feel this nervous. Not at anchor, for goodness' sake.'

'There is nothing to be afraid of,' he said over his shoulder.

Was it the river she was nervous of, she wondered suddenly, or being alone with Leo like this? She glanced at him quickly then she looked away a clutch of excitement in the pit of her stomach.

'The river is a wild moving creature,' he went on, 'but it is predictable within parameters. You need to study the tides, the winds. If you link it to the moon and the weather, if you study its birds, if you learn its moods it becomes a friend.'

She was smiling. 'That sounds poetic.'

'Sorry.'

'No. I like it. What about the mist?'

'Ah, the mist.' Behind him the kettle began to whistle shrilly. There was a pause while he reached for a dented tin of teabags and two mugs. Zoë clutched the mug gratefully, trying to ignore the momentary brush of his fingers as she took it.

'Well,' she repeated after a long silence. 'What about the mist?'

'It is the river's veil, the disguise beneath which she hides herself when her mood changes.'

'So it's a she now?'

'Indeed.' He came to sit next to her outside, with his own mug, blowing on the scalding tea. 'This boat is my mistress, but the river is our nemesis; our goddess.'

Their thighs were touching in the small space of the cockpit.

'Is that what Deben means, a goddess?'

He shook his head. 'A great many rivers in Britain are named as goddesses, like Sabrina, the Severn, but these rivers round here have descriptive names. The Stour means rough water; and Deben comes from the Old English word for a deep river.'

She shivered. 'That follows.'

'Not here. Not when the tide is out.'

'I went to Sutton Hoo,' she said at last. 'It was very strange. I could feel it, the magic of the Anglo-Saxons. Their artistic designs, their jewellery. Their poetry. I loved it. I'm beginning to realise this whole landscape is imbued with their legacy.'

He nodded. 'There was an Anglo-Saxon village here,' he waved towards the barns. 'The Hall, Timperton Hall, was built on the site of a Saxon hall.'

'And it's all gone. Nothing but shadows and memories in the poetry.'

'I like that. It's mysterious,' he said.

'Do you think our barns were built on Anglo-Saxon sites

as well? And your forge?' She was staring down into the water.

'I wouldn't be surprised.'

'And the ghost ship? Was that Anglo-Saxon?'

'Maybe. Maybe not. Maybe it was a Viking invader.'

She looked thoughtful. 'The Anglo-Saxons were here when Christianity came to England, weren't they?'

He nodded again. 'Christianity first came at the very end of the Roman period. But it took a long time to take hold here. Husbands and wives would be of different religions. Some people covered their options by setting up altars to both at the same time. It was a strange period. Some of our greatest and most beautiful Christian artefacts come from the Anglo-Saxons, like the Lindisfarne Gospels. Then the Vikings came and destroyed the monasteries; massacred the people along the east coast.' He fell silent, staring out over the water. Suddenly he pointed. 'Look. There's a heron. See him? In the shallows.'

She squinted, following his finger, and managed to locate the tall, statuesque bird standing motionless in the water.

'We call those chaps harnsers in Suffolk,' he said. 'It's a nice name.'

'Do you think that's an Anglo-Saxon word too?'

He smiled. 'Ah, that I don't know.'

The sunlight was falling low across the water. It was growing hazy as it grew colder.

'Do you race the *Curlew*?' she asked suddenly.

He laughed. 'No. I'm not the competitive type. Why?'

'Ken is. He is always looking for the chance to test himself against other people.'

'I'm afraid he will find me very boring then.' Leo gave a rueful grin. 'I do not compete; I do not race. My *Curlew* and I drift sleepily around watching birds and dreaming in the sunshine.'

'That sounds like my kind of sailing.'

'Then we must do it together some time.'

She looked at him and for a moment their eyes locked. As before, she looked away. She sipped her tea. 'This is a magic place, isn't it?'

'I think so.'

'Is that why it is so full of ghosts?'

'Maybe.'

She put down her mug on the seat beside her. 'Leo –'

'Hush.' He put down his own mug and leaned forward towards her. For a moment she hesitated, then she closed her eyes. She wanted more than anything to kiss him, to hold him. She had never felt like this before with anyone, even Ken. The strength of her longing was frightening.

'Zoë,' it was a whisper, 'is this what you want?'

'Yes –' The word was cut short as she felt his lips on hers. The kiss lasted a long time. When at length they drew apart they studied each other for what seemed an eternity, then she reached out for him again and pulled him towards her, needing to feel him holding her, his body against hers. She was the one leading, she was the one who scrabbled to undo her jacket and pull open her blouse, it was she who brought his hand up to her breast and pressed it against her hot skin. Together they slipped from the seat to the floor of the cockpit, then Leo half dragged half crawled with her towards the cabin. 'Come inside. Here.' The bunks were no use. They were too narrow. He pulled one of the long vinyl-covered cushions down on the floor in front of the chart table and pushed her down on it beneath him, pulling at the rest of her clothes. 'Zoë!'

'Don't! Don't say anything.' She reached for his mouth again, overwhelmed by the electricity between them. 'Oh God, please, yes!'

At last they rolled apart and lay together in the narrow space on the floor of the cabin. Zoë gave a long sigh. She lay looking up at the roof above her, where the reflections from the water outside flickered on the curved wood. All the warmth had gone from the light. It was green and sad. She could hear the slap of the tide against the boat's sides and feel its movement as it rode the water, gently lifting and dipping with the motion of the evening breeze. It was growing cold, her skin chilled after the heat of his body, but she didn't want to move.

'I suspect our tea has got cold,' Leo said at last. 'Shall I put the kettle back on?'

She nodded. 'I'm freezing.' She laughed. The words sounded incongruous after the heat of their lovemaking.

'I'll get your clothes. I'm afraid I haven't any blankets on the boat. They get too damp.' He sat up and cursed as he hit his elbow on the leg of the table. 'I hope Jade went home and didn't decide she felt well enough to follow us.'

He knelt up and stuck his head out of the cabin, staring round the cockpit. The landing stage was deserted. 'It's getting misty,' he said. He grabbed her clothes and pushed them down to her, then he reached for his own.

She pulled on her sweater. It was cold and slightly damp from the evening air. She forced her arms into the jacket and zipped it up as he pulled on his jeans. 'I've wanted to kiss you for such a long time,' she said suddenly. She reached up to his face and touched it gently.

He put his hand on her hair. 'And I you. You have very sexy eyes, Zoë.'

'I feel sexy all over.'

He laughed. 'I was coming to that slowly. What is it the poem says: "How do I love thee? Let me count the ways." We would need all night, of course.' He hesitated. 'Do you need to get back?'

For a moment the thought of Ken came between them.

Zoë shook her head. 'He's not there. He said he was going to be out late with a client.' She fell silent as she knelt unmoving on the cabin floor, shivering. 'I don't want to go yet.'

He held her gaze and she saw the amusement in his face. 'Even if it means rowing back in the dark?'

'I trust you.'

He sat down on the edge of the bunk and leaned forward to put an arm round her. 'I'm sorry there's nothing to eat or drink. Tea, though. I can make more tea.'

'It doesn't matter. I just want to be quiet here with you. Feel the magic.'

He squeezed her shoulder gently. She slumped sideways against his knees and they stayed like that for a long time, not speaking.

Slowly she became aware of the sounds around them, the gentle ripple and slap of little wavelets on the hull as the wind got up and with it the sigh of the pine branches in the wood behind them. From somewhere up there in the dark came the sharp cry of an owl.

It was full dark by the time Zoë reluctantly forced herself to move. 'It's time, Leo. I must get back. Ken will be worried if I'm not there.'

Leo said nothing. He straightened and quietly climbed across her to the cabin door. He went out into the cockpit and stood staring out across the river. The wind had died away again and there was a slight haze over the water. Far above a chilly half moon hung behind a gauzy swathe of cloud.

'Is there anything out there?' Zoë emerged behind him. He heard the slight tremor in her voice.

'Nothing at all,' he said quietly.

10

'Please, Eric, come to bed!' Edith clutched the bearskin bedcover round her shoulders. Under it she was naked. Outside the house an owl hooted in the trees.

Her husband was pacing up and down the small living space of their cottage, still fully dressed, every now and then pausing to aim a kick at the smouldering logs in their hearth.

'That sword is my masterpiece. It is the greatest blade I have made or ever will make!' he muttered furiously. It is called Destiny Maker and it is not destined to be buried in a sick man's grave! It is a weapon of war. It was made to win battles!'

'There is nothing you can do, Eric. The sword is delivered and paid for. It is the Lord Egbert's now, in life or in death, and it was for him to decide what should happen to it.' She tried to cling to his arm. 'Please, my darling, come to bed.'

He shook her off, not seeming to notice that she was even there except as a sounding board against which to hurl his invective. 'I have to do something! That heathen sorcerer put a spell on Lord Egbert. He must have done, to seduce him back to the old gods.' Suddenly the old gods were mocking him. They had tricked him, lured him on, promised him glory and fame in exchange for a renunciation of the Christian faith, even offering him a son. 'No Christian is buried with his sword!' he finished angrily.

'Are you sure?' She turned away, hurt by his rejection, feeling the chill of the night against her bare skin. She pulled the fur closer. 'I thought you loved me, Eric, I thought you needed me!' It was the eternal plea of the woman who has been set aside for more important things. It had no effect.

'I will go and speak to Hrotgar again!' He picked up his cloak and flung it round his shoulders.

'Eric!'

For one second he paused and looked at her in response to her cry. But his gaze went through her. He turned away and let himself out into the night.

'Where have you been?' Ken was sitting in the great room reading the paper. He looked up at her as she came in. He didn't seem overly concerned.

'I had a drink with Leo.' It seemed better to stick as close to the truth as possible. Strangely she didn't feel guilty. 'Did you hear about the standoff at the OK Corral? Jackson Watts took a rifle and more or less threatened Rosemary and her friend, Dottie, down at the copse. Leo and I went down to try and stop the massacre. Jade told us her brother had taken a gun and we were somewhat concerned.'

'Grief!' Ken went back to the paper. 'Sounds as though you've had more fun than me this evening.'

Zoë bit her lip. If he only knew. She waited for him to say something else but he didn't. He seemed immersed in the paper.

'I think I'll go up then,' she said after the silence stretched out between them for several seconds. 'I've had enough excitement for one evening.'

Ken stayed where he was, his eyes fixed on the correspondence page but he wasn't reading. He heard her sigh and turn away and head for the stairs. She went up slowly and walked along the landing towards their bedroom. One by one the upstairs lights went on, then he heard the bedroom door shut behind her. He lowered the paper onto the coffee table and sat staring at it unseeing.

He had been standing at the high window looking out into the dark wondering where she was when he had seen the two figures walking up from the river, shadowy outlines in the hazy moonlight. He had seen them pause at the gate into Leo's garden as the moon went behind a cloud. They had thought themselves safe in the darkness but the moon had sailed high again, flooding the garden with silvery light, and he had seen the lingering kiss.

Zoë had turned away at last and headed back towards their house across the grass, triggering the security lights as she approached the front door. The sudden illumination of her face had shown the dreamy happiness there. Abruptly he had turned away from the window and thrown himself down on the sofa, grabbing the paper. He had wondered if there was something going on for a while. He wasn't sure yet what he intended to do about it. The irony of the situation did not escape him, and he was aware that he was being hypocritical – after all, where had he been all day? – but that did not stop him feeling a wave of jealous fury of a strength that surprised him.

∪

'There's a message for you, Dan.' Benjamin held out his grubby hand. In it was a folded piece of paper. Dan stared at it suspiciously. 'Who gave you that?'

Benjamin looked mutinous.

Dan reached forward and grabbed him by the ear. 'Tell me!'

Ben squealed in protest. 'It was Pip, up at the Hall. He ran down this morning when I was laying the fire. It's from –'

'I can guess who it's from.' Dan released him. He turned away towards the anvil.

'Aren't you going to read it?' The boy was still holding it out.

'No.'

'But I'll be the one to get into trouble. Me or Pip.' The boy's eyes were wide with genuine fear. Dan stared down at him. Was there no one the bitch didn't terrorise with her selfish demands? He snatched the paper from Ben and took it to the doorway, unfolding it.

Dan, it said. *Be at the ruins of the old church at midday*. That was it. No signature. No please or thank you, just the raw command.

Dan scrunched it up and, turning, threw it into the furnace. 'Get blowing,' he said curtly. 'We have work to do.'

He did not let up all morning. The sun rose higher in the sky. Midday came and went. He ignored the bread and cheese which Susan brought for him and worked harder making the rims for the cartwheels which lay against the wall. The afternoon was well progressed when Lady Emily rode into the yard. Her face was tight with fury. She rode to the doorway of the forge and shouted for Dan from the saddle. He put down his hammer, wiping the sweat from his eyes. 'Go home, Ben,' he said sharply. 'I shan't need you again today.'

'But, there's more to do.' Ben shot a scared look at the woman on her horse.

'Go!'

The boy didn't wait to be told again. He scuttled out of the door, ducked behind the cob and ran round the back of the forge out of sight. Dan walked up to her and took the bridle in his hand. He turned the cob and led it towards the barn and in between the high doors. There he stopped.

'I told you, no more,' he said curtly.

'You will do as I say!' she answered. Her voice was icy.

210

In the corner stall Bella shifted restlessly. George had brought her in from the orchard earlier and filled her manger with chaff.

'Tell me something.' Dan stared up at her, his anger so great he was no longer capable of being careful how he chose his words. 'Why is it the squire isn't able to sire his own brats?'

Her eyes narrowed. 'That is none of your business.'

'Oh, I think it is my business, my lady. You come down here and you throw your rank in my face, and you give me orders which will destroy my marriage and you cheat on a good man and you make yourself a doxy and me into a liar and an adulterer, and you tell me it isn't my business!'

'He can't father a child,' she said quietly. 'Isn't that enough for you?'

'He fathered one on his first wife. Mrs Crosby was a good and gentle lady. She would never have cheated on him.'

He saw the colour flare into her cheeks. Her eyes were like slate. 'Things have happened since then which are not your concern.'

'If he's impotent, he will know any child you bear is not his.'

'He's not impotent.'

'Then?' He could feel his anger bubbling in his chest like molten metal.

'Suffice to say that he cannot father a child!'

'And he doesn't know this?'

'No.'

'So how is it that you know?'

'Because I can't conceive. Because nothing happens. Because I went to see someone –' She bit her lip as though regretting what she had said.

'A doctor?'

'No.' Her shoulders slumped.

'Who then? If you won't tell me this conversation ceases.'

211

Absent-mindedly he stroked the cob's nose as it grew restless, not taking his eyes off her face.

'If you must know it was a gypsy woman. She read my cards and she told me that I would never bear a child with my husband.' She glared at him defiantly.

'You took the word of a gypsy woman?' he echoed incredulously. Suddenly he began to laugh; it was a harsh and humourless sound. 'All this misery and anguish is because you consulted a gypsy fortune-teller!'

'She is good. She has a reputation across the county for her accuracy.' She raised her chin a fraction.

'And did she tell you that the poor mug you chose to father your child was going to refuse to act your stud any longer? And did she predict that he would threaten to tell your husband if you don't leave him alone; and did she tell you to go back to your fancy hall and your fancy sheets and your fancy life and stay away from the barnyard?' His face was white with anger.

She looked down at him with sudden rage in her face. 'Are you refusing to do as I ask?'

'Oh, yes, I'm refusing. The whole world knows what we've been doing, and probably why, and I'm not going to be a party to it any more. I have a wife and soon I will have a child. You go back to your husband, madam, and you work out your own destiny. If you are to have a child it will be with him, not me.'

Behind them Bella gave a nervous neigh. Emily turned to stare at her. 'What is that horse still doing here?'

'That horse is fine, my lady. You leave her be.' Dan gripped the rein of her cob again and, turning it, led her out of the barn into the fierce autumn sunlight. 'Go home, my lady.' He slapped the cob on its rump. It bucked, nearly unseating its rider.

Emily steadied herself, grabbing the neck strap, then she turned to look back at Dan. 'You will be sorry,' she said icily.

'So very sorry.' She raised her whip and brought it down hard on the cob's rump. This time she was ready when the horse began to buck. She drove it forward and cantered out of the yard, hooves slipping on the high cobbles, scattering the hens, leaving a whirl of dust behind her.

Ken did not come to bed with her that night and in the morning he had left before Zoë went downstairs. She saw his car keys had gone from the hook by the back door. She made herself some coffee and poured some muesli into a bowl, staring out of the window. It had occurred to her the night before to wonder if Ken was having an affair and to her surprise she realised that if he was she was strangely unbothered by the thought.

The Old Forge looked deserted. Odd how she could tell when Leo wasn't there; it wasn't just that the windows or doors were closed. Outwardly there wasn't much difference when he was there or not. It was as if the soul had gone out of the house. She stood staring out, wondering how she felt about what had happened. Her body was happy, there was no doubt about that. She had awoken to a tingling sensation of delight which permeated every inch of her as she lay in bed hugging to herself the memory of the day before. She had forgotten just how exciting sex could be. But what about Ken? Shouldn't she feel guilty? She picked up her bowl and walked through to the great room, staring out of the window and stopped in shock. There was a police car parked outside The Threshing Barn. 'Oh, no! Rosemary!' she said under her breath, and cursed silently as she saw two officers come out of Rosemary's door, pause as they pointed towards The Old Barn, and head directly towards Zoë. She returned her bowl of cereal to the kitchen untouched and went to the door to meet them, wondering what she was going to say.

They understood, they said, that she had been a witness

to the unprovoked attack on Mrs Formby and Mrs Salcombe the day before. Could she tell them what she saw? She led them indoors and they all sat down. One of the police officers produced a black notebook. She took a deep breath. Almost without realising it she knew she was not going to incriminate Jackson.

'First, it wasn't an attack. Someone was out shooting behind the copse in the field. I don't know what they shoot at this time of year – rabbits? pigeons? – certainly not people!' She smiled, hoping they would take that as a joke. 'I didn't see them, but I am fairly sure whoever it was wouldn't have expected to find anyone in the field. There is no public footpath there although Mrs Formby seems very anxious to prove that there used to be and she wants to reinstate it. As I understand it, part of her campaign is to walk the line of the path as often as possible to prove it is used.'

'And is it, apart from by her?' The younger police officer looked up from his notes.

'No, I don't think so. She got a group of people together the other day to walk it, but as far as I know the claim is hotly disputed by everyone locally, especially by the farmer who owns the land.'

'Is there any chance he would have shot at her, or in her direction to warn her off?'

'No!' Zoë shook her head. 'Absolutely not. He's a nice law-abiding man. We met him just recently. There is no way he would do anything like that, although I think he is planning to go to law about her claim.'

'And you haven't lived here very long yourself?'

'No. Only a few months.'

'Long enough to know if there are any feuds between neighbours?'

She gave a wry smile. 'We haven't any neighbours apart from this complex, and as far as I can see there aren't any feuds amongst us. We all get on quite well.'

214

'So, may I ask what you were doing in the field yesterday? Were you going to go and support Mrs Formby on her walk?'

'No.' She paused, wondering in sudden panic what to say. 'No, I was walking down the track, which is a public footpath, with another neighbour, Mr Logan, who lives across there in The Old Forge.' She gestured out of the window, and hoped that the heat she could feel in her cheeks at the mention of his name did not show. 'We were going down to the river but we heard the shots and the shouting, and we saw a new gap which Rosemary – Mrs Formby – had cut through Mr Turtill's hedge, and we ran over to see what was happening. She and her friend sounded very upset.'

'And did you see anybody else. The man with a gun?'

She shook her head.

'So it is possible he shot without realising that there was anyone in the field?'

'Yes. I'm sure that was what happened.'

'No one should use a firearm of course without being absolutely certain that they have a clear view,' the first police officer said at last, 'but it does sound as if there was every reason to suppose that the field was empty. We will of course have to go and speak to Mr Turtill. He has a licence to own various firearms, as most farmers do round here. And even if he wasn't out shooting himself he must know who was unless they were there without his permission. And we will speak to Mr Logan to make sure he confirms your story. Which I am sure he will.' He looked up at her and held her gaze. She gave a faint smile. The two men stood up. 'Thank you, Mrs Lloyd.'

'I'm sorry I couldn't be of more help.' She led the way to the front door.

She watched surreptitiously as they made their way down the path towards The Old Forge. As she had suspected, Leo seemed to be out. They knocked several times and waited then retraced their steps to their car. Moments later they had driven away.

Rosemary knocked at the door only five minutes after that. 'Did you tell them what happened?'

'I told them what we saw.'

'It was Turtill. It must have been. I'll see him in court over this!'

Zoë shook her head. 'You don't know who it was, Rosemary, and almost certainly it wasn't deliberate. Someone was out shooting pigeons. It was just unfortunate. They weren't expecting anyone to be in the field.'

Rosemary pursed her lips. 'Well, they will in future. This makes me even more determined to get that path made official again, so if Turtill thinks it is going to deter me if he shoots at us, he has another think coming!' She glanced towards the window. 'Where is Leo? The police didn't seem to find him at home.'

'I don't know where he is.' Zoë clenched her fists, trying to keep her voice steady.

'So where were you both going yesterday when you heard us in the field?'

'Down to Leo's boat.'

'Why?'

Zoë frowned and shook her head. 'We just thought it would be nice to walk down there. He wanted to collect something and I was on my own and thought it would be fun to stroll down with him, that's all.' Enough. Don't say any more. She took a deep breath. 'Forgive me, Rosemary, but I was going out. I need to go and change. This business with the police has set me back a bit.'

Rosemary sniffed. 'I'm sorry I'm sure. Next time someone tries to murder me I will remember to make sure it is convenient for you!' She swung towards the door and went out, slamming it behind her. Zoë stared after her, then she shook her head. Now she would have to go out whether she wanted to or not.

*   *   *

216

She met Leo in the Cake Shop in Woodbridge. 'Small world,' she said as she tapped him on the shoulder. She could have kicked herself for saying something so banal, but he didn't seem to mind. His smile was warm.

'Are you on your own?' he asked. 'I saw Ken go out about six o'clock this morning.'

'I didn't hear him leave. I don't know where he's gone.' She didn't want to talk about Ken.

'Then come for a picnic with me.' The queue was moving up and he was next. 'I'll buy us some goodies.'

She watched as he bought pasties and buns as well as a loaf of bread. When she had bought her own, they walked on down the Thoroughfare and bought a bottle of wine, glasses, some rich country cheese and, at her instigation, a bar of dark hazelnut chocolate, then they made their way back to the car park.

She followed him through a network of country lanes which nevertheless she thought was not very far from home until at last he pulled into a lay-by which just had room for both cars.

'This is a very special place,' he said as he came and helped her out. 'I've never brought anyone here before. I know it's on the map but people seldom seem to bother.'

'I'm honoured.' She smiled at him a little shyly.

He didn't waste time on conversation; pushing open a gate – Zoë noticed the overgrown footpath sign with a small grimace – he led the way up a small grassy meadow and into a wood. The leaves were already turning a rich russet, rustling in the breeze as they pushed their way along an overgrown path and then turned off it, through another gate, this one falling off its hinges. Behind it Zoë could see a ruined stone wall. Leo glanced over his shoulder and grinned. He seemed very pleased with himself. 'It still seems undiscovered, doesn't it? I am always afraid some awful Rosemary-type person will have been in and stuffed it full of signs and health and safety warnings or wired it off altogether.'

217

'What is it?' She followed him across the grass and gave a small gasp of delight as they emerged in a sheltered rectangle of walls, one of which contained a small rounded aperture which must once have held a window. In another was the remains of an arched doorway. 'It's a church!'

He nodded. 'This is our Anglo-Saxon church. Isn't it a gem?' He unslung his bag from his shoulder and dropped it on the grass. 'We are, in fact, very near home; the river is just over the hill there and the Hall is through the woodland that way, but there is no access from the farm any more. Don't tell Rosemary, whatever you do. The last thing we want is another crusade for a footpath.' He walked over to the wall and rested his hand on the pale stones. 'This is a magic, sacred spot. This is all that's left of our village. I don't go much on churches, not working churches anyway. But this is so special.'

'Why isn't it working any more?' Zoë put her hand near his on the stone which was warm in the sunlight and rough with lichen. 'What happened to it?'

'It's been a ruin since early medieval times, I believe. As I told you, there was an Anglo-Saxon settlement here, with the hall of the local leader probably under the foundations at Timperton. It seems to have been a flourishing community. One can see the outline of some of the buildings as crop marks from the air. I was shown some photos of them by a guy I met whose hobby is looking for archaeological remains. It is fascinating how much evidence there is of the past still there under the surface of the fields. The settlement vanished. It didn't survive as a village. As you see, the only thing left is the ruin of the church.'

She walked out into the centre of the grassy space and looked round. It was sheltered in here; there were elder trees heavy with berries growing inside what was left of the walls, and clumps of nettles interspersed with flowers. There were oxtongue and mayweed, mallow and a few little flowers of the most intense blue. She picked one and twirled it in her

218

fingers. 'What are these? There were great patches of them down by the landing stage a few weeks back. They are such a brilliant colour.'

He took it from her. 'This is called viper's bugloss,' he said. 'In ancient times it was said to be a cure for the bite of an adder.' He tucked it into her hair. 'It grows round here because it is so sandy. We'll make a country woman of you yet, Zoë Lloyd!' He bent to open the bag. 'Shall we picnic in here?'

'Wait. Not yet.' She put her hands on his shoulders. 'Leo –' She wasn't sure what to say next.

He bent forward and kissed her on the lips. 'Over here. In the corner. That is what is so special about this place. We won't be spied on.'

He caught her hand and pulled her with him. 'Only if you want to, of course.'

'Oh God, I want to!' She threw herself against him, reaching up for another kiss, feeling the puckered roughness and ivory smoothness of his scars under her lips. She tore at the buttons on her shirt and pulled it open, desperate to feel his hands on her breasts, and for a long time she was aware of nothing but the closeness and strength of this man and the neediness of her own body.

When at last she could speak she was lying on her back staring up at the sky, her eyes half closed against the glare. 'Do you think it is wrong doing this in a church?'

He was lying half across her, his fingers entwined in her hair and he bent to kiss her temple, smoothing back the short fair strands. 'No, I don't. It hasn't been a church for centuries. If this place is sacred to anything it is to the goddess of lust and lechery. She was called Frige by the Anglo-Saxons.' He laughed. 'Otherwise known as Frig. One of those words we learn as children and are told to forget!' He kissed her again.

Goddess of lust, but not love, she noticed, but she said nothing. What had happened between her and this man was nothing to do with love, he was right. It was an explosion of desire so powerful neither of them would have been able to fight it even if they had wanted to.

'Are you hungry?' He sat up at last and reached for his shirt.

She nodded and watched as he dressed and collected the picnic bag. She was still sitting cross-legged on the grass, naked. Some part of her saw herself do this and was shocked at her lack of modesty, but then some part of her was appalled by everything she had done over the last couple of days. She didn't mind. If she was going to feel guilt it could come later. For now she was all sensation and for the moment the sensation was hunger. She took the pasty he handed her and bit into the flaky pastry, feeling a cascade of crumbs falling onto her breasts. She didn't care. Gravy spilled over her chin and she left it there, tearing into the food. She was aware of him looking at her, amused, but she ignored him.

'To think,' he said quietly, 'when I first met you I had you down as a middle-class matron.'

She snorted. 'And you loathed me on sight.'

'Pretty much.'

'I am a middle-class matron,' she added after a few seconds' thought. 'I think I've been possessed.'

'No, you've been liberated.'

'By you?'

He considered for a moment. 'I'd like to think so, but no, I think it is something else.' He reached across for the bottle of wine and unscrewed the cap, pouring two glasses. 'Nicely *chambréed*. It has been lying in the sun.'

She took the glass he passed her and sipped. A splash of wine joined the gravy on her chin and he leaned forward, removing it with the corner of his thumb. 'Too messy!' he admonished gently.

She laughed. 'I feel as if I am part of some Impressionist painting. Manet or Monet or someone.'

'"*Déjeuner sur l'herbe*,"' he confirmed quietly. 'That was

220

Manet. Nude ladies and fully dressed gents. Interestingly Monet decided to do the same subject but with everyone dressed.' He grinned. 'It didn't work!'

'Actually, I feel like more of a Gauguin lady,' she put in. 'Angular, raw, earthy.'

They both looked up as a shadow passed over them – a cloud had obscured the sun and Zoë shivered. She hadn't noticed that the sunny afternoon had gone, the sky had grown strong and already there was a hint that the day was nearly over. Setting down the glass, she reached for her bra and her shirt. 'Time to get dressed.' Suddenly she was in a hurry to put her clothes on, embarrassed, afraid somebody would see her. Only when she was fully dressed did she relax again with an apologetic laugh. 'I'm afraid the middle-class matron suddenly kicked in. Aren't I a wimp!'

'A beautiful wimp.' He chuckled. He topped up her glass and handed it back to her.

'Leo, can I ask you something?' It was something she had never intended to ask but somehow she knew this was the moment. If she didn't do it now, then she never could.

He inclined his head sideways. 'Fire away.'

'Are you married?'

'Yes.'

'Divorced?'

'No.'

She drew her feet up and hugged her knees. 'Same as me then.'

'Same as you.'

'Children?'

For the first time he hesitated. 'Yes.'

She buried her head in her arms for a moment. 'Tell me what happened.'

'After the accident I drove her away. She was kind and understanding and patient, and I was a vile self-pitying fool. We had never really understood each other. I know cheating men always say that, but I expect it is always pretty true, if we're honest, and we had made a pretty good fist of it. Then somehow it all fell apart. She has never been up to The Old Forge, or on the *Curlew*. She has found a new man and I expect one day she will want a divorce, but it is up to her.'

'And the children?'

'Lucy and Jo. I love them dearly but they belong with their mum. I see them –' again he hesitated – 'fairly regularly and we had agreed that if and when they want to they will come up to stay in the holidays. I hope that will still happen one day.' His smile this time was more forced. 'I told her about you,' he paused and then went on, 'she is pleased – and incredulous – that I have found someone who . . .' He stopped.

'Who?'

'Who can put up with me. She wishes you luck.'

Zoë was taken aback for a moment, then she relaxed. The fact that he had an ex-wife and children had come as a shock. Why hadn't she asked before? Surely that very basic question was one everyone should ask before they embarked on an affair. And it was an affair, wasn't it? The fact that the ex-wife approved of her was even more of a shock, but on thinking about it she was pleased. It confirmed what a nice, honest man Leo was. Unlike her. She was the one being dishonest. She was the one keeping secrets – from Ken.

Leo was sitting, staring into space, sipping his wine with every sign of calm enjoyment, giving her time to assimilate what he had said. She climbed to her feet and, slipping on her shoes, she walked away from him slowly.

'I was looking this place up last night in one of my local history books.' Leo stood up and followed her. 'About twenty years ago they did some excavations in the fields between here and the Hall and it confirmed what the aerial photos showed. At some point in the dim and distant past there was quite a large settlement here,' he said.

'It's strange, isn't it, how villages just disappear?'

'There is always a reason. I read once about a lord of the manor who flattened his village for no better reason than that he didn't want to see it from his windows. It spoiled his view. There are other places where whole populations were wiped out by plague, and here on the east coast there was the constant threat of malaria.'

'So much tragedy. Imagine how awful it must have been for the people who lived there,' she mused. 'So, what happened here, do they know?'

'There was a massacre,' he said slowly. 'The Vikings came.'

They had wandered towards the end wall where the broken remains of the rounded arched window looked out onto an increasingly stormy sky.

A loud report, the sound of wood breaking, out amongst the trees made them both jump. Zoë looked round startled. 'Leo,' she whispered. 'There is someone there.'

I heard.' He set his glass down on the rough stone of the sill. 'Hello!' he called. 'Where are you? Come out.'

'Supposing Jade followed us. Or Jackson?'

'How could they follow us? We started from Woodbridge,' he said. He strode back to the entrance and looked out again into the woodland. 'Listen. The birds are singing happily. No alarm calls. There's no one here. And if there is, you've got your clothes on again.' He chuckled. 'It is getting cold now though, with the sun gone; I don't think it's coming out again today.'

It was the signal to leave. Outside the church wall a gust of wind tore through the wood, rustling the leaves; a dust devil spun into the air at the east end, seeming to hover for a moment in front of the broken arch of the window, and the space around them, only minutes before so safe and serene, was filled with the rush of squally rain and the scream of the wind, a scream which to Zoë, as she stared around terrified, sounded like the scream of a woman in agony.

* * *

223

The kitchen was cold and empty, the lights off. Ken had already seen that Zoë's car was missing when he had returned. He and Sylvia had spent the day having an enjoyable and somewhat exhausting time and then they had settled down to have a drink in front of the TV while they recovered. He had been reluctant to leave, but his conscience had reminded him that Zoë was probably on her own. He was angry to find that she was out. He could have stayed longer.

He walked over to the window to stare down at The Old Forge but there was no sign of life there either. He reached for the light switches. Rain was pouring down the window and it was prematurely dark. He picked up his mobile and dialled her number. Seconds later he heard the faint sound of ringing from upstairs. Taking the steps two at a time he ran up to their bedroom. Her phone was there lying on the bedside table. He stared at it for a moment angrily, then he turned and made his way back downstairs. The great room was full of shadows and it seemed unwelcoming. On an impulse he grabbed his jacket and went to the door. Perhaps Rosemary and Steve were in.

They were. Sitting on the sofa with a bottle of lager in his hand and the TV showing the early evening match, he managed to put his ill humour aside. Rosemary appeared with a plate of nibbles and put it down near the men then she went back to the table, which was spread with her maps and papers.

'Did Zoë tell you about what happened to Rosemary and Dottie?' Steve commented. His eyes were glued to the screen.

'The shooting?' Ken took another swig from the bottle. 'She mentioned it. We haven't had a chance to talk much for the last couple of days. I was away all yesterday and out early this morning.'

'Zoë and Leo were great. They came to our rescue,' Rosemary commented from the table. 'And Zoë gave evidence to the police this morning.'

Ken forced himself to keep his eyes on the screen. 'Where is Zoë, do you know? We keep missing each other.'

He felt Steve's eyes on him for a moment.

'She didn't say. I spoke to her this morning,' Rosemary said, her voice becoming frosty. 'She was in a rush to go out but she didn't say where.'

'Were she and Leo going out somewhere together?' Ken couldn't stop himself asking. Something in his tone of voice registered with both his listeners. Rosemary pushed back her chair and stood up. She came and stood in front of him. 'He went out very early. Long before her,' she said with sudden concern. 'The police wanted to speak to him to corroborate our stories, but they said there was no sign of him. He is often away for long periods, Ken. Truly, I don't think you have anything to worry about there.'

Ken felt a flash of irritation. 'I wasn't worrying! I was just wondering where she was! She left her mobile behind when she went out.'

He didn't stay long. The cosy reassurance of their company had gone and as soon as he had finished the lager he rose and made his excuses. He ran back through the rain and let himself into the house, aware that it was very quiet after the violence of the storm outside.

He stood for a moment listening. Zoë was right. It did feel as though there was someone else there. As though they were listening and waiting. Uncomfortably he walked to the doorway into the great room and peered in. He had left only one light on so the whole room was in deep shadow, the lines of the beams black treescapes in the darkness above him. He frowned at the sound of something moving nearby. He remembered what Zoë had said – *it sounds like a horse. I can hear the hooves on the cobbles, the snorting, the rattle of harness.* Oh God, he could hear it too. A horse was walking across the floor. Except it wasn't. This floor was polished wood except in that one small place where a sheet of plate glass had been let in to show the original surface a foot below the present level.

He spun round as there was a crash behind him. The kitchen door had opened and blown back against the wall. Zoë staggered in, her hair plastered against her head by the rain, her jacket dripping on the floor. She forced the door shut and shook herself like a dog. 'Hi, Ken. God what weather!'

'Where have you been?' he said. 'Did it not occur to you that I might be worried?'

'Sorry.' She pulled off her jacket. 'I went out in such a hurry this morning I left my mobile behind. I met someone in Woodbridge and we had lunch and went to do some sightseeing locally and then the storm came. I hadn't planned on being this late.' She hung her jacket on the hooks near the door. 'You've been so busy I didn't think you'd notice!' she added defensively. 'I have hardly seen you for the last couple of days.'

He looked away uncomfortably. 'I know. I'm sorry. I have been setting up a business contact in Ipswich.' It had always been easy to lie to her; something of which he was not proud. 'I wasn't sure if it would come off so I didn't want to say anything yet.' He gave her an apologetic grin. 'Do you want to go and get dry and I will get you a hot drink? Or some soup. What about some soup?' He glanced back into the great room and bit his lip. The sound of the horse walking across the floor had been his imagination. Of course it had.

U

Daniel stood in the doorway to the barn, staring across at the orchard, then he turned back inside and walked over to the empty stall. Behind him George appeared with a barrow. 'I couldn't stop them, Dan,' he said as he saw Dan standing there. 'They said Lady Emily had given orders for Bella to be taken up to the stables at the Hall. Zeph said she'd been here

226

long enough.' The man's face was heavy with sympathy. The undergroom was not one of his favourite people. The man was rough and had a cruel streak. He had all but dragged the horse out of the yard. 'I know you'd got fond of her, but when all's said and done she belongs up there.'

Daniel grimaced. As soon as he had seen the empty stall, swept and bare of buckets, he had known. He strode towards the great open doors. 'I'm going after her. There's no more use in that horse for riding. They don't need her up at the Hall.'

'Dan –' George called. 'Be careful. That woman is a schemer.'

Dan ignored him. He was already striding across the yard.

Sam, the head groom at the Hall, was watching Pip clean a saddle as Dan strode into the stables. He stood up. 'Go, Pip. Go and get your tea, lad,' he said sharply. The boy looked surprised. He threw down the soapy rag and with a glance at Dan scuttled out of sight.

'I know why you're here.' Sam put his hand on Dan's arm. 'I'm sorry. Her leg was broken. The knacker's taken her away.'

Dan stared at him in shock. 'Bella?' he whispered. He could feel a great sob rising in his chest. 'What do you mean, her leg was broken? How?'

Sam looked away. 'Just as she got here. She caught it in a rabbit hole.'

'Oh, she caught it in a rabbit hole, did she! And did you see it happen? Did you see it with your own eyes?' Dan shouted. 'No, I thought not. Happen they took a hammer to her, the bastards! Who was it? Zeph came down and took her. Was it him?' His voice broke. He was striding up and down the tack room, kicking at the floor. 'That poor horse. She was sweet and gentle, would never hurt a fly. She deserved better than that! That woman did this! Out of revenge. She knew I had grown fond of Bella. The bitch! The utter and complete bitch! Where is she? I will strangle her with my own hands!'

'Leave it be, Dan.' Sam folded his arms, leaning against a saddle tree. 'Come on, old friend. Let it go. You can't do anything. That mare is beyond pain now. She can't be hurt any more.'

'But I can!' Dan's face was white with rage.

'Aye, and the more you show you're hurt the more you play into her hands.' Sam reached into his pocket for a clay pipe and his baccy tin. Against the rules to smoke anywhere in the stables, but he packed the little bowl and lit up anyway. 'I'd heard you refused to play her game any more,' he said gently. 'She didn't take kindly to being refused, eh?' He shook his head, puffing out a small cloud of blue fragrant smoke. 'Let it be, Dan. Think of Susan. You don't want any more trouble.'

Dan paused and rubbed the back of his hand across his face, suddenly overwhelmed with sorrow. 'That mare was the kindest soul. She had grown to trust me.'

'And you gave her comfort and a good home for her last days, my friend.' Sam watched as Dan sat down on an upturned bucket and put his head in his hands. He said nothing, waiting for the spasm of grief to pass. He knew how the smith felt. Even a man who had been with horses all his life, seen them come and go, grew especially fond of some. He smoked quietly for a while, giving Dan some time to get a hold of himself.

'I let Zeph go today,' he said at last as he reached for more baccy. 'He wasn't suitable for this job. I told Mr Crosby I didn't want him working near my horses any more.' He concentrated on the bowl of the little pipe. 'Vicious streak. He'll not get another job as any kind of groom, I'll see to that.'

Outside the daylight was leaching out of the sky. In the stables nearby they could hear the sound of the horses moving restlessly back and forth. They always knew when one of their number had died.

* * *

In the drawing room in the Hall Emily was standing staring out of the window down towards the river. Night was creeping in and with it the slow cold mist which smelled of the sea. She wondered if Dan had heard about Bella yet. She gave a small angry smile of triumph. When he did he would realise that it did not pay to cross her. In future he would do as she ordered. Either that or it would be his fat common wife who would be the next to suffer.

She pulled her shawl tighter round her shoulders. She had changed into a tea gown and the room was growing cold. She stepped across to pull the bell for one of the maids. The fire was a miserable smouldering apology which failed to heat the room at all, and no one had brought the tea things. Going back to the window, she gave a last glance out towards the river. A pale square sail was slowly drifting up on the tide. She looked at it for a moment. There was the head of a great beast of some sort on the sail. A bear, she thought. How odd. She turned her back on the view. It was cold and depressing and somehow full of menace.

11

The hall had fallen silent at last. Men and women were sleeping on the benches, wrapped in their cloaks, and the great fire had died to a smouldering heap of embers. The air still held the smell of roasting meat, and the stench of fear. Pushing the door open Eric let himself in and crept past the first sleepers. Two wolfhounds were lying nearby in the rushes beneath the table. They looked up but made no sound.

The sword he had chosen, almost finished and set aside when he received the commission to make the Destiny Maker for Lord Egbert, was carefully secreted under his arm beneath his cloak as he made his way silently through the hall towards the back door which led to the lord's house. The candles had died. The only light came now from the occasional lamp which someone must have filled before they went to sleep. He reached the door and pushed gently, frowning as it creaked in the silence. Behind him someone let out a loud snore and he froze. Another man coughed and stirred and fell silent. The hall was strangely quiet considering there were so many people there. The shock of what had happened had fallen like a blanket over the whole company.

In the lord's bedchamber behind the mead hall two more lamps were lit. Eric could see the figure of the dead man lying in his bed. His hands were crossed on his chest and held between them he saw the hilt of the Destiny Maker. A figure was seated at his side in one of the great chairs which had been pulled up close to the bed. His wife was keeping watch. He scanned the room carefully. Where was the sorcerer? He couldn't see anyone else. There was no sign of Hrotgar and the shadows seemed empty.

His gaze came back to the Lady Hilda. Her head had drooped on her chest and she was swathed in a heavy cloak. Was she asleep? He took a small step forward and held his breath. She made no movement. Another step. He could smell the stench of death in the room and he gave an involuntary shudder.

There were other things there as well, he realised now his eyes were adjusting to the near darkness. Heathen amulets he himself had made for Lord Egbert. He had a vision suddenly of the fertility charms he had made years before at Egbert's insistence, charms to ensure his wife's fecundity. Eggs, a small silver hare and the figure of the goddess Frige, made of the living iron, and, in the tradition of the most ancient times, another figure, grotesque and swollen in belly and breasts, the mother goddess, shaped in his own forge, a talisman which would bring fertility to whichever woman touched it.

Lady Hilda had given them back to him and demanded they be melted down once their job was done and she had her sons. He had ignored her instructions, leaving the bag of charms in the cottage for his wife to find. He smiled in spite of himself. Again they had proved their power and Edith had conceived. He prayed to the one god and all the gods that this time they would be blessed with a living child. He shivered, wondering how the Lady Hilda could sit there in their presence. She must have loved her lord very much to suffer the indignities this sorcerer had inflicted on her over the years.

He glanced round again and jumped as the sleeping figure beside the bed let out a small gasping moan in her dream. He held his breath. Nothing moved; even the lamp flames were steady.

He tiptoed towards the bed and carefully drew back the bed cover, then he reached out to unclasp the man's hands from the hilt of the sword. The cold fingers were stiff; they held on tightly. Eric struggled, tugging hard, trying to force them apart. The woman beside the bed moaned again and shifted in her chair. He froze. Time passed and he waited, then he began to work on the fingers again, one by one freeing them from the hilt. Quietly he loosened the sword at last and lifted it away from the bed. Then he withdrew the replacement from beneath his cloak and carefully laid it on the man's body, trying to refold the hands. The fingers wouldn't bend back. Nervously he tried to force them to clasp the hilt of this unfinished sword but they refused. It was as if the man knew what was happening and rejected the substitute.

Sweat dripped from Eric's face. He could feel waves of panic beginning to build in his chest. He clenched his teeth desperately and with one last effort somehow folded the hands in place. He rested his own hand for a moment over the other man's loosely clasped fists and muttered words of blessing, then he turned away. He gathered up Destiny Maker and tucked it under his arm, then drawing his cloak around him he tiptoed away from the bed towards the door.

In the silent room the figure by the bed moved and stood up. Hilda stooped over the body of her husband and, bending, kissed his forehead. Then she drew the fur covers up over the sword and the clasped hands and tucked them tightly in to keep him safe. Only when she was satisfied that there was no sign of any interference did she resume her seat and quietly begin her prayers again.

'If you say a word about me or my affairs to anyone ever again or stick your spotty little nose into my business once more I will ring up Mum and tell her to come and fetch you,' Jackson yelled. 'Is that clear? And I will tell her you got chicken pox deliberately.'

It had taken Jackson and his sister three calls to convince Sharon not to come and fetch them when she heard about the chicken pox and she had rung every few hours since. Only her worry about Darren and Jamie being left alone with only their father to keep order prevented her from jumping into the four-by-four and racing back to fetch Jade home.

Jade sat on the kitchen chair without moving for several minutes after her brother slammed out of the house, trying very hard not to cry. She was feeling ill, her throat was sore and she was a little bit frightened. No adult had said anything to her about what had happened except her brother, to whom she had confessed her betrayal. 'If you had killed her you would have gone to prison,' she had wailed.

'We weren't going to kill her, you prize muppet!' he yelled back. 'Just scare her off.'

They had both seen the police car outside The Threshing Barn and seen the policemen go over to The Old Barn and then to The Old Forge. Jackson was white to the gills. He had already cleaned his gun and taken it upstairs to his father's gun cupboard where he had slotted it into the rack and locked the door on it. The key he had hidden under a floorboard in the family bathroom.

Miserably Jade let herself out and made her way over to The Old Forge. She knew Leo was out. She had seen him leave early on without coming over to see them, without thanking her and giving Jackson the bollocking he deserved.

She groped for the key in its hiding place in the flowerbed and let herself in. He was obviously coming back. He had left

233

stuff lying around and there was half a bottle of milk on the kitchen table next to a sketchpad covered in drawings and workings-out of some sort. She glanced at it, uninterested, and then made her way through the cottage to the stairs. She stood for a long time in Leo's bedroom, looking down towards the river. She could see the *Curlew* attached to her buoy in the freeway and she frowned.

She had followed him and the Zoë woman down there yesterday after the shooting incident, which she had watched from the shelter of the hedgerow. She had seen them talking and laughing and seen how he had helped her into the little dinghy and then into the cockpit of the boat where they had kissed. Watching from her concealment behind one of the ancient pines, Jade had felt a pang of excruciating jealousy which had deepened into fury and pain as she saw them begin to undress, there where anyone could see them and then as she watched they had disappeared into the cabin. A few minutes later she had seen the boat begin to rock up and down at its mooring. She wasn't born yesterday. She might be only eleven but she knew what was going on and her anger at Leo's betrayal was overwhelming.

She had made her way home and gone up to her bedroom where she had crawled, still fully dressed, under the bedclothes. Jackson had returned some time later but he didn't come up to see her. She hadn't told him about her role in the events of the day before till the next morning when she had found him in the kitchen. His anger at what he saw as her betrayal of him had simply added to her misery and rage.

She turned and looked at Leo's bedroom. Part of her wanted to smash it up, to damage his things, to rip up his pictures, to go out in the dinghy and put an axe through the *Curlew*'s hull so she sank. Absent-mindedly she scratched her face. Another part of her was already planning a far more satisfactory revenge. She was going to destroy her rival for his affections: Zoë.

Daniel was waiting for her. He stepped out of the shelter of the barn and seized the cob's bridle with one hand and her wrist with the other. Emily opened her mouth to scream, but he was too quick for her. Dragging her from the horse he clamped one hand across her lips.

With a panicky neigh the horse bolted.

'You vicious bitch! You couldn't let an innocent animal live. You thought I loved that horse so she had to pay with her life!' He released her with disgust. 'How could you? Have you not one smallest bit of compassion in your heart?'

Emily recovered her composure remarkably quickly. 'Do as I ask and there will be no need to prove to you just how little compassion I have!' she retorted. 'You need to learn to obey when the squire's lady gives you a command.'

He stared at her through narrowed eyes. 'You can't force a man to service you. Not even your poor husband. What would happen if I told him what had been going on? What do you reckon would happen to you then? He'd throw you out, that's what. Like the cheap doxy you are. You leave me and mine alone, my lady,' he emphasised the last two words with heavy sarcasm, 'or you will regret crossing me for the rest of your days. You've already cost one man his job.' He moved away from her. 'Leave us alone, do you hear me? If you threaten me again there will be trouble; I mean it. I will go to Mr Crosby and tell him everything! And don't imagine that he won't believe me, because he will. Every word.'

He strode away towards the forge leaving her standing where she was on the muddy track. He did not look back.

Zoë was sitting on the long sofa, her feet propped up on cushions, when Ken appeared the following evening. She was reading, the book in a pool of light from the lamp behind her, the rest of the room in semidarkness as the light faded in the sky. He glanced round the room cautiously. She saw the look. 'What? What are you looking for?'

'Nothing.' He came and sat beside her, pushing her legs over a little to make room. 'I've been hearing the horses too.' He gave a self-conscious half laugh.

Zoë hitched herself away from him. 'What kind of horses?'

'How do I know? A horse is a horse to me. It's just noises. Just the sound of hooves, that kind of sneezy sound they make, the chink of harness. I wonder if we are going mad!' He bent his head and ran his fingers through his hair.

'It's happening more and more often, isn't it?' she said dully.

'At first I thought it was your imagination.' He grimaced. 'But there is something in here, isn't there? Not the kids. Nothing to do with them. There is something restless about this place, as if it's waiting for something to happen.'

She stared at him and her mouth dropped open for a moment. 'You feel it too?'

'You know I do.' He stood up. 'Shall we make a project of finding some blinds or curtains or something for these windows? I feel really exposed in here as it gets dark.' He looked towards them with a shudder.

'Agreed,' she said. 'As soon as possible, right? I don't like the idea of people being able to look in on us. Anyone could be out there. That Jackson guy. I really didn't like him. Or any of those kids. Or burglars, for goodness' sake!'

'Or Leo,' Ken said softly.

She gave him a sharp look and hoped he didn't see the colour she could feel flooding into her face. 'Why Leo? What on earth makes you say that? He's not a peeping Tom!'

'No,' Ken said. 'No, I'm sure he's not.' There was a long pause. 'But he walks across the grass to the path down to the boats. I've seen him. If he uses his eyes at all he could hardly miss this great floodlit area of glass and everything we are doing behind it.'

'I suppose not.' She pulled herself to her feet. The conversation was becoming uncomfortable. It was the moment to mention Leo's hatred of all the floodlights, but she sensed it would not go down well.

She headed for the kitchen, and just as she reached the door she heard the noises herself. There were horses in the great room and over by the woodburner a hazy shimmering impression, just for a moment, of shadowy sheaves of hay, and harness hanging from pegs in the wall and the windows were no longer windows but huge double doors opening onto a yard which was bathed in moonlight.

'Ken.' Her voice came out croaky with sudden fear. 'Can you see it too?'

But it had gone. The room was as it ought to be and the only sound was from the TV as Ken picked up the remote and started flicking through the channels.

Later, in bed, he reached out for her. 'Darling, I know I haven't been very attentive lately.' He sounded embarrassed.

She rolled away from him. 'It doesn't matter. I haven't been in the mood either.' It was true, of course.

She felt him edge away from her again. He turned over onto his back and sighed. 'Old age, I suppose.' He gave a bitter snort of laughter.

'Speak for yourself!' She meant it to come out humorously but somehow it didn't. 'We've been under an awful lot of strain, Ken,' she went on after a moment. 'What with the move and everything. And neither of us has been sleeping properly. Look at your sleepwalking, for goodness' sake. We're tired and worn out. All we need is a bit of time.'

'You don't still want to move away, do you?' he said after a pause.

She lay still, staring at the ceiling. She wasn't sure what to say. To move would mean moving away from Leo. 'Perhaps we should give it a bit more time, as you said,' she whispered at last.

He didn't reply. She sensed he wasn't asleep, but she said no more and lay, eyes closed, trying to steady her own breathing.

The irony was that every bit of her body contradicted her claim to be tired. It was tingling with longing, alive, every portion of her skin reacting to the touch of the sheet, of her own arm as it brushed against her breast, the movement of one thigh against the other, the corner of the pillow nuzzling the back of her neck, but it wasn't Ken she was thinking about as she lay still beside him, terrified he might sense her arousal, it was Leo.

It was much later, when his body had at last relaxed into sleep and his breath was punctuated by a gentle snoring, that she gave up trying to sleep herself and climbed cautiously out of bed. She stood for a moment looking down at him in the dark, then she crept towards the door. Closing it carefully behind her she held her breath, listening. She was, she realised suddenly, scared of going downstairs in the dark, as much afraid of what lay down there as of waking Ken. She didn't want to put on the lights. She knew the light switch, bringing on banks of lights, both up here and below, made a loud enough noise to be heard in the bedroom if one was awake. The question was, was it loud enough to wake Ken?

She looked over the balustrade. There was no moonlight in the windows; the gardens were pitch black beyond the glass. A week or so ago she would have run down the stairs in the dark without a second thought, but now she hesitated. It was completely silent downstairs. They had let the wood-burner go out so there was no sound of shifting logs, no night sounds of wood or metal settling into the cold. She shivered. She hadn't dared to reach for her dressing gown in case she woke Ken; she was wearing a short silk nightdress which barely covered her bottom. She crept along the landing to the top of the staircase and peered down, reaching for the banisters. Then slowly she reached for the top step with her bare foot.

She was halfway down when she heard a sound. She froze. After a moment she heard it again. A gentle rattle broke the silence. It came from the direction of the kitchen. She realised her hand was clutching the wooden handrail so tightly it was hurting her fingers. She took another step down. Something about the noise made her suspicious. It had no ghostly feel. It sounded very real. And then as it came a third time, she realised what it was. Someone was trying the backdoor latch. She ran the rest of the way down and across the floor into the kitchen and paused there just inside the door listening. After a moment it came again and this time she could hear someone turning a key back and forth in the lock. She gave a grim smile. Thank goodness for the new lock. She was about to tear the bolt back and throw open the door when she became aware of how scantily clad she was. If it was Jackson she had no desire to confront him all but naked. The next best thing was to find out who it was. If she scared them off the chances were they would run round the front of the house and the floodlights would come on. If they didn't she could bring them on manually with the switch beside the back door.

Not turning on the kitchen lights, she banged hard on the door and then ran to the window so she could look out unseen. At first she thought nothing was happening, then after several seconds she saw a small figure running across the lawn. She was keeping to the dark area beyond the reach of the lights, but nevertheless just about visible. It wasn't Jackson. It was Jade.

'Gotcha!' she murmured. 'Little monkey!' She switched on the floodlights and watched the whole area swim into view. Jade had judged her flight perfectly. There was no sign of her.

'Zoë?' The voice behind her made her jump out of her

skin. She spun round. Ken was standing in the doorway, his hand on the kitchen light switch. 'What's going on?'

'Don't turn it on,' she cried. 'It was Jade. She was trying to get in with a key. They have obviously still got one.'

'Good thing I fitted the bolt and changed the lock, eh?' Ken came to stand beside her at the window. Outside the floodlights went out leaving the garden pitch black. 'A word with her parents tomorrow, do you think? On the phone.'

'She's supposed to be ill with chicken pox,' Zoë said thoughtfully. 'Presumably she's not feeling that ill.' She went over to the light switch, then she paused. 'I hate the thought of turning on the lights and being watched from outside as if we were a theatre set. Can we get blinds for the kitchen tomorrow as well?'

'Sure.' He was still staring out into the dark. 'I thought it wouldn't matter not having curtains and blinds in this place,' he said wistfully. 'It is supposed to be so private, but it isn't, is it?'

'Isolated is a better word,' Zoë put in. 'It is just us. This strange community on the edge of the river. Four houses, miles from the world. No village.' She thought back to Leo's description of the lost village on the hill and she shivered. There were goosepimples all over her arms and shoulders. 'I'm cold. I'm going back to bed. We'll deal with it all in the morning.'

Ken was about to follow her upstairs when he saw a bent horseshoe nail lying on the floor. He stopped dead, looking at it with distaste. After a moment he bent and picking it up between finger and thumb he threw it in the bin with a shiver. Upstairs, he went into the bathroom. When at last he emerged he lay down beside Zoë but he made no move towards her. It was a large bed. There were a least three feet between them. Zoë was lying with her back to him. Her eyes were open and she was staring at the window. There were curtains in their bedroom but they were open and she could see the stars, far away between the swathes of cloud.

Eric pushed his way into the cottage and stood just inside the door, his heart beating furiously. The sword was there, under his cloak. He didn't think anyone had seen him take it; no one had followed him from the hall, but they would guess it was him as soon as its loss was discovered.

'Eric?' Edith was lying in bed in the corner. 'Where have you been?'

It was pitch dark in the cottage apart from the dull red glow from the hearth where the fire was dying. She couldn't see his face; he was no more than a dark silhouette as he stood there, but she could sense his unease. She sat up and pulled a heavy rug around her shoulders.

'Don't bother yourself with where I've been,' he said gruffly. 'Go back to sleep.' He was staring round in the darkness, wondering where to hide it.

He could hear her moving. She was standing up. He could see her outline now, faintly, in the light of the embers, as she moved towards him. 'What happened?' She reached out to him. Almost instinctively she touched the sword hilt where it poked out from beneath his arm. 'Oh, Eric, what have you done?'

'I have done no more than was right. This sword was not made so it could be buried in the earth.'

'They will come here.' He could hear the fear in her voice.

'Do you think I don't know that?' He was whispering, his voice harsh. 'I will hide it. You know nothing. Go back to bed. If they come, say you haven't seen me; say you have been asleep.'

'But what are you going to do with it?'

'I will give it to Oswy. It will be up to him, as Lord Egbert's eldest son, to keep it or give it to his uncle. It needs to be blooded. It is the Destiny Maker!' His voice sounded desperate.

Her hand dropped to her side. Without a word she retreated to their bed and stood there, gazing down at it unseeing in the darkness. 'God go with you, husband mine,' she murmured.

He waited only another moment, then he turned and made for the door. She stood there a long time without moving, listening to the silence, then she turned towards the fire and squatted in front of it, holding out her hands to the dying warmth. Tears were running down her cheeks.

Leo woke suddenly with a shout of panic. He clutched at the bed covers, trying to remember where he was and what had happened. He had been dreaming. He must have been dreaming, but he couldn't grasp the dream. It was slipping away even as he tried to hold on to it. It was about a sword. A special sword – but it had gone. He sat up, feeling the sweat cooling on his face, and swung his legs out of bed and standing up staggered to the bathroom. He filled his cupped hands with cold water and splashed his face several times, willing his pulse to steady. Glancing up at his face in the mirror he scowled. It still took him by surprise sometimes, that hideous swathe of scars, that demonic twist to his features.

He turned towards the door, pulled the switch cord to extinguish the light and walked back into his bedroom. Jade was sitting on the end of his bed.

'My God, Jade, what on earth are you doing here!'

She grinned wanly. 'I couldn't sleep. Neither could you, obviously.'

'You've got to go. You've got to go now, Jade.' He reached for his shirt hurriedly and pulled it on, followed by his jeans. Thank Christ he was wearing his boxer shorts. More often than not he slept naked.

'Why?' She raised her chin a fraction. 'You never minded me coming here before.'

'Well, I do when it's,' he glanced at his wristwatch, 'two thirty in the morning! What are you thinking coming here like this now? Is something wrong?'

She shrugged.

'Jade?' He felt better now he was dressed. He looked at her face. There was a swathe of spots across her forehead and another over her chin. She had obviously been scratching them; one or two were bleeding. 'Have you got calamine for that rash?'

He saw her mouth turn down. 'I look awful.'

'It won't last long. But you mustn't scratch them. Come on downstairs. I'll make you a hot drink, then you must go home.'

He led the way towards the stairs. 'Jade?'

She was standing looking down at his bed. 'She came up here.'

'Who?'

'That Zoë woman. I told you.'

'Yes. She was looking for me.' He paused in the doorway. 'She found you.' Her voice was listless.

'Yes, in the end.' He could hear alarm bells ringing somewhere in the back of his head. 'Come on Jade. Let's get a hot drink.' He walked a few steps down the narrow twisting stairs, but still she didn't move.

'I saw you on the boat,' she said after a pause.

'Well, I'm often on the boat.' He had stopped and was looking up and back over his shoulder.

'With her.'

Bugger! He closed his eyes as a spasm of anxiety and genuine sorrow went through him. 'Jade, love, that was adult stuff. Her and me. It's got nothing to do with you. You and me, we're still best mates.'

She didn't react.

He considered for a moment wondering what it was best to do, then he turned his back on her and went on

243

downstairs to the kitchen. He switched on all the lights and reached for the kettle. It was a long time before she appeared.

'OK?' he grinned at her.

She shook her head. She had been crying and her eyes were red. 'Does Ken know about what you do with his wife?' she asked. There was an unpleasant harshness to her voice.

Double bugger! She wasn't going to leave this alone.

'No, he doesn't.'

'So you don't want me to tell him.'

'No I don't.'

She perched on one of the stools and folded her arms. 'It'll cost you.'

He gave a rueful grin. 'I thought it might.' He switched on the kettle. 'What's the going rate for silence?'

'I haven't decided yet.' Again there was a hardness there he didn't like. 'I'll have to think about that one.'

He looked at her sternly and she met his gaze without flinching. 'The price will be very high,' she said. She went to the door, pulled it open and went out without saying goodbye.

Leo sat where he was without moving for several minutes, listening to the kettle as it came to the boil. It switched itself off but he made no move towards it. Eventually he stood up, turned out the lights and retraced his steps towards the staircase. He went up with a heavy heart. Whatever had happened between him and Jade had caused an irreparable rift in their relationship and for that he was sorry. She had been a good and loyal mate. He would not have had her hurt for the world.

U

Emily was pacing up and down the morning room, her hands clenched in the folds of her skirt, her face pinched and white. She reached the far edge of the carpet and turned to walk back towards the window. She was halfway back again when the door opened and her husband appeared.

'What is it? Beaton said you wished to see me?' He turned and closed the door behind him. 'Emily, what has happened?'

She shook her head, for a moment incapable of speech, and tears began to trickle down her cheeks. She sat down on one of the chairs which flanked the fireplace and shook her head inconsolably.

Henry was looking alarmed. He went to stand beside her and reached down to take her hand. 'What is it, my darling?'

She sniffed. 'I've been assaulted.' It was a barely audible whisper. Her hand in his was shaking.

For a moment he didn't react. He stared down at the top of her head incredulously, then he dropped her hand. 'What did you say?'

She looked up at last, and her eyes were swimming with tears. 'I've been assaulted, Henry. I'm so sorry. I didn't know what to do. What to tell you. I was so afraid. Afraid of you and afraid of,' her voice broke and for a moment she couldn't finish the sentence, 'afraid of him.'

'Who? Who assaulted you?' His voice echoed round the room.

'Daniel Smith.' Again, it was barely audible.

'And what,' he hesitated, closing his eyes for a moment. 'what – exactly – did he do?'

'He raped me.'

He walked away from her and stood, staring out of the window. She raised her eyes, watching him. 'He said,' she added with a pitiful wail, 'that if I told you he would say I instigated it, that I had been encouraging him.'

'And had you?' He swung round, his face hard.

'No! Of course not. How could you say that?' She stood up, wringing her hands. 'Henry, I love you. I had just lost your child. I was vulnerable and ill and miserable.'

'And where were you when this happened?'

She hesitated. 'I had been down to the forge to discuss the disposal of my horse. Bella. She had to be put down.'

'Why?'

'She broke a leg.'

'When you were riding her?'

'No.' She shook her head. 'I wasn't there. I had told Sam I wanted her brought back up here to the stables and she put her foot down a rabbit hole in the park. The undergroom was leading her. Dan came up to see what had happened.'

'Dan?'

She bit her lip. 'Daniel.'

'And why were you alone with him?'

'Sam turned Zeph off. He blamed him for the accident.' She glanced up through eyelashes sparkling with tears. 'Zeph was angry.' She shook her head. 'They were all angry. Poor Bella.'

'Why in God's name would a groom take a horse anywhere near the rabbit warren? And why has no one told me all this? When did it happen?'

'A day or so ago.'

'And when did Daniel Smith,' he paused, unable to bring himself to say the word for a moment, 'rape you?'

'Afterwards. He was angry and upset. We were talking alone.' She put her hands to her face, aware that her hair was beginning to shake loose from its combs. 'He has always found me attractive.'

'There cannot be a man alive who would not find you attractive, my dear,' he said grimly. 'That does not give them leave to touch you, never mind –' he took a deep breath – 'assault you. Why did you not tell me at once?'

'I was frightened.'

'Of me?'

She nodded submissively. 'I was afraid you would think me in some way – damaged – Henry.' She clutched her shawl around her tightly. 'Will you sack him?'

He narrowed his eyes. 'Sack him!' he echoed. 'I hardly think that sacking would be sufficient. I will see to it that he is punished, have no fear. Leave me now.'

'But Henry –'

'Leave me!' It was a roar of anger.

She ran towards the door and pulled it open. Beaton was standing outside, a handful of letters in his hand. 'Beaton, is that you?' Henry called from inside the room. 'Come in here.'

Beaton glanced sideways at Emily and walked into the morning room, closing the door behind him. 'You called, sir?'

'Indeed I did –'

Emily heard no more. She walked slowly upstairs towards her bedroom, her tears already dry. Her anguished expression had been transformed into one of hard satisfaction.

Pushing open the door she found Molly standing by the bed. 'What are you doing here, girl?'

'I was checking the fire was laid and the flowers fresh, my lady.'

'I am sure everything is perfect. Leave me.'

'Yes, my lady.' Molly shot her a look of acute dislike. It was lost on Emily, who had walked across to the window. Outside, the river was covered in swathes of white mist. Beyond the trees a sail had appeared. She watched it as it moved slowly up-river, at times almost invisible, at others hazily spotlit by the weak sun. On the huge square expanse of sail she could see clearly the head of a dragon.

The cars for all four properties were garaged in a range of converted cart sheds some fifty yards up the drive. There was space for at least ten cars; Rosemary and Steve's blue Nissan Micra, and Jackson's black Corsa were there, as was Zoë's small silver Audi and Leo's ancient Land Rover, but there were several empty spaces. Zoë was about to climb into her car when Leo appeared round the corner of the garages. He had his own car key in his hand. He glanced round. 'Ken?' he said.

She shook her head. 'He went out early.'

'I need to talk to you.' He ducked into the shadows. 'We have a problem. Jade saw us on the boat.'

'Oh God!' She threw her bag onto the passenger seat of the Audi and leaned on the car drumming her fingers on the roof. She was thinking hard. 'Did she see us doing anything incriminating?'

'Yes.'

'And she's going to tell?'

'She's considering her options.'

'Shit!'

'As you say.'

'What do we do?'

'I shall try and head her off at the pass. But meanwhile we need to deny everything and get our story straight. Yes, you did come on the boat with me. No we didn't do anything we need be ashamed off. She misconstrued the situation, that's all. Will Ken believe that?'

'I'm not sure.' She sighed.

'Where is he today?'

'Ipswich. He won't be back till late.' She no longer believed in the business contact in Ipswich, but she found she didn't mind. Leo was grinning suddenly and she felt her heart begin to thump with excitement.

'Feel like an assignation? Then we can get our story straight at the same time,' he said.

She nodded. 'For some insane reason I seem unable to resist your invitation.'

'Ditto. I will meet you in an hour at the car park in Woodbridge. Give me five minutes to get away now in case she's watching.' He opened the door of the Land Rover and hauled himself in. Raising his hand he drove off in a cloud of blue smoke. Zoë glanced round warily. Was someone watching – Jade? Jackson? The whole place seemed deserted.

The turning area in front of the garages was still cobbled. She walked out, feeling her shoes slipping uncomfortably on the stones, and turned round in a full circle, scanning every bay of the cart shed, every shadowed corner. A spray of sow-thistle nodded against the wall, the seed heads white and fluffy, the flowers a vivid yellow against the old red stone.

There was no one there. When she climbed into the car ten minutes later and drove slowly out onto the driveway through the fields she was fairly certain no one had been watching.

'Have you ever made a sword?' Lying in Leo's arms, Zoë was staring at the clouds racing overhead.

'Why do you ask?' He glanced across at her.

'I don't know. I just wondered.'

He grimaced. 'I have, as it happens. Or at least, I helped someone make one, a long time ago. He was an Anglo-Saxon re-enactor, and he was determined to do everything accurately so he brought me the instructions and we made the thing together. It was a fabulous object.'

'What happened to it?'

'I don't know. As far as I recall he used it in battle – a mock battle, but I suppose the sword wouldn't have known that. It held up. It was a good sword. That was shortly before . . .' His voice trailed away.

'Shortly before?'

'Shortly before my accident. My forge was closed. I lost touch with my customers. I moved away.'

'And now?' She rolled towards him.

'Now?'

'What do you do now? And don't say, "this and that".'

She punched him on the shoulder.

He smiled, throwing his arm across his eyes. 'This and that just about covers it. I illustrate books. I draw things.'

'Things?'

'Things.' He rolled out of reach and climbed to his feet,

reaching for his sweater. 'People contact me. Sometimes publishers; sometimes authors. I work freelance.'

'It sounds interesting.'

'It is, I never know what I'll be doing next.' He shrugged and grabbing his jacket he pulled it on as he walked away from her.

She dressed quickly. It was cold once she was sitting up. The wind which had seemed negligible when she was lying down pressed tightly against his hot skin was stronger now and there was a breath of autumn to it which had not been there earlier. She pulled on her sweater and then reached for her scarf. The sun went in, and black cloud shadows were racing across the grass throwing jagged templates of the ruined walls at her feet.

Staring up, they both saw a large bird fly overhead. It circled once above them then angled off towards the west.

Outside the wall, hidden in the thicket of brambles, Jackson Watts smiled grimly to himself. He slid his camera into the canvas bag on his shoulder and quietly began to make his way out of the undergrowth, retracing his steps across the scrub and woodland to the lay-by where he had left his car half a mile down the lane. By the time Zoë reached home his Corsa, with its alloy go-faster wheels and souped-up engine, was back in its place; she had no reason to think it had gone out at all.

Leo did not come home until much later that evening, long after Zoë and Ken were poring over a sample book of curtain materials. Ken had borrowed a ladder from Steve and nailed an old bedspread across the large barn window. It gave them at least an illusion of privacy and could be caught back with a tie. Ken had brought home some samples and a pile of catalogues from his visit to Woodbridge. He was feeling quietly satisfied that he had remembered, and from Steve and

Rosemary he had obtained the name of a woman who would make their curtains for them. She had performed the same task for The Threshing Barn. 'These huge windows are fabulous in the daytime,' Rosemary had agreed with a rueful nod, 'but in the winter when it is dark outside, I don't like it at all. I don't blame you for feeling a bit vulnerable. We put something up in the first month.'

Ken glanced at Zoë as she flipped through the samples. She had caught the sun during the afternoon; there was a glow to her complexion he hadn't noticed there for a long time, even after they had been sailing. She was still a good-looking woman, his wife. She felt his eyes on her and glanced up. A quick flash of anxiety seemed to cross her face, then she had looked away again. She pushed away the samples. 'I want something absolutely plain. These patterns wouldn't suit the room at all. We have to keep the utilitarian austerity of the place.'

She was of course right. He had always admired her taste, her judgments were usually spot on. 'What colour, do you reckon?'

There was no answer. 'Zoë?'

She was staring past him into the depths of the room. All the colour had leached from her face. For a moment he found he couldn't breathe. He didn't want to see whatever it was she was looking at. Slowly he turned his head.

12

It was still dark when Hrotgar burst into the cottage, a flaming brand in his hand to light his way. He held it up and surveyed the single room. 'Where is it?' he shouted. 'Edith! Where is Eric? Where is the sword?'

She had finally fallen asleep after lying for hours listening to the call of an owl quartering the woods behind the forge and she was genuinely frightened and confused as she swam up from the depths of her dream. She grabbed the bed covers and held them against her as she sat up, staring at the angry man who stood in the middle of the room, the wild shadows dancing round him.

'I don't know,' she stammered. 'I don't know where he is. What has happened?'

Hrotgar moved towards her. 'Don't pretend!' he shouted. 'Eric has stolen back the sword. I know it was him. Who else would dare?'

She shook her head. 'I don't know what you are talking about,' she repeated. 'I'm sorry. He didn't come back last night. He was up at the hall.'

'And so were you,' Hrotgar shouted. He came very close,

thrusting his face into hers, the flaming brand held dangerously close to the roof thatch. 'Don't pretend you didn't hear him. He was angry. He confronted the sorcerer. The man has cast the runes. He said it was taken by Eric and he said the sword was here.'

She looked at him, terrified. 'It's not here. It can't be here. I don't know where it is, I swear it by Our Lady's mantle.' She shrank back in the bed. 'Please, leave.'

'Don't you understand?' He turned and hurled the brand into the hearth where it smouldered for a few seconds and then died. The room was suddenly almost dark. He turned back and grabbed her arm. 'He's a dead man. What he has done is sacrilege. He has taken grave goods already sworn to the gods!' He paused, seemingly in despair, and she saw him shaking his head, his profile dark against the dim glow from the embers. 'There is nothing to be done then. I am too late. It will be up to others to find him. Of course, that means,' he was suddenly breathing heavily, his words catching in his throat, 'that you can at last be mine.' He stepped towards her and before she could dodge away from him he thrust her back on the bed, throwing his weight down on top of her, stifling her scream with his hand. In the hearth the brand ignited an unburned section of dry apple branch and the room was suddenly lit by the flickering flames, which cast shadows over the walls and filled the air with sweet smoky perfume.

By the river Eric had thrust the sword, wrapped in a heavy piece of sacking, into a hole in the bank. He dragged a handful of undergrowth over it and wedged moss and weed into the gaps. Satisfied it couldn't be seen, he glanced round yet again to make sure he had not been overlooked, then he crept away towards the village. He passed his cottage and for a moment he paused. Surely he had closed the door behind him? He looked at it puzzled, then he shook his head slowly.

All was quiet. For now he had other places to be. He needed to find the Lord Egbert's brother and consult him on what was to be done and he must go to the church and speak to Father Wulfric. Surely the Christian God had magic enough to defeat this Saxon sorcerer and negate his curses. He glanced up as a bird flew overhead in the dark, and as he heard its lonely piping call he crossed himself, something he had not done for a long time. It was an omen. Almost, he stopped; almost, he diverted back to his cottage and the forge, but the call of his duty to the family of Lord Egbert was strong and with an effort of will he forced himself to walk on up the track towards the mead hall and the thegn's house.

As soon as they were in full sight, he stopped. The great doors at the end of the hall were open and he could see the light from a hundred torches pouring out into the darkness. Men and women were running around and he could hear the shouting from where he was. There was no shelter on the track. He glanced round, then he loped sideways in the shadows towards one of the great oak trees standing on the edge of the small field. He took cover behind it then peered out again, narrowing his eyes against the flare of lights, trying to make out what was happening. Had they discovered the loss of the sword already? He measured the distance from his hiding place to the next tree and, ducking away from the cover, sprinted towards it. He could hear the shouting more clearly now, but still he couldn't make out the words. He glanced behind him towards the village but the cottages there were all in darkness. Most of the people were up at the hall. Far away in the south-east a pale line of light was appearing on the horizon. Soon it would be dawn.

U

Sam was standing in Henry Crosby's office, twisting his cap between his fingers. He had never seen the squire looking so angry or so ill.

'I understand you let Zeph go. May I ask why?'

Sam's face darkened. 'I have on several occasions found him less than satisfactory; then I had reason to suspect him of an act of downright vicious cruelty to one of the horses. I will not tolerate such behaviour in my stable.'

'We are talking about my wife's mare, Bella,' Henry said.

'Yes, sir.'

'I had understood that he was careless rather than deliberately cruel.'

'Is that what Lady Emily said, sir?'

Something about the way Sam said the words made Henry pause. 'That is what my wife told me.'

Sam kept his face impassive. 'With all due respect, sir, she was not there. She did not see the mare.'

'I see.' Henry looked thoughtful. 'I am sure you did right, Sam. I would never challenge your judgement. I assume you sent Zeph off without a reference? Do you know where he has gone?'

'Back to Ipswich, I would guess, sir. He'll find work on the barges easily enough. I don't care what he does as long as he never works with animals again.'

'Indeed.' Henry Crosby paused for several seconds. 'All right. You may go, Sam. Thank you.'

Sam hesitated, changed his mind about whatever he was going to say and turned to the door. Outside he rammed his cap back on his head and headed for the kitchen.

Molly was down at the forge cottage with her sister. Susan was pale and uncomfortable as she walked up and down the small parlour floor. 'Why won't it come?' She put her hands to her back again and groaned. 'I can't bear it!'

Molly shook her head. 'Have you asked Betsy? There must be something you can take to bring the baby on.'

'She suggested raspberry leaf tea. I've taken it. I've drunk pitchers full of it.'

'Where's Dan? The forge was empty when I came past.'

Susan bit her lip. 'He's been acting peculiar these last few days. Something has upset him.'

'Of course it has.' Molly glanced at her sideways. 'You do know they killed that mare, Bella? Had the knacker to her. Said she broke a leg. That must have upset him after he had worked so hard on her. He was fond of her, wasn't he?' She shook her head.

Susan stared at her. 'I didn't know they killed Bella! Why didn't Dan tell me?'

'Probably trying to save you any more upset.'

'Was it that woman?'

Molly laughed. 'Oh, yes. 'Course it was. I reckon she did it to pay Dan back. You know word is, in the servants' hall, that Dan refused her when she came back to him. She was spitting nails. He loves you, Susan. He's not going to let her get her claws into him again.'

'Then where is he?' Susan's eyes filled with tears.

'Maybe he's up the fields with George. They're busy this time of year.' Molly glanced at the window where the sun was shining through the dusty pane. Normally Susan would rather have died than allow a speck of dust in her precious parlour. 'Do you want to go for a small walk outside in the fresh air?' she asked tentatively. 'I have to be going back soon. I only managed to get away because Mrs Field wanted me to drop some things in on Jessie Turtill. I need to get back before her ladyship finds out I'm overdue back at the hall, but I could spare a few minutes.'

Susan shook her head. 'You go, Moll. I don't want you getting in trouble. I'll be all right here. Dan will turn up soon enough.'

'What is it? What can you see?' Ken whispered. He could feel the uneasiness in the air; the tension which was almost like an electrical charge, but he couldn't see anything.

'There,' Zoë whispered. 'There is a man standing there.'

'Where?' Ken was paralysed with terror suddenly. His eyes darted back and forth as he tried to pinpoint whatever it was she was seeing. 'What sort of man?'

'He's shadowy; tall, working clothes. I can't really see his face. He's there, where the floor section is exposed. It's the floor from his time.'

Silently and very slowly she stood up, then with an exclamation of annoyance she shook her head. 'No, he's gone.'

Ken stared at her. 'Aren't you scared?'

She gave a small self-conscious smile. 'I am usually when I sense things, but do you know, I wasn't. Not this time. He was too wispy and shadowy. And he was just standing there. I didn't sense any danger from him. He didn't know we were here. It was just as though the light was suddenly shining through a crack in the old barn walls and catching him as he went about his business. Why should he be frightening?'

'Most people would be terrified.'

'I'm not most people.'

'No.' He paused. 'No, you're not.'

'We should be pleased about the things that make us special, Ken,' she said gently.

'And this is Leo's philosophy, is it?' Ken couldn't keep a sudden bitterness out of his tone. Zoë stared at him. For a moment neither of them said anything.

'I don't know what Leo's philosophy, as you call it, has to do with any of this,' she said at last.

She walked towards the stairs.

Ken sighed. He swept all the samples and books and catalogues into a pile. Not for the first time he wished he hadn't given up smoking. Now would be the perfect moment to go outside and have a cigarette under the stars. Anything to get out of the house.

*　*　*

257

Jackson was in his father's den. He had spent a fruitful morning with the photoprinter and had a bulging envelope full of incriminating pictures to show for it. He grinned to himself and glanced at his watch. Mike would be over in a minute; he was going to enjoy looking at the fruits of Jackson's labours while they decided the best use they could make of their evidence. That was a bonus. The real purpose of Mike's visit was to plan the next step in their war against Rosemary Formby.

It only occurred to him for a brief second to wonder where his sister was. She wasn't there, getting in his hair, which was the main thing.

Jade was watching The Old Barn. Zoë was still inside, but Ken had gone out early again. She had watched him open the door and stand there, taking deep breaths of the cold morning air, then he had banged the door shut, unnecessarily loudly, in her opinion, and walked off to find his car. She had crept after him to make sure he was actually off the property and seen him stand for a long time deep in thought in front of Leo's old muddy Land Rover. She smiled. So he did know. Pity. She would have liked to break the news to him herself. But then there was still plenty she could do to spoil Zoë's life.

She heard the distant sound of a motorbike and drew back out of sight behind the cart shed as Mike Turtill appeared down the drive. Her face darkened. She didn't like Mike, and if he was going to see Jackson, it meant she would have to stay away.

Leo was home, but did she want to go and see Leo? Her visits to him were spoiled now. And anyway, no doubt he would soon be joining up with Zoë.

She was right. Within half an hour she saw them both walking down the path towards the river. Once they were on the *Curlew* they would be out of her reach. Her skills had

258

not proceeded as far as electronic bugging though for a moment the idea appealed to her. It never occurred to her that her brother might be on the same quest and that for future reference he would probably be quite capable of thinking of a way to organise surveillance of the boat.

Leo grinned as he helped Zoë on board. 'Are you thinking what I'm thinking? The woods are full of busy little eyes, watching.'

Zoë nodded. 'Wretched girl.'

'We'll cast off and drift down river a little way. I don't know how far she is prepared to follow, but she can't drive yet, thank God, and I trust she isn't going to leap into one of the family boats and row after us.' He gestured towards the two large dinghies upturned on the mud of the foreshore a little further down river. 'Are you up for a bit of a sail?'

Zoë nodded gamely. 'The wind isn't too strong; and I trust you.'

He smiled. 'You sit still in the corner there and leave it to me. *Curlew* and I know each other well. We'll give you a nice gentle ride.'

As the sail filled and the boat drew away down river Leo glanced back at the landing stage. Jade was standing there in full sight. The expression on her face was one of total devastation. He was standing, the tiller in one hand, the main sheet in the other, one bare foot on the seat. Zoë was staring ahead, her hair blowing round her face. She hadn't looked back and so hadn't seen the small figure behind them, for which he was glad. Once again he was troubled by his own sense of guilt that somehow he was betraying Jade, though why, he wasn't sure. He felt no guilt at all about Ken. Zoë was a free agent. It was up to her what she did or didn't do with her husband and with her neighbours.

They lowered the sails and dropped anchor a while later off a small wooded bay. There was no sign of any houses or roads nearby and one or two buoys, which showed it must be an anchorage of sorts, were vacant. The breeze was gentle and the sun was warm as they slid into the bottom of the cockpit out of sight.

Later, when they were eating their picnic of French bread and cheese and sipping white wine from the glasses that Leo had tucked into the top of his backpack she told him about the ghostly appearance the night before. 'It was nothing to do with Jade. I could see him clearly. Well, not clearly, but enough to know that there was someone there.' She shivered and reached for her jacket. 'It's weird. I don't think he is trying to contact me; I don't think he is aware of anything. He is just there, like the walls and the floor.'

'Trapped in time and space.' Leo was leaning back, his bare feet on the seat opposite. 'Don't some people say that ghosts are nothing but visual echoes? There is nothing there to be scared of.'

'I wasn't scared this time.' She leaned across and cut herself another piece of cheese. 'It all fits together. We can hear horses sometimes, and the clanking of harness. It's a kind of window into the past of the barn. I would love to know who they were; what their names were; what their story was.'

'You should ask Bill Turtill. His family have lived here for generations. He was telling me the other day. His great-great-grandfather, I think it was, was farm manager when the Crosbys at the Hall owned all the land, and his father and grandfather before him had worked for the family, probably going back years.'

Zoë nodded. 'I went to the library and looked it up. The whole set-up came to an end I think around the First World War.'

'That's right. Then Bill's grandfather bought the farm in the twenties or thirties. It was the Depression and I suspect land prices were at an all-time low and nobody wanted it so he probably got it for a song. They have worked very hard to make a go of it. Penny is going to start doing bed and breakfasts next year so they are doing up the farmhouse as well.'

'And has Bill got a son to come after him?'

'Do I hear a hint of sexism there?' Leo laughed. 'What about a daughter? Actually he's got one of each, but I don't think either is showing any interest at the moment. It must be heartbreaking when generations of links to the soil come to an end.'

'Going back to my ghost,' Zoë said after a moment. 'He must have worked for one of the Turtills. Isn't that strange? And he must have worked with horses.'

'Which were shod in my cottage. Or at least the forge part of it.' Leo stretched lazily. 'I like that sense of continuity. It is something that is being lost everywhere. One more generation and it will be gone for good.' He glanced up at the pennant at the mast head as the halyards and stays rattled in a sudden change of wind. 'So,' he went on after a moment. 'You don't know where Ken is going on these day-long forays of his?'

Zoë shook her head.

'And you're not even remotely interested?'

She gave a wry laugh. 'I suppose I should be, but if it allows me to do this, then no, I'm not.'

'You don't think he has a fancy woman?'

'I had begun to wonder. But if he has, good luck to him. I'm pretty sure he's had them before.'

Leo sat up and looked at her. 'You are a remarkable woman.'

'I've been bewitched by my pirate smith.'

He put his head on one side. 'That's how you think of me?'

She nodded. 'Seriously, Leo, something has happened to me. I was in danger of becoming a middle-aged boring housewife. That was how you saw me, wasn't it, when we first met? You said so. And you have turned me into someone quite different.'

'A sexy sea gypsy!' He grinned.

'I wish!'

'It's true.' He looked her up and down lazily. 'I think the next thing is to get rid of some of your respectable clothes and kit you out with bright colours and plunging necklines.'

'That would shock Ken.'

'You're going to have to leave him, you know.'

Zoë froze. 'That's not part of the deal, Leo.'

'Why not?'

She shook her head again. 'It's too soon. I am having enough trouble getting my head round what is happening now, today, yesterday. I hardly know you, Leo. Not really.'

'I don't think you know yourself,' he said gently. When she didn't reply he went on, 'I wasn't suggesting you move in with me, Zoë. I am not in the market for any kind of lasting relationship at the moment. I still have too many commitments I can't sort out yet in my own head. You and me, it's fun and it's daring and it's exciting, but it can't be for ever. I am sorry if I misled you.'

She was looking out towards the far bank of the river and seemed lost in thought. 'No,' she said after a pause. 'You haven't misled me.'

'You will still have to leave him. He is stifling you.'

'So, what do you suggest I should I do?'

'Pack a bag, buy a ticket. Head for distant climes. Adventure. You haven't any kids, have you, so you've no ties.'

She bit her lip, suddenly terrified she was going to cry. 'Supposing I want ties? I would have loved to have kids.' She gave a small half laugh. 'I only realised it very recently. Perhaps I could have your kid. A pirate's baby. No ties, no claims, a wild child who will travel with me.'

For a moment they were looking at each other rather too hard and the moment had stretched out too long. Zoë broke the gaze and looked away from him. 'No. Come to think of it, definitely not. I'm not ready for that. No way. I haven't been a wild child myself yet. You're right. What I need is adventure. Shall we sail some more? The tide is turning. You see, I do know something about the river. But I don't want to be out here when the mist comes. That might be an adventure too far.'

U

Henry Crosby was sitting in a waterfront alehouse in Ipswich. It was somewhere men went sometimes to find work on the barges or in the docks. It had taken several days for his informant to find the whereabouts of Zephaniah Fry and another to set up this meeting and come down on the train. He was seated at a corner table in the darkest area of the bar, two tankards of ale in front of him on the table. When the man appeared he seemed to hesitate for several seconds as he peered round the room, then he walked over. Henry pointed at the stool opposite him and the man sat down. He was young, strong, his clothes worn, his neckerchief a dirty red above the threadbare shirt. 'I have a job for you,' Henry said. 'No questions asked or answered. You do it and then you leave for London with the next tide. I have a contact in Rotherhithe who will give you a job there.'

Zeph reached for the tankard opposite him and drank half of the contents down in one swill. He had not so far said a word.

'I want a man killed.' Henry's eyes were fixed on his face. Zeph made no sign at all.

'The man who was to blame for your dismissal. Daniel Smith. I want it done quickly and quietly. I want people to think that he killed himself, do you understand? I want no fuss and I want no recriminations. But,' he held up his hand as Zeph was about to drain the second half of his drink, 'I want Daniel to know why he is dying. I want him to know and to regret and to go to hell aware that he dies by my orders. Is that clear?'

Zeph drank. He rubbed his sleeve across his mouth and then he nodded.

'Aren't you going to ask me what you have to say to him?'

Zeph gave an unpleasant leer. 'I presume this is something to do with him bedding your wife.'

Henry flushed a deep uncomfortable red. 'Is there no one who doesn't know about it?'

Zeph shook his head. 'She wasn't too fussy who knew.'

'Well, I shall deal with her myself. Your job is to finish off her lover. Can you do it?'

The nod was instant. 'I've got no reason to like Dan Smith. I can do it. How much?'

Henry reached into an inner pocket and produced a small bag of coins. He put it on the table. 'Half now and half when the job is done, plus your passage to London.'

Zeph slid the bag into the front of his shirt and gave a gap-toothed grin. 'I'll take another pint of that ale, if it's all the same to you, Mr Henry, and then I will be on my way.' He beckoned the pot boy and pointed at the empty tankard. After he had drunk it he stood up and without a word he left the bar, effortlessly blending with the crowds around him and disappearing into the street outside.

Henry sat at the table for a while longer, staring down into the drink before him. Eventually he stood up, leaving it all but untouched, and walked slowly towards the door. A woman standing near the fire had been watching him. She seized the tankard and drained it down. She belched loudly and raised it in salute towards his retreating back. 'Thanks, mister,' she called. He didn't hear her.

It was nearly dark when the *Curlew* nosed up to her buoy and drifted to a stop. Smoothly and efficiently Leo stowed the sails, tidied the decks and lowered his bag down into the dinghy. 'OK. Ready?' he said.

Zoë had been watching him as she sat languidly in the corner of the cockpit. It was cold now, and she had put on his jacket over hers at his insistence, but she made no offer of help. She was enjoying the quiet competence of the man. The *Curlew* had no engine, but she had come up to her mooring under sail as easily and accurately as ever the *Lady Grace* did with the full noise and fuss and smell of a diesel engine. In the silence, she could hear the ripple of the water against the hull, and somewhere nearby the echoing call of a redshank.

She had had plenty of time to think that afternoon and to realise that she had fallen deeply in love with Leo Logan. She had also realised that almost certainly he was not in love with her. If she wanted to be with him on any level she would have to settle for what he offered, the excitement of an affair, fantastic sex and a new and very different outlook on life, but would that be enough for her? She wasn't sure. And what about Ken?

She stood up and taking his hand let him help her over the side and down into the small dinghy which had been waiting attached to the buoy. They had timed it just right. In another half an hour the water would be too low to reach the landing stage with any dignity. Leo paddled them across the intervening strip of water, again so silently she could barely hear the drip of water from the oar. 'You are used to doing everything quietly,' she commented at last. Her own voice seemed strident against the night.

He grinned. 'No need for noise.' He spun the boat round and brought it in close so all she had to do was reach up and cling to the rungs of the short ladder.

Climbing up, she stood upright and glanced round. Was Jade there, waiting for them? The place seemed deserted. Below her Leo tied up the dinghy and followed her onto the bank. 'No sign of her?'

'I don't think so.'

'Do you want to go up ahead of me?'

She shook her head. 'I've no problem about where I've been. What I've been doing, perhaps.'

They emerged from the woods and began to walk across the parkland towards the barns which lay as black shadows in the dusk. As they drew closer the security lights of The Threshing Barn came on. The curtains were open and Zoë could clearly see Rosemary and Steve standing in the room. Both had turned and looked out as the gardens outside were flooded suddenly with light. Zoë raised a hand in greeting. 'I think she should draw the curtains,' she said. 'If there was someone out here who wanted to take pot shots at them they are sitting targets like that.'

The Old Barn, she realised was in darkness. Obviously Ken had not yet returned from wherever it was he had gone.

'I don't think those boys were intending to murder her.' Leo stopped. 'But it is a point worth making to her next time you see her. She's an arrogant woman. I don't think she realises how much local opinion is against her on this one.' He gave her a quick smile and turned away across the grass towards The Old Forge without any further goodbyes. She watched him fade out of the range of the lights and out of sight in the darkness. She stood still, undecided for a few moments, then she turned towards The Threshing Barn. Rosemary had seen her. There was no point in denying where she had been and it might be a good moment to make her point about the lights. Besides, she didn't feel like going home to an empty building. Not yet.

Rosemary opened the door to her with a warm smile. 'We saw you with Leo,' she said.

'I went sailing with him,' Zoë said, following her in. 'He is giving me some lessons so I am not so scared when I go with Ken. Ken is too competitive for me. Everything has to be pushed to the limit. With Leo we just drift around. He is letting me get my sea legs slowly.'

266

She saw Rosemary glance at Steve and ignored the look, accepting the glass of wine which Steve pressed on her. 'So where is Ken?' Rosemary asked as they were all seated in front of the TV. The sound had been lowered and no one seemed to be watching it.

'God knows! He's involved in some contract, I think.' Zoë glanced over her shoulder at the window. 'You know Ken was telling you about our curtain problem. Leo and I were just saying how exposed these barns are at night. You can see every detail of this room from outside.' She hesitated. 'I know it seems crazy to even think it, but after what happened about the footpath, do you think it might be sensible to draw yours?'

Steve leaped to his feet. 'She's right! We've got so used to the long summer evenings we haven't realised how quickly the nights are drawing in.' They all looked round at the blackness outside the windows. The lights outside had gone off and all was dark. Steve went over to the curtains and reached for the pull cords. In a moment the whole area was hidden by a swathe of bright red poppies. Zoë thought of her discussion with Ken about curtain material and hid a smile. It didn't matter what the curtains looked like, and in fact they were rather jolly, and the room was cosy and warm and safe.

Outside, Jackson and Mike were walking across the grass towards the cart sheds where Mike had left his bike, careful to keep out of range of the movement detectors which set off the lights. They saw the curtains shut across the window.

'All set for tomorrow?' Jackson said jubilantly.

'All set!' Both boys laughed and, heading away from the barns into the darkness, they exchanged a high five.

'Say a word of what has happened between us and Eric will die.' Hrotgar had murmured the words so close to her ear

267

she had felt the heat of his breath on her hair. 'This is between you and me, and you were willing, do not deny it.' He sat up and pulled on his trousers. 'I know he stole the sword. If he returns it, then he may survive the anger of the old gods. I don't know how they function, but the sorcerer saw at once what had happened. He cast the runes and divined who had taken it and he called out curses on Eric's head. His eyes sent out shafts of fire and his lips spewed poison.' He drew on his tunic and climbed off the bed. He stood looking down at her. 'He said that the sisters of wyrd will decide whether Eric lives or dies – but to my mind your husband's fate is in your hands. Remember that well, Edith.'

He swung towards the door and disappeared, leaving her cowering on the bed. Her body was covered in bruises; she had fought him with every ounce of her strength. Eric would know what had happened as soon as he saw her. With a murmur of fear she huddled into the corner of the bed cradling her belly, praying that her child had not been harmed, and at last the tears came.

It was a long time before she got up and went outside to find a bucket of water to wash herself. She pulled her clothes on over her wet and shivering body and realised that her gown was torn and her mantle had ripped away from the brooch that had held it closed, the brooch that Eric had made her. She fumbled with the material, trying to find it, but it was missing. She spent a long time groping around in the dark of the bed, and then on the floor, and retrieved it at last from the basket of logs beside the hearth. She held it against her cheek, pressing the intricate silver knotwork into her skin as though it would heal the bruises which had spread over one side of her face. Later she would make a salve from some of the herbs which hung above her head, plantain, meadowsweet, agrimony, vervain, comfrey. Until then the silver would suffice. Almost silently she began to recite the words of the healing charm to herself. It comforted her a little.

When the door opened she turned half-afraid, half-eager. 'Eric!' She needed him so badly to hold her.

The figure that appeared was shorter than her husband, outlined against the first streaks of dawn light.

'Hrotgar?' Her anguished whisper made almost no sound.

He walked over to her and stood looking at her for a long moment. 'I made a mistake,' he said slowly. 'I can't allow you to tell Eric what has happened.'

She tried to run but there was nowhere to go. Stooping, he picked up something heavy from the hearth and raising his hand he brought it crashing down on her head.

Outside it was slowly growing light, and there was still no sign of Eric.

There was no need to spy out the land. Zeph knew every inch of the estate and the farm buildings. He had hitched a lift to Woodbridge with a carter, hiked across the fields, and spent the night in the ruins of the old church out of the worst of the wind. Just before first light he made his way cautiously down towards the barns and hid behind one of the hayricks, grateful for the shelter as he settled down to wait for the farm to spring to life. George brought two of the shire horses out first, harnessed and ready to put in the shafts of the largest wagon; he saw the older man, Robert, emerge to give him a hand, grumbling and easing his coat on more comfortably as he tested the traces and helped back the horses into place. It was full daylight before Ben appeared from his mother's cottage up the lane, still munching on a wedge of bread. He opened the door into the forge and pushed it wide, allowing the fitful daylight to illuminate the piles of horse-shoes, the anvil and the cold fire. His job was to rake out the ashes and start up the furnace. Today was going to be busy. They were going to make hinges for the new gates. There was no sign of Dan.

Zeph settled further into the back of the haystack, trying to find some warmth there. He felt in his pocket for the remains of the pasty he had bought the day before and slowly began to munch. Ben was obviously expecting Dan. His gaze moved lazily to the forge cottage, which showed no signs of life. There was no smoke coming from the chimney and the curtains in the front room were closed. He took another mouthful of the cold greasy pastry and settled back. He was in no hurry.

Dan was rubbing Susan's back. As soon as Betsy arrived to stay with her he would get to the forge. He was late. He had made his wife a drink of raspberry leaf tea as Betsy had instructed and sat on the bed as she drank it. Her face was white with fatigue and every now and then she groaned a little. She had eaten nothing for two days. 'There's another pain coming,' she whispered, her voice weak with exhaustion.

'Don't you fret, my girl,' Dan whispered back. 'Betsy will be here in a while and she said we'd send Ben for the midwife if nothing happens this morning.'

'There's something wrong, Dan, I know there is.' She reached for the mug of tea. 'The pains aren't coming properly. They should be regular by now.'

'Maybe the babe is just not ready to come yet. Betsy said it was early.' He leaned forward and kissed her forehead. It was clammy and her hair was plastered to her scalp with sweat. He got up and went to the basin on the side table, rinsing out a washcloth to sponge her face and hands.

'You're good to me, Dan Smith.' She smiled up at him. 'You get you out to the forge. I'll be fine here for a while.'

'Are you sure?' He stood up again with alacrity. 'Betsy won't be long, and Mr Turtill said Jessie would look in on

270

you this morning as well. She's had six of her own so she'll know how things are with you.' He reached his coat off the back of the door. 'You look after yourself, my dear, and I will come in and see you a bit later.'

He walked through into the parlour, noticing how cheerless it was with the curtains still closed and no Susan to put fresh flowers in the little blue jug she kept for the purpose on the windowsill. He pulled back the curtains and looked at the dead daisies with a grimace. The water they were standing in was rank. He pulled open the front door and tossed the contents of the jug out onto the path, then he set the empty jug down on the table. He would pick her some flowers from the hedgerow when he came in to see her later in the morning.

Zeph saw the door open and he narrowed his eyes, trying to see better. It had begun to rain and he could feel the damp seeping into his jacket. He finished the last mouthful of his pasty and wiped his hands on his trousers, checking in his pocket for the snare he had brought with him. It was a piece of equipment he had often used in the fields round the hall, catching rabbits mostly, but sometimes a fox. One of them had bitten off its own paw in an attempt to free itself from the wire, but it hadn't escaped far. He had found it nearby dead, lying in a pool of its own blood. Last night he had adapted the snare, twisting each end of the wire over a small piece of wood to help give him purchase. Anything else he might need he would find in the barn.

He watched Dan pause and glance back at the cottage, then he pulled the door shut behind him and walked quickly down the path to the forge where Ben had already started the fire. The blue fragrant smoke from the oak chippings he was using as kindling was drifting straight up into the dank still air. Dan disappeared inside and Zeph settled back. Nothing would happen until the horses had gone to the

271

fields with George and Robert, the dairy maids had left with their buckets to see to the milking cows and the yard was deserted. Whatever was going on in the cottage would like as not distract Betsy if she came down from the farm cottages later.

The clouds were lifting a little and there was a patch or two of blue in the sky. Every now and then he heard the sound of hammering from the forge. A couple of hens were pecking round his feet; he clapped his hands at them and they flew up squawking.

It was a long time before Dan appeared in the doorway and headed towards the barn, as Zeph had known he would. There were always things to be mended, harness to be reinforced, tools to be reforged, and George often left the items to be seen to stacked just inside the doorway. It had been during those visits to the barn that Dan had taken the opportunity to stroke Bella and murmur in her ear, giving her a handful of oats. There was always the chance that he might have sent Ben to collect the repair jobs, but Zeph knew his man. Dan was methodical, doing things in the right order, and in the same way each day. He would have bet good money on the fact that Dan would come himself while the fire was steadily building its heat, and he was right. Silent as a shadow Zeph slipped from behind his hayrick and headed for the side door to the barn, groping in his pocket as he did so until his fingers closed around the wire.

Zoë woke with a start. She was clutching her stomach, groaning in agony as she ran towards the bathroom, leaving Ken sitting up sleepily staring after her. He lay back as she disappeared inside and slammed the door and reached for the pillow, clutching it over his head, not wanting to hear the sounds of her vomiting, but there was a long silence, followed at last by the splash of the shower.

She stared at herself in the mirror over the wash basin for a long time, waiting to see if she was going to be sick, until it dawned on her that there was nothing wrong. The stomach pains which had woken her had vanished. They were part of her dream.

She had straightened up at last and pushed her hair back from her forehead. Then she tore off her nightdress and headed into the shower. She was bathed in sweat and exhausted. In her dream she had been in labour and she had known she was going to die.

When at last she emerged from the bathroom Ken had disappeared. He had left a note on the kitchen worktop: *Sorry you're not well. Maybe you should call the doctor? I have to be in Ipswich by nine but I will ring later to see how you are.*

She screwed up the note and threw it in the bin.

Leo put two slices of toast under the grill for her and pushed down the filter in the coffee jug. 'You dreamed you were having a baby?' He had been working in his garden when she arrived. With one look at her face he had thrust his spade into the earth and abandoned it. Within seconds of them going inside a robin had appropriated the handle as a perch.

She nodded. 'It was awful, Leo. There was something wrong and there were people all round and they knew it was all going terribly badly and there was no doctor and the midwife was useless. She knew next to nothing. My neighbour knew more than she did.' She grabbed the cup of coffee he poured her. 'I woke up in such agony I couldn't believe it.'

'That must have scared Ken,' he observed dryly.

'Ken didn't hang around to find out what was wrong. When I got out of the shower he had gone. He left a note telling me to call the doctor.'

'Sympathetic chap.'

She took a deep breath. 'I'm still a bit shaky, if I'm honest.'

'Have something to eat and you'll feel better. It's an odd

thing to dream. But of course we were talking about kids yesterday.' He glanced at her as he shoved a pot of marmalade towards her on the work surface, pushing aside a sketchbook and pencils as he did so. She put her hand on his arm to stop him and flipped open the cover of the book. Inside on the front page there were several small sketches of a heron. She looked at them closely. 'These are lovely. Harnsers.' She remembered the word. 'Did you do them?'

He gave a resigned nod, removed the book from her hands and tossed it behind him onto the table. 'Eat.'

'You have so many hidden talents.'

He grinned. 'Maybe. You concentrate on the talents you know about.'

'OK. But first tell me something. When I said I dreamed I was pregnant you didn't seem surprised.'

He shook his head, suddenly sober. 'There seems to be a pattern emerging. I didn't want to say anything to you in case it upset you and I suppose I wanted to see what happened.' He stared down at the table for a moment, deep in thought. 'Eat your breakfast, then we'll talk about it. First I want to find one or two books to show you.'

In spite of herself she was hungry. As she ate the toast she looked at his sketchbook while he was out of the room. It was full of pencil drawings of birds. On the bookshelf behind the table she found a stack of other sketchbooks. All birds, some pen and ink, some watercolour, some with notes in small cramped writing of details of plumage and where he had seen them. There were, she noticed, small paintboxes and bottles of ink on the windowsill between the pot plants.

On the corner of the table was a jam jar containing brushes and pencils. She just had time to replace the sketchbooks on the shelf when she heard him coming back. Under his arm there were three old volumes with torn dust jackets. He grinned at her. 'As you have probably guessed my current assignment is a birdbook.' He had seen her looking at them. 'I sometimes think I have managed to move sideways into the most wonderful job in the world. Now,' he put the books down on the table, 'as you know I've read a bit about the history of this estate; and I've collected a few books about it when I've found them in second-hand bookshops and car boot sales. It's fascinating. One of the things that intrigues me is the number of times the ghosts are mentioned.'

Zoë closed her eyes in a gesture of denial. 'Tell me,' she said resignedly.

'You already know about your house – The Old Barn. Then there are supposed to be ghosts here in the forge, and down at the water's edge, and in the Hall itself. There isn't much more to tell. No details.' He hesitated. 'There is something else, though. People have nightmares here.'

'Great!' She shuddered. 'You mean, not just us. Sometimes I think I'm beginning to hate this place!'

'Aren't you even a little bit intrigued?'

'No. I'm scared.'

'No, you're not. Not my Zoë. You are a brave lady with an enquiring mind. What you want to know is how and why it happens. So, I think you should know, for what it's worth, that it is one of the things that tipped your predecessors over into leaving. Sarah was pregnant when they left. She kept on having dreams like the one you described. Everyone thought it was because she was scared of being pregnant. Her sister had died in childbirth and she had said she would never have children herself. Then it happened. She was quite pleased at first, then the dreams started and she became more and more freaked out by them.'

'You seem to have known them quite well,' Zoë commented curiously. 'I thought you didn't rate them very highly as neighbours.'

'I didn't. I didn't like Dave. And they chickened out. They should have waited to see what was going to happen.'

'A research project.'

'Yes.' He smiled. 'If you like. Go on, you'd like to know, wouldn't you? What happened.'

'I can guess what happened. Some poor woman who lived round here – presumably she didn't live in the barn itself – was pregnant and very afraid. She probably died in childbirth.' She shuddered again. 'And her poor spirit is wailing from the rooftops about it and has been ever since. It is gross!'

He looked up at her from the book he was perusing. 'You don't sound very sympathetic.'

'I'm sorry.' She sat down abruptly on one of the seats by his window. 'You're right. That sounded awful. It's just that it was too close. I was her.' She reached for the coffee pot and poured herself a refill. 'Is this why Ken was sleepwalking, do you suppose? Is it all part of it?'

Shaking his head, Leo helped himself to the last drops of coffee, real coffee. He had not made the mistake of offering her instant again. 'Dave never mentioned sleepwalking. Has Ken mentioned nightmares?'

'No.'

'I don't think all this applies to the other barns. It is specific to yours. Threshing was built in the sixteenth century, I think, so it's not as old as yours. And The Summer Barn was later than that. I think they put it up as a granary at the beginning of the nineteenth with lots of extensions later. Yours was the one the planning people made all the fuss about when they submitted the plans for conversion. If I were you I would want to know more. How else can you lay the ghost? The trouble is that there is often no record of the names of the people who worked on the farms. We know the Turtills were here, but unless there is reason to list the other inhabitants we will never know who they were.'

She was becoming intrigued inspite of herself. 'There is the Census. That must tell at least who was here every ten years since the first, and it's online now.'

Leo applauded silently. 'What a fantastic point! I shall look it up. Just out of curiosity.' He glanced at his watch. 'I'm really sorry, Zoë, but I've got to go out soon. Can we meet up to talk about this tomorrow perhaps?'

Zoë jumped to her feet. 'I'm sorry. I never thought.'

'It's OK.' He laid his hand on her arm. 'Just an appointment I can't miss. Row out to *Curlew*, if you like. Veg out away from the world. I do that often. It is so peaceful down there.'

She shook her head. 'That might be lesson ten, but I think it's too soon to go on my own. Don't worry. There is a lot to do at home.'

He held out one of the books. 'Some bedside reading?'

'No way!'

He laughed. 'OK. See you tomorrow, then.' Walking with her to the door he watched as she crossed his garden and let herself out of the gate. Then he turned back to the kitchen. 'Jade?' He opened the back door. 'You can come out now.'

There was a scuffling in the flowerbed and a red-faced Jade emerged from behind his lavender bush. He could smell the fragrance of the plant on her as she came and stood on his doorstep looking sheepish. 'How did you know I was there?' she asked crossly.

'I can see through walls.'

'And you sent her away.'

'I told her I was going out. How much of that did you hear?'

'All of it.' She stared at him defiantly.

'Liar.'

She smiled cheekily. 'You don't know how much I heard.'

'I can have a good guess. Did you hear the bit about the police looking for your brother?'

'No.' She went white.

'Well, they will be if he doesn't behave himself. So you get home now and tell him.'

277

'But I thought you might take me for a sail.'

'Not today. I'm sorry.'

'But you took her.' The resentment was obvious.

'I will take you, but today I have to go out. If you had heard every word of our conversation you would know that that is what I told Zoë and the same applies to you. I am busy today so scram!'

Her face was transformed into a scowl. 'Can I stay here and wait for you?'

'No. I'm sorry.'

She turned sulkily towards the door.

'Jade!' he called after her. 'Key?' He held out his hand.

She scowled even harder. Reluctantly she put her hand into her jeans pocket and produced a key on a keyring with a small pink plastic teddy bear fob. He opened the ring with his fingernail and took off the key, then he gave her back the bear. 'Put your own door key on that, OK?'

She stuck out her tongue at him and headed for home. He waited until she was halfway across the grass before he closed the door and double-locked it. He didn't trust her an inch. There would be backup keys and probably back-ups of the backups, if he knew anything about her at all. He wondered where she got the money to have all these keys cut.

Zoë paused as she got to the front door of The Old Barn and turned to look back at The Old Forge. She was in time to see Jade heading across the grass towards home and she gave a quick, irritated smile. You had to give it to the girl. She was nothing if not persistent. She stood by the door weeding one of her tubs, the one which contained pink geraniums and ivies and Michaelmas daisies, until she saw Leo come out. He had a portfolio under his arm. She watched as he turned and double-locked the front door – a wise move, in her opinion – and then he headed up the path towards the garages. So, he really was going out. Comforted that he had not been making some excuse, she turned and let herself into her own door, bolting it behind her with the thought that if Jade was at a loose end she might find the idea of neighbour-baiting an appealing one. She walked through into the great room and stopped dead.

Ken was there standing by the woodburner. With him were John and Amanda Danvers.

'Surprise!' Ken announced triumphantly. 'You didn't suspect, did you? They've come up for your birthday.'

'My birthday!' Zoë echoed. She felt weirdly out of sync. The two faces looking at her were like strangers.

'Zoë, love! You look completely gobsmacked!' Amanda let out a peal of laughter. She was dressed in an immaculate blue-striped top and skin-tight navy jeans with stack-heeled red sandals. Slim as ever, and with a neat bob of dark hair, she immediately made Zoë feel dowdy. She moved forward and gave Zoë a hug. 'Ken told us you didn't suspect a thing. Isn't it wonderful? So much fun – and this place is completely magical. Glorious!'

'Zoë, darling.' John stepped forward, as always quieter, lower key than his wife. He kissed her cheek and reached for her hand. 'So, how is wildest Suffolk? Are you settling in?' Far taller than the rest of them, he was a rangy, angular man, slightly stooped, with a mop of untidy grey hair and gold-rimmed glasses.

He had always been more observant than his wife; he would have spotted the dark rings under her eyes, the moment of something like terror she had felt as she registered the people standing in the room, before she had actually recognised them.

'It's been quite a gear change, coming up here,' she said quietly. 'I expect Ken has told you.'

'Ken has been raving about it all,' Amanda said. 'We've been following his emails avidly and reading his blog. So many adventures, and your own mooring at the end of the garden. We can't wait to see how *Lady Grace* has fitted in. I do hope we can go out in her soon.'

So Ken had been emailing them. Zoë was trying desperately to readjust, to put Leo and Jade and the dream out of her mind and concentrate suddenly on practicalities, like preparing a bedroom for unexpected visitors. And a blog. She didn't know he wrote a blog. She realised suddenly how out of touch she had become since they had moved. She couldn't even remember when she had last checked her email.

As if reading her thoughts Ken broke in, 'Your room is ready, folks. As it was all a surprise for Zo, I made up the bed last night after she was asleep. I was terrified she would hear me and think I was the ghost.'

'The ghost?' Amanda's eyes rounded. 'You have a ghost?'

Zoë and Ken exchanged glances. It took only a fraction of a second but John saw it. 'My goodness, you have.' He looked at his wife. 'I hope you've got your ghost-busting hat on, darling. Amanda's a dab hand with ghosts, did you know?' He turned back to Ken and Zoë.

Zoë finally gathered her wits. 'Well, you'll have plenty to practise on here. But first things first. Let us show you your room. Once you've settled in we'll have plenty of time to catch up.'

'And we're going to start with a pub lunch,' Ken said. 'No cooking for Zo today.' He gave her a smile.

'But my birthday is not for three days.' Zoë had finally worked it out. She was appalled to find she hadn't even known what day it was today!

'No matter, darling.' Amanda pounced and gave her another hug. 'Every day is going to be a birthday for you this week. We are going to see to that, aren't we, John?'

Zoë smiled. It had suddenly dawned on her. Ken must have asked them up in an attempt to cheer her up, to distract her. She wasn't sure whether to be angry or touched that he should have thought of it.

Eric had guessed at once that he was a marked man. He watched from the edge of the woodland as it grew light, screwing up his eyes, trying to make sense of the scurrying forms which emerged from the mist and then disappeared again. He could see the forge from here, a solid form which from time to time dissolved into the shadows. By now there should be smoke emerging from the roof, but it looked bleak and almost abandoned. He thought about Edith for a moment, alone and worried about him, no doubt, but treasuring within her the hope of their future child. He wondered if Hrotgar had been there looking for him. Almost certainly. It was the obvious place to start the search. Luckily she knew nothing and would have told him nothing even had she known where her husband had hidden the sword.

He ducked back into full shadow and retraced his steps into the woods; from there he took a narrow path through the undergrowth, heading round the village to the east. Once well out of sight of village and hall he cut back up through the paddocks with grazing oxen, and the strip fields, their parallel turf divisions exaggerated in the half-light. He moved along the headlands and across a horse enclosure, making for the little church. Father Wulfric would help him.

He pushed open the door, wincing as it creaked loudly on its hinges. Father Wulfric was kneeling before the altar, deep in prayer.

'Father?' Eric's voice was hoarse after the night out in the damp woods.

The old priest paused, ended his prayer and crossed himself. He rose to his feet with a groan as his aching knees protested at the sudden movement. 'I thought you might come to see me, my son.'

'What shall I do, father?' Eric knelt before him.

'You have the sword safe?'

Eric nodded.

'I have prayed for an answer to your question since the Lady Hilda came to see me this morning. As soon as they found the sword had been replaced there was an outcry. The heathen sorcerer says that the runes you carved at his command dedicated the sword to his gods of war, but that it was for our Lord Egbert to carry the sword to the Otherworld.' The old man shuddered.

'I don't want my sword committed to the flames on an old man's bier.'

The priest shook his head. 'Nor to the earth. I know not yet what plans they have for the disposal of his body. The Lady Hilda, it appears, has no say in the matter.'

'So it would be best to pass the sword on to Oswy as Lord Egbert's heir, or to his brother?'

Father Wulfric nodded. He had no intention of telling the swordsmith of the threats that had been made against him. No doubt the man could guess as much himself. The entire village was dividing. Hidden allegiances and jealousies were surfacing. He knew the swordsmith had changed his beliefs and followed the old religion, but now he was wavering. Others who were openly Christian had harboured secret longings for the old ways. Whilst some dithered, the Christian majority was ranging itself against a hothead bunch who, attracted to the ideas of the old religion, as tradition demanded followed the leadership of their lord. If Egbert worshipped in the old religion then so did they. Peace against war. Why was it always thus? He glanced up at the small round-topped window behind the altar and sighed. This small precious house of God was so frail a refuge, for Eric or for himself. He shivered, his old bones protesting against the cold damp heart of this place. 'Go, my son, and fetch the sword and bring it here just after dark tonight. I will see to it that Oswald is here. He has sworn to protect the rights of his brother's sons until they are old enough to bear a sword themselves. Once he has it the responsibility is passed on and you can rest more easily.' He hesitated. 'Do not trust too much, Eric. There are those you might consider friends who conspire against you.'

Eric frowned. 'Who?'

Wulfric shook his head. 'Walls have ears. I dare not speak names out loud.'

'And yet you tell me to come here, out loud. And you tell me to give the sword to Oswald, out loud!' Eric was staring round, suddenly very afraid. 'Who is here?'

'No one but God, my son,' Wulfric said equably. 'I watch; I listen. People don't always even notice I'm there. They talk unrestrainedly in the hall and in the village.' He sighed. 'They plan to bury him in the tumulus down in the field on the river's edge, where his ancestors were buried before him.' He sighed again. 'They would deny him any hope of heaven. But then he rejected that himself when he refused baptism. The heathen belief is that he will lie there, his soul anchored to his body, ready to talk to whoever asks if they placate him with offerings. An ancestor to whom all will turn when they are in need.'

Eric shuddered. He crossed himself again, astonished to find how naturally the comforting gesture returned to him. 'It seems I did all I could to help him, by inscribing the sword with runes which the sorcerer prescribed.'

'I doubt if you knew the implications of what you were doing,' Wulfric reassured him. 'Or of the magical practices that have been going on openly in Lord Egbert's house. He claimed many years ago that it was his devotion to the goddess Frige which enabled the Lady Hilda to conceive three sons when she had been feared barren. She denies this. She has come to me in anguish and contrition, afraid that what they had done under the blessing of heathen idols had caused her to give birth to three healthy sons and for that she would be damned for ever to the deepest of hells. As you know, the Lord saw fit to take one of those sons at birth and it was the shock of that which showed her the error of her ways in allowing her marriage bed to be defiled by these idols, but, for all her repentance and prayer, there has been much to displease Our Lord since in her household.'

Eric said nothing. He didn't know what to say. It was he who had made the idols for her, at the thegn's insistence, the eggs, the fertile hare, the small slender statue of Frige, but also and most powerfully of all, the figure of the mother goddess with her swollen stomach and pendulous breasts.

Hilda's payment to the gods had been made in full, poor woman, and Eric had taken them home and there one day Edith had found them in the bag he had carried them in as, if he was honest with himself, he had hoped she might. She knew at once what they were and assumed he had made them for her. Christian though she was, she had put them in a basket on the cottage hearth and from time to time he suspected they were secreted in their bed. Her barrenness ended. She conceived at once, but the baby died. Again and again her babies were born before time and lived only a few hours or they were born dead. He begged her to let him melt down the idols but she refused and he had no heart to insist. Even now they sat on his hearth at home and now at last once again they had worked and his wife was with child.

Wulfric put his hand on the other man's forehead, sensing this new pain as the memory hit Eric fully, but not understanding it. 'Bless you, my son,' he murmured. 'I sense your repentance. God will listen to your prayers. Now go and stay hidden until tonight, and then do as I say. Bring the sword here to the house of God.'

U

Stooping to pick up the broken harness pieces, Dan glanced up at the empty stall where Bella had so recently stood. He had grown used to hearing her friendly greetings as he walked in and seeing her excitement as the time for her to be turned into the orchard came near. He bit his lip and bent, scooping the chain into his arms from the dusty floor. He heard the movement behind him too late. A shadow seemed to envelop him, he felt arms around his neck and then the choking cut of the wire around his throat. He fought for only a few seconds, grasping desperately to get a purchase on the wire before it cut too deep, but he couldn't free himself. The man behind him was too strong. As the world went black he felt the warmth of his own blood as it flowed from his neck. His hands fell away from the wire, his frantic struggles stopped at last and he fell to the floor.

He never saw who it was who killed him.

Zeph stood looking down at the body for several seconds with a smile of grim satisfaction and only then did he remember the instructions to make it clear to Dan why he had to die. He gave a sneer. 'I reckon you knew why, my friend!' he murmured. He bent and got hold of the body under the arms and dragged it to one side. It would be clear enough to anyone who looked that the man had been killed but he would at least make a show of pretending that this was a suicide. He groped in his pocket for the note Mr Henry had given him and slid it into the dead man's pocket, then he looked round. He had been in the old barn often enough to know that George and Robert kept all sorts of tools and harness hanging from lines of old nails on the walls. He grabbed a coil of rope and tossed one end up over a beam. At the other end he made a noose which he put around Dan's neck. For a moment it almost hid the deep cut left when he pulled away the wire. Sweating profusely, he dragged Dan up onto a pile of hay bales, secured the end of the rope, then kicked away the top bale. The body fell and hung for a moment, the feet only inches from the ground, swinging gently against the wall. It was enough.

He slid out of the shadows into the bright sunlight outside and round the back of the yard, seen only by the hens scratching in the dust. In the barn the rope creaked once or twice as it tightened further round the beam, then all was still.

Jade was sitting cross-legged on her bed staring down at something lying in front of her on the pink bedcover. She was sucking her thumb, something she only did now when she was sure no one could see, fitting her front teeth comfortably into the groove below her nail. The item lying on the bedspread was a squat rounded figure, some three inches high and two inches across which, if one screwed up one's eyes and defocused, could look like the torso of a woman with a fat stomach and huge breasts. She had found this ages ago when searching the hedge near Leo's house for a cricket ball which the boys had lost. They had promised her ten pence if she found the ball. Which she did. She had promptly threatened to throw it in the river unless her prize money was increased to fifty pence, and she still regarded that as one of her first successful business deals.

The figure was metal and had been a rather nasty corroded green colour when she had found it near the old well. She had washed it and then cleaned it using some old Brasso she had found under the sink. It cleaned up remarkably well, but there was something intensely unpleasant about it. It was ugly. It had a nasty feel. She reached out with her fingertip and then withdrew it without actually touching it. Normally she kept it in a box in the bottom drawer of her bedside cabinet, swathed in bubble wrap. She was pretty sure it was something a witch had once used to curse people. Once or twice she had been on the point of asking Leo about it; she was sure it was the sort of thing he would know, but as quickly she had reached the conclusion that like all adults when confronted with one of her finds, he would have immediately decided that she was not the person to keep it. If it was valuable he would insist it was given to the museum; if it was just a mass of old metal he would probably chuck it in the river. If it was truly evil, he would – what would he do? She chewed her thumbnail. She had been right not to show it to him because now, at last, she had a use for it. If it was used to curse people, why didn't she try it out and see if it still worked. She smiled to herself. The thing was, where to put it to maximum effect?

She cocked her head to one side, listening. Mike Turtill was there downstairs with Jackson. She wondered suddenly what they were planning. Scooping the figure back into its wrapping and putting it carefully into its box so that she didn't actually have to touch it, she slid off the bed and returned it to its drawer. Then she crept to the door and opened it. A little eavesdropping would help to pass the time before she went downstairs and demanded that they provide her with something to eat.

What she heard made her smile.

'Dad is going to plough the field in the next day or so. That will make her wild!' Mike was saying.

The boys were in the kitchen. The fridge door was open and Jackson was rummaging through the contents. He was assembling enough butter and cheese and eggs and bacon on the worktop to feed an army. 'When is her next walkies with her friends?' he asked.

'Don't know. I thought we might delegate that bit of under-cover work to the child.'

Jade closed her eyes and squirmed with fury. She hated Mike Turtill, but for the moment she was prepared to shelve her resentment and go with this idea. It proved they appreci-ated her skills.

'He's going to leave it as rough as possible,' Mike went on

with a chuckle. He leaned towards Sharon's fruit bowl and grabbed a banana. 'We can only hope she breaks her ankle.'

'Or her bloody neck! There must be other things we can do. Scare her away altogether. What about some more haunting? I don't think it's worked with the new people in The Old Barn but we can leave that for now. They sussed us out pretty quickly anyway. And I reckon they don't much like our Rosemary either.'

'They were helped by the weirdo.' Mike stretched over and dipped the end of the banana in the open jar of mayonnaise.

'Jade thinks he's having an affair with Mrs Old Barn,' Jackson commented. He was slapping piles of cheese and ham onto squares of white bread.

Jade frowned. She hadn't said a word to her brother about what she had discovered. Then she remembered, she had mentioned her suspicions long before she had had any proof. That had been what her friend, Holly, called her intuition. She was astounded to realise that Jackson had obviously listened to what she had said, and taken it on board. Mentally she awarded him a mark for his acuity.

Jackson was anointing his masterpiece with mayonnaise. 'Yuk! How could she let him touch her? He looks completely gross with all those scars.'

'Perhaps she likes mingers.'

That was too much for Jade. 'Don't you call my friend a minger!' She burst into the kitchen and glared at both boys. 'He's a really nice person.'

'Oh, yeah?' Jackson was unfazed by her sudden appearance. 'Here. You'd better eat something.' Suddenly remembering his *loco*-parental responsibilities, he sawed his enormous sandwich in half and pushed a bit towards her. She gazed at it for a moment, tempted to reject it on principle, then overwhelmed with hunger, grabbed it. She took a huge bite. The boys watched her chew.

'So, how much of what we were saying did you hear?' Jackson asked nonchalantly when he judged her once more capable of speech.

'Enough.' She grinned cheekily.

'Price of silence?'

'I'll think about it.' She saw the surprise and then suspicion in his face and took another bite.

'I heard you were ill,' Mike said at last. 'I take it you're feeling better?'

She nodded. It was, she realised, true.

'So, are you up for doing a bit of spying for us?' Jackson asked. 'Find out when Rosemary is going to take her little band of walkers back to Mike's field.'

'I'll try.' She shrugged. 'It's not always easy. They don't trust me any more.'

Both boys laughed. 'I'm not surprised.'

'In exchange I'm going to want you both to do something for me.' She shook her head and raised her hand. 'I don't know what yet. There is someone I want to fix, big time.'

Jackson didn't seem surprised that his scrap of a sister should be waging war; he even guessed who it was she was out to get and why, but he said nothing. 'I'm sure we can help you there, sis.'

She beamed at him. 'Good.' She turned and headed for the door. 'That sandwich was disgusting,' she added as an afterthought over her shoulder. 'It will give you cholesterol, eating all that fat.'

U

Benjamin had used the bellows with gusto, fanning the fire to a white heat. He stopped and wiped his forehead with the back of his arm then he looked round, puzzled. Dan had been gone a long time. At twelve years old Ben was proud of his position as bellows boy to the smith, who was already training him in the trade. He walked over to

289

the door and stood looking out across the yard. The place was deserted except for the hens, as usual scratching happily about amongst the ears of corn which Betsy had thrown them earlier. He turned towards the cottage. Had Dan's missus called him back there? He would have heard. The door was closed and he could hear nothing coming from inside. He wandered out into the yard and then headed for the old barn.

He stopped in the doorway, looking inside. Motes of sunlight were slanting across the floor and the place seemed empty. He frowned. He could see the heap of chain lying on the cobbles and beside it a large patch of what looked like blood. The boy froze. 'Dan?' he called nervously. 'Dan, you there?' He looked fearfully at the blood; it was smeared and there were drag marks on the floor heading towards the side of the aisle. He took a step or two further in, staring round. At first he didn't see it, then he moved forward again and stopped, immobilised by shock. Dan was hanging from a beam near the side of the barn, his legs trailing on the floor, a hay bale lying out of place near him. The front of his shirt was soaked in drying blood, his face was contorted, his eyes bulging and sightless. For a long time the world seemed to stand still as the boy stared at the man who was his employer and his friend, then he crumpled to the ground, catatonic with shock.

For a while he rocked himself to and fro, moaning, then at last he tried to pull himself together and stood up on shaky legs making his way backwards out of the barn, his eyes still fixed on Dan's face, before he turned and stared round wildly for help. He looked at the cottage and knew instinctively he couldn't go there. He would probably never go there again. With a sob he realised that there was no one nearby to help him. The men were in the fields. There was nothing for it but to go and find them. With one last look over his shoulder he headed for the gate into the lane and began to run.

At the Hall Lady Emily was sitting in the morning room with her husband. She glanced at him and then looked away. On her knee lay a piece of embroidery. The fabric was crushed, the stitches messy. She wanted to hurl the whole silly piece of nonsense into the fire but she didn't dare. Henry's face was a study of dark anger, and had been for several days. He had barked at her the day she had told him she was going riding and forbidden her to go to the stables; later he had come to her room and forbidden her to go out at all. He had called Molly and told her to sit with her mistress to keep her company and later had come back and dismissed the woman before sitting down himself across the fire from her.

'Is there anything wrong, Henry?' she had asked timidly.

'Anything wrong?' he had shouted. 'You tell me that you have been raped and you ask me if there is anything wrong?'

'What have you done about Daniel?' she said at last.

'That is none of your business. He is to be punished.'

'Has he been dismissed?' She leaned forward a little and he saw the sudden spark in her eyes.

'I will see that he never works again.' He set his lips in a thin line. 'That is enough. Get on with your embroidery.'

She saw him glance at her handiwork with disdain and she bit her lip. She had never been a good needlewoman; she remembered screaming at various nursery maids who had tried to teach her to sew as a child. Reluctantly she picked up the frame again and began to stab at the design with stitches of pale blue silk. It was only a short time before she pricked herself and with an exclamation of pain and annoyance saw the bloody stain spread across the spray of flowers.

Zoë asked Rosemary and Steve to join the four of them for supper that night and laid the table in the window of the great room. Ken was at his jovial best, playing host with alacrity as she retreated to the kitchen to put the finishing touches to the meal. She drew the new blind on the kitchen window and bolted the back door; they had already agreed to leave the large window unscreened as a huge harvest moon floated up into view. With several people there she didn't feel so exposed and their guests were enchanted with the whole feel of living in a barn.

She heard a roar of laughter from next door and smiled. They were all enjoying themselves; drinks were flowing freely and the meal was nearly ready. There was a rustle in the doorway and Amanda appeared. She was carrying two glasses. 'We can't have the cook slaving away in here without a drink,' she announced. 'Come on. Stop for a minute. We need to talk on our own. What's going on? You can tell me.' She hitched herself onto the edge of the pine table and picked a salad leaf out of one of the hors-d'oeuvre bowls. She began to nibble it tentatively and grimaced. 'I hate rabbit food! I hope you've got something meaningful to eat with this.'

Zoë laughed. 'Don't worry. I remembered your appetite. I'm afraid it is out of the freezer, but you will like it, I promise.' She set down her oven gloves and picked up the glass. 'God, I need this.'

'So, what is going on?'

'Ken loves it here. I don't.'

'Ah.'

'I've nothing to do. There is no job for me here. I don't know people. I've no backup.'

'So, what's wrong with them?' Amanda nodded backwards towards the door to the great room.

'Nothing. They are a bit boring and a bit obsessive. Has Rosemary started on about her wretched footpaths yet?'

'Oh, yes.' Amanda looked heavenwards. 'We heard about that in the first five minutes. The gentlemen have steered her away from the subject, I am pleased to say. Ken keeps plying her with gin; I doubt if she will still be coherent by the time we eat.'

'The food won't be long.'

'That wasn't a hint. I want to know, Zo, what is it? OK, so you don't like the house, but there is something up between you and Ken. Something else, isn't there?'

Zoë gave a quiet laugh. 'I had forgotten how perspicacious you are.'

'So, who is he?'

Zoë stared at her. 'How did you know?'

'Because I am perspicacious!' She leaned forward. 'Come on, spill the beans.'

Zoë glanced towards the door. 'You won't say anything.'

'You know me better than that.'

'It's the man next door. No,' she giggled at Amanda's expression, 'not Steve, bless him. Next door across there.' She waved her arm towards the window. 'He's a maverick ex-blacksmith, scarred in body and soul.'

'Wow!' Amanda's eyes widened.

'And he is a fantastic lover! Is that too much information?'

'No such thing, dear. Go on!'

'There is no future in it.'

'Ah. He's married?'

'I'm not even sure about that. He has an ex, but he is a free spirit now. And he is cultivating mine.'

'Your free spirit?'

'Yes.

'In that case, he has my total support. We all love Ken dearly, but he has never been the man for you.'

Zoë stared at her. 'Why did you never say anything?'

'Not my place. It was something you had to see for yourself. So what happens next?'

Zoë shook her head. 'I've no idea.'

293

'Just concentrate on the illicit sex. It is so much more exciting than the marital kind.'

'Amanda?'

'We are not talking about me, dear. Now, what about this food. Can I help? Then tomorrow you will have to introduce me to your Lothario so I can give him my full approval. We need to get rid of the men. No problem there, of course. We will send them to sea in the boat!'

Zoë was laughing. 'You are good for me, Amanda. I needed cheering up so badly.'

'Doesn't sound like that to me. OK. No more for now in case the walls have ears. Which reminds me, you need to tell me about your ghost. That is a suitable subject for public discussion, I take it?'

Zoë nodded. 'We've both felt things, seen things. Through there, in the great room.'

'The great room!' Amanda giggled. 'Well, I suppose it is hard to call it anything else. It really is barn-like, isn't it. What do you see?'

'Perhaps I shouldn't tell you. Wait for your famous knack to kick in. I didn't even know you had ghost-hunting skills.'

Amanda sobered for a moment. 'It's not something I talk about. Or enjoy. It is just one of those weird things that I seem to have a facility for. Sensing things. But I didn't when we walked in, so maybe that is a comfort for you.'

Zoë was loading a tray with the small bowls of hors-d'oeuvres. 'Can you take this through?' She reached for a jug of dressing. 'You didn't feel anything at all?' she said. Her tone was carefully neutral.

'No.' Amanda reached for the tray. 'Perhaps I'll go in there later when everyone else has gone to bed. That's a good time to feel things. There is too much noise going on there now.'

Zoë nodded. She was unconvinced.

'Fantastic nosh, Zoë, old girl!' John said some time later. He rubbed his stomach and grinned at her. 'You've lost none of your skill at cooking, I'm glad to see.'

Zoë smiled. 'Thanks, John. I don't see why I should have. This is Suffolk, not Mars.'

She paused. The room was growing colder although the woodburner was glowing with heat. Outside the moon was shining down across the gardens and there was a suspiciously frostlike glitter on the grass. She shivered. 'Is everyone warm enough?'

Amanda's cheeks were glowing; Rosemary, Steve and Ken were engaged in a heated conversation down the other end of the table. No one seemed to hear her question.

She could feel her eyes drawn to the far corner of the room where the panel was let into the floor. There was a focus of energy there, a vortex of swirling mist and suddenly she could hear the creak of a slowly swinging rope. She blinked. It was the heat, the food and wine; her head was throbbing and they had left the lights dim on the far side of the room, concentrating on lighting the table with candles. She heard the knife drop from her hand onto the plate with a clatter.

'Zoë?' John's voice sounded a long way away. 'Zoë, are you all right?'

She knew what the rope was; on the end there was a noose. Someone had died, hanging from the beam. She could hear the creak of the thick strands tightening, the scrape of heels on the floor, the wind in the straw which whisked across the floor as a dust devil spun in through the doors and was gone, and the squawk of a suddenly panicked hen. She felt herself stand up, pushing her chair away. She turned away from the table, staring at the spot where the body hung, swinging gently, slumped against the hay bales from which it had fallen.

'Zoë? What's wrong?' There was silence round the table

now. She heard other chairs pushed back. Someone had come and put their arm round her shoulders. 'Zoë?'

'Leave her!' That was Ken, suddenly authoritative. Then he was there. He was trying to lead her somewhere. She resisted, her eyes still fixed on the scene, trying to focus, trying to make it more solid, trying to understand what had happened.

'Murder,' she murmured. 'It was murder.'

'Oh my God!' Amanda's voice was shrill. 'What do we do?'

'I thought you were the expert, honey!' That was John. She couldn't engage with them. She was somewhere else, but not somewhere else. The scene still hovered there, the silence behind the quiet ordinary sounds of the deserted barn almost tangible around her. No one spoke. She took a step forward and Ken's restraining arm fell away. She was completely focused on the scene before her. Why did no one come? But someone had come. A boy was standing in the doorway looking towards the body. It shouldn't be a child who found him; that was all wrong. That was cruel. She saw the boy move forward, his eyes rounded, then she saw him fall to the ground.

'No!' she screamed.

There was a resounding silence in the room. The scene had vanished. Now the barn walls were again painted; pictures hung on the spaces between the great vertical beams where once horse collars and nosebags and bait sieves had hung, the floor was shiny wood, covered in rugs, the underfloor locked away beneath its glass. She staggered forward a few steps and collapsed on the sofa nearest the woodburner. She was shaking.

Slowly she raised her head and looked round. The other five people in the room were standing round her in a semi-circle, their faces a picture of concern and fear and horror respectively. 'Sorry,' she stammered. 'Not sure what happened there.' Her hands were clutched together in her lap. She glanced nervously over her shoulder at the corner of the room but normality seemed to have returned.

'Can you tell us what happened?' Rosemary came and sat on the sofa next to her.

'The usual.' Zoë gave a shaky smile.

'More than the usual,' Rosemary persisted. 'You said there was a murder?'

Zoë closed her eyes. She nodded. Then she shook her head. 'I don't know. I don't know what I said. He was hanging, from the beam.' She glanced up. All eyes followed her gaze.

'Oh my God,' Amanda whispered again.

'I'm so sorry.' Zoë rubbed her face hard with her hands. 'It has never happened before like this. We've sensed things; we've seen things, but not like this.' She was shivering violently suddenly.

Without comment Ken walked over to the tray of drinks on the side table and poured a slug of whisky into a tumbler. 'Here.' He pressed it into her hands. 'It will make you feel better.'

She took a sip. 'He was swinging, so gently. I could hear the rope creaking; his legs were dragging on the floor. If he had stood up he could have taken the weight. He was dead before –' She shook her head and took another sip.

'No horses this time?' Ken said softly.

She shook her head. 'No horses.' She sniffed. 'Then a boy walked in and saw him.'

'So,' John said abruptly. 'I thought you were the expert.' He was looking at his wife. 'What's going on?'

Amanda shook her head. 'I don't know. I felt nothing; I saw nothing.' She was standing looking down at Zoë, an expression of awed concern on her face. 'I'm a fraud. I must be. I've never experienced anything like that.'

Ken looked at Rosemary and then Steve. 'Did this happen to our predecessors? Is this what finally drove them away?'

Steve nodded. 'I suppose so. They didn't tell us in detail.

We thought it was the kids next door. To be honest, we never really believed them.'

'Can you tell us what "the usual" is?' John said suddenly. 'Not all of us are in the loop here. What do you see normally?' He couldn't keep the disbelief out of his voice.

'Just barn stuff,' Ken said calmly. 'We hear things mostly. Horses clip-clopping across the cobbles, hens, we see dusty visions of the past sort of hanging in the sunbeams.'

Zoë looked up. 'That's exactly it,' she said huskily. 'It is like a film projected into the space around us. Nothing scary. Not as such. But this time I could see someone. And it was awful. He was hanging from the beam –' Her voice broke and she fought back her tears. 'A boy came in and saw him,' she whispered. 'He collapsed on the floor, then it all stopped.'

No one said anything. Zoë was aware of the others exchanging glances. 'Sorry,' she said at last. 'A bit of a conversation stopper. That's what happens when you come out into the deepest countryside, folks!' She looked from John to Amanda with a shaky smile. 'Ignore me. I've gone all weird. Rosemary has noticed it setting in. It's the curse of The Old Barn syndrome!'

Rosemary managed a smile. 'I'm afraid she's right. These old places have such an amazing atmosphere, don't they? You will sleep well, my dears, don't doubt it.' She leaned forward and put her hand over Amanda's. 'There is nothing to fear. Have you met Leo yet?' She nodded towards the window. 'Our other neighbour? He is the expert on all this history – he's been here longer than any of the rest of us – he will tell you about the ghosts.'

Amanda looked at Zoë and raised an eyebrow. Zoë looked away. Rosemary saw the exchange. 'You've heard about him, I expect. An interesting man,' she went on relentlessly. 'Did he show you his books, Zoë? He's an expert on our best ghost of all. It is a ship.'

'A ship?' John interrupted. 'Now that is interesting. That's our kind of ghost, eh, Ken?' He laughed. 'This conversation is getting altogether too serious for my peace of mind. I suggest we broach that interesting bottle we bought you folks. What do you say?' He stood up and walked across to the table by the far wall where Ken had left several expensive carrier bags which their guests had presented them with on arrival. He rummaged through them and produced a bottle of brandy. 'Glasses?' he demanded.

Ken got up and headed for the kitchen. He paused beside Zoë and put his hand on her shoulder. 'OK?' he whispered.

She looked up and nodded. 'OK,' she replied.

In The Old Forge Leo was standing in his kitchen. He had turned out the lights and was standing at the window looking down towards the river. In the moonlight a hazy mist was forming over the water. He was waiting for the ship to appear. He could sense its presence, feel the chill that accompanied it as it drifted up the river. Zoë had asked him if it was a portent of evil. He shivered. What else could it be?

13

Eric cradled the sword in his arms as he carried it up through the wood, swathed in a length of cloth he had brought with him for the purpose. Every now and then he paused, every sense straining to hear or see anything suspicious. All was silent in the darkness. There was no moon or stars. The sky was steeped in cloud. He kept well away from the village. He wanted there to be no possibility of involving Edith in what he had done any more than he had already. He picked his way surefooted through the undergrowth and stopped again at the edge of the wood, staring out at the darker silhouette which was the squat solid outline of the little church. There were no lights showing in the small high windows.

He crept forward and ran the last few paces, crouching against the northern wall, several feet from the door. Again, nothing. He waited until his breathing had steadied. Somewhere below in the woodland he heard an owl calling, the haunting sound echoing in the silence. After a long pause he heard the answering call of its mate, sharp and loud, very close. He stood with his back to the wall, his eyes the only part of him that moved. Was that an owl, or the signal of a man?

Some instinct was telling him to be wary, that all was not well. Surely Father Wulfric would not betray him? Soundlessly he squatted down and put his bundle carefully on the ground, pushing it in amongst the long grasses against the wall. He straightened up and again waited, holding his breath. Again he heard the hoot of the owl. The sound was further away now, more wavering. There was no answer from its mate. He took a step closer to the door, and then another and then he heard the sound of horses, the thump of their hooves on the dry ground, the chink of harness.

He retreated into the shadows of the wild rose bushes beyond the track which led to the door and waited. Three men rode up and slid from their mounts. One remained with the horses, the other two approached the door and banged on it loudly. There was no reply. Eric waited, straining his eyes in the darkness. He could see the outline of the horses, the shape of the man holding them; the other two had vanished against the more intense dark of the shadows in the lee of the church wall. The two men by the door held a whispered consultation – he could hear their murmuring but nothing of what they said – then they banged again and he heard them rattle the handle, the great iron ring which he himself had wrought when Father Wulfric had taken over the church.

The door was not bolted. He heard the creak as it opened and saw the faint glow of candlelight spilling out into the darkness, then he heard the first cry of alarm. He pulled back, watching. The man holding the horses led them closer, right up to the door, and Eric heard him call out. Inside there was silence. Eric felt himself grow cold. For a while nothing happened, then the two men reappeared, silhouettes against the golden light. They grabbed their horses' reins and flung themselves into the saddle. In seconds all three had galloped away.

Bending low, Eric ran towards the door, his heart thudding

with alarm. He paused as he reached the threshold, staring into the church. Father Wulfric was lying on the ground in front of the altar. His eyes were open, an expression of such horror on his face that Eric blenched. The old man's woollen robe was soaked in blood; there was no sign of the weapon which had killed him.

It took Eric only three heartbeats to take in the scene before he turned away. He ducked out of the light, ran round to find the sword where he had left it and fled towards the darkness of the woods, clutching it in his arms. It was a long time before he stopped running. He was breathless, blind from the sweat which trickled into his eyes, not even knowing where he was as he slumped to a halt, his back against the trunk of a tree, and rested there, his chest heaving, the sword still held tightly in his arms. Below him, the tide was running slowly up the river, licking at the mud banks, combing out the tresses of weed. There was no sound now from the owls.

It was a long time later that he heard the bell clanging frantically from the small belfry on the end of the church. Someone had found the body and was summoning help.

In the barn Amanda lay staring up at the ceiling of their bedroom. She had been intensely disappointed to find it was a comparatively ordinary room at the back of the building. It had a no doubt beautiful view, but from what she could see in the moonlight, it faced across the fields. There was no sign of the river. It had been very late when the party had at last broken up and Rosemary and Steve had made their way out into a night, suddenly illuminated by the cold white lights clicking on beneath the eaves, floodlighting the lawns. It had been fun in the end, Zoë's weird turn neutralised by the liberal doses which Ken had poured of their expensive brandy. She frowned in irritation as John beside her let out a particularly resonant snore. Alcohol always did that to him.

However tired she was she was not going to sleep now. She sat up and swung her feet to the floor, grabbing her dressing gown.

The landing was in darkness. She felt her way towards the staircase and began to make her way down. The great room was warm from the fire in the woodburner. The glass doors showed a deep glow. She could still smell the range of smells from the evening; the faint residue of cooking, the warm pungency of Ken's wine, the sharper notes of the brandy, the light traces of the women's scent. At the bottom of the stairs she paused and stared round, her eyes becoming used to the faint light from the fire, and soundlessly she subsided to sit down on the lowest step, her bare feet on the wood floor, her hand on the turned oak post at the base of the banisters. Quietly she began to try to still her thoughts, to tune in to whatever unhappy spirit haunted this place. She had been extremely miffed to find she had sensed nothing of the turmoil which had obviously left its mark here. Why had she not picked up on it? She prided herself on her sensitivity.

She waited, her eyes fixed on the stove, watching the flickering fire behind the glass. A log slipped slightly and banged against the doors and she jumped. Her attention wavered a little towards the table over by the far wall and she debated the idea of going to pour herself another small libation from the brandy bottle. It was a tempting thought but she didn't move. Her sleepiness was beginning to over-whelm her. Her head nodded and just for a moment she rested it in the cradle of her arms on her knees.

U

They cut Dan's body down and laid him in the straw. Then they dispatched Robert up to the Hall, riding on one of the Suffolks, the harness bouncing loose on the horse's fat rump as it trotted heavily up the drive. While George and John

303

the cowman waited with the body, Ben stayed outside in the sun. He had stopped sobbing now and sat, a small frozen figure, arms hugging his thin body, on an upturned bucket near the pump. The two men debated urgently what to do about Susan. 'She has to know,' George said firmly. 'Poor woman can't be left in ignorance.' Both men glanced towards the open door and the forge on the far side of the yard.

John breathed out heavily between his teeth. 'Reckon your missus will be with her. You go and have a word and see what she thinks.'

George nodded. 'Should we cover him, do you think?'

John went over to the stall where Bella had been stabled, and gathered up the old horse blanket which had been thrown over the wooden partition. He laid it gently over their friend and pulled it up over the face, shaking his head sadly as George walked slowly over to the cottage behind the forge.

It was a long time before he returned. When he did he was alone. He laid his hand gently on the boy's head as he passed him, then he went into the barn and grimaced at John. 'The baby is on its way. Betsy said not to say a word. She's calling for him and we've had to say he's been sent off to town. Poor Susan.' He shook his head. 'Betsy says it's not looking good. Baby's breached. Jessie is there and they've sent for Mother Bartle.'

The men shook their heads soberly. Mary Bartle, down in the village, combined the role of midwife with that of laying out the dead.

'No word from the Hall?' George went on.

'Nothing yet.' John groped in his pocket for his pipe. 'I reckon I might take the boy back to his mum. You'll watch him?' He meant Dan. George nodded.

It was a while before the squire arrived riding the cob; not far behind him Sam was driving the squire's valet, William Mayhew, and Robert in the dog cart. The men walked into the barn.

'Dear God! What happened?' Squire Crosby stood looking down at the blanket. George pulled it back. 'We reckon someone killed him,' he said succinctly.

Henry Crosby looked at him sharply. 'Nonsense. Who would do such a thing?' He studied Dan's face. 'Surely, the man hanged himself.'

'He didn't hang,' George said quietly. 'Someone cut his throat. Look at all the blood. Besides, his feet were on the ground.'

Henry Crosby moved a step forward. His own face had darkened to a deep shade of red. 'Nonsense I said! He's hanged himself. Look at the noose, the rope round the beam. Did he leave a note?'

George looked uncomfortable. 'Not that I can see.'

'Search his pockets, man. It's obvious what he's done. He couldn't live with the crime he had committed.' He glared round. The men behind him all looked at the ground. John shuffled his feet. It was George who reluctantly pulled the blanket back further and gingerly inserted his hand into Dan's pockets one by one. The note was in the pocket of his leather jerkin. He drew it out with two fingers and held it up reluctantly.

'Give it to me.' Henry Crosby was sweating.

George held it out to him. All the men were watching intently as the squire unfolded it. '"I can't go on",' he read. "What I did was a crime I can't live with. I pray that God will forgive me."' He snorted with disgust and screwed up the note, throwing it down on the ground. 'I hope God will do so, but I doubt it,' he said firmly. 'So, what to do with him?'

'Shall I go for the police, sir?' George asked.

The squire shook his head. 'No need for that. We can clearly see what happened. We'll sort this out ourselves. How is his wife?' He looked round at the men.

'Not good, sir. My missus and Mrs Turtill are with her and

they've sent for Mother Bartle. Susan is very poorly,' George replied.

'Then for her sake we will sort this out ourselves. As Justice of the Peace I will authorise his burial. As a suicide he cannot rest in consecrated ground so we will bury him ourselves.' Henry Crosby's face was hard and his voice firm. 'You men will dig the grave. The sooner the matter is dealt with the better for everyone, particularly his wife. See to it tonight.'

'But, sir –' George and Robert protested with one voice.

'Enough! Deal with it quickly and discreetly. You understand what that means? No one must ever hear about this. For his wife's sake. Tell her there was an accident, or that he has run away and deserted her. She will have to leave the cottage, but I will allow her to remain until she is churched. She can think herself lucky for that.' He turned to Mayhew, who was standing behind the others, his face as white as a sheet. 'See to it that they deal with this quickly. And you, Sam, help to arrange it. Put him in the spinney in Dead Man's Field.' He gave a sharp snort of laughter. 'That seems appropriate. This matter will never be mentioned again, do you understand? I do not wish my wife to come to hear about it from anyone but me. Is that clearly understood?' He looked at each man in turn, then he walked out of the barn.

The men looked at each other. 'The callous bastard,' Sam said softly. They stood in silence watching as the squire swung himself up onto his horse and trotted across the yard and up the track towards the Hall.

'What do we do?' Robert asked.

'We do as we're told,' Sam replied. 'What choice have we got?'

Amanda awoke to find herself sitting at the foot of the stairs in the dark. She had an agonisingly stiff neck and she was very cold. The fire still glowed in the woodburner but the heat was less intense now. Outside the window the moon was high in the sky; the lights were off and the garden lit by an ethereal gauzy moonlight. She hauled herself to her feet and stood for a moment clinging to the newel post, staring round. She had been dreaming but the dream had gone. Staggering slightly from stiffness she walked across to the window and stared out. It was unbelievably beautiful out there, magical even. She could see the great trees down on the far side of the lawns, the milky mist lying over the water and there drifting up-river a huge square-rigged sail. It didn't occur to her until much later to wonder why the sail billowed as if before a strong wind, when the night outside was so still the dew was turning drop by drop into the first sparkling frost of autumn.

Jade was sitting at Leo's table next morning when he came down for breakfast. 'I thought I told you to give me *all* your keys.'

She assumed a look of outraged innocence. 'I forgot I had another one. Sorry.'

He held out his hand. 'Give it here.' At this rate he would have to change the locks, like the Lloyds.

She shook her head. 'You still owe me.' She had helped herself to a bowl of muesli and drowned it in milk. 'This tastes shitty. Like cardboard.'

'And I suppose you are going to chuck it out and waste it.'

She shook her head. 'I'm hungry.'

'Will wonders never cease. Is Jackson not feeding you?'

She grinned. 'I keep out of his way. He's busy.'

'That's a frightening thought. Busy with what?'

'Plans. The footpath woman is going to have another meeting tomorrow out in the field.' It had been so easy to find out it was pathetic. The woman talked about it incessantly and loudly on the phone, and the phone was near the window. She didn't even use her mobile so she could walk about. She had rung all her troublemaking friends and discussed it with each one of them, planning it as though it was a war campaign instead of a silly little walk.

'And what is Jackson going to do?'

'Mike's dad is ploughing it up today. That'll piss them off, big time. We're going to watch.'

'Just watch?'

'Yeah. What else?'

'It sounds a bit too passive for you lot.'

She took a huge mouthful of cereal and found herself unable to talk for several seconds. Chewing hard, she watched Leo fill the kettle. 'We reckon,' she said at last, 'that she will call the police again.'

'Or Bill Turtill will. It is his field, after all.'

'Whatever.' She took another mouthful. He had a feeling that she was actually enjoying the stuff, but he wisely said nothing.

'Did you know your girlfriend has guests over at the Old Barn?' Jade went on. 'I watched them last night. They had a dinner party. All posh with candles and loads of knives and forks and glasses and stuff. It smelled really nice.'

Leo shook his head. 'So you poor little soul pressed your nose to the windows and watched the rich people eat? Don't give me that one, Jade. Your mum and dad could buy the Lloyds out ten times over and still have too much change to count.'

Jade grinned at him and he realised too late he should have denied the girlfriend tag at once. He decided to leave it. What was the point? She knew what was happening. 'So, what were the friends like?' he asked, curious in spite of himself.

'Nice. John and Amanda.' She pronounced the names with exaggerated care. 'They bought them loads of bottles of plonk. And later, after they had all gone to bed,' Jade glanced at him archly, 'Amanda came downstairs and sat on the bottom step all by herself in the dark. Do you reckon she's in love with Ken?'

He glanced at her, suspicious at the look of bland innocence on her face as she took another mouthful of his muesli. 'I have no idea,' he said. He hoped his tone was repressive enough to deter further speculation.

'She just sat there for a long time in the dark, then she walked across to the window and stared out at the moonlight all dreamily.'

'Moonlight can be very beautiful, Jade.' She had obviously found a way to circumnavigate their damn floodlights. He should warn Zoë that their every move was being spied on. 'Do you never just stand and stare up at the moon and dream?'

She shook her head. 'Why would I?'

'Why indeed.' He smiled tolerantly.

'As *she's* busy,' Jade went on suddenly, 'you could take me out on your boat.'

He was tempted. He wondered if he could by any means possible instil even a small amount of poetic soul into the child. 'Have you learned to swim?'

'Yes.' She looked him in the eye.

He knew she must be lying. 'Would you wear a life jacket the whole time and do as you're told?'

Her whole face was lighting up with excitement as he spoke. 'I promise!' For the first time in a long time there was a genuine ring of sincerity in her voice. He noted it carefully. It would be useful to remember it for future use.

'You will have to get Jackson's approval. He is in charge of you, isn't he? Officially.'

'I'll get him to write a note for you.' She abandoned her bowl and spoon and was dancing round him.

He realised at once the scope for loopholes. 'I will need to speak to him on the phone.' Forgery was probably one of her specialities.

Her face fell. 'He's gone out.'

'He's got a mobile.'

She scowled.

'No call, no trip.'

It was surprisingly easy. The voice on the end of the phone was undoubtedly Jackson. He was distracted and somewhere noisy – Ipswich, at a guess. He had no time for niceties. 'Try not to drown her, yeah?' was his response before he ended the call.

Leo gazed at the phone helplessly as he replaced it on the table. 'It sounds as though it's OK,' he said.

To his astonishment she did as she was told and proved to be a natural sailor. She was used to the river in her father's large motor boat, but the silence and the sensitivity of travelling under sail enchanted her. She had no qualms about the weather. There was a brisk wind blowing and the *Curlew* heeled over as they beat down-river, the slap of the waves against the prow and the spray in their faces. He was tempted to take the boat out beyond the bar into the sea, but in the end he resisted. He could see the white-topped rollers in the distance; he would have to insist she wear a safety line and instinctively he knew that would spoil it all for her. Hauling the boat round he put the helm up and headed back up-river. 'Enjoying yourself?' he asked at last.

She nodded, her eyes sparkling. 'I'm a better sailor than her,' she said.

He groaned inwardly. 'You're a better sailor than a lot of people I know. You should ask your dad if he would get you a dinghy – a little Topper or something – and you could have some lessons up at the club. Then you could sail on your own.'

She narrowed her eyes. 'You like sailing alone best?'

He nodded. 'I'm afraid I do. I like my own company. I like to watch the weather and the birds and the water. The river is endlessly fascinating.'

This time she didn't scoff. She frowned as though trying to understand. 'Because it's different colours all the time.'

Yes! He almost punched the air in delight. 'And different textures, different moods. Like a woman.' He grinned.

'Because of the weather.' She was being very literal, concentrating.

'Indeed. And the tide and the season.'

'Did you tell *her* all this?'

He sighed. 'Zoë understands about the tides and the winds. She is used to sailing.'

'Then why is she scared?'

Leo frowned. How did she know that? Had he told her? 'Because Ken likes racing. He likes pushing the boat to the limit. He sometimes does dangerous things.'

She was silent for a while. 'I would never be scared,' she said at last.

'No, I don't suppose you would. That is why I think you should learn to sail properly. Next summer holidays perhaps. You should ask your mum and dad.'

He adjusted the main sheet. The wind was dropping and they were moving more slowly, feeling the pull of the tide against them. He glanced behind and felt himself grow cold. A thick wall of mist was drifting towards them up the main channel.

♘

'See here,' George glanced up at Fred Turtill as they stooped together over Dan's body. 'Under the rope. His throat's been cut.'

Fred nodded slowly. 'Nobody ever bled to death by hanging,' he said quietly. 'Poor lad.'

'Reckon that bitch of a wife of his was behind it?' Robert had walked up behind them. He was carrying two horse blankets. They all knew who he meant.

'Molly said the mistress told gov'nor that she'd been raped,' Sam put in.

'That's a lie!'

'We all know it was a lie. But who would have done this?'
They stood in silence for a while.

'Squire went to Ipswich last week. A few days after I sent
Zeph packing for beating that horse to death,' Sam said at last.
His voice was very quiet. 'My son Walt works as a carter in
Ipswich. He saw Zeph catch a lift back to Woodbridge yesterday.'

The men looked at each other.

'Well, if it was him, he'll be long gone over the fields. I'll
put word out and see what happens,' Fred put in. 'In the
meantime, lads, we've no alternative but to do what the
governor wants, I reckon. Put old Dan in Dead Man's Field,
and we'll say a prayer over him ourselves.'

There was a sound behind them and they all turned. It
was Betsy. She was looking at the blanket-covered figure on
the ground. She shook her head. 'Poor soul,' she said. There
were tears in her eyes. 'The babe is dead,' she went on softly.
'He never lived to open his eyes. Maybe he should go in with
his da'.'

'And Susan?'

'I've not told her. She's beyond hearing. I doubt if she will
last the day.'

Sam scrabbled at his cap and pulled it off. 'Dear Lord, may
they rest in peace.'

The other men removed their caps as well, standing in a
semi-circle, their heads bowed.

There was a long silence and it was William Mayhew who
spoke out at last. 'Where is this Dead Man's Field, then?
Seems someone's been buried there before?'

George shook his head. 'Not in my time. It's always been
called that far as I know.'

Fred Turtill nodded. 'Even in my grandfather's day. Since
time before time, I reckon. It's a good place to put the poor
lad. Peaceful. No one's ever interfered with that ground.
People don't go there. Not from the village or the farm.'

'But what about justice?' Robert said suddenly. 'Isn't anyone going to see Dan gets justice?'

'Oh, yes.' Sam broke the silence that followed. His voice was heavy with anger. 'We'll see whoever did this gets his deserts. Or hers.'

In the quiet of the afternoon the barn drew the heavy shadows into itself. They put all the farm horses out in the orchard and chased the hens away then they walked two by two down to the field with spades over their shoulders.

In the afternoon Molly came to see her sister and stayed with her, crying. As the sun set Betsy and Jessie Turtill folded Susan's hands around her dead child and closed her eyes for the last time. For her there would be the last journey in the wagon behind the Suffolks, her baby with her in the coffin and a service in the village church. It was better that way than laying the child in unconsecrated earth.

Betsy elected to take the first turn to watch with the bodies. The women had gone round the cottage opening all the windows to allow poor Susan's soul to go on its way, then she waited until Jessie had gone, taking Molly with her back to the farmhouse, before she turned to the bedside cabinet, the one her husband had made with his own hands as a wedding gift for the couple all those years ago. She pulled open the door and ducked down to feel inside.

Susan had told her what to do if anything happened to her. Right at the back, wrapped in an old woollen scarf was the small rounded lump of metal which looked uncommonly like a woman's body with swollen stomach and bulging breasts and buttocks. The goddess Frige, Mother Bartle had told them, a fertility charm made long years ago in their own forge and hidden near the well so every generation of women who had need of it could be told where to find it. They hadn't asked her how she knew or why she had taken custody of the thing, but she had given it to Susan, and Susan with a

313

superstitious shiver had put it in her feather bed and within a few months she was with child after so many years of trying.

Betsy looked down at the figure in her hands with intense dislike. Susan had been so happy. But in the end it had killed her. She wrapped it more closely in the scarf, careful not to touch the metal with her hands, and carried it outside. The yard was quiet, the men all gone down to the field. This was women's magic. She carried it across the garden and down the side of the forge and groped amongst the stones near the well head. The cavity was there, just as she had been told it would be, near the hedge. She tucked the figure in and filled up the space with stones, finishing it off with some earth, then she rubbed her hands together with a shudder. She contemplated dipping the bucket so she could wash them more thoroughly, but then she thought of poor Susan lying all alone in her bedroom and she turned back towards the cottage.

Mother Bartle had told them she had promised the figurine to Lady Emily in her turn and asked the women to find it. Betsy had felt the old woman's eyes on her and was sure that she had blushed, but she had given her word to Susan. Emily Crosby would never have it. The woman would die barren, she would make sure of that. She gave a grim smile. It was time to go inside and light the candles.

Zoë knocked on the door again and with a sigh moved around to the kitchen window to peer in. She could see signs of breakfast having been eaten – two bowls on the worktop, two mugs on the draining board, the breadboard full of crumbs and a roll of kitchen foil lying on the table. He had made sandwiches and gone out with someone else. She was completely unprepared for the wave of primitive jealousy which swept through her at the thought, and for a moment had to support herself against the wall, stunned by the fact that she was shaking all over. She glanced back at The Old Barn. There were still no signs of life, but if someone had woken up they could make themselves fresh coffee. She had no desire to see any of them at the moment, not after the previous night's horror.

She let herself out of the garden and followed the path down towards the landing stage. From halfway through the wood she could see down towards the anchorage. *Curlew* wasn't there. He had gone sailing.

Depressed, she went on down the path. Leo's little dinghy was bobby merrily out in the fairway, attached to his buoy. Their own was upside down on the beach where Ken had left it. Thoughtfully she sat down on the edge of the landing stage in her favourite place, legs dangling over the water. The tide was dropping slowly, leaving wet iridescent weed clinging to the wooden piles. She could see a heron standing in the water on the far side of the river, studying the reflections around him.

Leo had taken Jade. The thought flashed through her mind with sudden certainty. The child had been pestering him to go sailing for ages and she was in the blackmail business; Leo probably realised they had visitors and had decided it was a good time to take Jade out when she was preoccupied and couldn't go with him. It made her feel better to have worked it out, but she still missed him with a physical ache which astonished her. He wouldn't have guessed how much she needed to talk to him, to be with him, or, she realised suddenly, how much she needed to talk about what had happened the night before; the hanged man.

The laughing call of a gull close overhead jerked her out of her thoughts and she realised she had been sitting there a long time. It was cold this close to the water, even in the bright sunlight, and the wind had strengthened. She climbed to her feet, aware that nearby she could hear the drone of an engine, and she looked up through the wood, surprised. Slowly she retraced her steps up the path, and at the top she took the left-hand fork up the track towards the fields. Her gull had joined a cloud of noisy birds which were following a tractor as it made its cumbersome way down the field, the plough behind it turning the stubble over in huge shining swathes of mud.

Zoë smiled. Rosemary would be furious, and she couldn't help feeling a little pleased that Bill Turtill had outmanoeuvred the woman. The great walk was planned for the next day. By then the whole field would be impassable. Bill had spotted her and she saw him raise a hand. She waved back and retraced her steps down through the wood to the path which led up to their own grounds.

When she reached home the others were seated round the table in the kitchen. 'John and I thought we'd go sailing this morning,' Ken greeted her. 'Can you girls amuse yourselves for the day?'

'I think we can do that,' Zoë said coldly. Did he realise how patronising he sounded? She glanced at Amanda and grinned at her. 'The little women will find something to do, I'm sure,' she said. She fluttered her eyelashes in what was supposed to be demure acquiescence.

'So, are you going to introduce me to your lover?' Amanda asked as soon as the door had closed on the men with their load of sailing gear and food.

Zoë shook her head. 'Sadly he's gone sailing too. I went down to the mooring and the *Curlew* wasn't there.'

Amanda screwed up her nose. 'Pity. Never mind, there is something I want to tell you. I came down last night after you were all in bed. I was a bit puzzled as to why I hadn't felt anything. You know. Your ghosts.' She slid off the stool she was sitting on and led the way through to the great room. 'You have a window in the floor there, in the corner. A window into the past.'

316

Zoë, following her reluctantly, gave a wan smile. 'I've begun thinking of it like that too.'

'Can we do Ouija? I've brought the letters with me.'

Zoë looked at her, dismayed. 'I don't know. I'm not sure I want to. Up to now the noises and things have been friendly, reassuring even. But yesterday it was horrible.'

'Better to know what the story is.'

'Is it? Are you sure?'

'Of course. I know what to do if anything happens.'

Zoë threw herself down on the sofa near the woodburner. 'What do you mean, if anything happens?'

'If we have a visitor.'

'Oh God, Amanda. No. I don't think so. I really don't.'

'Come on, you used to be up for it when we did it on the boat.'

'There weren't any ghosts on your boat, Amanda. This is very different. We were messing around then. None of it was real.'

'What do you mean, none of it was real?' For a moment Amanda looked really angry.

'Well.' Zoë bit her lip. 'Sorry. Of course it was. It's just that that was fun and seemed harmless at the time, and now I've experienced stuff which feels so different. It's like opening a window – a trapdoor – and peering through into the past when something happened which was so awful that its echo has remained here, attached to the house we live in, through centuries. Last night I felt –' She paused, aware of Amanda's eyes fixed on her face.

'You felt what?' Amanda asked.

'I felt that it would take a very small movement, a very small adjustment – I don't know what the right word is – to make it all spill out into our lives. And I am afraid that using the Ouija board might just be the trigger he is waiting for.'

'He?'

'The dead man.'

Amanda was silent for a few seconds. She wrinkled her nose. 'I know what to do if he appears. I've read books on this. We just talk to him and ask him what it is he wants us to know and we ask him to go, to move on. To return to the light.'

'And it's that easy?'

'It sounds easy.'

'So you've never actually tried it?'

Amanda shook her head. She went to stand near the viewing panel in the floor. 'If he wants the truth to be known it must be something awful. Did he hang himself or was he murdered? He wants to tell us his story.'

'Can you sense that?'

Amanda said nothing for a long time. 'No,' she whispered at last. 'I can't sense anything, that's why I want to use the Ouija. I'll tell you something else odd, though.' She walked away from the corner and went towards the window. 'When I was down here last night I was looking out at the river in the moonlight and I saw a great ship coming up in full sail. It looked –'

'Like a Viking ship,' Zoë finished the sentence for her. She stood up and joined Amanda by the window. 'So, you have seen a ghost after all.'

'Are the two things connected, do you think?' Amanda asked at last when Zoë had finished telling her the story.

'Who knows? The ship has been seen on and off for centuries, as far as I can gather.'

'And seeing it is a warning?'

'No one seems to know that either.' Zoë looked down across the river. 'It worries me, though, with the chaps sailing down there.'

'Especially your chap,' Amanda said softly.

Zoë smiled. 'All of them.'

'Come on, Zoë, let's see what's going on.' Amanda headed for the stairs. 'Fetch a tumbler and I will get my cards.'

She laid them on the coffee table in a circle, the letters A to Z and a *Yes* and a *No*, with the upturned tumbler in the middle. Zoë looked at the layout unhappily. 'I'm still not sure this is a good idea.'

'It's a perfect idea. We will find out what's going on. Come over here and put your finger on the glass and we'll ask.

'We know there are people here who want to talk to us,' she said once Zoë had joined her at the table. 'And if we can we want to help. Please, tell us if you would like us to continue.'

She waited, her gaze on the tumbler, her finger lightly placed on top next to Zoë's. Nothing happened.

'It's not going to work,' Zoë said after a full minute had passed.

'Sssh! Wait.' Amanda shook her head. 'Are you there?' she asked again. 'We can sense you are restless and unhappy. It may be that we can help.'

Out in the fields Bill Turtill began to turn the tractor as he reached the copse, careful to avoid catching the plough in the tangled wire around it. He was wearing ear protectors and didn't realise he had snagged a blade round something heavy till he felt the tractor lurch. He turned round with a frown to look at the deep parallel furrows neatly radiating back behind him and then reached forward to cut the engine. In seconds he was down from the high seat in the cab and striding back to see what had happened.

14

Eric crept through the darkness towards his own cottage, holding his breath. He had returned the sword to its hiding place in the river bank. There was nowhere else to go now but home. The village slept in the moonlight and he could see no signs of life. One of his neighbour's dogs started up and barked as he crept past and he stopped gesturing to it to keep quiet. It ran to him, tail wagging, then returned to its bed under the eaves of the house and settled again to its watch.

The door of his cottage was closed. There was no light inside, but by now Edith would be in bed. He pushed open the door and listened. There was a total silence indoors which frightened him. He glanced at the hearth and saw that the fire was out. 'Edith?' he called anxiously. 'Edith, are you there?'

There was no reply. The cottage was empty after all. Turning away from the doorway he glanced round at the other cottages. His friend and neighbour, Cerdic the wheelwright, was awake. He could see the light of his fire through the cracks in his door. He could trust him not to betray him so he knocked and begged a firebrand. 'Where is Edith?' he asked.

Gudrun peered past her husband. She was wrapped in a shawl against the night air. 'I've not seen her since the night Lord Egbert died,' she said. 'We thought she had gone away with you.'

He retraced his steps to his cottage with the light in his hand and this time he went in.

He paused just inside the doorway, and only now could he smell the violence and the blood. His heart thudding with apprehension in the darkness, he piled kindling in the hearth from the basket and thrust in the glowing brand. As the flames took and the light spread round the cottage he turned and surveyed the scene.

Edith was lying on the bed, so still, so slender he had not at first seen her form amongst the rumpled bedclothes. He could see at once she was dead. Her tunic had been torn down the front, and the skirt was pushed up above her hips. He could see the bruises on her wrists where she had struggled, but the blow that killed her was on her forehead, a great bloody dent which must have crushed her skull. Lying on the pillow next to her was the weapon the man had used. It was the figurine of the pregnant goddess, snatched from the basket on the hearth. He could see the blood on it, with strands of Edith's beautiful hair entangled with it. Eric picked it up and stared at it in the flickering light of the flames, then he turned and hurled it out of the door with a wild oath. The amulet which was supposed to confer life had taken it cruelly and obscenely. The work of his own hands had killed the most precious thing in his life and, with her, her unborn child.

With tears scalding his eyes he turned and ran blindly from the house, aware of Gudrun and her husband standing in the doorway of their own cottage, watching. He ignored them, hurtling down towards the river. Throwing himself down on his knees he fumbled amongst the moss and leaves to find the sword and, drawing it out, he gazed at it for a long moment. He was tempted to throw it into the cold clean water, but that would serve no purpose.

Gudrun's screams as she went in and found Edith's body had brought other neighbours to the cottage. The cry had been taken up and passed from house to house until the whole village was gathered there in horror. Eric strode through them without looking left or right, the sword in his hand, and took the path up to the mead hall.

Pushing open the great doors he marched in and looked round. 'Hrotgar?' He did not know who had killed his wife but he had a very good idea. It mattered not. Hrotgar was the go-between, the man who had forced him to forge the iron, to carve the runes, to mutter the charms over the gleaming blade. He strode through the hall towards the thegn's house and pushed back the door. Lady Hilda wasn't there. Two strangers stood beside the body which was now dressed in chain armour, the head covered by Egbert's ornate helmet and ready for burial. Eric stared round. 'Where is Hrotgar?'

'I am here.' The man appeared quietly behind him. He looked pale but defiant as he saw the sword and he smiled coldly. 'I am glad you saw fit to bring it back. We are ready for the burial now. It must be returned to Lord Egbert.'

Eric stared at him unmoving for a moment, then he spoke in a voice which was barely more than a whisper. 'Did you kill my wife?' He fixed the other man with a gaze which didn't waver and saw the uncertainty and fear flash through Hrotgar's eyes. 'You lusted after her, don't deny it, the whole village knew it. While I was away you went to my house, and you raped my pregnant wife and then you killed her.' He paused.

Hrotgar seemed incapable of speech.

'I have come to give this sword to the man who commissioned it as is its due, but first, I will blood it as tradition demands.' He raised the sword, holding it with both hands before him, and before the man could move, thrust it straight into Hrotgar's chest. The two men sitting on either side of the body leaped to their feet but they were far too late. Hrotgar clutched at the sword with a horrible gurgling noise in his throat, collapsed onto his knees and then sprawled at Eric's feet.

Zoë and Amanda stared down at the broken tumbler lying on the floorboards, then looked at each other.

'I'll get the dustpan.' Zoë stood up.

'No, wait.' Amanda seized her wrist. 'He's pretty angry. Let's try again while he's here.'

Zoë stared round. 'Nobody's here, Amanda. We were pushing the glass too hard.'

Amanda shook her head. 'I was hardly touching it. And neither were you. One can tell when people are cheating, and we had no reason to cheat. Get another glass. Please. Let's try. You do want to know who this poor guy was, don't you?'

With a sigh Zoë went to fetch the dustpan and swept up the pieces of glass, then she collected another tumbler and set it upside down in the middle of the circle of letters. She resumed her seat. 'Go on,' she said. 'You ask, you're the psychic one.' She put her finger on the glass.

Amanda was about to contradict, to point out that it was Zoë who saw the ghosts, but changing her mind she leaned forward instead and put her finger lightly next to Zoë's. 'We want to help. If there is something you want us to know, please tell us.'

The glass began to move. Both women watched it carefully.

'Will you tell us your name?' Amanda asked.

The glass began to circle the letters in a strangely forceful way. 'I'm not doing anything,' Zoë whispered.

'Nor am I.' The glass slid round at increasing speed then stopped suddenly.

'D,' Amanda whispered.

The glass moved on. 'A.' Zoë was breathless now. Her hand was shaking.

'N,' Amanda said after a moment.

The glass became still. 'Dan? Your name is Dan?'

Nothing happened.

'How can we help you, Dan?' She glanced at Zoë. 'Did Zoë see you? Did you hang yourself, Dan?'

The glass was suddenly reanimated. It shot across the table and stopped opposite the card which said, *No*.

'Did someone murder you, Dan?' Finally Zoë plucked up the courage to ask the question. 'Yes,' she murmured as the glass slid jerkily sideways. 'Do you want us to know who killed you?'

The glass was off again.

E. M. I. L.Y.

Zoë and Amanda looked at each other. 'You were murdered by someone called Emily?' Amanda asked, puzzled.

'Yes.' The glass almost fell off the table again.

They both looked up startled as on the far side of the room the door from the kitchen opened.

'What in the world are you doing?' Rosemary appeared. In her hand there was a pot of azaleas.

Zoë groaned inwardly. 'Rosemary, I'm sorry, we didn't hear you knock.'

It sounded rude, but she was, she realised a bit embarrassed at being caught at such a stupid pastime. Rosemary approached the table. 'Ouija board. I always thought that was terribly dangerous. Isn't it supposed to ask in the devil? I'm surprised you would do something like that here.' She set down the plant. 'I just came over to say thank you for last night. It was such fun.' Her eyes hadn't left the table. 'Can I be very rude and ask if I can join in?'

Amanda glanced up at Zoë, a query in her gaze. Zoë laughed uncomfortably. 'I don't see why not. The more the merrier.'

Rosemary sat down at the end of the table. 'Is there anyone there?' she asked. She was addressing Amanda.

Amanda nodded. 'He's called Dan, and he was murdered, so he says, by a woman called Emily.'

Rosemary's eyes rounded. 'When did he live?'

'We haven't asked.'

'You need some numbers.' Rosemary jumped up again. 'Have you a piece of paper, Zoë, I'll make some.'

With numbers one to ten included in the circle they began again.

'Can you tell us the date you died, Dan,' Amanda asked.

One. Eight. The two numbers came swiftly, then the glass was still again.

'Eighteen,' Amanda said. 'Eighteen what?'

There was no answer.

'Did you live here, Dan?' she asked at last.

Again, no answer.

'He's gone.' Zoë leaned back and put her hands in her lap. 'I reckon he's tired. It probably takes quite an effort to do that, if it was real. Was it real, do you think?'

The two other women sat back as well. 'It felt it,' Amanda said at last. 'How intriguing. How are we going to find out who they were?'

'We can ask again another time.' Rosemary stood up. 'I'm sorry to intrude. I have to go. I just came over to say thank you. Tomorrow I have a large group of friends coming over. We are going to walk the footpath. I don't suppose either of you would like to join us?'

Zoë shook her head. 'I'm sorry, no,' she said firmly.

'You should, you know. People have to stand up for their rights.' Rosemary headed for the door.

The other two watched her leave.

'Weird woman,' Amanda said as soon as they had watched her cross the grass towards her house.

'Obsessive and irrational,' Zoë said with a sigh. She was gazing out of the window now, down towards the river. 'It's got very misty down there,' she said. 'I hope the chaps are all right.'

'They can't get lost. It's a river!'

Zoë shook her head. 'It's not the river I'm worried about.' She stood up. 'I'm going to make some coffee.'

Amanda followed her into the kitchen. She had begun to empty the dishwasher while Zoë made the coffee when there was a loud crash from next door. Both women stopped what they were doing and looked towards the doorway. The second tumbler had fallen to the floorboards and smashed. Scattered amongst the slivers of glass were the letters and numbers which they had left lying in a circle on the table and three rusty horseshoe nails.

No one stopped him. He turned and fled from the lord's chamber and through the hall, past the benches and tables, past the baskets of logs being brought in for the next evening's feast, past a group of women huddled together whispering by the embers of the fire. He wrenched open the door and ran out into the night. A dog barked and at last someone challenged him out of the darkness but he was already off the path and out of sight amongst the houses on the side of the hill. He headed for the river, vaulting fences, scattering pigs and sheep and horses as he ran. No one prevented him. By the time the alarm had been raised he would be far away. There was nothing to keep him now. He was without a lord, without allegiance, without the woman he loved. He was passing the granary stores now and he ducked inside out of sight as he saw a group of men walking up through the village towards him. These men were his friends. Or were they? Had they known what Hrotgar planned? Everyone had known that the reeve lusted after the smith's wife. But no one surely had known that he would rape and kill her.

He felt a great sob lodged in his chest and he screwed up his eyes, trying to swallow it as he caught his breath, keeping silence until the men had passed. He heard the sober sounds of their conversation but he couldn't make out the words. He waited in the dark, breathing in the warm floury smell of the sacks stacked around him until the conversation had died away and there was silence. He looked up at the beams of the roof above his head. It was dark and safe in here beneath the snug thatch of sedge, but he couldn't stay, however tempted he was to crawl in among the sacks. Soon someone would raise the hue and cry, and the dogs would find him even if the men didn't.

He looked out, took a deep breath and ran, heading for the woods beyond the village and, beyond them, the wild heathland.

Even when he was safe he lingered. He couldn't bear to go before he saw what happened to the sword. Circling round, he crept back along the river and then he climbed into one of the ancient oaks on the edge of the field where the burial was to take place, and waited as the sun climbed in the sky. The old tumulus had been opened and a grave dug deep in its centre. He could see the cold shadows filling the deep declivity, saw how large it was, how neatly made ready. The earth which would fill it again had been laid carefully on some matting some distance away and he saw the spades waiting to fill it in standing like sentinels impaled in the soil.

It was full light before he saw them carry the Lord Egbert down from the village on his bier, and with him a line of men, carrying baskets filled with the selection of items chosen to make his journey to the other world more comfortable. There was food and wine, there were boxes of finery, there were weapons, but nowhere could he see the sword. The body was laid in the grave and only then did Eric see, as they pulled back the great bearskin that covered him, that the sword was strapped to his waist. He bit his lip as he saw it there, powerful and heavy, lying against the body of a weak and wasted man. He clutched at the trunk of the tree, feeling his nails split and tear in the bark. They were bringing something else now, something long and heavy on another stretcher carried by four men. He caught his breath. It was the body of Hrotgar. They laid him at his lord's feet, a servant to accompany him to the Otherworld.

Eric could hardly breathe. His eyes were full of tears. So, the village was united now. They did honour to their lord, but also to this man who had murdered Edith, and one amongst them had gone further in their sacrilege and murdered Father Wulfric. It was an outrage. The whole village was cursed by their actions. They sanctioned a pagan burial and they sanctioned a murderer's passage on to the Otherworld. His eyes wandered over the crowd who were standing round watching in silence. Hrotgar's wife was there in the front. She was sobbing quietly, holding the hands of his two small children, the woman who had been Edith's friend, who had sympathised over her childlessness, who had been her confidante. He pressed his forehead against the tree's rough branches and suppressed a sob.

He saw the sorcerer, Anlaf, now, no longer a shadowy dweller of the woods but a pagan priest, dressed in all his finery. With Father Wulfric gone, this man no longer had a rival. If there were Christians present they were saying nothing, watching in silence. He could hear snatches of the incantation the man was chanting.

Closing his eyes, he rested his head against the trunk of the tree and waited.

Much later he climbed down from the tree and walked over to the grave. He stood looking at the burial mound in the moonlight without moving. All the mourners had gone and he could hear the sounds of music now and then, carried on the wind from the hall up above on the hill. The whole village was there, seeing Lord Egbert off in style.

He wondered what was going to happen to Edith. Was she still lying in the cottage or had her family taken her body to the church? But then with Father Wulfric dead who would say the mass for her soul? He shivered. He would never know. There would be no return for him. He was a marked man. Whatever happened now it would not matter to him. He had to leave and be long gone by morning.

Wisps of mist were curling round the boat now, licking at the mast, beginning to obscure the burgee at the top. Leo tightened the mainsheet and put the tiller up a fraction, trying to get the last inch of speed from the old girl. Jade had fallen silent. Every now and then she glanced over her shoulder and he could see the apprehension in her face. 'There's nothing out there, is there?' she said at last. 'I don't want no ghost ships following us.'

'I can't see any ghost ships.' He grinned. 'Surely the intrepid Jade Watts isn't scared?'

'No. Course not.' She was sitting on the far side of the cockpit from him, clutching the jib sheet.

'A bit tighter, Jade. It will give us that inch of speed. I want us back at that mooring while we can still see it. If we end up by the Tide Mill we'll be in trouble and they'll try and charge us a parking fee.' He joked.

'There's no other boats out here.'

'That's good, surely.'

'I mean real ones. Where are they?'

'More sensible than us. We should have come back a smidgeon earlier.'

'What's a smidgeon?'

'Something a bit smaller than you.'

She looked back at him sternly. 'You're making fun.'

'Yup.'

She pulled the sheet a bit tighter and the boat slowed.

'Too much. As you were.' He was staring ahead, trying to make out any landmarks. 'I should be able to see the *Lady Grace*. She's not here.'

'So we're back?'

'I reckon. Can you make out the landing stage? When it's sunny we can see The Old Barn and The Old Forge from here.' He was heading in slowly towards the bank. 'Drop the rope, Jade, and pick up the boathook there. See if you can hook it through the top of the buoy as we come alongside. Don't worry if you can't, and don't fall overboard.'

He came up into wind and let the boat drift gently towards its berth.

'Got it!' It was a crow of triumph.

'Well done.' He let out a sigh of relief. In seconds he had the boat secure and the mainsail down. 'Just sit still, love, will you? I don't want to lose you at the last minute and I do want to do this as quickly as possible.' They still had to negotiate the last few yards in the dinghy and he could feel a cold prickle at the back of his neck which he disliked intensely. It was a feeling he had learned not to ignore. He reached for the sail ties. That would be enough. He could come out and neaten up and put the sail covers on tomorrow when the sun came out. For now it was enough to bring her to a standstill.

Out in the river he heard a splash.

'What was that?' Jade stared round, her eyes huge.

'Fish, I expect. Come on. Down into the dinghy with you.'

'I don't want to. I'm scared.'

He stared out into the fog. He could see nothing now but a few feet of still water round the boat. What wind there had been had dropped.

'I'm not having a scaredy-cat on my crew,' he said briskly.

'Over you go. Carefully. And sit in the stern.' He could hear the squeak of oars, the flap of canvas, the sounds of a large sailing ship coming to a halt nearby. 'Now, Jade!'

She almost fell into the bottom of the small boat and scrabbled on her hands and knees to the back, clutching the sides, which were wet and cold and slippery from the fog. The small boat rocked wildly as Leo climbed down after her and grabbed for the oars, slipping them into the rowlocks, heaving the boat round with one strong pull before rowing hard for the landing stage. He rowed straight on past it, aiming for the bank until the boat grounded, shipped the oars and leaped over the side, pulling the boat, with Jade still in it, up onto the mud and shingle beach. His jeans were wet to the thigh. 'Out.'

She didn't need asking twice. Scrambling over the side she caught his hand and the two of them raced for the trees. He hadn't even paused to tie up the boat.

Behind them the river settled into silence. Little wavelets rippled up the beach and somewhere nearby a lonely oyster-catcher whistled as it plodded up the tideline probing its beak into the mud.

Leo took her to the door of The Summer Barn but she wouldn't let him go any further. 'I'm OK now. Sorry I was such a wuss!'

'We were both wusses,' he said with a relieved smile. 'Let me see you go inside and lock the door behind you. When is Jackson going to be back?'

'Dunno. I'll have had a hot bath by then and clean clothes.' They both looked down at their respective wet and muddy jeans.

'I hope you won't catch a chill,' he added with a grin.

'If I do, I'll sue.' She bent to search under the mat for the key and produced it with a flourish. 'Simple when you know where to look,' she said. A moment later she had disappeared inside and slammed the door in his face.

He walked back across the grass. Already he could barely see as far as his own house. The fog was a real sea fret, heavy with the green cold scents of the deep northern oceans. He shuddered. They had only just got back in time.

Half an hour later he was showered and in dry clothes, and feeling thoroughly ashamed of himself. The boat they had heard must have been the *Lady Grace* coming back to her moorings. He glanced out of the window up towards The Old Barn and wondered if he ought to go over and make sure things were all right; then he decided against it. The Lloyds had visitors and the last thing they would want would be the neighbour from hell knocking on the door. Better go into his studio and do some work. He gave one last glance out towards the river. The fog was so thick now he couldn't even see the trees on the far side of his garden.

U

They were all uneasy, glancing round, acutely aware of the strange atmosphere. An uncanny silence hung over the copse. The mound within it was darkly brooding. There was no wind and the evening was totally silent, holding its breath. Down on the river the tide crept up slowly without a ripple.

It was after sunset when the five men walked slowly across the field, spades on their shoulders, a heavy silence hanging over them. Fred Turtill led the way across the stubble and stopped at last as they reached the edge of the copse. Night was approaching and a slight mist was beginning to form over the river. 'Where shall we put him, lads?' He spoke quietly as though afraid of being overheard. Nearby a crow called loudly into the silence, and he glanced across the field in time to see the shadowy shape of the great black bird vanish into the trees.

They made their way tentatively into the deeper shadow of the copse and stopped where the nettles and brambles tangled into a natural barrier around the foot of the mound.

'I don't like this,' George murmured. 'It's not right.'

'No. It's not. So, do you want to lose your jobs?' Fred replied. 'He would fit us up as soon as look at us and we all know it. Our word against that of the local JP?'

They nodded in resignation.

'So, where are we going to put Dan?' George pushed his way into the undergrowth and levered it back with his spade. 'It will be the devil's own job trying to dig a grave in here.'

'We could put him in the mound,' William Mayhew said quietly. 'Whoever is buried there won't mind sharing after all this time.'

The men all turned to look at the tumulus and George shivered. 'The Dead Man.'

'When did he go in, do you reckon?'

'Long enough ago not to worry about sharing his bed.'

'And his ghost?' Again the shiver. 'You reckon that won't mind?'

The men fell silent.

'It's the only way.' Fred tried to insert his spade into the soil. 'This is like iron down here, but here,' he did the same thing on the slope of the mound and the spade went in with relative ease, 'this is softer.'

'Here it is then,' Sam spoke up suddenly. 'Let's get it done and over with.' He thrust his spade into the ground next to Fred's. 'It will be a softer resting place for poor Dan, but I doubt he'll lie easy all the same.'

They had been digging for some time when one of the spades struck metal. They stopped and peered down into the deepening hole. Two of the men had brought lanterns and the flickering shadows ran crazily up the trees and across the ground as they worked. George picked up one and held it down into the cavity. 'There's a bowl down here, and a jug,' he whispered. 'And other stuff.'

'No bones, thank the Lord!' Sam murmured. He knelt down and reached in. 'It's treasure, that's what it is.' He held up the bowl. It was dented and blackened. He scratched it with his thumbnail. 'Silver.'

'And look at this.' Fred squatted down and reached over. He drew out a long, rusted and corroded blade. 'It's a sword.' The men stared at it in awe.

'Put it back!' Robert straightened. 'Put it back. Don't you see. This was buried with a man to see him into the next world. We've hit the dead man's grave. God save us all, we've gone in and disturbed the grave itself.'

They stared in silence for a moment. Fred was still holding the corroded hilt. In the lantern light they could all see the designs carved on it, almost obscured beneath the lumps of corrosion. He rose, holding it in both hands, then jumped lightly down into the grave. 'I'll put it back. I'll put it all back, and I'll rebury the sword here. I reckon Dan has as much right as any to lie here too – a man who worked with iron, he would have appreciated the skill that went into making this.'

The others nodded. They carefully put all the items back in the soil and filled it in, then they set to to finish the grave before retracing their steps towards the barn.

By the light of the lanterns they laid Dan's body on a door and carried him slowly back across the field as a huge red moon rose out of the trees, and laid him, reverently wrapped in the two horse blankets, in the grave. Fred Turtill stood forward and said the Lord's Prayer, and George laid Dan's hammer and fire tongs and rasp beside him. They stood for many minutes, not moving, then at last with heavy hearts they began to throw the soil in over him. On the top of the grave Sam stood the little blue jug which Susan had loved so much, filled with Michaelmas daisies from her garden. 'I reckon Susan would have wanted that,' he murmured, almost embarrassed by the gesture, but the other men merely nodded their approval. Above them the moon was climbing out of the mist, turning from red to silver against the indigo sky.

Out in the river the longship drifted to a standstill and unseen hands lowered the sail bit by bit towards the deck. William Mayhew saw it first. Dropping his spade, he stood back from the grave and stared down at the water, then silently he pointed. The others followed the direction of his finger, also staring.

'It's a sign,' Fred said at last. They stood shoulder to shoulder, watching. The ship was hazy, an insubstantial shape against the reflections and the moon shadows in the water.

'There's no one on her,' Robert whispered.

They were all river men, born and bred within sight and smell of the tidal mud and weed. They had all heard the legend of the ship. 'Dan drew a picture of her not so long ago,' George whispered. 'Do you reckon it's come for him?'

'Do you think we should weigh him down with something?' Robert said. 'I don't figure the poor chap would want to go with them.'

They laid their spades over the grave; iron to bring protection, oak handles to hold him close, and each man muttered a prayer, then quickly and quietly, without a backward glance at the river, they melted away into the night leaving the copse in Dead Man's Field to its silence.

Bill Turtill pulled the tangle of spades out from under the plough and looked at them in puzzlement. They were old, pitted and rusty, the handles mostly rotted away. What were they doing there on the edge of the copse? He stopped to examine the shares of his plough and then walked on up the side of the wire. He had caught one of the spades with the end share and the others had pulled free with it. Shaking his head he threw the whole rusty mess back over the wire and went up to haul himself back into the tractor cab. Behind him the freshly turned sods gleamed in the sunshine and he smiled quietly. He would like to see anyone try and walk over that lot.

He restarted the engine, watching the flock of gulls rise and wheel behind him and engaged gear. Part of him had expected the Formby woman to have arrived by now, waving her arms around and spitting fury about her footpath. He was pleased Zoë Lloyd hadn't given him away. It had given him a fright seeing her standing there in the shadow of the hedge, watching him, but she had waved in a friendly fashion and obviously she had said nothing. Mentally he awarded her a gold star for neighbourliness. And talking of neighbours, he must remember to tell Penny to ring Lesley Inworth and spread the word around that tomorrow they could do with some help up here. The more people there were to see off Rosemary and her walkers the better. In ten minutes he had drawn away up the hill out of sight of the copse and had settled again to concentrating on keeping his furrows straight. He did not give the ancient spades or the copse where he had thrown them another thought.

Behind him the cloud of gulls scattered across the field.

♆

Lady Emily was sitting by the window staring out at the garden. It seemed like only a short time earlier that she had been watching the gardeners working, bringing in the bedding plants before the winter set in. Now the mist had closed in and night was near. A huge orange moon was floating over the river. She shivered. The house was very quiet. She had rung the bell for Molly but no one had come. The fire had burned low and the room was growing cold. She wanted the curtains closed on the night. She stood up and walked over to the fireplace, pulling the bell again, hearing it jangle faintly in the depths of the house. Surely someone could hear it. Going over to the door she pulled it open and looked out. The hall was dark. No one had lit the lamps. The other rooms appeared to be empty. She didn't know where Henry was.

'Mrs Field? Beaton?' she called. There must be servants around. There were always servants around, ready to do her bidding. She took a step out into the hall, then she changed her mind. It was dark and it was cold out there. Better to stay in the drawing room. She went back to the bell and rang it again, hard.

It was full dark when Henry came in, carrying a candle. He stood in the doorway holding it up high and looked in. She was sitting huddled on a chair, a silk shawl wrapped round her shoulders. 'Where have you been?' she asked in relief. She stood up. 'Where are the servants? I have rung and rung the bell. I shall send Molly away. I shall send them all away!' She fell silent, seeing his face by the light of the candle. It was very grim.

'Molly will not be waiting on you tonight,' he said. His voice was cold. 'She is staying down at the farmhouse with the Turtills. Her sister, Susan Smith, died this afternoon, in childbirth. I understand most of the servants are down at the farm, paying their respects. I have told Beaton we will not require them tonight.' He took the candle out of its candlestick and held it down to the fire. After a moment the kindling caught and small flames began to lick at the logs which had been laid ready early that morning. 'Molly will be returning to her parents' farm after the funeral.'

She was staring at him in silence. 'Susan died,' she said at last, her voice husky, repeating the words as though unable to believe them. 'And the baby?'

'Dead.'

'And –' It was a whisper. Her voice faded and she said nothing more. Her husband ignored her. He bent to pile on more logs and then walked over to pull the curtains across. 'Are you capable of finding us food in the kitchen?' he asked as he came back to the fire.

She shook her head. 'Are all the servants gone?'

'All.' He set his lips in a tight line. 'It is no less than I would expect. Susan was well liked by most people. Her death is a tragedy.'

'Yes.' Again it was a whisper.

'You will represent us at the funeral.'

'No!' She turned on him. 'No, you can't make me go to that.'

'It is the least you can do, Emily.' He glared at her so coldly and with such hatred that for the first time she realised with absolute certainty that he knew. He knew her story of rape was a lie. She fell back into one of the chairs by the fire, drawing her shawl tightly around her shoulders and closed her eyes. Tears had always won him over in the past; this time, it dawned on her suddenly, her tears were real and this time they would have no effect.

15

They had had a wonderful day's sailing, heading out of the mouth of the river and along the coast for a while before turning back; Ken had timed it meticulously this time and they crossed the bar without incident as the light began to fade in the sky. He had become aware of the great bank of sea mist behind them between one moment and the next. Glancing back as he felt the breath of ice-cold wind on his cheek, he had felt his eyes widen in horror.

John was on the foredeck coiling down the ends of the halyards, neatening everything up. He hadn't noticed.

'John,' Ken called. His companion showed no sign of hearing him and he realised he was whispering. 'John,' he called again, louder this time. John looked up. 'Get back here, fast.'

Now John had seen it too. He saw the look of incredulity on his friend's face, before he edged down the side deck and jumped down into the cockpit next to him. 'Where did that come from! Bloody hell, that was fast. Shit!'

'Shit indeed.' Ken felt the cold mist on his face now, tendrils weaving round them in the cockpit. He could smell the ice and the deep seas of the north. He was frantically scrabbling with the key to the engine. He turned it. The engine struggled to turn over again and again but refused to catch.

'Take it easy. Use the pre-heat button. Try again,' John murmured. He was staring at the bank of fog in astonishment. 'Can we outrun it even with the engine?' He reached into the cabin for his windcheater and dragged it on over his head, shivering.

'Almost no chance.' Ken grimaced. The battery was failing. He gave up with an exclamation of disgust and went back to the tiller. 'They come from nowhere, these sea mists, and move fast, creeping in over the land as well.' He groped for his mobile. He wasn't sure who he was going to call. Zoë. She would know what to do; not about the engine; about the fog. He needed to tell someone what was happening. He put it to his ear. Silence. He checked the screen. No signal.

'Should we anchor till it's gone? We'll be sailing blind otherwise,' John suggested quietly.

Ken could feel a tightness in his chest now and he knew it was panic. It wasn't the fog which scared him, it was the ship which came with it. It was already too late to try and outrun it if it came; the wind was dropping. In seconds it would have gone altogether. They were being carried by the tide and they had already lost steerage. 'I'll head out of the main channel and we'll try and pick up a buoy. There is quite an extensive anchorage along here.' He glanced back apprehensively. The mist was all round them now. He was beginning to lose his sense of direction. He leaned forward to look at the compass mounted on its binnacle near the cabin door and felt his stomach lurch in panic. 'John, take a look at this. What's going on –'

John came to stand beside him. 'Crikey, Moses!' The needle was spinning round in circles.

He saw John look round too and for the first time there

was a flash of fear in his face. 'Shall I go forward and find the anchor?'

Ken shook his head. 'It's in the locker. There's no time.' There was something out there behind them, he was sure of it. But which way was behind them? They seemed to have come to a standstill now. The water was calm as glass and they were enveloped in a strange, muffling silence. He had a feeling the boat was beginning to spin like the compass. And then he heard it, the unmistakable sound of oars, the thunder of a huge sail in a powerful wind and near them on the starboard bow the sudden dark silhouette of a longship. Ken frantically pushed the tiller over hard and at the same moment he felt the deep keel of the *Lady Grace* catch on the bottom. She shook herself loose, floated free again for a few seconds and then she caught fast. They were trapped.

Both men moved instinctively forward, trying to shake her free but she didn't move. 'The tide is rising,' John whispered. 'It won't be long before we float again.'

His voice died away as he saw the longship coming closer. 'It's moving fast,' he whispered. 'Under sail. Where is it finding the wind?' He glanced up at their own burgee, barely visible as the mist wreathed round them, but enough to see it hanging limp at the masthead.

Ken didn't answer. His eyes were riveted to the great ship as it came closer to them. He put his hand to his chest. He was finding it hard to breathe. He could see the details now. The sail with the huge head on it, a fire-breathing dragon; and he could see the lines of shields along the deck, the oars, working in unison, the vast curved prow, slicing through the mist as it held its course up-river. He jumped as he felt John beside him again.

'There are no men,' John whispered, his mouth close to Ken's ear. 'Look, there are no men on board!'

Ken closed his eyes. His head was buzzing strangely. He felt dizzy and sick. He took a deep breath of the cloying heavy mist, choked and clutched at John's arm. It was the last thing he remembered.

Leo woke to the sound of the telephone. He switched on the light and grabbed his watch. It was midnight. When he answered the call it was Zoë.

'I'm sorry it's so late, but Ken and John went sailing this morning. They aren't back yet. We can't raise them on their mobiles. I don't know what to do.'

Leo lay back on his pillow, the receiver in his hand, and groaned inwardly. He shook his head to clear it. He had only been asleep an hour and his brains felt like cotton wool. 'Did they say what their plans were?'

'Not really. We expected them back long before this.'

'Do you want me to call the coastguard?

'I don't know.' Her voice was subdued. 'We could go down and look at the mooring? See if there is any sign?' She sounded desperate.

He gave another inward groan. His bedroom had never seemed so safe and cosy. Reluctantly he hauled himself out of bed and walked over to the window, pulling back the curtains and staring down at the river. The mist seemed to have gone. The moon had moved round and the trees on the point were throwing long shadows over the water.

'I'll go,' he said at last. 'You stay where you are.'

'No.' Her voice sharpened. 'No, Leo. I'll come with you.' The line went dead.

He threw on his clothes and pulled a heavy sweater and jacket over his shirt, then he ran down the stairs. Zoë was waiting outside the back door. He glanced past her as he opened it. 'Your friend?'

'I've persuaded her to stay by the phone. She'll call my mobile if there is any news. They have probably been becalmed somewhere, or stopped at a pub and decided it was sensible to stay put till it got light, but –' She looked up at

342

him pleadingly. 'I've got a bad feeling about this. About the ghost ship.'

He was rooting about on the worktop for a torch. Finding it amongst the litter of painting things and cooking implements and books he switched it on and checked the beam. 'OK. Let's go.'

As he pulled the door closed behind him he threw a glance over towards the barns. He hoped Jade was in bed and asleep. All he needed was to have her see him and Zoë set off into the dark and decide to come and throw a spanner in the works. He left the torch off. There was enough moonlight for them to follow the path down towards the landing stage. The night was cold and sharp, the grass wet with dew and the silence was intense.

Zoë hadn't uttered a word since he had opened the door. At the top of the path down through the wood he stopped and stared down. In the moonlight he could see the *Curlew* clearly, lying quietly to her buoy. The tide was low now and it was obvious that she was the only boat at the anchorage. He said nothing, setting off again. Halfway down he felt Zoë groping for his hand. He grasped her fingers in his own and went on without pausing, almost dragging her over the rough parts of the path where she hesitated in the darkness. Once at the bottom he stopped on the edge of the river. The mud glittered in the moonlight and a breath of wind stroked his face. 'They are obviously not here. Do you want us to go out after them?'

'In the *Curlew*?'

'How else? She doesn't draw more than a couple of feet.'

He heard the quick intake of breath as she struggled with her fear. 'Is there any point?'

'Not really. But it would be an adventure.'

'There isn't enough wind,' she said slowly. 'Is there?'

He laughed softly. 'The wind is off the land; it's with the tide. We could get down to the mouth of the river. We might have to take up a mooring and wait for the tide to turn before we could get back. If we dry out it won't matter. *Curlew* has twin keels. She won't lie over on the mud. Have you got your mobile safe?'

Her hand went to her pocket.

'Is it charged?'

She nodded.

'Then it's up to you. You can come with me, or I can go on my own and you can go home and wait for me to phone you if I find anything.'

'You don't think he's in danger, do you?'

He shook his head. 'This is not the back of beyond. If anything had happened to them you would have been told.'

'Unless it was the ghost ship.'

He was silent for a moment. 'I am not sure what the ghost ship means. It is scary, yes, but has it ever harmed anyone? If people had been abducted we would know about it.' He was not going to mention his encounter with Jade beside him, the terror he had felt, the abject way they had fled. Nor would he be able to explain the state he had left *Curlew* in.

There was barely enough water now to float the dinghy. They stood looking at it as it lay on the beach, the oars still protruding from the rowlocks. 'I took Jade out earlier,' he said at last. 'We came back in a hurry. She was afraid we wouldn't get back before Jackson arrived.'

'You took her out without permission?'

'No, I spoke to him first, but she seems very keen on avoiding him. I don't think she's afraid of him, she just ducks out of trouble where possible.' He saw the fleeting smile on Zoë's face and nodded. 'Wise child, but then I suspect they don't really act as any kind of brake on each other's schemes.' He bent and half-lifted, half-pulled the prow of the little boat round, shipping the oars and pushing it with a grunt towards the water line. 'Are you coming?'

He saw the fear in her face, then the sudden look of determination. 'I'm coming.'

'Good girl.' He grinned.

'If I wasn't so scared I would tell you not to be patronising.'

'Then I'm glad you're scared. I was actually impressed by your bravery. Hop in. There's no point in us both getting muddy.'

In ten minutes they were aboard the *Curlew* and Leo was hauling up the sail. He was right. There was enough wind to carry them out into the centre of the fairway and hold course. 'Keep your eyes peeled. If they have anchored somewhere we don't want to sail past them.'

He settled himself in the cockpit, the tiller under his arm, the main sheet in the other hand. 'Grab a rug from the cabin if you're cold. The river is chilly at night.' The boat was gaining speed. He could feel her waking up under his hands. Strange how good it felt to have Zoë there, though she had none of the natural wild enjoyment that Jade had displayed.

'Is the mist coming back?' She was staring forward past the sail. He could hear the fear in her voice.

'If it is, we'll sail straight through it.'

She didn't answer and he laughed. 'Come on, Zoë, courage! We are intrepidly going to the rescue! Lifeboat, that's us!'

'I'll feel such a fool if they've checked into a pub somewhere and are fast asleep.'

'If they are we'll have a legitimate cause to ask why the hell they didn't ring. They must know you'll be worrying.'

They fell silent, Leo enjoying the feel of the wind on his face, Zoë staring out into the dark. He had clamped the jib sheet round a cleat and she sat, her hands tucked into the pockets of her jacket, the collar pulled up round her ears as she scanned the banks for any sign of the *Lady Grace*. What she wanted more than anything was to stop, for them to moor somewhere and lower the sail and go into the cabin out of the cold and for him to make love to her. Under her breath she was cursing Ken. He knew how worried they would be, of course he did, but what would he do if they found

345

him? When he saw her sailing with Leo, in the early hours of the morning . . .

'The tide is dropping fast.' Leo's voice broke through her thoughts. 'We'll need to tie up somewhere before we reach the bar and wait for it to turn. There's not enough wind to take us home against it.'

She felt a shaft of excitement knife through her. She looked back at him and smiled. 'Sounds good to me. If they've gone out to sea we would never find them.'

'Do you want to try?' He laughed mischievously.

'No!' She shuffled backwards, so she was sitting opposite him. 'I want to stop.'

He held her gaze for a moment. 'So do I.'

They picked up a buoy at a mooring upstream from Felixstowe Ferry. 'It's unlikely anyone will come back here tonight. If they do they will swear at us immoderately and we will grovel our apologies and scuttle off into the night.' He was making all fast. 'We'll be off soon anyway. As soon as the tide has turned and there is enough wind to make headway.'

'Shall I ring Amanda?'

'You'd better. Reassure her, though. Because we haven't found them doesn't mean there is anything wrong. As I said, if anything was we would have heard, I promise you.' He glanced round the cockpit, checking that all was secure, then he leaned forward to push open the cabin door. 'After you,' he gestured. 'We'll have a midnight feast and then,' he paused, 'rest, perhaps, until dawn.'

U

Once again Henry did not come to her bed that night. Somehow she had undressed alone in the cold room and pulled on her nightgown, then she had crawled under the coverlet, leaving the oil lamp burning on the table near the door. She woke several times during the night, acutely aware of the silence in the house and gave up trying to sleep in the end, lying watching the lamp begin to flicker and die, then later the dawn begin to filter through the curtains as she lay, listening to the sad song of a robin serenading summer's end on the pergola outside in the rose garden until at last she began fitfully to doze.

She lay in bed a long time next morning, hoping someone would come. The sun had risen and was shining strongly through the curtains, throwing patterns of light onto the carpet. The room was growing warm now, and before long, she knew, she was going to have to use the chamber pot. She slid out of the bed and glanced underneath. The pot wasn't there. She closed her eyes for a moment in frustrated fury, then reached for her shawl. There was nothing for it. She was going to have to go to the privy.

The door to Henry's dressing room from her bedroom had been locked. The other door which led onto the corridor was open, she saw, as she went past. His bed did not look as though it had been slept in. She was filled suddenly with a feeling of panic. Had she been all alone in the huge house all night? Was she all alone now? Where had all the servants gone? What if they never came back?

Rosemary had set the alarm for five thirty. As it rang she groped in the darkness for the button and switched it off. Steve lay with his back to her, snoring. She reached out and shook his shoulder. He groaned. 'Steve, come on. Get up! You know what we've got to do.'

There was no answer. She sat up, beginning to regret her plan. It was cold in the room – the central heating hadn't kicked in yet and it was still pitch dark outside. Still, the plan was a good one. It had to be done. She punched Steve, harder this time. 'Come on. I want you awake by the time I'm dressed.'

She didn't turn on the bedroom light. Even with the curtains drawn someone might be awake and see that they were too. She grabbed her clothes and retreated to the bathroom where she showered and dressed in jeans and a thick sweater. When she returned to the bedside Steve had pulled the duvet up over his head.

'I'm not coming,' he groaned when she seized it again and shook it. 'It's a mad idea. Stupid.'

She left him. Downstairs she grabbed a mug of instant coffee, pulled on her jacket and picked up the bag she had left by the door the night before, then she let herself out into the dark and switched on her torch. By the time she was halfway to Dead Man's Field there was a faint lightness appearing in the eastern sky. She began to make her way towards the field and paused, puzzled by the darker lines of blackness across the grass in front of her. Then she realised. It had been ploughed. The bastard! She swung the torch round. He had done about three-quarters of the field. The tractor with the plough lying behind it was parked in the corner by the hedge. She gave a cold smile. If he thought that would stop them he had another think coming; she would be back later with all her supporters and he had left enough unploughed for them to walk across easily.

Heading towards the copse in the middle of the field she found there was enough dim light to make her way without the torch. She shivered, thrusting her gloved hands into her pockets. The wind was cold. The last few days had been so warm one forgot that autumn was well under way and that a hint of winter was already there in the east. Soon the weather would break and fewer people would be interested in walking. It was imperative to get this footpath walked and marked before the really wet weather set in.

She reached the edge of the scrub and stopped, groping for the torch again, shining it in amongst the tangle of brambles and shrubs. She could see guelder-rose berries there and dogwood, and clusters of hawthorn, rich red in the torchlight, and round the edge of the copse the tangled strands of barbed wire. She put down her bag and rummaged in it for the wire cutters. Better to do this now, to open the path and make it easy for the others. It would hold things up if they had to do it with Turtill there shouting about damage to his property. If there was a fuss she could always point out that he hadn't challenged her while she was clearing the path before, another sign that he didn't really believe he was in the right to deny her entrance. She reached her gloved hand in amongst the rusty wire and snipped several pieces away. Then she cut back some brambles. Somewhere nearby a pheasant got up with a shriek of panic and flapped away into the darkness.

Some of the wire had been pulled away from the posts it was stapled to and the posts, rotten and collapsing, had pulled out of the ground. She shone her torch carefully along them. It looked as though someone else had been here trying to clear an entrance. She smiled. More evidence. Tomorrow – no, later today – she would bring her camera to prove it. She pulled the wire back and threw several bits of rotting post aside, then she shone her torch into the centre of the thicket. She could see the so-called burial mound clearly now. It wasn't nearly as impressive as the name suggested. Only a few feet high and covered with nettles, it couldn't have been more than twenty feet in diameter. She shone the torch around its perimeter and there were the tell-tale signs of a narrow path through the long grass at its base. The torch showed up some rabbit droppings and further on something larger deposited by a fox or a badger. Never mind. It was a path of sorts.

She stepped over the wire and followed the path round, snipping back the brambles as she went. Halfway round, the path veered left and she gave a small whistle of triumph. It was heading out of the copse again, down in the direction of the far side of the field just as she would have expected.

She followed it, still using her torch although the daylight was stronger now. There at the edge of the copse she saw the deep furrows of the plough had come close to the edge, so close in fact that it had run into the copse itself, dragging the wire away from the posts again.

She stood surveying the damage; the posts had snapped off and the wire had been wrenched free and folded back, probably by Bill Turtill himself. She traced it with the torch light and saw part of one of the posts levered back out of the earth; nearby there were a couple of rusty spades. She smiled. More proof that there had been access to this area in the past. She remembered her phone and fished it out of her pocket. She could use it to photograph the site, just in case Bill was tempted to arrive early and move the evidence. She clicked the camera several times, blinking to adjust her eyes after the flash, then she stopped and pulled at the spades to arrange them in a closer group. They were hooked up with some other piece of metal, a crowbar of sorts. She bent and pulled it free. It was thin and rusty but still incredibly sharp and she let out an exclamation as it cut through her glove and sliced her palm. She cursed and threw the thing down, then took a picture of it before stashing her phone back in her pocket and looking for a wad of tissues to stanch the blood soaking through her glove.

Suddenly she bent and picked it up again, looking at it closely; it had a crosspiece at the handle, and a strange corroded lump on a short narrow shaft above that. She gasped in sudden realisation. She was holding an ancient sword. The wood around her seemed to be holding its breath. She was intensely aware suddenly of the silence and she shivered. She looked over at the mound. Beyond the brambles and nettles it looked higher than before; a definite shape. Man-made, not just some natural lump in the field. And she was holding in her hand proof of the fact that this was some kind of burial mound, evidence which would hold up the order

350

confirming the footpath. She glared at it. If she left it lying around, or if she threw it back into the undergrowth there was always the chance that someone would come across it with a metal detector. On impulse she tucked it into her bag. She would dump it somewhere else on the way home.

She glanced round, as she pulled the bag onto her shoulder, the sword sticking out of the top. She had her evidence of a right of way, and she had cleared access for the path. The light was growing. It would soon be sunrise. She could see a line of crimson appearing along the horizon to the south-east. She switched off her torch and listened for a minute, suddenly aware of a noise deep in the copse. It sounded like a groan. She froze, conscious of a sudden prickling at the back of her neck, then she thought of the animal track through the copse and smiled. It was a fox or a badger coming back to its lair. She stood still, listening. The wind had got up now and the leaves above her head were rustling; she could hear nothing else. Time to go back. She didn't want to be seen out at this hour. As it was, Turtill would probably notice nothing if he came up later in the morning and by then it would be too late for him to deny there was a path; it would be there for all to see.

Carefully she retraced her steps, conscious of how heavy the sword was on her shoulder and as she came to the edge of the copse she paused again, glancing back uncomfortably. She had the strangest feeling that she was being watched. She swallowed hard, amazed to find she was feeling scared. There was no one around but as the wind dropped again she was very conscious of the absolute silence in the trees around her. Not even a bird made a sound. She took a step forward and heard a twig snap under her foot. It sounded deafening. Then in the distance she heard a horn. Not a car horn, not a hunting horn, it was more musical than that and it sounded like a warning, drifting up from the river. A fog horn, that was it, though it wasn't foggy up here in the field.

She glanced down through the trees, still dark where the dawn light hadn't reached. It was foggy there. Thick fog. Here, on the edge of the copse, the whole world seemed to be draped suddenly in spiders' webs, hung with diamond dewdrops. She shivered. Time to go home. She was, she admitted as she hurried forward again, rather pleased that when she returned in three hours' time she would be in the company of at least a couple of dozen other people, probably more.

Ken stuck his head out of the cabin door and glanced round the *Lady Grace*'s cockpit. With her single dagger keel she lay at an impossible angle on the mud. He glanced at his watch, screwing up his eyes to read the time. The tide must have turned. In fact he could see the water now, a dark shadow at the periphery of his vision. It was lighter now, dawn creeping imperceptibly up the sky out to sea. It was still a long way off sunrise. There was no sign of the mist or the ship it had brought with it.

He hauled himself out of the door and pushed it closed behind him. John was still asleep, though how he had managed it wedged so uncomfortably between bunk and cabin wall he wasn't sure. He propped himself up on the lower of the cockpit seats and stared out. Birds were beginning to stir. He heard a lonely whistle somewhere out on the mud and saw the silhouette of a small wader already stalking across the wet surface close to the boat, probing swiftly for food amongst the shallow running channels of water. He looked at his watch again. Time was out of kilter. Was it morning or evening? Suddenly he wasn't sure. The tide was in the wrong place, surely. He found he was shivering violently.

Suddenly remembering, he groped in his pocket for his mobile. There was a good signal now, and he had missed four calls, all from Zoë. He glanced again at his watch and then he called her back. She did not pick up. With a frown he dialled the house phone. It was a long time before Amanda answered. She was frantic and she was alone.

It was another hour before there was enough water to lift them off the mud. Ken made no attempt to sail. The engine started first go.

Amanda was waiting for them on the landing stage. Her face was white and strained and there were huge dark rings under her eyes. 'She went off with Leo to look for you.'

Ken had already noticed the *Curlew* was absent. 'When did they leave?'

'I don't know. I was asleep. Quite late. We were frantic with worry about you both and I wanted to call the police or the coastguard or something. She said to leave it for a while because of the tides and things, and I went upstairs to lie down. I must have fallen asleep almost at once. I feel awful. I slept right through till you rang.'

John grimaced. 'So much for wifely concern!'

'You were worn out,' Ken said placatingly.

'We were stuck on the mud without any mobile reception,' John went on. 'I am so sorry. The last thing we wanted was to worry you.'

'And now Zoë is missing,' Amanda went on. 'This guy she's with, Leo, I take it he is an experienced sailor?'

'Oh yes, he's experienced all right,' Ken replied grimly.

They all turned to survey the river. It was deserted.

Neither man had mentioned the ghost ship as they came back up the river. It wasn't until they had tied up to the buoy and were pulling in the dinghy that Ken had glanced at John. 'Best not mention what happened last night,' he said. 'We don't want to scare anyone.'

John nodded. 'I was hoping that bit was a hallucination,' he said.

'Let's agree that it was.' Ken gave a tight smile. 'All part of the romance of this lovely coast, eh?'

The three of them walked up to the house and let themselves in. Ken paused on the threshold and looked round as if half hoping Zoë would have returned. They could have landed further down-river and come back by road or something, but the house was silent.

Amanda shivered. She had long ago moved all traces of the séance, but she was intensely aware of the possibility of a presence in the great room. The two men had disappeared upstairs for a shower and, at least in John's case, some sleep. Within minutes she was alone again.

She went outside and walked down the path and over the grass towards The Old Forge. Pushing open the gate, she went up to the front door and knocked. There was no reply; she walked round to the back of the building and rattled the handle of the back door. To her surprise it opened easily. She stepped in.

'Hello? Anyone there?'

The kitchen was a mess. The supper dishes were stacked in the sink – a meal for one, she noted, but a messy cook. She stood looking round. Attractively untidy, she decided. Artistic, but not contrived to be so. The real thing. Painting materials, cooking stuff – he was a real cook, there were herbs and olive oil and other tell-tale signs of someone who did the genuine thing, and a pleasant smell of spices and coffee and something sharp – presumably turpentine. Intrigued she went over to the bookshelf. She liked kitchens with bookshelves, particularly when the books weren't only cookery books. Here there were local guides, a tide table, catalogues of seeds and computer software, a telephone directory, all sorts. She moved along to the table on which lay a pile of sketches.

'What are you doing in here?'

Amanda jumped out of her skin at the child's voice so close beside her. She stared at the small skinny girl in the T-shirt and jeans. She had huge grey eyes, red hair and freckles, and her face had a sprinkling of pockmarks which looked angry and painful. This was obviously the notorious Jade about whom they had heard at the dinner party. 'I'm looking for Leo,' she answered as she recovered her composure.

'He's not here.'

'Where is he, do you know?'

The child shook her head.

'I'm staying with Zoë and Ken across the grass there.' Amanda waved towards the window.

'I know who you are. I watched you through the window,' the child said.

Amanda hid a smile. 'Well, Leo went out last night to look for Ken and my husband, John, after they went sailing together. We were worried when they didn't come back last night. It appears they got stuck on the mud and they have just got back safely. I was worried that there was no sign of Leo or Zoë and I came over to see if they were back too.'

'Zoë?' The girl's eyes narrowed. 'Zoë went with him on the *Curlew*?'

'You know her?' Better make sure . . .

'Of course I do.'

'You live next door, right?'

'We live at The Summer Barn.'

Amanda smiled. 'What a lovely name.'

Jade gave her a look of deep scorn. 'When did they go?'

'Last night some time. Zoë's not answering her mobile.'

'Mobiles don't work in some places.'

'I'm sure they are fine, we were just a bit worried.'

Jade reached into the pocket of her jeans and pulled out her own mobile. She had Leo on speed dial, Amanda noted. After a few seconds she threw down the phone with a scowl. 'It's switched off.'

'I'm sure they're OK. I haven't met Leo yet. Is he nice?'

Amanda was making conversation but the suspicion in the girl's face was suddenly razor-sharp.

'What's Zoë told you?'

'Nothing much.'

'She should leave him alone. She's got a husband.'

Amanda hesitated. The girl was radiating hatred. 'I got the impression Leo was helping her get over her worries about sailing. I don't think it's any more than that,' she said gently.

'Then you don't know nothing,' Jade shot back. 'They sleep together.'

Amanda's expression remained carefully impassive. 'Are you sure?' She kept her voice level. They had obviously been extremely careless.

'I've seen them.'

'And have you told anyone?'

'Not yet.' Jade pursed her lips. 'But if he's taken her out on *Curlew* all night that's what they're doing. And it was me he was going to take sailing again.' Suddenly the hurt child was showing through. But not for long. 'I'm going to stop them,' she said. 'I'm going to make it so he never looks at her again. You tell her if she's your friend. You tell her if she goes near Leo any more I am going to screw up her life for ever.'

Amanda hoped the horror didn't show on her face. 'That sounds a bit extreme,' she responded as casually as she could.

'I'm an extreme person.' There wasn't a trace of humour in the child's face. 'Leo's mine.'

Amanda looked at her in concern. 'Does he know this is how you feel?'

For the first time Jade looked uncertain, then she nodded.

'And have you told Zoë?'

Jade shrugged. 'She knows.'

'And your family? What do they think?'

'None of their business.'

'But your mother and father know Leo, don't they?'

'They're not here.'

'You're not living here alone?'

'My brother is here.' The girl was looking sulky now. 'He's supposed to be looking after me but he's busy. He's always out with Mike Turtill.'

'And Leo is the only one who cares?' Amanda felt a sudden wave of compassion for this lonely wayward girl.

She looked defensive. 'I don't need anyone else.'

'Why aren't you at school, Jade?'

She smirked. 'I've got chicken pox. Have you had it? If you haven't you'll catch it.' There was something undeniably malicious in her tone.

Amanda smiled. 'I got it when I was at school. It's horrid, isn't it. Very itchy.' She glanced towards the door. 'Well. I had better get back. Are you going to wait for them here?'

Jade nodded.

'OK, well, tell them we were worried, will you?'

She could feel the girl's eyes watching her from the window, all the way back across the grass, and it gave her the creeps. She wondered if Zoë realised what a potentially vicious little enemy she had.

On impulse she turned left and took the path back down to the river. There was still no sign of the *Curlew* so she sat on a fallen log on the edge of the wood and settled down to wait.

Mike Turtill slithered to a halt on his motorbike, climbed off and felt with his foot for the stand. He was sweating inside his leathers and with a glance up at the sun he unzipped the jacket and pulled it off. Leaving it draped over the bike he headed for The Summer Barn. 'Jackson?' He pushed open the kitchen door and walked in, the buckles on his boots rattling as he moved.

'Jackson, mate?'

The other boy appeared. He was tousled from bed, dressed only in some tatty jeans. His feet were bare. 'What?'

'It's today. That woman is bringing her group of walkers down to the field today.'

'I know. Jade told me. Bitch.' Jackson scratched his head. It wasn't clear whether the insult was aimed at his sister or at Rosemary. Probably the latter, Mike concluded.

'Well, get your gear on, man. We're going down there. Dad ploughed it yesterday but he didn't finish the whole field. I said I'd do it.'

'Plough it?' Jackson was incredulous. 'Do you know how?'

'Course I do. Even you know how to drive a tractor. Surely you haven't forgotten.'

'That was when we were kids.'

'Well, we're not kids now. This is war. Dad doesn't want a confrontation but he said he would call the police if they push it.' Mike opened the fridge and rummaged through the contents. 'Go on. Get some shoes on at least, then we'll go down there. I'll have some breakfast while you shower. Man, you smell minging!' He had pulled out a carton of milk and looked round vaguely for something that might resemble cornflakes. 'Where is your little sister, anyway?'

'Gawd knows.'

'She's not out with that paedo again, is she? If I was your mum I'd be seriously worried about the amount of time she spends round there.'

Jackson frowned. 'He gives me the creeps.' He paused. He had spent a long time wondering what to do with the photos he had taken of Leo and Zoë and had in the end put them in an envelope and stuck them through the door of the local paper. Only one edition had appeared since he had done it and there had been no sign of the headline he had hoped for, but weeklies obviously worked more slowly than dailies. Leo's prowess with Zoë would seem to contradict the suspicion that he might fancy a skinny little girl like his sister. But you never knew. 'You don't really think that's what he's after, do you?'

Mike sniggered. 'If she was my sister I'd make sure he never went near her or any other woman ever again.'

His response was eminently satisfying. Jackson preened himself quietly. As he headed for the stairs he gave his friend a jaunty thumbs up.

It was twenty minutes before the two young men set off for the field on foot. They had disappeared behind the hedge on the track long before the first car drew up outside Rosemary's and the passengers began to unload their day-sacks and walking poles. Rosemary opened the door and ushered them in. 'We're starting at eleven,' she announced, 'so come in and have some refreshment. As soon as everyone is here we will begin our walk.' She had a clipboard with a list of names. Ticking off the newcomers she waved them towards the kitchen table where there was a selection of Thermoses with various hot drinks, and plates of biscuits. Within the next forty minutes or so the kitchen had begun to fill up.

Down on the field Jackson had hauled himself up onto the gate to watch as Mike set off up the field with the tractor dragging the five-furrow plough behind him. Already the seagulls had appeared and were screaming and diving over the newly turned earth. Jackson grinned. At the first sign of the walkers in the lane behind him he would signal Mike. The plan was for Mike to drive towards them and scatter them if they set foot on the field. He grinned. He was going to enjoy this. He tipped the last dregs of lager down his throat and reached into Mike's bag for another can. It made a very acceptable breakfast.

U

Emily pulled on her cloak against the brisk cold wind and made her way out towards the stables. Whatever else happened Sam would not leave the horses unfed. Sure enough she could hear the sound of buckets clanking and the splash of water from the pump as she walked into the stableyard and stood looking round. Pip the stableboy was hefting a large pail towards the end box, the water splashing over his boots. 'Boy!' Her sharp call made him drop the bucket with a cry of alarm. Water sluiced over his feet and across the cobbles. 'Where is Sam?'

'I am here, my lady.' Sam appeared from the door of the harness room. 'Fill it again, lad,' he said gently. 'And you can give Prince his oats if you would.' He walked towards her as the boy carried the empty bucket back towards the pump.

'What can I do for you, my lady?' He met her gaze steadily. She noted how exhausted he looked and realised she had never actually bothered to look at him before with such care. 'I understand Susan Smith has died,' she said. 'I am sorry to hear that. How is,' she hesitated, 'how is Daniel taking it?'

Sam tightened his lips. 'I haven't seen him,' he said. He turned away and began to walk towards the hayloft.

'Sam, wait!' she called. 'I haven't told you that you could go. I shall require the cob to be brought round later this morning. That is if,' again she hesitated, 'if my husband hasn't taken him out.' She was very conscious that the boy had stopped by the pump. He was making no attempt to fill the bucket. He had put it down and was staring at her over his shoulder.

'I drove your husband to the railway station this morning, my lady,' Sam said curtly. 'The horse is tired, but if it is really urgent I suppose I can saddle him for you.'

'The railway station?' She tried to hide her panic. 'Why? Where was he going?'

'He did not tell me, my lady.' Sam bent and picked up one of Pip's buckets. 'Would you like me to saddle the cob for you later?'

'No.' She shook her head. 'No, don't bother.' She turned and walked away though the archway which led to the drive and the front of the house.

When she went back in she knew at once the servants had returned. She still didn't know where they had been, but someone had lit the fire in the morning room and there were fresh flowers in a vase on the windowsill. As she pulled off her cloak Mrs Field appeared behind her.

'My lady.' Mrs Field dropped a small curtsey. 'Mr Henry asked that you be informed that he has gone away for a few days.' The woman's eyes were carefully expressionless.

Emily bit her lip. She wondered suddenly how many of the servants knew of her meetings with Daniel. Before, she hadn't cared if they knew or not as long as Henry didn't find out, but now she had told him about the rape, it occurred to her to wonder if the backstairs gossip had seized on what had been happening, and how near they had been to the truth. As Mrs Field made no attempt to take it from her she threw her cloak over the back of the sofa. 'I was so sorry to hear about Susan,' she said with an effort. 'I understand that Molly will not be returning for a few days.'

'Molly has left your service for good, my lady,' Mrs Field said evenly. 'Mr Henry has been informed.' Emily was searching for some response when Mrs Field went on, 'Do you require a notice to be put in the local paper that you need a new maid?'

'In the paper?' Emily cried. 'Surely there are staff here who could be trained up? One of the parlour maids, or someone from the village.'

'I will ask, my lady, but I think it is unlikely any of the housemaids will want to change their duties.' She was a large woman with greying hair piled untidily under her cap. Her apron was creased, Emily realised suddenly, and she had missed a button on the front of her dress. She had never seen her looking less than immaculate before, and she was suddenly intimidated by the expression on the woman's face.

'Whatever you feel would be best, Mrs Field,' she said meekly.

'I will have your lunch brought to the morning room later,' Mrs Field went on. 'I am sure you agree there is no need to use the dining room if you are alone.'

Alone. The word sound bleak and angry. As the door closed behind her Emily sat down on the edge of a chair, her hands clasped in her lap, and stared at the fire. It was already dying back. Whoever had lit it had put only a couple of logs on. Alone – with an empty womb and a husband who hated and despised her.

She wondered briefly where Daniel was. In his cottage presumably. She frowned. She missed him. Not just his body, but his edgy challenging obedience. If Henry was away and she was very, very careful perhaps she could engineer a meeting between them after a suitable time had passed to enable him to grieve for his wife. She wasn't inhuman. She would allow him his grieving. She sat up straighter and felt her spirits lift. It was a plan she could work on.

In the kitchen Mrs Field sat down at the table and glared at Mrs Davy, the cook, who took a step back as she met her gaze. 'I've just spoken to that woman,' Mrs Field said. 'It was all I could do to keep my hands from her throat!' She wiped her hands on her apron as though trying to clean off the very mention of her employer's wife. 'She doesn't know he's dead, so she's expecting to see him, I could see it in her eyes.'

Mrs Davy shook her head. 'Someone is bound to say something. How does Mr Henry think we are all going to keep silent?'

Beaton had told them all the night before in the servants' hall, after the men had buried Daniel, and that officially at least Dan had killed himself. It was clear he did not believe it, and he did not expect them to either, and he had repeated

Mr Henry's instructions that his wife was not to be told anything.

'She's missing Molly already,' Mrs Field went on. 'I told her we would have to post an advertisement. She didn't like that, I can tell you.'

'No one round here would work for her ever again,' Mrs Davy said, nodding. 'Poor Susan. And poor, poor Daniel.'

They were silent for a full minute, then Mrs Davy turned back towards the range. 'I'll give her soup and a bit of bread for her luncheon. See how she likes that,' she said viciously. 'And I'll spit in the soup!'

Mrs Field looked shocked but she said nothing. It was no more than the woman deserved.

16

Leo woke suddenly and stared round the cabin. He could see the reflections of the sunlit water dancing on the ceiling and hear the contented murmur of feeding birds on the mudflats outside. He stretched contentedly. He loved this moment in the day when he was down on the boat; it was utterly peaceful.

He glanced sideways and stretched out his hand. On the narrow bunk there had barely been room for the two of them, but that hardly mattered. By the time they had fallen asleep they were so closely entwined they had taken up no more space than one body on the mattress.

She was not there beside him. He sat up, looking round. The cabin door was shut and when he peered through the portholes he couldn't see her. In a moment of sheer terror he was out of bed and pulling open the door. He stared round the cockpit. It was empty. He turned and peered forward over the cabin roof and at last he saw her, perched on the fore-deck, sitting with her legs hanging over the side. Her hair was tousled in the wind and she was looking completely relaxed and happy, one arm linked loosely round the starboard shrouds. He relaxed. He watched her for several minutes, the sunlight playing over the planes of her face as she stared off into the distance, her hair a tangle of spun-gold threads, then he ducked into the cabin and rummaged for one of his sketchbooks. He wanted to capture her like that as she was, unself-conscious and free.

He was jolted out of his reverie by the ringing of a phone. She heard it too and glanced back. 'Is that mine?'

'I'm afraid so.' He cursed silently. 'Shall I turn it off?'

But she had already scrambled to her feet and was coming back. She jumped down into the cockpit. Her feet were bare and her jeans rolled up almost to the knees. The early morning sunlight had reawakened her summer tan; he could see the tiny gold hairs on her legs. He found the sight unbearably erotic. 'They'll be worried. I ought to answer.'

The phone stopped ringing. She ducked into the cabin and found her bag on the floor with her jacket; rummaging for her mobile she peered at it. 'It was Ken.'

'So the ghost boat didn't get him.' Leo smiled, astonished at the pang of jealousy he felt.

'Not unless that was a ghost ringing.' She grinned. She pressed a button and waited for it to connect. 'Ken? Where are you? Are you OK?'

Leo turned away with a sigh.

Picking up their mooring again beside the *Lady Grace*, Leo rowed Zoë ashore and then made his excuses. He couldn't bear the thought of seeing her with the others, not now. He rowed back to the boat and picked up his sketchbook again.

The area in front of The Threshing Barn was busy. Zoë stared as she walked up across the grass. There must have been at least half a dozen cars parked on the gravel outside and it was thronged with people. 'Oh, Rosemary!' she muttered as she saw the day-sacks and the walking sticks. She headed towards her own front door, her head resolutely down and made it without being accosted by her neighbours.

'So, you dark horse, where have you been?' Amanda was in the kitchen.

'Looking for Ken and John, as you well know.' Zoë dropped her bag on the table.

'All night?' Amanda asked casually.

'All night.' Zoë smiled. 'Ken phoned just now. He said he and John were in Woodbridge. I gather they are getting the ingredients for a barbecue.'

'And they won't be long.' Amanda grinned. 'If I were you, I'd go up and have a shower and try and wipe that smile off your face before they get back.' As Zoë headed upstairs she called after her. 'Where is Leo, by the way?'

'On the boat. He didn't feel like meeting everyone.'

Amanda nodded. 'I'm not surprised. Go on up. We'll talk when you are respectable.' As Zoë ran upstairs she walked over to the window and stared out at the crowd of people outside the barn on the other side of the lawn. Life was obviously not dull in this part of the world.

Jade was sitting on her bed looking at the squat figure of the woman. She had washed it yet again and carefully dried it and sat it down in the middle of the piece of bubblewrap, then she had washed her own hands again, unable to suppress a shudder at the feel of the cold iron. It was evil, she was sure of it, very heavy for its size and very, very old.

She heard a shout in the distance and she slid off the bed to go and look out of the window. From her room you couldn't see the front of the barn or the neighbours but she knew what it was. Mrs Formby and her walkers. She smiled. Jackson and Mike had gone out early and the field would be all ploughed up by now, and Mike's mum was going to come down with some of her friends from the village to help see off these people. The Turtills were furious.

Strangers had no right to come and try and change things. The village had been the same for hundreds of years. Everyone knew where things were and everyone liked Mike's dad.

It didn't occur to her that she too was a stranger. As was Leo. Her eyes narrowed as she suddenly thought about him and Zoë. But then her plans for Zoë were almost complete. She looked back towards the bed with an expression which would have shocked to the core any adult seeing it.

He had watched so carefully he knew exactly where to dig, and he had seen the men discard their spades. Perhaps they meant to return later to neaten the job they had done, to firm down the soil and to trim the edges of the mound. Whatever the reason he blessed them silently. Tearing off his tunic he threw it on the ground and lifted the first spade, thrusting it into the earth. He dug for a long time, burrowing sideways into the soft soil, throwing the earth over his shoulder, making no attempt to hide what he was doing. If he had time he would make good the grave later; he had respect for Lord Egbert, but not at the expense of Destiny Maker. The sandy earth collapsed and subsided as he dug on, but he ignored it, scraping it aside, throwing it behind him, digging on and on until he came at last to the first of the group of earthenware jars which had been left to refresh the dead man. He paused, leaning on his spade. He was already on the second; the first had snapped when he was halfway into the mound. He had no fear of Lord Egbert's spirit, nor of the curses he had heard the sorcerer declaim on any who disturbed the grave. The magic of the sword, the magic of the smith who wrought the alchemy which turned ore to iron in the secret heart of the fire more than protected him.

To reach Lord Egbert he had to pass the man who had been laid at his feet. He stood looking down at Hrotgar impassively, taking in the sunken features, the rigid limbs, the wide eyes which no one had been able to close. There was no sign of the great bloody wound in his chest. All had been washed and cleaned and he had been dressed in his finest cloak. His gaze went back to the open eyes, covered in soil, the dirt on his hands; this man had been a Christian and he had been laid in the grave of a follower of Woden. He smiled grimly. Hrotgar was there to serve his lord. To serve his lord he had colluded in the making of a pagan sword. It was only right that his had been the blood to bathe the blade.

He wasn't sure why he wanted it so badly. What was there left to live for? His lord and his wife were gone. Neither his village nor his family would ever have him back. In their eyes he was guilty of murder, however justified it may have been. But the sword would live on. He would see to that. In his hands it would live up to its name.

He threw a spadeful of earth onto Hrotgar's face with a sardonic grin. Unshriven and in a state of mortal sin the man would go to Hell. Or, in the wake of his pagan lord perhaps he would go to the Otherworld of the Saxon gods and grovel before Woden himself. Wherever he went Eric hoped his immortal soul would suffer the agonies of the damned.

It took only a short time to dig his way into the mound to the place where Egbert lay, and there, beside him, lay Destiny Maker, already dulled by the weight of the earth. He pulled it from its scabbard with a smile and stroked the blade with the edge of his thumb. A thin line of blood appeared. It was still as sharp as when it had left his workshop.

Laying it gently on the ground he picked up the spade and began to infill the earth once more. It took longer than he expected, but at last it was done and he had scraped the last traces of soil off the grass. No doubt in daylight it would be obvious what had happened but by then he would be long gone.

Suddenly exhausted he sat down there in the darkness and took the sword on his knee. He glanced up, seeking the moon, but the clouds had gathered and there was no trace of it. The darkness was absolute. With a heavy sigh of exhaustion he lay back on the ground and just for a moment closed his eyes.

It was the breath of ice-cold air which made him stir. He sat up suddenly, wondering what had awoken him. The night was still, but far away on the wind he could hear the beat of music coming from the mead hall where the villagers still drank to their lord's memory. Standing up stiffly he turned and looked down towards the river.

A thick mist was drifting up through the trees towards him, wreathing round the branches, already licking at the newly settled earth of the mound in the centre of the field where he stood. He couldn't see the water now; all was silent. He took a step away, the sword in his arms, suddenly alert. He could see movement down at the landing stage where the fishermen had left their boats to attend the funeral rites.

Another craft was nosing up-river, a large craft with a huge sail. Hesitating, he drew back and watched. It was far larger than any local fishing vessel or even one of the traders. He strained his eyes. As the mist thinned for a moment and the moon appeared he could see quite clearly. The sail was being lowered. The ship swarmed with men. He took a few steps closer and peered through the trees, trying to see more clearly in the moonlight. They had waited for darkness before they came ashore. He felt his blood run cold. He could see the glint of soft moonlight on armour, and on the great curved beak of a head at the prow of the ship. They were very quiet.

They were Danes.

'Jesus Christ save us all,' he murmured. He turned towards the village and looked up the hill where the sound of music still carried on the wind. The people up there had been his friends; amongst them were members of his family and

369

Edith's. Her sister, her mother. Gudrun. Lady Hilda. He had to warn them or they would all be massacred.

Hefting the heavy sword onto his shoulder he began to run, as silent as a shadow, up the field.

'Tell me, are you planning on walking clean over the top of the burial mound?' Dottie and Arthur were standing next to Rosemary as they watched the group finishing their coffees. Dottie spoke softly, her eyes fixed on the others; there were people in the group she didn't recognise. Youngsters. Some had the light of zeal in their eyes, others looked rather more sinister.

'If necessary.' Rosemary folded her arms. She hadn't picked up her own walking pole yet; it lay with Steve's and several others against the fence near the front door. She sighed. Her head was splitting and she could barely see straight. On her return three hours before she had abandoned the idea of going back to bed. Putting on the kettle for some strong coffee, she had taken the sword out of her daysack and wrapped it in a towel, then she had stood indecisively wondering where to hide it. Suddenly she smiled. Leo's. What more natural, if anyone asked, than that he would have picked it up and stashed it away somewhere. If there was any trouble at any time it would be for him to sort out. Pulling open the door, she had crept outside and headed across the grass towards the forge. Halfway there she stopped suddenly. A small figure was walking surreptitiously up the path just ahead of her. Jade. Rosemary ducked sideways behind the hedge that divided their garden from that of the Lloyds and on impulse thrust the sword in under it. She pulled away the towel and left it there. In five minutes she was back in the kitchen sipping the scalding coffee.

She nodded at Dottie. 'We will look to see where the traces of the original path run. On the map it seems to go clean over the top of it, but we may find that it skirts it.' She smiled a little smugly.

'And you have checked that this is not some sort of national monument? If it is an archaeological site we don't want to infringe any by-laws. We are awfully near Sutton Hoo here.'

'If it was like Sutton Hoo there would be clearly signposted access,' Rosemary retorted. She felt a slight pang of guilt at the thought of the old sword now lying under her neighbour's hedge and the fact that the site was clearly marked on the largest scale Ordnance Survey maps. Well, if no one else had registered the fact, she was certainly not going to point it out. 'If you ask me it is just the remains of a refuse dump. Anything more important would hardly be fenced off with rusty wire.'

'And you checked with the council?'

'I have informed them what we are doing. I have told them the path has been deliberately blocked. I have followed all the correct procedures, I assure you.' Rosemary narrowed her eyes. 'Don't tell me you are having second thoughts.'

Dottie pursed her lips. 'I was a bit shocked at the strength of feeling about this walk in the pub last night. There seems to be a huge amount of resentment in the village at newcomers coming in and stirring up the status quo.'

'You're not a newcomer.'

'No. But we aren't local either.' Dottie shook her head. 'Our neighbours accept us and I think they like us. I don't want to spoil that relationship. It's different for us. We live in the middle of the village. We know people.'

'If you don't want to come, don't,' Rosemary interrupted impatiently. 'I thought you and Jim were with me on this one, but it makes no difference to me. There are a great many people who care about our liberties here. We won't miss you. I thought you were someone who stands up for the little people against landowners.'

'Bill Turtill is hardly a rampant landowner, Rosemary. His

371

family may have been here generations, but he is a hard-working farmer and much respected locally. He does things for the village.'

'Then he should go just that bit further!' Rosemary sniffed. She bent to pick up her pole. 'Right, I think we are about ready. I am doing this for the people of Britain, Dottie,' she commented. 'As you well know, without people like me we would lose all our rights of access. There should be no corner of the country where we cannot go.'

Dottie stood back without a word. She watched as the group formed into a loose-knit crocodile behind Rosemary and Steve and began to walk across the lawns towards the lane.

Jim approached his wife, hanging back with her. 'Second thoughts?'

She nodded. 'I agree with so much she says usually, but this time I think she's got it wrong.'

'Dead Man's Field,' Jim said with an exaggerated shiver. 'If there is some dead Anglo-Saxon buried in that mound he's not going to be pleased about all those people walking all over him.'

She nodded slowly. 'And what is more I think the village is right. There has been a tradition of not walking in that field. It feels like sacrilege.'

'Shall we go home?'

She glanced after the others and then she gave a small, almost embarrassed nod. They stood and watched as the group of people walked purposefully towards the hedge. One by one they disappeared through the gate and out of sight. Only when the last one had gone did Jim and Dottie turn and head back towards their car.

'There's a couple of people wimping out,' Ken said slowly. They were all standing at the window watching. 'Does Bill know what is about to hit him?'

'He knows,' Zoë said. The barbecue had been lit; it would take a couple of hours for it to get going. The meat and sausages were in the fridge and Amanda had made a jug of Pimm's.

'Shall we go down to see the fun?'

'I'm tempted.' Zoë glanced at Amanda. 'We've lots of time before lunch. What about you? Who wants to see an agrarian uprising in action?'

'I do!' John put up his hand. 'I had no idea you all had such fun out in the sticks. It beats our part of the world for entertainment value. Which side are we on?'

'Not theirs.' Amanda nodded her head towards the disappearing crowd.

'Too right. Up with the landowners!' He grinned. 'I never thought I would hear myself say that. But it seems to me there are hundreds of footpath signs all over the place. More than enough for everyone.'

'There are,' Zoë put in. 'It's just this one woman with a crusader complex. I expect her dad told her to keep off the flowerbeds when she was a child and she has been stamping round having tantrums about being told to keep off other people's property ever since.'

They walked down the field and turned into the lane, keeping well behind the stragglers. In the distance they could hear the sound of a tractor.

Behind them Jade had slipped out of the door of The Summer Barn with a smile. The whole area was deserted; every building, including Leo's – she had checked earlier to see if he was back. There was no one anywhere. On her shoulder she was carrying an ecological and environmental Fair Trade-cotton shopping bag she had found on the back of the kitchen door. Her mother never used it. She skirted the deserted smoking barbecue with a critical glance at the charcoal and cautiously headed towards The Old Barn. They had left the door on the latch. She noted that they had changed the lock and there was a new bolt on the inside and she gave a little sneer. All those precautions and they had left it unlocked!

Pushing her way into the kitchen she surveyed it critically. It was immaculately tidy. Someone had loaded the dishwasher and it was quietly swishing in the corner.

Creeping through into the great room she studied it carefully too. Nothing was out of place. She had seen them all walk away across the grass but even so she was very careful. She tiptoed up the stairs and along the landing to the master bedroom and pushed open the door. It was not so tidy here. The bed was unmade and a towel lay on the floor. She screwed up her nose and walking towards the bed she sniffed cautiously like a small animal. As she had suspected, he had got up late and left it a mess. She could smell the freshly applied aftershave. So, he slept on the side nearest the bathroom, which meant *she* slept nearer the window. She moved round to the far side of the bed and pulled back the covers.

She could smell Zoë's perfume now; she recognised it. She scowled. Groping in her bag she brought out the metal figurine and carefully tucked it under the mattress. Then she jumped on the bed to test if Zoë would realise it was there. She could feel it easily. She frowned. Plan B. She would have to put it under the bed. It would hopefully be as efficient, though it might take longer. She would have to take the risk that it would be found if anyone zealously vacuumed the room.

She retrieved it and pushed it right under the bed, so that it rested underneath the pillow where Zoë's head would lie, then carefully she straightened the sheets and the duvet. The bed looked wrong with the other side rumpled so she straightened that as well. He would never remember. Her mother said men never remembered things like that. Then she walked to the end of the bed and raised her hands above her head.

'Great goddess,' she intoned solemnly. 'I want you to destroy this woman. Take her away. Make her leave. Fill this house with bad things and make the Lloyds go away.' She paused. 'Amen,' she added. She waited, half-expecting something to happen at once, aware that she was for the first time feeling a little scared. There had been no doubt of the power of the figure in her mind, but now that she had unleashed it on the unsuspecting Zoë she wondered if she had gone too far. 'I don't want her to die,' she added under her breath. 'At least —' At least what? Actually she would be very pleased if she did die. That would get rid of her for good. She bit her lip surprised at her own daring, and even more surprised when she realised that actually she didn't care.

She heard a sound behind her and she spun round. There was no one there. She could feel her heart thumping with fright. It was already working. She had to get out of there. The room was filling with magic. Bad magic.

Running out of the bedroom, leaving the bag lying on the floor, she fled down the landing towards the staircase. At the top of the stairs she paused and looked round. Even from up here she could sense that suddenly there was a strange feeling in the room below. As if it were full of people; people she couldn't see. She could hear a faint stirring, sense a crowd, smell the warmth of hay and horses and she had the feeling that someone was looking up at her. Her mouth went dry and she realised it was hard to breathe. All her bravura had gone. She had never been so frightened in her life. She looked round desperately and realised suddenly that she had to go down the stairs, into the midst of whatever was going on; there was no other way out.

She glanced over her shoulder. She could go back, run down the landing, hide. Hide where? In one of the bedrooms? But then what would happen when they came back? Zoë and Ken would catch her. She was looking backwards and forwards like a small hunted animal, frozen with fear. She had started something, switched something on which she knew suddenly she would not be able to stop.

She wanted Leo. He would know what to do, but how could she reach him? He was out on the boat still, and even if he came back he wouldn't know where she was. She heard herself give a small whimper and immediately, as though the sound had broken a spell, everything around her was normal again. She stood still, not daring to move, then slowly she walked to the balustrade and looked down into the room beneath. It was quiet again. She could hear nothing but her own harsh breathing.

She turned and ran back to the stairs, fled down them and across the great room to the kitchen. In there she pulled open the door and ran out, leaving it open behind her and tore across the grass towards The Old Forge. There, she scrabbled for the key under the flower pot. It had gone. With a small sob she remembered Leo taking it away from her and putting it into his pocket. She pressed herself against the door trying to catch her breath, then she sank down on the doorstep, huddled against the wood which was warm in the sunlight. She was safe there and soon, very soon, he would come back and find her.

Eric was gasping for breath as he reached the outlying cottages of the village. They were deserted. Everyone was up at the hall, and from where he stood he could see the light streaming from the open doors, hear the sound of the lyre and the horn carried on the wind. He glanced behind him. There was no sign yet of the men from the ship. All was quiet, any sound masked by the roar of the rising wind in the trees along the river. The earlier mist had gone. The first of the autumn gales had set in with a vengeance as rags of black cloud raced across the moon's face.

The door to his own house was closed. He thrust it open

and peered in. All was totally dark. There was no fire. His wife's body had gone. He paused a moment, head bowed, to wish her on her way wherever they had taken her, then he ducked out of the building again and pulled the door closed behind him. He would never set foot there again.

He set off up the track, pausing to push open one or two further doors as he passed to make sure the houses were empty. He could hear the animals moving restlessly in their pens; they sensed something was wrong. Nearby a dog was howling. He stopped to cut through the leash which tied it to a ring in the doorpost and it vanished into the night.

There were guards outside the door to the hall. They saw him coming and drew their swords. 'Stop!' he shouted. 'Let me speak. Tell them inside. The Vikings are in the river. They have landed below the field of the dead. Tell everyone to flee.' He bent over, trying to regain his breath.

One of the men began to head towards him threateningly. 'Murderer! Traitor! You laid hands on Hrotgar and you must pay with your life!' he shouted.

The other hesitated, taking in what Eric had shouted. 'Vikings?' the man repeated.

'Vikings!' Eric pulled Destiny Maker off his shoulder and held it out before him. Both men skidded to a halt. 'Tell them,' Eric yelled in anguish, 'for God's sake, tell them! They have to run!'

One of the men turned and ran towards the hall, disappearing inside as Eric felt the first blow between his shoulder blades. As he staggered forward with a gasp he realised two other men had appeared from the shadows. Destiny Maker flew out of his hand and disappeared into the dark. His arms were wrenched behind him and he felt a thong being slipped around his wrists. 'Take him away and secure him. The Lord Oswald will deal with him when the mourning is over,' someone called.

'Stop! Listen!' Eric screamed. 'The Viking host is here. In

the river. Can no one understand me? What is the matter with you? Tell them! You must flee, all of you. Protect your women and children!'

The blow that silenced him came from behind. For a moment his head rang like a great bell, then all went black. As they dragged him away he heard a voice as if from a million miles away saying, 'Did you hear what he said? Vikings!' There was a note of fear.

'Rubbish,' came the reply, then all he knew was that his legs were dragging on the ground and he was being taken away and thrown into the dark, and a door was barricaded from the outside.

The group of walkers paused in the lane by the gap in the hedge which Rosemary had cut. Bill had obviously found it and filled the gap with a roll of wire. With an exclamation of irritation she moved forward and reached for her gloves. 'Can someone give me a hand pulling it out of the way? Wretched man!'

No one volunteered for a moment and at last it was Steve who stepped towards her and reached gingerly for a handhold which wouldn't lacerate his fingers. 'I'm afraid this is a sign of the opposition we are going to encounter,' she called over her shoulder. 'I am glad you are all wearing boots, as you can see they have ploughed the land to make things as difficult for us as possible. And it's not going to work.' She helped Steve haul the wire out of the hedge and he pushed it back from the opening, then they led the way through the gap. The soil was newly turned into huge smooth slices of mud, the giant furrows rolling like waves across the field, and as the others followed her through the hedge they could all see the tractor still moving steadily away into the distance. To walk towards the centre on the line of Rosemary's putative path involved treading diagonally across the muddy wasteland, something which was going to prove uncomfortable and exhausting. There was a murmur of anger as they set off.

Behind them another group of people had appeared at the top of the lane. Lesley Inworth and Penny Turtill had marshalled their supporters and were heading down towards the field.

'What are we going to do?' Lesley asked breathlessly, trying to keep up. 'There are an awful lot of them.' At least two dozen as far as she could see as they set out in a straggling line across the furrows. 'Are we going to lie down and make them walk over us?'

There was an appreciative wave of laughter from the half-dozen or so men and women following them. Lesley spotted the Lloyds' party walking towards them and waved. 'We need support! We are outnumbered!' she called.

John looked at Ken and grinned. 'I'm up for it! Are we allowed to hit them?'

'No.' Lesley heard him as the two parties converged. 'Sadly not.'

'We can talk and shout and argue; we can get in the way. We can take photos of any damage they do,' Penny said. 'They are trespassing and if they don't leave when we ask we can contact the police. I hope it doesn't come to that, but if necessary that is what I am going to do.'

'Where is Bill?' Lesley asked suddenly. 'He should be here.'

'I thought he was down with the tractor,' Penny replied, shading her eyes, staring down the field. 'That's Mike,' she said. 'So, where is Bill?' She set off down the field striding purposefully over the furrows. The others followed.

Amanda found herself next to Zoë. 'Isn't Leo joining us?'

Zoë shook her head. 'He would hate this. I should imagine he's still down on the boat.'

'And the fearsome child?'

Zoë laughed. 'No idea.'

Amanda was already breathless from the unaccustomed

strenuousness of the walk. 'Look, I didn't get the chance to mention it before, but I had a talk with Jade when you were with Leo. She is venomously jealous. You want to watch out for her.'

Zoë smiled. 'I don't think I need to be terrified. She's only eleven, Amanda.'

'I wouldn't underestimate her. As far as she is concerned he is her property.'

'You discussed me with her?'

'It was the other way round. She told me to warn you off.'

Zoë fell silent. 'The whole family are a bit odd,' she said after a while. 'On top of that, she has been left far too much to her own devices. I think Leo is the only person who has ever taken any notice of her.'

The others had slowed as they reached the centre of the field at last, closing up with Rosemary's party, who had formed a solid phalanx at the edge of the trees. 'Here,' Rosemary was saying, 'I removed the wire which was blocking the way. Luckily it had already been cut.' She stared defiantly at Penny. 'And I found a path leading directly into and through the copse, just as I thought. It hasn't been ploughed or interfered with so it is easy to see where it led. Directly in the direction we knew it would down to the far corner of the field and out onto the path near the landing stage.'

'And why, Rosemary, would anyone want to go to the landing stage apart from us?' Ken asked sharply. 'With all due respect, it is private. As we have told you before, it says so in our deeds as I'm sure it does in yours.'

Rosemary flushed with anger. 'The ownership of the landing stage is irrelevant here. In the past it belonged to everyone.'

'So your next target is to end its privacy and allow the general public access?'

'No, I –'

'Then what are they going to do when they get here, Rosemary? Turn round and go back again?' Penny asked.

'No, they will follow the track round. That is a public footpath already.'

'And that public footpath is enough for them going up that way, but not any use coming down?'

'That is not the point!' Rosemary retorted. 'As will be seen when the council replies to my demand that the path be reinstated.' She turned away. 'Enough. Come on. Follow me and you will all see for yourselves how the path is clearly still there for all to see in the copse.'

Leo paused at the top of the track and glanced left towards the field. He could hear the sound of the tractor clearly now, see the clouds of following gulls over the tops of the trees. He smiled. So Bill was ploughing the field; he doubted if it would thwart Rosemary but it would make it uncomfortable for them to walk over, and as far as he remembered farmers had the right anyway to plough up public footpaths in the course of their legitimate activities as long as they reinstated them fairly soon afterwards.

Unable to resist the temptation of seeing what was going on, he walked slowly up to the gate to watch. They were all there, the occupants of the barns, except – he found himself checking automatically – Jade was nowhere to be seen. His gaze went back to Zoë, who was standing with another woman, presumably Amanda, a little apart from the others, obviously there, like him, to observe and not take part. Zoë glanced up suddenly as though aware of his eyes on her and he saw her look towards him. He smiled. There was no denying the link between them. Amanda turned to see who Zoë was looking at, then he saw Ken look round as well. His personality was obviously magnetic this morning! He lifted a hand. Only Zoë waved back. He saw Ken scowl and turn away.

His glance strayed back to the copse where Rosemary's group of followers was gathering. He screwed up his eyes against the glare of the sun, conscious suddenly that something was different about the place. Normally he didn't notice it; there was no need. He had never walked in the field, and he didn't often walk down the lane either, but the copse in the centre of the newly ploughed land seemed larger than usual. He could see an odd shimmer of light over it. Had she been in there and cut down some trees? Surely even Rosemary wasn't capable of such a thing? The air was vibrating slightly over the trees, like a mirage; it looked strangely sinister. Leaning on the gate he found he couldn't drag his eyes away.

Mike Turtill drew the tractor to a halt near the gate where Jackson was waiting and carefully engaged the lever to lift the plough. The blades rose slowly out of the earth and came to a stop at a forty-five degree angle behind the tractor.

'That's it. All done. Beautiful job, though I says it myself.' He slid down from the high seat and walked round to the back, leaving the engine running and the cab door open. 'Just checking all is well then I'll head back with it and park up.'

'No.' Jackson shook his head. 'The plan was you'd drive at them and scatter them! Give them a fright!'

Mike shook his head. 'Too dangerous, mate. Look I'll take it over there and leave it by the hedge, then I'll come back and find you and we can go and join the fray. We can cause enough chaos without trying to murder them!'

Jackson laughed. He was standing near the huge offside back wheel, another can of lager in his hand. 'Why not? Can't think of anything I'd like more.' He chucked the can into the hedge and patted the tyre. 'I think there's a bit more fun to be had with this baby first, though.' He reached up for the footplate and scrambled nimbly into the cab.

'Oi!' Mike ducked away from his examination of the linkage behind the tractor. 'Get down. You're not allowed up there!'

'Course I am. As you reminded me, your dad taught me.' Jackson leaned forward and put his hands on the wheel, then he reached for the gear lever.

'No, Jackson, get off!' Mike was really worried now. He leaned in and tried to wrench open the door but already Jackson had the tractor moving. Mike leaped out of the way just in time. 'Stop!' he shouted. 'You can't drive it like that. You fucking idiot!' The tractor was gaining speed, the plough with its huge metal shares, like giant teeth still raised behind it, swinging crazily as it headed across the furrows towards the group of walkers.

'Through here.' Rosemary had located the place where she had cut the wire. She ushered her group through the gap and into the shadows of the trees. 'See there. A path, just as I said.' She gestured at the narrow animal track which in daylight was barely visible in the long grass. 'It skirts the bottom of the burial mound, if that is what it is, so if people are worried about desecrating the place, they needn't be.' She laughed uncomfortably. The strange feeling from the cold early dawn was still there. Restless, angry; almost threatening. Wondering if anyone else could feel it, she glanced round and noticed the tractor getting closer. The engine was straining, deafeningly loud now, black smoke pouring from the exhaust stack above the cab as it hurtled across the field towards them lurching uncontrollably over the furrows.

'Bloody fool,' someone said. 'If he's not careful he'll flatten his precious mound!' The group moved back as one the way they had come through the gap in the wire and back to the field to watch.

'It's not Bill,' Steve shouted. 'It's that idiot Watts boy! For God's sake, what does he think he's doing?'

17

Emily was standing in the stables, looking at the cob who was pulling at a hay net as Pip brushed down the stall next door. The boy had been whistling until she came in. Now he was sullenly silent, his back turned resolutely towards her as he worked. She noticed the cob had turned its head towards her briefly, laid back its ears and rolled its eyes. So, even the horse hated her.

Sam walked down the long line of empty stalls and stopped beside her. 'Can I help you, my lady?'

She nodded. 'I want to ride. Will you have him saddled for me, please?'

Sam turned and looked at the horse then he turned back to her. 'I am sorry, my lady, he has cast a shoe. No one can use him until he has been to the farrier.'

'Then why not take him down there?'

There was a long pause. 'There is no one there to shoe him, my lady. I understand Mr Henry has advertised for a new farrier and blacksmith for the farm, but until one is found, we have to wait until someone is free to walk him up to the village to see Jo Wicks.'

Emily was staring at him. 'Where is Daniel?'

Sam pressed his lips together. 'I understand you will have to ask Mr Henry that, my lady.'

'But my husband isn't here.'

'No, my lady.' Sam turned away and walked swiftly back down the line of stalls and out into the yard. Pip pushed at his broom, paused to splash some water over the cobbles and swept again, harder.

Emily walked back to the house and in through the front door. There she rang the bell. It was a long time before Beaton appeared.

'Do you know when my husband is returning?' she asked.

He inclined his head slightly towards her. 'I am sorry, my lady. He did not inform me.'

'Are there no horses I can ride?'

'That is for Sam to say, my lady, but I understand not.'

'Who is shoeing the working horses?'

'I am afraid that is not my department, my lady. I have no idea.'

'I gather Daniel has left our service.'

She was watching his face closely and she saw the slight wince as he turned away. 'I oversee the house servants, my lady. I have no idea what happens down on the farm.'

'But that's not true, is it?' she insisted. 'You all know everything. I am the only one who doesn't. I have no maid, Mrs Field tells me nothing, I am alone here and now I am a prisoner in my own house!'

'You are no prisoner, my lady.' Beaton carefully schooled his features. 'There is nothing to stop you walking outside.'

'Then I will. I will walk down to the farm. I cannot believe the Turtills have gone as well.'

'I am sure not, my lady.' He paused. 'Will that be all, my lady?'

Her anger gave her the energy to walk the first half-mile. After that she slowed, regretting her high-heeled boots, but she was determined not to give in. In fact she had no alternative. It was clear there was no other way of either reaching the farm, or of returning home after her visit.

The farmhouse was up a short track some quarter of a mile above the yard and the smithy. She paused at the fork in the drive, looking down towards the barns. From there she could see the yard. It was deserted. The forge and the cottage behind it were closed up, the curtains in the cottage pulled across the windows. There was no sign of anyone in the yard. She could see an empty hay wagon pulled up against the wall of the old barn. One of the wheels was missing; there was a pile of bricks under the axle holding the wagon level.

Jessie Turtill was in the kitchen of the farmhouse talking to Sarah, one of the maids. She turned as Lady Emily appeared at the door and dropped a perfunctory curtsey. 'My lady, I didn't know you were coming. Please, go through to the parlour. You shouldn't come into the kitchen. Fred is in the backhouse, I'll call him.'

'No!' Emily walked into the room and threw her gloves down on the kitchen table. 'No, it is you I want to talk to. The girl can go.'

Jessie frowned, but she nodded at Sarah, who vanished through a back door into the dairy. Jessie waited. She was a large woman in her mid-forties with work-roughened hands and greying hair under her cap, but for all the hostility in her face, her eyes were kind.

'I have come to see you, Jessie, because no one else will be honest with me,' Emily said at last. There was a note of desperation in her voice. 'My husband has gone away, I'm not sure where; my maid, Molly, has left my service as you know, the servants will not talk to me and I understand there is no horse I can ride.' She paused. 'Because Daniel has gone.' The final words came out in a whisper.

'And what did you want from me, my lady?' Jessie asked at last.

'The truth.' Emily had been looking down at the table, unconsciously noting how spotlessly clean it was. There was nothing on it but her grey silk gloves. 'Where has Daniel gone?'

Jessie tightened her lips. For a moment she said nothing, then she nodded as though coming to a decision in her own mind. 'Your husband gave orders that no one should tell you, my lady,' she said at last, 'in case you were upset. But as Mr Henry has remained away so long, I see nothing for it but to tell you. Daniel died, my lady.'

Emily clenched her fists in her skirt, but she said nothing, her eyes on the floor. Jessie waited, watching her. It was several seconds before Emily at last looked up. 'How?' she whispered. 'How did he die?'

'I understand it was some sort of accident, my lady.' Jessie was not going to be the one to tell her what had happened. 'The men are understandably upset.'

'Was it the wagon? I saw the wheel was missing.'

'No, my lady. Not the wagon.'

'What then? Do they think it was my fault?' she whispered again.

'As to that, my lady, you would have to ask them,' Jessie said. 'Suffice to say that he is with his Susan and the babe in heaven.'

'Of course.' Emily picked up the gloves and began shredding the fine silk between her fingers. She took a deep breath. 'When is the funeral?' She was finding it hard to speak. 'My husband said I should represent him when Susan and the baby were buried?'

'It is on Tuesday, my lady.' Jessie hesitated. She softened her voice a little. 'I understand it will be a family affair, my lady. I don't think it would be appropriate for you to go under the circumstances.'

'Under the circumstances?' Emily echoed. 'And Daniel? He is to be buried with them?'

Jessie looked for the first time disconcerted. 'I understand not, my lady. He has been buried privately.'

'Privately?' Emily looked up again. 'What does that mean?'

'It is not for me to say, my lady. I don't know anything about it –' Jessie broke off as the door opened and her husband walked in.

'Lady Emily,' he said curtly. 'I am afraid I must ask you to leave. As for the funeral, I understand there will not be any vehicles available to collect anyone from the Hall.'

'Of course.' Emily turned towards the outside door. She tried to muster a little dignity as she paused and gave a faint smile. 'Thank you, Jessie.' She ignored the woman's husband completely.

She waited until she was out of sight of the farmhouse before she stopped. She leaned on the fence which bounded the south park of the Hall and stared out at the sheep grazing in the sunshine. She would never see Daniel again. The information was only slowly sinking in, though somewhere deep inside her, she knew she had suspected this, and, a thought not to be faced yet, that his death might have something to do with Henry. What had she expected him to do when she accused Daniel of raping her? In her anger and spite had she considered for a single moment what her husband' s reaction might be? She took a deep breath, aware suddenly of how much her feet were hurting in the boots. She would miss Daniel's ministrations. She smiled a little, remembering how he had pulled off her riding boots for her, how he had removed all her clothes, the touch of his body on hers and, as it finally dawned on her that he would never touch her again, at last the tears began to flow. There would never be another man save her husband, of that she was certain. Henry would see to that. As she leaned on the fence and sobbed, her sorrow was all for herself. Not once did she give another thought to Susan or the baby, or to Daniel and how he might have died.

The group of walkers had spread sideways outside the wire as the tractor approached. 'Don't let him scare you!' Rosemary cried. 'He wants to see us run. We won't give him the satisfaction!' She stood, hands on hips in front of the rest of the group, glaring at Jackson as he approached. Far behind him, Mike Turtill was running as best he could over the furrows trying to catch up.

Jackson smirked as he focused on the people ahead of him. He was not slowing down. He clutched the steering wheel tightly, leaning forward to peer out of the windscreen, judging the distance carefully. At the very last moment, as he was nearly on them, he swung the wheel sharply to the left. He was close enough to see Rosemary's face, her mouth open in fury or fear, he wasn't sure which. He saw the other figures round her and he let out an exultant whoop as the tractor veered violently away from her and he headed up the furrows towards the gate.

Behind him the huge plough swung out to the right. It caught Rosemary only a glancing blow but she went down like a stalk of grass. For a moment no one moved. The tractor hurtled on up the field, Jackson, oblivious to the damage he had done, still at the wheel.

'Oh God!' Steve fell on his knees beside his wife. 'Rosemary?' He caught her hand, staring down at her in disbelief, seeing only the curtain of blood which had engulfed her head. Behind him the secretary of the walking group, Dave Roberts, had reached for his mobile and was already dialling for an ambulance. Across the field Ken and John had broken into a run with Zoë and Amanda behind them.

Dave's wife, Jan, knelt beside Steve and gently pushed him back. 'Is she breathing?' She reached over to feel for a pulse and took her hand away sticky with blood. 'I can't feel anything. Here, I'll start CPR.' She glanced up at Dave. 'Tell them it's bad – a blow to the head – and tell them there's no vehicular access. Maybe this is one for the air ambulance,' she commanded, her years as a St John Ambulance volunteer automatically kicking in as the others stood around too stunned to move.

Zoë was staring down at Rosemary as Mike arrived, so out of breath he couldn't speak. When he did, he was incoherent. 'I told him not to.' The words tumbled over each other. 'He was drunk. He just wanted to frighten her. He didn't mean to hit her.' He was looking down at Rosemary lying on the path in a pool of blood, then he turned and gazed up the field. The tractor had disappeared over the line of the horizon but they could still hear the roar of the engine. It went on and on as if it was going to race around the field for ever, then abruptly it stopped. The silence was absolute, broken only by the keening cry of a gull in the wind.

'Somebody had better ring Bill,' Ken murmured. He glanced up as Leo appeared to stand behind them, his face grim. On his way back to The Old Forge he had seen what happened from the gate. 'I will.' He reached into his pocket for his mobile. 'I have the number here.'

The rest of the group stood in silence. One woman was crying softly; two others turned their backs and moved away a little, their arms around one another, faces white.

'She's dead, isn't she?' Steve whispered. He was still clutching Rosemary's hand.

'Not if I have anything to do with it,' Jan said robustly between chest compressions. 'Cover her up with something to keep her warm. The rest of you stand back. Give me some space.'

It was the sword. She shouldn't have moved the sword.

Rosemary was vaguely aware that she was lying on the ground; something had hit her; she didn't know what. It was silent there in the field and the ground was surprisingly comfortable. She was almost floating, but there was danger nearby. She had felt the tension around the burial mound, been aware that she had done something terribly wrong in touching the sword, taking it away. It was protected by special charms, runes of immense power. She could see the man who had put it there, his face strong, weatherbeaten, his cloak of animal furs, a necklace of amber beads round his neck. His eyes were like shards of flint as he looked down at her.

I didn't mean to take it away. She was repeating the words in her head. I'm sorry. I didn't know.

Ignorance was no defence. The coiling spiral of curses which bound the sword to its owner had been activated. Where was he? Who was he? She was too tired to wonder any more. I could fetch it. Bring it back. I hid it nearby. I wanted the path to go through unhindered. I'm sorry.

There was a strange roaring in her head. She tried to open her eyelids but they wouldn't obey her. She could feel a sudden wind round the place where she lay and she could see the trees in her mind, bending, sweeping, mourning the loss of the sword.

A great yellow bird had come to collect her, take her to hell, but she wouldn't go to hell. She was doomed. Cursed. She had meddled in things which didn't concern her.

I'm sorry. I shouldn't have touched it.

She could hear voices. She was being lifted up now. Her head hurt. The man with the flint eyes was near her, watching, his hands lifted to tighten the curse.

I can tell you where the sword is. I know it's safe. I didn't damage it. It was so old. I wrapped it carefully.

They were carrying her away from the wood now. It was a helicopter not a bird; she could hear a police siren, she was safe. But the man with the flint eyes was still there with her. He was following. His curses were circling her like smoke. There was to be no escape. She had touched the sword. She had defiled the grave.

* * *

Jade woke suddenly as the yellow helicopter swung low overhead and roared away to the west. She had fallen asleep on The Old Forge doorstep, sitting beside Leo's abandoned gumboots and his garden fork. She stood up slowly and stretched painfully. Her head hurt from where it had rested against the wood of the doorframe and she was hungry. She looked at her wristwatch. It was lunchtime. So, where was Leo? She squinted up at the vanishing speck in the sky. The air ambulance had been very close and very low. Had there been an accident down on the river? She scowled. It wouldn't have been him. He was much too careful with his boat.

She tiptoed through his garden and glanced back to check that he hadn't arrived and gone in through the front door, not realising that she was there. But no, the place was still deserted. Then she spotted a group of people walking up across the lawns towards the barns. She frowned. There were a lot of them – a couple of dozen or so. They paused outside Steve and Rosemary's, then they began to break up. Most were finding their way back to the cars which had been parked outside The Summer Barn; some were heading round the back towards the garage area, and four, no, five of them were heading towards the Lloyds'. She screwed up her eyes. Yes, Zoë and Ken were there and the other couple staying with them, and another man. She ran forward a few steps. It was Leo.

'Hello, Jade.' Amanda saw her first. 'Are you going to join us for lunch?' She glanced at Zoë. 'Does she know what's happened?' she mouthed.

Zoë shrugged. 'Leo, will you stay? Please. Tell Jade that Jackson has had to go away.'

It seemed wrong to resume their plans, to activate the smouldering barbecue, to fetch the food from the fridge and bring out the glasses, but all the other participants in the morning's activities had gone now and what else was there to do? Rosemary had been stabilised at the scene of the accident

392

and flown to hospital. Steve and Bill Turtill, who had driven back from a meeting with his solicitor, had followed in a police car. Jackson had been arrested and that meant that Jade was, technically at least, alone. Leo sat with her on the wall at the edge of the terrace and spoke to her quietly. 'We've rung your mum and dad, Jade. They will be here soon.'

Her face was white and pinched and she was strangely silent. 'I saw the helicopter. It went right over The Old Forge,' she said at last. 'Will Rosemary die?'

'We hope not.' He shook his head. 'She has had a very bad head injury but she was breathing again when they took her to hospital.'

'And Jackson did it?'

'He didn't mean to, Jade. He wanted to scare them, that's all.'

'He'll go to prison, won't he?' She seemed matter-of-fact about it rather than worried.

'I don't know. It was an accident, but he shouldn't have been driving when he had been drinking.'

'It was only a tractor.'

'A tractor is a very dangerous thing if you're not in proper control of it.' He looked up as John approached with a glass of Pimm's and another of squash for Jade. John sat on the wall next to him. 'Did you hear what Rosemary said when they put her in the 'copter?' he murmured.

Leo shook his head. 'I thought she was out cold.'

'She was, but she seemed to be trying to say something about you.'

'Me?'

'You would know what to do with the sword.'

'Sword?'

John nodded. 'Zoë, you heard her, didn't you?'

Zoë glanced at Ken and then came over. 'She was delirious, John. I don't think it meant anything. But yes, she said Leo several times and what sounded like sword.' She shivered. 'I wish someone would let us know how she is.'

'Bill is going to ring Penny when he hears and she will tell us.' Ken had followed Zoë over. He glared at Leo. 'I gather you spent the night with my wife.'

Jade slid off the wall where she had been sitting next to Leo, swinging her legs. 'Why? Why did you spend the night with her?' she yelled at Leo. She pummelled him on the chest with her fists. 'If you had stayed here none of this would have happened!'

'Jade, love –' Amanda went over and put her arm round Jade's thin shoulders but the girl threw her off.

'Don't touch me!' she snapped. She turned to Zoë and glared at her. 'It's no good. Something awful is going to happen to you too. I've put a spell on you and there is nothing you can do about it. You are going to die, just like Rosemary!' With a sob she turned and ran away from them, heading towards home.

'Leave her.' Amanda put out her hand and grabbed Leo's arm as he began to follow her. 'It's all been an awful shock for her. Give her a bit of time. If her parents are coming they are the ones to look after her.'

Leo subsided onto the wall and nodded. 'Poor kid.' He glanced at Zoë. 'Don't let her frighten you.'

Zoë gave a faint smile. 'I'm not.'

'I think it's time you left,' Ken said, meeting Leo's eye. 'Don't you?'

'Ken!' Zoë protested, but Leo stood up.

'You are probably right.' He winked at Zoë. 'You know where I am.' Seconds later he had vaulted the low wall and was striding across the grass.

Zoë turned and walked into the house. No one followed her. She went through the kitchen and into the great room half-expecting to feel it ringing with the shockwaves of what had happened but there was nothing.

She ran upstairs and into her and Ken's bedroom and stood looking round. It felt different; uneasy. Had the wretched child been in there? She stooped and picked up the cotton bag lying on the floor near the bed. Where had that come from? Jade? Or Ken? She threw it down on the chair. She walked into the bathroom and washed her face, then she went over to the window and looked down at the other three standing awkwardly round the barbecue. They weren't talking. Amanda was turning the sausages with the tongs while the two men appeared to have abandoned the Pimm's in favour of bottles of lager. She turned away with a sigh and threw herself down on the bed, unaware of the sinister object which had been placed beneath it. In minutes she had drifted off to sleep.

When she woke it was dark. She lay still, aware only that she had had the strangest dream: she was pregnant, heavily pregnant, and she could feel the baby moving inside her. Her hand went to her belly and she stroked it sleepily. It was completely flat. Her hand fell away and for a moment she found she was fighting the most enormous disappointment. She lay gazing round the bedroom blindly, battling with her tears; it was several minutes before she levered herself out of bed and turned on the light. It was just after seven. She had slept for hours.

Leaning over the banisters she could see that the lights were on and the TV was playing quietly in the corner. There was no sign of the others. She changed quickly into jeans and a thick sweater and ran down the stairs. The whole place seemed deserted. Then she spotted the note.

Hi Zoë, so sorry about everything that has happened. Don't know where Ken is. John and I have talked and we thought it was probably better if we gave you some space so we are heading home. I will ring you tomorrow.
   Lots of love, Manda.
   PS in your shoes I would climb aboard the lugger!!

Zoë smiled in spite of herself. Did that last cryptic comment mean what she thought it meant? She looked round again. So, where was Ken? Suddenly she didn't want to know.

She grabbed the torch out of the drawer, reached up and turned off the master switch for the floodlights, then she opened the door.

Picking her way across the grass, she headed for the hedge which separated their garden from that of The Threshing Barn next door. She glanced up at the Formbys'. All the lights there were off. The Watts's car was outside The Summer Barn and the lights there were on behind the drawn curtains, so at least Jade wasn't alone. She wondered what had happened to Jackson. She hoped Rosemary was OK. Following the beam of her torch she went towards the gap in the hedge and it was then that she spotted the long metal shape lying half hidden under the leaves. She paused and trained the beam on it, then she squatted down and reached out to pick it up. She knew at once what it was. A sword. The sword.

Leo laid it reverently on his worktop and reached for a magnifying glass from one of the shelves. He had locked the door after she came in and drawn the blinds. 'We don't want any more small eyes peering in at the windows, making trouble,' he said. He pointed at a stool and she perched on it obediently.

'It is a sword, isn't it?' she said after a long silence.

He was carefully examining the blade in front of him. It was rusted and corroded but the basic sword shape was clear to see. 'I can see carving here and traces of inlay on the hilt,' he breathed. 'This is, or was, exquisite workmanship.'

'Is it like the ones they found at Sutton Hoo?' she whispered.

'It might be. My guess is that it came from the burial mound out there; and that it is a burial mound with a pretty rich and important guy buried in it.' He laid down the magnifying glass and looked at her. 'How on earth did it get into your hedge?'

'Rosemary? She mentioned a sword. And she mentioned you, Leo. She said you would know what to do with it. As they were putting her into the air ambulance.' She shrugged. 'Do you think she found it when she was poking round in Dead Man's Field? Either that or she saw it in her hedge and recognised it. Perhaps someone else had hidden it there. Perhaps they meant to come back for it.'

'Jackson?'

'Maybe. Or one of the walkers this afternoon.' She leaned forward and touched it tentatively with a finger.

There was another long silence. Leo reached for his magnifying glass again. 'This shouldn't have been removed from wherever it was found. It is probably unbelievably valuable. It needs research. It needs restoration.'

She gave a faint smile. 'And let me guess. You're the man to do it, right?'

He laughed. 'I would love to, in theory.' He shook his head. 'But this is very specialised work. And I would need a proper forge. Something I don't intend to have ever again. And a laboratory of some sort, I would think. No, I fear we are going to have to hand this over to the experts.'

With a sigh he stood up and walked across to the window. 'It's so dark out there. The whole place is deserted.'

'Not quite. Sharon and Jeff seem to be back, thank goodness. Poor things. What a catastrophe to come back to.'

Picking up a paper bag from the worktop he put it on the table. 'Doughnuts,' he said, sitting down. 'I bought them this morning and forgot all about them. Have one.' He bent over the sword again. Zoë rummaged in the bag and took one out. She was ravenous, she realised.

'I had a call from Bill, just before you came,' Leo said suddenly. 'Steve rang him from the hospital.'

'And?'

'Rosemary is in intensive care. She is in a coma and will almost certainly need brain surgery.'

'Oh God.' Zoë looked up at him. She put down the doughnut. 'Supposing she doesn't make it?'

He shook his head sadly. 'Let's hope for the best. That's all we can do.'

Flecks of rust and soil had crumbled off the sword as it lay on the table and there was a litter of dead leaves and dried plant stalks lying around it as Leo lifted the sword up, turned it gently over and began to examine the other side. Zoë watched as he picked up the magnifying glass again. He held the blade angled so that the light from the lamp caught it. 'It's hard to see, but there are inscriptions on the blade; the pommel is in better condition. It is clearer here.' He squinted as he looked more closely. 'It was a beautiful piece of craftsmanship.'

'So, it is very old?'

'Oh, yes.' He lifted his head and smiled at her. 'I am pretty sure it is Anglo-Saxon. It's pattern welded. That means the blade is made in a particular way; it made them very strong. And these are runes. I've seen enough of them in the museums – and at Sutton Hoo, of course. I don't know how one dates it, but it must be at least a thousand years old.'

They both sat and stared at it. 'I would so love to keep this, just for a while. Do some research on it myself,' Leo went on. There was a wistful note in his voice.

'It can't have just been lost, so it must have been buried with its owner,' Zoë said at last. 'Do you think he was a king?'

Leo shrugged. 'I doubt it. There is only one burial mound down there, as far as we know, isn't there? And it isn't very large. It couldn't have had a boat in it. Could it?' He looked at her again and smiled.

'No, but it could be to do with that ghost ship, couldn't

it?' Zoë replied after another pause. 'Oh, Leo, it might be all tied up in some way.'

As she looked down at the sword, the phone in her pocket chimed. She pulled it out and glanced at it. 'It's from Ken. He's not coming back tonight,' she said.

'Does he say why?'

'The project he's working on in Ipswich; apparently they phoned him and asked him to go over there urgently.'

'Do you believe him?'

She sighed. 'I don't know.'

'But it means you can stay here.'

For a moment they held each other's gaze, then she smiled. 'Yes, please.' She switched off the phone.

'Excellent.' He grinned.

They both looked down at the sword again. Zoë could see the remains of the engravings now her eyes were getting used to interpreting the corroded blade with its nodules and grooves and ragged edges.

'It seems awful for it to be taken away from the man who owned it. It must have been his most treasured possession.' She sighed. 'I am always a bit sad when I see things in museums which have been removed from graves. It seems wrong to treat somewhere sacred as if it were a treasure hoard.'

He nodded. 'It has always been that way. Remember Egypt? The tombs in the Valley of the Kings were robbed as often as not by the very men who dug them.'

'It doesn't mean we have to rob this one, though, does it?'

He held her gaze and after a moment, he laughed. 'Are you suggesting we take this back? Rebury it?' He looked back at the sword. 'It is so special. Imagine how it looked when it was new,' he said. There was a touch of awe in his voice. 'I wonder if that would be the right thing, to rebury it?'

'I think so.' She nodded. 'Have you got a camera? You can take lots of photos of it for your research, but I think it ought to go back with its owner.' She gave a sudden quick shiver. 'It feels wrong to have taken it away. I think that's what Rosemary meant.' She reached out to it again, then withdrew her hand without touching it. 'Supposing it is cursed, Leo. Supposing anyone who touches it is cursed?'

He cocked an eyebrow at her. 'Is there a reason you are saying that? Can you feel something?'

'I don't know.' For a moment she looked almost miserable. 'Yes, I suppose I can.'

'It could be true, of course,' he said thoughtfully. 'In all kinds of cultures they would use magic to protect the dead – either to discourage people from grave robbing, or to make sure the dead stayed dead and didn't come back to haunt the living.'

'Like poor Dan.'

He looked startled. 'Ah, Dan, the ghost in your barn. You don't really believe that, do you? Ouija boards?'

'No,' she heard the uncertainty in her own voice. 'I don't think so, but it was strange. It was so – definite. So real.'

'Well, your so-called psychic friend has gone, so we'll never know on that score.' He paused. 'We need someone who can read the runes.'

'Are they clear enough to see?' She came closer.

He looked up, reached across and kissed her. 'You taste of sugar.'

'Eat yours, then you will too.'

He reached into the bag and added a shower of sugar crystals to the mess of soil and rust on the newspaper in front of him.

'There is a shop in Woodbridge which sells runes and things in little bags,' she went on. 'They would have a book.'

'No need. I've got books on runes somewhere,' he said. 'I studied Anglo-Saxon at university. But it was a long time ago.'

She stared up at him again. 'You are amazing. Is there anything you can't do?'

He laughed. 'Not a lot.'

'Let's rebury it, Leo.' Suddenly her eyes were shining. 'It would be the right thing to take it back, wouldn't it? Please. Then it is up to the ancient gods, whoever they were. If the sword is ever found again someone else will decide its fate.'

'If we got caught it would take an awful lot of explaining.'

She stood up and walked round the table to him, putting her arms round him. 'No problem. We won't get caught!'

In the field the burial mound of the Lord Egbert and his servant Hrotgar lay unnoticed by the passing Danish horde. Under the soil the death treasure lay untouched, but Destiny Maker, the best and greatest sword made by Eric the sword-smith, was not there.

After the ill-omened barbecue that afternoon John and Amanda had said they wanted to rest for a while, and as Zoë was asleep, Ken had walked up the fields away from the river. He needed to be alone. An awful lot had happened in the last twenty-four hours and his head was reeling. He walked for a long time, conscious that he was probably going round in circles, and found himself eventually in the spot where he had woken from his sleepwalking incident. He knew now it was a ruined church; he had traced his route on a local map. It was an Anglo-Saxon church and had been destroyed, so the legend went, during a Viking raid in the ninth century. It seemed odd that it had never been rebuilt, but then after the raid there was no village left any more.

He sat down on a low pile of flints, the remnant of an ancient wall, and heaved a long sigh. The idyll he and Zoë had promised themselves was over almost before it had begun. He knew it and so obviously did she. His first wave of fury at suspecting she was having an affair with the man next door had begun to subside. After all, if he was honest the passion between him and her was long gone; he had been selfish persuading her to come here, trying to bully her into sailing when he knew she was frightened of the water, forcing her to abandon her job and her friends and – he had to acknowledge that was a part of it – the chance of a family. And what had he done when he arrived? He had found himself a girlfriend in Woodbridge. He smiled at the thought. Zoë hadn't any idea, of course, but subconsciously perhaps she had guessed. Otherwise why would she turn to that man – what was it Jackson called him, the freak? – to comfort herself?

Jackson.

His thoughts turned to Rosemary. Poor woman. He wondered if she would make it. What a can of worms he had moved them into. And it had all seemed so peaceful!

An hour later he had returned to the barn, seen no sign of any of the others, and tiptoed out to the garage. Collecting his car he headed off towards Woodbridge. Sylvia was home and he was in need of some TLC. The rest of them could go to hell. He would text Zoë later on the pretext that he was going to stay overnight in Ipswich and let her know he wasn't coming home.

After the accident the police had secured the scene with blue and white tape which fluttered in the breeze, and returned later in the afternoon with a team of investigators to try to piece together what had happened. It seemed straightforward. Jackson Watts had taken the tractor without permission, having imbibed a good deal of lager, and had driven it deliberately at a bunch of walkers with a view to scaring them off Mr Turtill's field. The witness statements were all fairly consistent. He had driven without due care and attention and in order to intimidate but in all probability he had not intended to cause injury or loss of life. He had steered away from the group of walkers at the last moment and in the normal course of events he would have missed them. The injuries to Mrs Formby were caused by the plough which had swung loose behind the tractor. Engineers were checking the hydraulics which lifted the blades out of the soil, but it seemed clear that it was the erratic driving and the incorrect use of the machine which had caused it to lurch in the way it did.

The photographer ducked under the tape, into the edge of the copse with his camera. He took pictures of the cut wire and the trampled nettles. It had to be remembered that these people were trespassing on private land. He leaned forward and took several more pictures, then he noticed the old spades. They looked as though they had been there a while. He leaned in and pulled one out of the brambles with a gloved hand. The rusty old blade was half buried and it tore up some grass with it, leaving a square of exposed soil. He leaned closer. A couple of twigs, bleached and stained, had emerged from the earth. And another. He caught his breath, and leaned down, gently filtering the soil with his fingers. They were ribs. He scraped a bit more of the soil and found several vertebrae. He worked his way upward slowly and there it was. A human skull. 'No wonder it's called Dead Man's field,' he muttered. He backed out of the undergrowth and looked round for his colleague. 'Over here, mate. You are not going to believe this, but I've found a body.'

18

Zoë woke and for a moment she didn't know where she was. She stretched luxuriously, then she remembered Leo. She put her hand out to his side of the bed but there was no one there. The sheet was cold.

'Leo!' She sat up in the dark.

'It's all right. I'm here.'

She could see him now, a silhouette against his bedroom window. He was staring out into the night.

'Couldn't you sleep?'

He turned away from the window and, coming over to the bed, sat down beside her. Leaning down, he kissed her long and hard. She put her arms round his neck. 'Come back to bed.'

'In a minute.' He stood up again. 'Zoë, there is something I want to discuss with you.'

'What?' She felt herself tense with apprehension at the sudden change in his mood.

'I've been planning a trip on *Curlew*, the last of the season.'

'And?' She felt suddenly cold.

'And, I haven't mentioned it because I didn't know how

my work was going to pan out – there is always an element of uncertainty when one is a freelance.' He moved away from her, back to the window. 'I have a couple of weeks coming up. I want to go, get away from all this, and I want you to come with me.'

'Me?'

'You.'

'But I can't!'

'Because of Ken?'

'Yes, of course because of Ken.'

There was a long silence in the room, then he laughed quietly. 'Zoë, you are in my bed, in my bedroom. Ken is not really a factor in this, is he?'

She didn't answer.

'Do you want to come?' he said at last.

'You know I do.'

'Even if it means sailing across the North Sea?'

'In *Curlew*?' It was a horrified whisper.

'In *Curlew*. You could learn to be a pirate's moll!' He grinned. 'Have you got a passport?'

'Of course I have.' Her brain was whirling. She pushed herself up against the pillows.

'I'll take you shopping in Holland; or we'll jump on the train once we're over there and go to Paris. Get you those gypsy clothes. Set the real Zoë free.'

'Leo.' She shook her head. 'I would so love to. It sounds so exciting. Indiana Jones. Enid Blyton! But the truth is, I'm scared.'

'No you're not. You are a brave, gutsy lady. All you've been waiting for is someone to suggest it!'

'But I hate sailing. You know I do.'

'Not with me.'

'With you it's been in the river.'

'And you've passed the test. Promotion. Leo's sea school is next.' He lifted the curtain and stared out again, then he turned back to her. 'And I tell you what. If we decided to rebury the sword, that would be a test of our nerve and derring-do. How about that? Would that give you time to think? But it can't be too long. The weather will change soon and then the chance will have gone.'

Behind him down on the river the mist was growing thicker. In the silence of the night as the tide rose, carrying the deep sea water up the channel once more, the shadow of the great long ship headed in across the bar on its journey towards death and destruction.

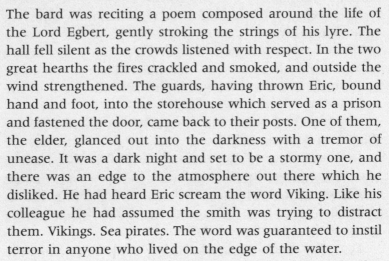

The bard was reciting a poem composed around the life of the Lord Egbert, gently stroking the strings of his lyre. The hall fell silent as the crowds listened with respect. In the two great hearths the fires crackled and smoked, and outside the wind strengthened. The guards, having thrown Eric, bound hand and foot, into the storehouse which served as a prison and fastened the door, came back to their posts. One of them, the elder, glanced out into the darkness with a tremor of unease. It was a dark night and set to be a stormy one, and there was an edge to the atmosphere out there which he disliked. He had heard Eric scream the word Viking. Like his colleague he had assumed the smith was trying to distract them. Vikings. Sea pirates. The word was guaranteed to instil terror in anyone who lived on the edge of the water.

The moonlight was patchy, clouds streaming across the sky. Surely no ship could come up-river in this weather? But then earlier the night had been still, the river shrouded in fog, fog which had dissipated at last with the first gentle breezes coming from the south-east. Restlessly he put his hand on his sword and loosened it in the scabbard. His companion was staring in through the door, straining to listen to the eulogy declaimed by the man standing on the dais in the distance, all his attention on the words and music, his back to the night.

In the darkness of his prison Eric was fighting his bonds furiously, working his hands loose as he wriggled towards the wall, searching for something sharp to help him saw through the ropes. They had tied him hurriedly and carelessly. The end of the knot worked free and he felt it loosen. With a grunt of satisfaction he struggled some more and at last his hands were free. He bent to untie his ankles, then he set to, to force open the door. It was taking too long. He groaned with impatience. Any moment the invaders would be on them, and everyone was unprepared. He could hear the music, the sudden cheering from the hall. They hadn't understood his warning.

He launched himself at the door afresh, frantically throwing himself against it. It hadn't been built as a prison; it was a storehouse. Eventually the hinges gave with a splintering sound, tearing away from the doorframe. The men on guard at the door could not have failed to hear the crash of the door falling, but it was too late.

The attack was swift and deadly. Below the hall on the flank of the low hillside the invaders streamed through the village with yells of fury, naked swords in their hands, ransacking the cottages as they went. Between one moment and next, or so it seemed, the night was lit with fire as thatched roofs were put to the torch, flames and sparks roaring up into the night sky.

As the smell of burning reached upwards and stained the clouds red, the men turned away from the looted, ruined cottages and began to stream up the hill towards the mead hall. Beneath their helmets their faces were wild and contorted, the pupils of their eyes pinpoints against the blaze. Eric had heard descriptions of attacks like this, men with their wits crazed, berserker, the scop had called it, mad with battle rage in the service of their god, Odin, oblivious to pain, without fear, bent only on joining their god in Valhalla.

He stared round frantically and to his amazement he saw

Destiny Maker lying on the ground where it had fallen from his hand, the blade reflecting the deep scarlet of the flames which lit the night. Stooping, he picked it up, the glittering hilt solid in his hand, and he turned to face the enemy.

He had an instant to tighten his grip on Destiny Maker and raise it above his head as the vanguard of the Danish horde reached him and the roar of battle broke about his ears. He was without armour, he had no shield, but his fury and despair were for a while more than a match for the men who attacked him.

The two men at the doors of the mead hall died instantly but their killers turned to find Eric behind them. Both fell, their last sight the flames reflected in the flailing blade. Exhausted, blinded by sweat, Eric turned and found himself face to face with a huge man, moustached, helmeted, dressed in heavy armour, a shield on his arm. The man raised his sword and Eric took the chance, pushing his own blade into the vulnerable spot under the man's armpit. The giant gave a groan and staggered, then he fell.

Outnumbered and overwhelmed at last Eric, for all his bravery, stood no chance. He fell, a curtain of blood veiling his eyes, and collapsed on the ground only a few feet from the door of the hall. The howling mob of invaders had closed on the building, barricading the doors shut. Inside the music and cheers had long ago turned to screams. As the building was set alight and those inside realised there would be no escape, those screams grew ever more desperate but Eric did not hear them. He was dead.

U

Emily was finding it harder and harder to sleep. Each morning she rose before it grew light and sat, wrapped in a thick shawl, in a chair facing the window watching the sunrise. Only when she had heard the servants stirring in the house below did she creep back to bed and pretend to be asleep, and when whichever housemaid had been allocated to her that day knocked on the door and came in to light the fire, she lay with her eyes closed until the girl had finished and crept out again.

Finally she wrote to her father, begging him to send a carriage for her, telling him that Henry had been called away and she was alone and unhappy. She left the letter on the salver in the hall; later that day it had gone. She hoped that someone had taken it to the post.

There was still no word from Henry. The funeral had taken place. The whole household had gone to it except for her. They returned, sad, dressed in black, and did not speak to her; she didn't ask about it.

Three days later she rose early as was her custom, but this time she dressed. She went slowly down the broad flight of stairs wearing her outdoor boots, her coat, her hat and she set off down the drive in the almost-light of a cold dawn. It took her half an hour to walk down to the farmyard. There was no one about, which seemed strange. Surely the men should be at work by now? She frowned. She could hear the restless stirrings in the henhouse, the contented snorts of pigs from the sties behind the summer barn, and somewhere a robin was singing its sad thready song into the dawn. She walked across to the forge and pushed open the door. It was cold, the floor swept clean, the tools hung in neat rows on the wall, the firebed empty.

'Dan?' she whispered.

There was no reply.

She walked out and went round to the cottage. She didn't try the door. The place was obviously empty, the curtains closed, the chimney cold. She supposed that Fred Turtill would hire a new smith soon and the man would move his family into the forge. She shivered and suddenly she stopped. Was that a face at one of the windows? A young woman, with long blonde hair fastened in a thick heavy plait which swung forward over her shoulder. Emily stared at her for several seconds and then the woman had gone. She stood rooted to the spot staring at the window but there was no one there. The cottage was empty. It was her imagination.

She walked slowly across the yard to the old barn and, with difficulty pushing open one of the tall heavy doors, she peered inside. The huge space was full of shadows. She gazed round. Half the barn was stacked now with sacks of stored barley and wheat; there were machines parked in there too, a thresher, a plough, a harrow, scythes, rakes, a dray. Why was there no one about? The horses were there in the line of stalls, the shires, the cart horses, the Suffolks. The animals stirred uneasily as she appeared and she saw their ears flick back towards her momentarily before they returned to pulling at the hay in the racks. They were uninterested in her arrival, waiting for George and the men, waiting for the day's work to begin. Poor Bella had spent her last days in one of those stalls. She sighed. If she had only left the horse here; ignored it; ignored him.

She walked right into the barn and stood looking round uneasily. She would be the first to acknowledge that she wasn't usually a sensitive woman, but in here she could feel something, a frisson of fear, an echo of violence. Was it in here he had died? One of the horses let out a piercing whinny and stamped its hoof, and she jumped, her heart thudding with fright. Defiantly she took a couple of steps forward, her gaze fixed steadfastly on the horse. She could hear the sparrows twittering outside now, pecking in the chaff which was blowing round the yard. She took another step and an owl launched itself silently from a high rafter and flew towards the door past her. She could feel her mouth growing dry. It was as if the whole building was trying to scare her away. She took another step forward and then froze. From somewhere nearby she could hear a baby crying.

She clenched her fists. She was not going to run away.

There were babies aplenty on the estate, surely there were. This was not Susan's baby. It couldn't have been Susan's baby; she had heard that it had not drawn breath. Looking round wildly she waited to hear the cry again, but there was complete silence in the barn. Even the horses had for a moment stopped their restless movements and appeared to be listening too.

'Dan?' Her sudden desperate cry echoed up into the roof space. 'Dan, I'm sorry.'

There was no answer.

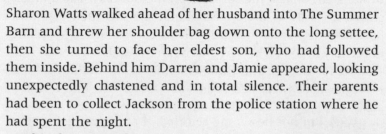

Sharon Watts walked ahead of her husband into The Summer Barn and threw her shoulder bag down onto the long settee, then she turned to face her eldest son, who had followed them inside. Behind him Darren and Jamie appeared, looking unexpectedly chastened and in total silence. Their parents had been to collect Jackson from the police station where he had spent the night.

'This does it, Jackson. We are taking you home and you are never, ever, coming down to this godforsaken place again. You put it on the market tomorrow, Jeff, do you hear me?' Sharon spun round and strode across to the bar. Helping herself to a hefty slug of neat vodka she stood for a moment swilling it round in her mouth. 'Arrested! Charged with causing grievous bodily harm and God knows what! Attempted murder probably, of that poor woman next door! And then on top of everything, you have to accuse that decent man across there, who has taken more trouble with Jade than you ever did, of being a paedo! I just don't believe it. What did you think that would achieve? It was hardly going to divert attention from what you'd done.'

They had spent two hours in the police station at the end of which they had agreed to guarantee bail for their eldest son, and persuaded him to admit there was no truth in his charge against Leo.

It was only now that Sharon thought to look round the house. 'So where is she?' She walked across to the bottom of the stairs and looking up, shrieked at the top of her voice, 'Jade?'

There was no answer. She ran up the stairs and disappeared along the landing while the four men of her family stood in silence looking at each other. Darren and Jamie caught each other's eyes and sniggered; their father gave them a look which silenced them totally.

It was several minutes before Sharon reappeared followed by a bleary-eyed Jade. 'She was still asleep.' She turned on Jackson. 'On top of everything else I gather you've been leaving your baby sister alone in this house.'

'No. That's the point!' Jackson defended himself at last. 'She is always out. Round at The Old Forge.' He glared at Jade.

'Well, I'm not now,' she retorted. 'I am never going there again.'

'Why?' Sharon looked at her suspiciously.

'You tell Ma,' Jackson put in. 'Tell her what happened. That filthy bastard touched you up, didn't he? No one believed me when I told the police.'

Jade paused. A calculating look crossed her face. She was thinking of Zoë and the tender glance Leo had given her. Her mouth tightened into a thin line. She wasn't sure why Jackson was making the accusation, but suddenly it opened all kinds of possibilities for revenge. 'That's right. I thought I could trust him but I couldn't. He wanted me to go into his bedroom.' She looked down primly. 'I wouldn't; I knew what he wanted.'

Sharon said nothing. She was scanning her daughter's face suspiciously. 'Are you prepared to swear that on your grandmother's grave?'

412

Jade blanched. 'He's always been very nice to me,' she protested. 'Too nice. He fancies me rotten.'

'You lying little brat!' Jamie put in. 'Leo's a decent guy and you have pursued him without stopping ever since we bought this house, hasn't she, Dal?' He looked at his brother with such ferocity that Darren could only nod support. 'He was kind to you because he was sorry for you. He'd never fancy you in a million years. And I happen to know he's got a wife and kids, so there.'

'He hasn't!' Jade went white to the gills.

'He has. And he thinks you're a damn nuisance.'

'How do you know all this, Jamie?' his father asked suddenly.

Jamie went red. 'I was listening outside the door one day when Jade was in there. Like Jacko, I was a bit worried about him. He's an old guy and he's definitely weird, but he's no paedo. He was nice to her and gave her some juice and tried to persuade her to go and she wouldn't and he was pretty fed up about it. Then after she had gone at last, there was a phone call and I heard him talking to this woman and he asked her if she wanted a divorce and he told her he still loved her and he talked about his kids. There is no way he would ever, ever fancy Jade. She's just a kid and a pain in the arse at that.'

Jade went scarlet. With a small yelp of distress she turned and fled up the stairs. The house shook as her bedroom door slammed.

'Poor kid,' Jeff said quietly. 'It will be a long time before she forgives you that one, son.' He glared at the boy.

'Right, that's it, we are going home. Now,' Sharon said with a groan. 'This minute. Pack the car. I've had enough.'

'But, Mum,' Jackson protested.

'But Mum nothing!' Sharon shouted at him. 'We gave an undertaking to the police, if you remember, to take you home and keep you there.'

*　　*　　*

413

Upstairs Jade had buried her face in her pillow.

When the sobs had subsided at last she lay still, exhausted, and it was then she remembered her curse. She sat up, sniffing, and her face broke into a slow smile. Zoë was going to get pregnant by her horrible husband. She was going to get fat and ugly and puke all the time and Leo would hate her. He wouldn't even want to look at her and then she was going to die while she was having the baby. It was all part of her magic spell, and her spells at school had never failed.

Well, not really, so there was no reason to think this one would. It had started when someone called her a witch. 'I'll show you, you cow,' she had screamed back in fury. Later that day the girl had slipped and broken her ankle in the playground. Jade's reputation was made.

When he returned the next morning Ken sat for several long minutes in the car, his eyes closed, then at last he climbed out, the newspaper in his hand. He had seen the Watts's car outside their house and decided not to go over. What was there to say?

The story had made all the nationals. Most of them had covered what had happened in great detail, spread over two pages. According to the ones he had seen, Rosemary was in hospital in a coma and they were waiting to decide whether or not to operate. They said Jackson had been arrested and charged, but they didn't say with what. There was a photo of the tractor and the offending plough and another of a police car. He gave a grim smile. Sylvia was a stringer for the local weekly. Her story would contain far more than this one, thanks to him. He hoped no one would guess where she had got her facts.

The morning was cold, blowy, with a heavy cloud cover as he walked from the garage towards the barn. He and Sylvia had talked long and seriously the night before, after which, decisions if not made, then at least mooted, he had spent the night with her. Now he was not feeling so certain about anything. After all, he hadn't known her all that long and he had felt this strange euphoria before when he had started a new relationship. Never make promises, surely he should know that by now.

He stood outside the door, rattling the keys in his fist, putting off the moment. Behind him the whole place had a deserted feel. He glanced at his watch. It was after ten. Usually there were people about by now, especially at a weekend. But of course there was no one to be about. Steve would be in hospital with Rosemary; and as for the Watts, their car was outside but their front door was tightly shut.

He glanced over his shoulder. The Old Forge looked locked up and deserted as well. He walked into the kitchen and glanced round. The whole place was silent. Throwing down the paper, he rested his hand briefly on the kettle. Cold. Then he saw the note on the worktop. It was from Amanda to Zoë. He read it and felt a pang of guilt. So, the Danvers had left, presumably the day before, and he hadn't been there to say goodbye. He hadn't even realised that they had gone. He had noticed that their car was no longer parked against the wall in the garage yard but he had thought nothing of it, expecting to see it somewhere near the front door.

'Zoë?' he called. He walked through to the great room and looked round. From the chill in the air he could feel the woodburner was out. The place felt unsettled, unhappy.

He ran up the stairs two at a time and pushed open the door into their bedroom. It too was deserted.

Her car had still been there in the garage, so she must be around. He walked over to the bed and stood looking down at it, guessing sourly that it had not been slept in last night. After all, he had messaged her, told her he wouldn't be coming back. With Amanda and John gone what had there

415

been to keep her here, with lover boy right there on the doorstep? Suddenly that cryptic PS in Amanda's note made sense. She had gone with Leo.

He glanced round again, then, without quite knowing why, he bent and glanced underneath the bed. There was something there, pushed in near the skirting board. He climbed stiffly down onto his knees and reached in to pull it out. It was small and metallic and very heavy. Retrieving it he stood up and gazed at it in puzzlement. It was a round lump of iron, roughly shaped into the torso of a woman with huge breasts and buttocks. He shuddered. What on earth was such a grotesque thing doing under their bed?

He put the figurine down on Zoë's bedside table and went into the bathroom. Her toothbrush and make up were gone. He narrowed his eyes suspiciously and began a more serious search of the room. He was right. She had taken her handbag, her running shoes, a few clothes and, as far as he could see, her sailing gear.

For a moment his rage and jealousy were overwhelming; it was a while before he realised the irony of it all. He had come home to tell her he had found someone else. Whether or not he stayed with Sylvia would remain to be seen; what was certain was that he wanted a divorce and if he was honest with himself he had wanted one for some time. Perhaps even before they had moved. Perhaps the move had been a way of putting off the moment when he would have to decide, a chance to give them both a last crack at the marriage. But it hadn't worked. If anything it had emphasised the differences between them. So why did he mind so much that she had made the same decision? He should be pleased. It would make life so much easier.

He sat downstairs in the great room for a long time, feeling strangely deflated. He had wound himself up to tell her, to reason with her, to face her tears and pleas, and she had not been there to listen. She had spent the night with another man. He was being illogical and hypocritical and he knew it. But still it hurt.

Later he walked down to the landing stage and looked out towards the mooring buoys. *Lady Grace* and *Curlew* lay as though quietly asleep in the grey water. Wherever she was, she and Leo were not on the boat.

He walked back up the lane past the scene of yesterday's debacle in the field and stopped in astonishment. The whole burial mound had been encircled with blue police ribbon, and there were two four-wheel-drive cars and a black van drawn up in the field. Someone had rolled a rough track across the furrows so they could get close to the copse. He could see several people busy in amongst the trees. Curious, he walked over the mud towards them. One of the men straightened from his examination of the ground and came to meet him. 'Can I help you, sir?'

Ken looked past him at the undergrowth. It had all been cut back now and there were floodlights trained on the ground. In the centre of the excavated patch of earth he could see a small blue jug, incongruous anywhere but especially at the scene of so much tragedy. 'I'm sorry. I was here yesterday when the accident happened. I live here.' He waved across the field towards the barns. 'I wondered what was going on. Did Rosemary – Mrs Formby – is she all right?'

'I understand Mrs Formby is seriously ill. You would have to enquire at the hospital.'

'So, what is all this?' Ken stared at him suspiciously.

'We have found a body, sir, buried in the mound.'

Ken felt a shiver run across his shoulders. 'An Anglo-Saxon body?'

'No, sir. The doctor said he thought it was probably far more recent than that, a hundred years or so, maybe. We still need to finish photographing the scene of yesterday's accident, then we will hand over to the coroner's department.

417

They will probably bring in forensic archaeologists, then we'll know for sure.'

U

There had been no reply to her letter to her father and miserably Emily had written again. This time she gave it to one of the visiting tradesmen, with a large tip to persuade him to deliver it to the post. When she had an answer, she told him, she would give him as much again.

It was the fourth time she had visited the barn. Each time it was just after dawn, before the activity of the farm started in earnest. Once she had mistimed it and seen George and Robert harnessing the two Suffolk punches to the dray. She had waited, hidden behind the smith's cottage, until they had disappeared up the lane, perched on the high seat behind the horses, then she had gone down to the yard. There was no one there. Young Benjamin, the boy who had been training with Daniel, who had hoped one day to be a smith himself, had gone. It was one of the undermaids who had told her, breaking the rule which seemed to apply at the Hall now, that no one should speak to her. She had felt that it would be permissible in order to pass on the news, with malicious venom in her voice, that he had run away, unable to get over the trauma of finding Dan's body. His mother was distraught and the whole countryside had turned out to search for him but they had found no trace.

Emily walked into the barn and stood there hopelessly, not even knowing why she had come. Was his spirit there, waiting for her? The living were no longer prepared to talk to her, so perhaps the dead would do so.

There was a rustling in the straw bales and she jumped back as a large rat ran across the floor.

Daniel wasn't there. There was no one there, just a huge barn, piled high with the year's harvest, which, in the wind which was whipping across the countryside, was creaking like a ship at sea.

She turned back towards the doors and stopped in fright. There was a figure standing in the doorway. She couldn't see who it was. It was dark in the barn; there was no sunlight outside. A shower of rain was sweeping across the yard.

'Dan?' She whispered the word under her breath and felt the hammer of fright under her ribs.

The figure moved forward a couple of steps and she narrowed her eyes, trying to make out his face. It wasn't Dan. He wasn't tall enough to be Dan, and Dan was dead. She shook her head slightly. Her veil was thick. She couldn't see properly.

'Who are you?' she called out. 'What is your business here?'

There was another sound, behind her this time, and she spun round.

The shadows were suddenly thick around her, the wind whisking at the wisps of hay, filling the place with dust. The barn was overwhelmed with the roar of the storm and the rain, slanting across the yard, rattling on the cobbles and on the roof above her head. The noise was deafening. Slowly she put her hands to her ears. As she closed her eyes to block out the chaos around her she felt the sudden vicious pressure of hands around her throat. There was no time to scream, no time to struggle. In seconds the world had gone black.

Zoë and Leo headed cautiously through the trees. Leo was carrying a canvas sail bag in which he had put the sword, carefully wrapped in newspaper. They skirted down towards the landing stage, which was deserted. There was no sign of anyone there, or on the track. They followed it towards Dead Man's Field, keeping in the lee of the hedge, carefully peering round each bend as they approached the gate. From there they could see down to the copse.

'The police are still there!' Leo ducked back out of sight.

'They can't be!'

'They are. There are two cars and lots of tape. We can't bury the sword with them there.'

Zoë grabbed his hand and pulled him back down the lane. 'Wait here with the sword. I'll go and ask them what's happening,' she said.

Leo sighed unhappily. 'I hope this doesn't mean Rosemary has died. Would they accuse Jackson of murder? Surely not. It was a stupid accident and she was trespassing on someone else's land.'

'He drove straight at her, Leo.' She turned and looked back towards the centre of the field. 'We don't want to be caught with the sword. They might think we looted it or something. You wait here out of sight. I'll go and see if they'll tell me anything.'

There were flames licking the surface of the mound. Rosemary shuddered. She hadn't realised that there were people standing round, watching, when she had taken the sword. Shadowy people, ancient people, called from the distances to guard it. They did not want her to take it. They were angry. They had called on her to leave it but she had not heard them. She had taken it away and lost it.

Where had she put it? If she could only remember. Her head hurt. She knew that much. It was hot and that was her punishment for moving the sword. She could not move her hands or feet; she could hear nothing and her eyes wouldn't open. Perhaps she wasn't there at all, in her body.

Was she dead? She could see her body lying there in the bed. There were all sorts of tubes attached to her, screens beeping beside her, bandages around her head and someone sitting there, in the corner of the room. Who was it? Not Steve. No one she knew. She felt a shaft of fear run through her body. There were other people there, people from the burial mound, the guardians, still watching, but now they were watching her. They wanted the sword. She had to tell them where it was and she didn't know, and in the meantime the mound was burning, flames licking across the soil, lightning flickering across the sky, illuminating the trees.

The Lord Egbert was angry. He couldn't rest in peace. His burial place was an entrance to the other world, a sacred place, and it had been violated. Rosemary could see him, waiting for the sword to return. She could see the others there with him, one of them had been buried at his feet; they were waiting too, but the sword was not there and she didn't know where it was and she was terrified.

The runes had spoken. Until it was returned she could not be free. Until it was returned it was her fate to be guilty of sin, shut up in dwelling-places of devils, bound in bonds of hell, and tormented with evil . . .

'Leo!' He was dozing, sitting on the verge, and suddenly Zoë was there beside him. She was panting, glancing over her shoulder. 'This way. Quickly.'

He scrambled up and followed her without pausing to question her. Bending low so they were hidden by the hedge they slipped along the field and cut across the corner, out of sight of the burial mound and the men standing round it.

She pulled him off the path and into the wood, turning away from the river and running as fast as she could ahead of him now away from the barns, along the top of the ridge to where the trees were thicker and gave better cover. Only then did she slow down and bend double, trying to regain her breath.

He slid to the ground beside her, panting. 'What happened? Why are we running?'

They had both looked back. The woods were silent. She shook her head. 'Ken is around here. I didn't want him to see us. Not yet. Not like this. I've got to think how to talk to him. I spoke to the men and they said he had been up there only an hour ago. Rosemary is still in a coma as far as they know. They've found a body, Leo! A man's body buried in the mound.'

'The owner of the sword.'

She shook her head. 'They think it's Victorian. They are waiting for someone to come and look at it officially, but the police photographer said it had had its neck broken. It's Dan! It must be. The man I saw hanging. The man from the séance!'

'You don't know that.'

'I do. Who else could it be? How many Victorian men round here were murdered?' She realised her hands were shaking. 'I am sure it's him. It's all coming together, don't you see? That's why he appeared. He knew people were poking round his grave. We have to do something, Leo. He wants us to find out what happened.'

Leo shook his head slowly. Then he looked up, staring up into the branches of the great pine above their heads. 'First things first. Are they keeping watch over the site?'

'They must be. There is tape everywhere and a tent over the diggings so we can't rebury the sword. Even if we managed to get it into the grave, they will find it straight away. The man I spoke to was talking about archaeologists digging up the mound, taking the body away and then searching to see if it was originally an Anglo-Saxon burial. Apparently the local historians are very excited. They have always known about the site, it's even on some maps, but this has reawakened interest in it, and it is now considered endangered because of Rosemary's demand that it be recognised as a public footpath.'

Leo sighed. 'So does that mean we can't bury the sword even if we wanted to?'

She shrugged her shoulders. 'It changes our options. We could still take it to the museum. I would have to explain where I found it but I've nothing to hide. It wasn't me that stole it in the first place. Or you keep it after all and do your own research.' She shook her head. 'They are going to dig up this whole place now; the poor man whose grave it is will be stuck in a museum! I think that is awful. Leo!' She hesitated, then she went on, suddenly certain that she was right. 'I am probably being stupid and romantic and unscientific, but I think in some ways it would almost be better to give it to the ancient gods than let it go to a museum; we could send it to a watery grave. In the river!'

'No!' The scream echoed through Rosemary's head. 'No, you have to put it back. You have to! Until you put it back, I am in hell!'

There was no one to hear her scream. A nurse noted a sudden irregularity in her pulse, visible on one of the screens, that was all. It lasted a fraction of a second, and was gone.

19

Henry Crosby had hired a trap to bring him from the station and sent it away at the front door. He walked into the hall and, putting down his valise, stared round. He put his hat and gloves onto the hall stand and frowned. There were no servants to answer the doorbell. No one there at all. He walked towards the morning room and threw open the door. Despite the coldness of the morning no one had lit a fire in the grate and the room had an unlived-in feel. He strode across to the fireplace and rang the bell. He could hear it jangling in the depths of the house.

For a long time no one came, then at last he heard the scurry of feet. A flustered parlour maid appeared in the doorway. 'Oh, sir, oh, sir, I'm sorry, sir!' She bobbed a curtsey. 'We didn't know you was here, sir.'

He turned and looked at her. 'No matter. Make up the fire and tell Beaton to come here.'

The girl hesitated, as though unable to decide which to do first. He sighed impatiently. 'Call Beaton, girl. Now.'

He stood staring down at the rent table in the centre of

the room as he waited. The magazines laid out on it were out of date and there was dust on the surface.

Beaton arrived at last, as flustered as the girl had been. 'Mr Henry, sir. I'm sorry. I received no word that you were returning.'

'I shouldn't need to send word,' Henry retorted. 'What in the world has been going on here, man? The place is a mess.' He ran a critical finger through the dust and left a straight line across the inlaid leather centre of the table. 'See to it that the fires are lit and the place is cleaned. And tell my wife I want to speak to her in here.'

Beaton shuffled his feet uncomfortably. 'Lady Emily hasn't been home, sir, for several days.'

Henry spun to face him. 'What do you mean she hasn't been home?'

'Her ladyship was in the habit of going for walks in the morning, sir. She was unable to ride as the cob is lame, so she walked a little before breakfast each day.'

'And?'

'And on Tuesday the new girl, Sally, told me that her mistress had not returned by lunchtime. I was concerned, sir, and sent the servants out to look for her, but no trace of her was found and I decided, that is, we decided,' he hesitated, 'that she had walked into the village, sir, and from there obtained a lift to the railway station. I understand she had been unhappy here on her own for so long, Mr Henry,' Beaton raised his chin a little, 'and had written to ask her father to send for her.'

Henry met his eye thoughtfully. 'I see. Then we should contact her father and make sure she arrived safely. I will write at once. Send Mayhew to me, if you will, and make sure the servants see to the house.'

Bill Turtill was standing looking down into the grave. The

call had come early in the morning and he had met the coroner's car at the corner of the field. The two men strode across the muddy furrows, both wearing boots and thick jackets against the wind and rain. A tent had been erected over most of the mound and inside it was lit by high-powered lamps. Two men and a woman were working on the site, sifting through the soil with small brushes and implements that looked like scalpels.

'Another body, you say?' Bill scratched his head.

'Lying near the original fellow.' One of the archaeologists, Colin Hall, adjusted one of the lamps slightly. 'This one is female and I am hopeful we will get an identification. There is jewellery and the remnants of her boots.'

'Lady Emily Crosby,' Bill said slowly. 'It must be. She lived up at the Hall in the mid-nineteenth century. My great-great-however-many greats grandfather was farm manager here at the time and the story was handed down. She disappeared without trace and was never seen again. There was a hell of a stink about it. Rewards offered, accusations. Tremendous scandal. I understand she had been having an affair with one of the farm labourers and he disappeared around the same time. The theory was they had run away together.'

'So you think this chap here,' David Swinburne, the coroner, waved in the direction of the other skeleton, 'is her lover?' He had pulled out a notebook and scribbled down the name. The presence of the coroner in person was, he had explained, the result of the exceptional historical interest of this case.

Bill was silent for several seconds. 'Might be.'

'So, who killed them?' Swinburne asked.

'You don't think it was a suicide pact?'

'Not unless they buried themselves first.'

'Look at her finger bones here.' Mel Parker, the second archaeologist looked up. 'She's wearing a wedding ring, two other small diamond rings, a gold bracelet, and there, round her neck, a gold chain with a locket on it. So, it wasn't a robbery.'

There was a patter of rain against the sides of the tent. Bill shivered. 'I remember my grandfather talking about this when I was a nipper. I wish I had listened more carefully. Her husband lived here for years and years on his own after she disappeared. I don't think he ever remarried. He was the last of the Crosbys. After that the Hall passed to some distant relation, if I remember right. It's in some history book Penny's got at home. I'll see if I can find it. Or Lesley Inworth might know. She lives at the Hall and she's taken a bit of an interest in the history of the place.'

He squatted down on his haunches and looked more closely at the skeleton in the grave in front of him. 'So, is there no Anglo-Saxon king, then?'

Colin shook his head. 'Oh, I think this is originally an Anglo-Saxon burial; we've found one or two artefacts to substantiate that story.' He waved behind him where a make-shift table displayed some muddy lumps of metal and pottery. 'But I doubt if he'll turn out to be a king. And if Sutton Hoo is anything to go by there won't be much left of the body after so long. We've got to get these two out first, then we'll work our way into the site. He may have been cremated, in which case he'll be in a pot. Or there may be more grave goods. That will tell us more about him.'

'And no one can insist on a footpath crossing over the top of this place?'

The man laughed grimly. 'I doubt it. How is the lady who was hurt, do you know?'

'She's had an operation to remove a blood clot on the brain. I understand they are keeping her unconscious for the time being.'

'Nasty business.' David Swinburne frowned unhappily. 'These bloody people who insist on rights of way for no reason at all! Who in God's name would want to walk across

427

here anyway?' He gave a theatrical shudder as another gust of wind rattled the walls of the tent.

'It's all about levelling,' Mel commented. She brushed another bit of soil gently from the woman's skull. 'The perceived rights of the people versus the hated rich landowners.'

'Well, if you think I'm a rich landowner!' Bill folded his arms.

'No, we can see you're not.' Colin laughed gently. 'Not with those holes in your wellies, mate!'

The others stared down at Bill's feet. He grinned. 'I'm sorry Mrs Formby was hurt, very sorry, but that woman was the most dreadful pain. She's not local – they've only lived here about ten minutes – but she was prepared to argue the toss with everyone else, people from the village who have been here generations, local historians, the nice woman from the council who came up to have a look, people who have known all these paths like the back of their hands all their lives. They all told her there had never been a path here, everyone said the same!'

'Well, some good has come out of all this,' Mel reminded them quietly. 'We have found these two poor souls and maybe they would never have been discovered but for Mrs Formby.'

Leo looked out of the window. 'I can see Ken going into your house.' He turned to her. 'Do you want to go and speak to him?'

She shook her head. 'Not yet.'

'Did you leave him a message last night?'

Again, the shake of the head.

'Isn't the poor guy going to wonder where you are? He will be worried.'

She hesitated for a moment.

'You could find out what is going on, Zoë.' He sounded stern. 'See how Rosemary is. See if there is any news about Jackson.'

'And tell Ken I might be going away for a couple of weeks?'

He held her gaze. 'Are you sure?'

'I'm sure I want to leave Ken for a while. To think. I'm not sure about crossing the North Sea.'

'Fair enough. Little by little.' Leo gave an encouraging nod.

Ken was standing in the middle of the great room when she walked in. He turned at the sound of her step and she saw an odd mixture of expressions in his eyes. Relief, and was it disappointment?

'Hi.' She stopped in the doorway.

'Where have you been? With him, I suppose.'

She tried to read his expression and failed. 'I've come to collect some stuff, Ken, then I'm going away for a bit.'

'You're leaving me?'

She nodded. 'I'm sorry.'

'You're going with him?' He gave a curt nod towards the window.

'For now. Not necessarily for ever. I need some space. Time to work out what I really want from life.' She sighed. 'We haven't been happy for a long time, Ken, have we? Not really happy. I know you feel the same. After all, I'm not the only one who's been out all night.'

He looked away abruptly.

'There is someone else, isn't there?' she went on. 'There is always someone else.'

He didn't bother to deny it. He nodded reluctantly.

'So, why don't we settle this in a civilised way? There's been enough unhappiness in this building.' She glanced towards the corner. The whole room was dull and quiet. She felt nothing out of the ordinary. 'Let's take some time to think things through, Ken. Then we can discuss it when we've had some time apart.'

He nodded. 'Where are you going?' he said after a pause.

'I don't know yet. I wanted to make sure everything here

429

was all right. With you and with Rosemary. And Jackson. What has happened about him?'

Ken threw himself down on the sofa. 'He's been given bail. He's been charged with aggravated something or other and causing grievous bodily harm.' He reached for the newspaper and passed it to her. 'I gather Rosemary is still in a coma so it depends what happens to her. The Watts have all gone back to their house in Basildon. Sharon came down and rounded up the whole family including Jade. She was a sight to behold. The matriarch in full sail; and Steve is spending most of his time at the hospital. So where are you going? You're not going to move into The Old Forge!'

'No, we're going away. Just for a couple of weeks. It doesn't matter where. I haven't decided for sure what I am going to do in the end.' She was silent for a moment. Was that true? 'What about you,' she went on at last 'will you stay here? You are the only person left.'

He shook his head. 'I'll go too. It's lonely and a bit bleak, if I'm honest.'

She glanced at him, sadly. 'So, you'll go to her. What is her name?'

'Sylvia. We met her at the sailing club the first week or so we moved here. Then I met her again when I was shopping for the bolts for the door.' He gave a small ironic laugh.' She's a journalist.'

'And she lives locally?'

'Woodbridge. I didn't plan it, Zoë.'

'I don't suppose you did,' she said bleakly. 'Any more than I did.'

'I'll go and stay with her for a bit, until we know what is happening.'

'We'll have to think about the house.'

He shook his head. 'Not yet. It's too soon.' Hauling himself to his feet he walked across to the corner and stood looking down at the floor where the inset of plate glass showed the old brickwork underneath. 'All the unhappiness, the ghosts, the atmosphere, comes up through here. It's a porthole into the past. It ought to be filled in; sealed down for ever.'

Zoë nodded. 'You're right, it should.'

'Did you hear about the other body at the grave?' he said after a pause. 'I can't help wondering . . . It couldn't be our murder victim, could it? Dan? The man who you think was hanged in this house. Who was it Amanda said had killed him? Emily, that was it. Someone called Emily. I almost blurted it out to the policeman, but common sense kicked in. The so-called message of a so-called ghost, interpreted by an eccentric woman with an Ouija board would not be considered useful police evidence. He would have had me certified.' He walked over to the window and stared out. 'Manda rang,' he said suddenly. 'I told her you had probably taken her advice and gone with him.' He gave a wry laugh at her puzzled expression. 'You left her note behind. "Once aboard the lugger", remember? It took her ten seconds to work out what was going on. It took me a bit longer, but I got there. I hope he makes you happy, Zo, I really do. I'm sure he's a nice guy.'

'Thank you.'

Restlessly he headed for the kitchen. 'I'll make some coffee while you pack your stuff,' he called over his shoulder, then he stopped in the doorway. 'Zoë, why did you put that god-awful doll thing under our bed?'

She stared at him. 'Doll?'

He nodded. 'Horrible, primitive thing. Not your scene, I would have thought.'

She shook her head, puzzled. 'It's nothing to do with me, I assure you.' She felt a sudden whisper of cold cross her shoulder blades. 'Where is it? Show me.'

Ken produced the small bundle, wrapped in a dishcloth and unwrapping it, put it down on the table in front of her. She stared at it for a long time, not touching it. He was careful not to touch it either, she noticed. 'I've never seen it before,' she said at last. She shuddered. 'It looks like some grotesque fertility doll from the museum. Look at that stomach and breasts. Ugh!'

'Do you think Jade left it there?' he asked suddenly. 'She's been in and out of the house. She was very jealous, wasn't she, of you and Leo? In which case it might not be for fertility which would in any case be pointless. It is probably cursed.' They looked at each other.

Pointless. The words echoed bleakly in Zoë's head for several seconds before she dismissed them angrily.

'I'll chuck it away,' he said. 'Don't worry. I doubt if that little minx is much of a witch.'

Something awful is going to happen to you too. I've put a spell on you and there is nothing you can do about it. You are going to die, just like Rosemary!

Jade's tearful words echoed suddenly in Zoë's head and she shivered. 'Throw it in the river. I think it's the best place for some of the old junk floating round these barns. End the cycle.' She sighed unhappily. 'It's all tied up, isn't it? The memories, the ghosts, the Viking ship, Dan. Emily. It all needs to be exorcised and forgotten.' She shivered again.

'It's all centred on that mound down in the field,' Ken said thoughtfully. 'I have a feeling it's Rosemary who stirred it all up, and it's Rosemary who is paying the price.'

Rosemary who moved the sword.

Zoë stared down at the table bleakly. 'Is she going to die?'

'No one knows, unless they've told Steve. Bill rang. He told me the poor guy is completely beside himself. She irritated the daylights out of him, but at base I think he actually adores her.' He leaned forward and picked up the figure from the coffee table, using the dishcloth again to save himself from touching it. 'OK, this is for the river, then.'

'Thank you.' She looked up at him. 'You're a nice man, Ken. I wish it had worked out for us.'

'We can still be friends?'

She nodded. 'I hope so.'

'Me too.'

U

The earl, it appeared, had heard nothing from his daughter for many months. On his arrival, his displeasure at her disappearance was felt by the whole household. The staff at the Hall, cross-questioned about any letters Lady Emily might have written, knew nothing of who might have posted them or where they might have gone. The countryside was searched again, more thoroughly this time.

The earl demanded they send for the police. A detective inspector was brought from London and he spent two weeks in the area and interviewed everyone at the Hall, on the home farm, in the village and in the outlying farms. No one had seen Lady Emily on the day she had disappeared. It appeared that no one had driven her to the station and the station master was prepared to swear she had not bought a ticket there. Fred and Jessie Turtill were questioned twice, because they admitted that she had come down to the farmhouse before the funeral of Susan Smith. The inspector was no fool. He knew someone, perhaps everyone, was lying, and he was sure the lady was dead, but there was no proof, no body and no way of breaking the silence which surrounded the subject. Eventually he admitted to Squire Crosby and to the earl that he had failed to find any answers to the mystery.

'Bloody bumpkins!' he muttered to himself as he was driven to the station in the pony trap. He'd come across these small country communities before with their blank stares and their dumb silence. That was the problem with these people. Close as a rat's arse. Clammed up shut with their secrets.

The night the inspector left for London on the train from Ipswich Henry walked down to the river alone. He stood on one of the narrow shingle beaches looking out across the water and drew on his cigar, watching the fragrant blue smoke rise up into the evening sky. His father-in-law had left that morning in his landau. The subject of Emily's disappearance was closed.

'So, it's all worked out for the best,' Zoë said as she finished telling Leo what had happened. She reached up and kissed him.

He put his arm round her and drew her close. 'I'm almost disappointed. Fleeing from the irate husband with my pirate moll would have made it an even more exciting adventure. Now it seems he is donating you to the cause!'

She made as if to slap him. 'I haven't said I'm going yet. Not to sea.'

He smiled. 'So we're not going to voyage to distant parts?'

She shrugged. 'I am so tempted. I want an adventure. I want to buy those bright clothes you mentioned in some far-away bazaar!' Her eyes sparkled. 'But I am not sure about crossing the sea in a small boat, however expert her skipper.'

'Supposing we go down-river, wait for a calm day, nip out into the sea and toss a coin as to whether we turn left or right or go straight ahead, and see where we get to. There are exotic shops this side of the gannets' bath as well. How would that do you?'

'What's the gannets' bath?' She was delighted with the term.

'It's what the Anglo-Saxons called the North Sea. In *The Anglo-Saxon Chronicle*.'

'It's wonderful.'

'OK. So, you agree?'

She nodded.

'It's a done deal,' he said. 'But first we have to make a final decision about this.' He indicated the sword on the kitchen table. He had unwrapped it again. 'While I was waiting for you I tried to copy down some of the runes and I've taken some photos though they don't show up too well on screen; they are easier to see in daylight. Look.' He had a couple of books open on the table. They showed pictures of the runes. This one is thorn, which represents the forces of chaos and evil. It is perhaps a warning. And this is *eoh*, which seems to signify a weapon, and is something to do with deflection of magic, but best of all,' he grinned, 'I especially like this one. See? It's called Ken. It means enlightenment.'

She laughed. 'Poor Ken. Well, he's enlightened now.' She ran her hand lightly over the blade. 'Do you think the runes tell you whose it was? Who made it?'

'Possibly.' He exhaled slowly. 'Smiths were magicians in a way. Alchemists. They had a very powerful reputation for their skills in creating iron from fire. I used to think I had some special link into the past when I first became a smith.' He shook his head and in his turn reached out to touch the blade. 'Maybe this sword was made here, on this site. It's possible there has been a forge here for more than a thousand years.' He glanced up at her, almost embarrassed. 'A few weeks ago, I dreamed about a sword. I can't remember what it was about, but –' he stopped abruptly. 'Perhaps it was this one.'

Zoë looked up at him. 'That is incredible. Wonderful.'

'It makes it all the more important we do the right thing.' Yes, it would be romantic to throw it in the river, but wouldn't that be sacrilege? There is so much history here.'

She narrowed her eyes. 'You want to keep it, don't you?'

'Only for a while, to do more research.'

'And what about the curses you told me about? Which protected the graves.'

'Ah, the curses.' He stood up. 'I've found my old books on the Anglo-Saxons. Here's my copy of *Beowulf*. I've looked it up. Listen to this.' He picked up a slim paperback from the litter of books and papers on the kitchen table; on the cover there was a picture of the iconic helmet from Sutton Hoo. The book was old, the pages discoloured and loose. 'Here we are, listen to this:

'Goblets, flagons, dishes, and rich swords lay beside it, eaten with rust, as they had lain buried in the bosom of the earth for a thousand years. For the vast golden heritage of the ancients had been secured by a spell. No one might lay a finger on the treasure-house unless God Himself, true lord of victories and protector of men, allowed the hoard to be unsealed by a man of His own choice – whoever He thought fit.'

He laid down the book and smiled at her. 'Obviously God did not consider Jackson or Rosemary or whoever found the sword to be the man of his choice. Wonderful stuff. This book was my mother's first. She loved poetry; she was a clever lady.'

'And she encouraged you to read it?'

He nodded. 'I enjoyed it all so much I went on to study English at uni. Fat lot of use it was in my career, but it gave me a wonderful background against which to live my life.' He shook his head. 'Fine mess I made of that, though, come to think of it.'

'So you read it in the original at university?' She brought him back to the subject firmly.

'In Anglo-Saxon? I did, actually.'

'And can you still speak it?'

He shook his head. 'It's a difficult language. And not one I practise regularly.'

'It could have been useful.' She smiled. 'I had a vision of you standing on the prow of the *Curlew* declaiming to the ancient gods.'

'And warning off the ghost ship?'

She nodded.

'I haven't read the best bit yet,' he went on. 'Or perhaps the worst, depending on one's point of view. Here: ". . . the princes who placed their treasure there had pronounced a solemn curse on it which was to last until doomsday that whoever rifled the place should be guilty of sin, shut up in dwelling places of devils, bound in bonds of hell, and tormented with evil."' He put down the book. 'Strong stuff.'

'Poor Rosemary. I hope the devils realise it wasn't me who took it,' Zoë said dryly.

He stood up and began rewrapping the sword carefully. 'They will. I have made an executive decision. We will hang on to this for the time being. There will be plenty of time to decide what to do with it later.'

'So, you don't think it's cursed?'

'Oh, I'm sure it is.'

'And you're not afraid?' She could feel her own fear suddenly as she looked down at the parcel laying between them.

He smiled and shook his head. 'Superstitious nonsense! Besides, as you say, we're not the ones defiling the grave.'

Her skeleton lay on the slab in the mortuary with a certain degree of elegance. Her bones were small and fragile, her teeth in excellent condition. Beside her the remains of her riding boots and her jewellery had been placed neatly in two boxes. Next to them was a swathe of her light chestnut hair which had remained strangely untouched by its time under-ground. On the slab next to her lay the skeleton of the unknown man. He was tall, and had been strongly built. His boots too had survived in part. He had no jewellery but they had found some working tools buried with him, a hammer, tongs, two horseshoes and a handful of nails, and surmised that he might have been a blacksmith.

Sylvia Sands, in her capacity as a freelance reporter on the local paper, came down to look at the bodies and interview the archaeologists and the archaeo-pathologist who had joined them. After speaking to Ken she had been to the library and surfed the Internet and was piecing together the story. 'She disappeared in the winter of 1865. Three months before, the blacksmith on the estate, Daniel Smith, had also vanished, although there was a rumour that he had died in an accident on the farm. His wife, Susan, was buried with her still-born baby in the church in the village but there was no sign of his grave anywhere.'

She peered at the empty eye sockets of the woman's skeleton and shivered. 'She was the second wife of the squire, and she was supposed to have been very beautiful.' She glanced sideways at the chestnut hair. 'Do you think they were lovers? Would someone from the Hall fall in love with a lowly blacksmith? Did she kill herself to be with him?'

'Not unless she strangled herself,' Doug Freeman the pathologist put in. 'See here, the hyoid bone is fractured. Same with him. I would bet money they were both killed by the same person. Professional killer. Good at his job.'

She peered at the bone he was indicating with his gloved hand. 'But they could have hanged themselves.'

'Possible, I suppose. But unlikely. If they did, why were they buried out there in the field?'

'Because suicides couldn't be buried in consecrated ground and an ancient burial site was the nearest they could think of?' Sylvia was thinking aloud. 'But murder does seem more likely. So was it the husband?' She moved across to inspect the male skeleton. 'I gather he was the main suspect, though he had an alibi; he was in London when she disappeared, but he was around when this guy vanished.'

'I doubt if the husband was a professional killer,' Doug said thoughtfully. 'I've looked it up too. He was a country squire! He could have paid someone to do it, though.' He shook his head morosely. 'I don't suppose we'll ever know.'

'What will happen to the bodies?' Sylvia was looking at the jewellery now. The rings were tiny; the wedding ring would barely slip on her little finger. 'Will they be buried together?'

'There are no descendants to pay for a funeral, so I doubt it. They'll probably end up in cardboard boxes in an archive somewhere.'

She looked up, shocked. 'You mean they won't rebury them?

'I doubt it. Are you going out to the mound again tomorrow?' He looked at Colin Hall, who was standing beside him.

Colin nodded. 'We have to go very carefully there. If it is like Sutton Hoo there may be a sand body and nothing more.'

'A sand body?' Sylvia looked puzzled.

'The actual body has gone and there is just an imprint of where it was.'

'Where would the body have gone? You mean it's been stolen?'

'No. The sandy soil contains chemicals which would have dissolved it. It would have disappeared and just left a shape in the sand where it lay.'

'Wow.' Sylvia made a note. 'That is spooky. Amazing. But his belongings are still there, is that right?'

The men nodded. 'They've found a few things already.'

'But why weren't these two sand bodies?'

'They've only been there a hundred and fifty years or so. An Anglo-Saxon warrior – you can add a nought on the end of that.'

As Sylvia left the building she pulled out her mobile. 'Ken, thank you so much for the tip-off about the burial mound. It's the most amazing story. I've spoken to my editor and he wants me to do a feature.' She paused. 'Can I mention your ghosts? Your Ouija lady seems to have been spot on. He was called Daniel Smith and she was Lady Emily Crosby, and we have stumbled on a Victorian murder mystery.'

20

Sharon opened her front door to the police at two o'clock that afternoon. A man and a woman, both astonishingly young, stood uncomfortably on her doorstep and asked to come in. She led them into her lounge and sat them on the huge settee in the bay window. 'So, what is this about?' She could feel her panic rising and she clenched her fists in the pockets of her jeans. 'Rosemary's snuffed it, has she?'

The younger police officer, Anna Briggs, looked puzzled. 'I beg your pardon?'

'Isn't that why you've come? To tell me Rosemary Formby has died?'

Anna glanced at her colleague, Andy Nailer, in evident confusion. 'I'm afraid I don't know anything about Rosemary Formby, Mrs Watts.'

Sharon cast her eyes up towards the ceiling. 'Gawd help us; so much for joined up policing. Then why have you come?'

'We've received some information, Mrs Watts, regarding your daughter, Jade,' Andy said solemnly. 'A suggestion has been received that she has been seen in the company of a man suspected of being a paedophile.'

Sharon stared from one to the other. 'No!' She narrowed her lips angrily. 'That is not true. I thought we made it clear that my son made that accusation out of spite. There is no foundation to it whatsoever.'

Anna glanced at her colleague. 'You know the man concerned?'

'Leo Logan? I know him, and I have already told the police in Woodbridge that I would trust him with my life – and with my daughter,' she added. 'Jackson had no business saying that and he is sorry.'

'Jackson?' Andy queried.

'My eldest son. Isn't this what this is all about? He thought he would drop Leo in it. Leo is a nice man.'

'I appreciate that you like and trust Mr Logan, but it is often the nicest men who are guilty,' Anna said grimly. 'We are going to have to make further enquiries about this, Mrs Watts. As our colleagues in Suffolk have passed on the information and contacted social services we are bound to follow it up. And we would like to talk to your daughter, if we may. In your presence, obviously.'

Sharon looked from one to the other. 'I'm ringing my husband,' she said at last. 'You can't do anything till he gets here.'

Jade, unusually demure in a pink T-shirt and short frilly skirt, with on her feet mock-satin slippers with roses on the toe, sat on the edge of the sofa between her mother and father and smiled angelically at the two police officers. She was impressed that Jackson's anonymous phone call to the police that morning had had a result so quickly. He hadn't wanted to do it. She had had to threaten him with the information that she had heard him and Mike planning to shoot Rosemary. That knowledge would make the tractor accident look as though it was deliberate. Jackson, already in a state of nervous collapse, had caved in at once and made the call.

'I liked Leo so much,' Jade said with a sly glance at her mother. 'My parents didn't have much time for me, so I often went round to see him and he gave me biscuits and presents and took me on his boat.'

'Alone?' Anna said with a frown.

'Just him and me, yes.' Jade smiled.

'And did he ever –' Anna paused, 'touch you inappropriately, Jade?'

Jade smiled again. 'He put his hand on my bottom,' she said a little smugly. 'I told him I didn't like it.'

'Jade?' Sharon said warningly. 'If we find out you've been lying –'

'I'm not lying,' Jade replied. 'He did touch me. Often,' she added defiantly. 'Will he go to prison?'

Andy nodded. 'I think he probably will, Jade. Don't you worry. It's not going to happen to you again.' He glanced up over her head at her mother. 'We will need her to be examined, Mrs Watts.'

Sharon looked at Jeff. She appeared to be stunned. 'Of course,' Jeff said quietly. 'If this is true, I will kill him.'

'No need, Mr Watts,' Andy put in quickly. 'We will deal with the matter.'

'What do you mean, examined?' Jade put in suddenly.

'You will have to talk to a doctor, Jade,' Sharon said. She was tight-lipped. 'I will come with you. I can, can't I?' she asked Anna, who nodded.

'Of course.'

Jade looked wary. 'Why a doctor?'

'To see if Leo has hurt you.'

'He didn't hurt me,' Jade said quickly. 'I don't need to see a doctor.'

'I'm afraid it's the law, Jade,' Anna put in firmly. 'It won't hurt.'

'Hurt?' Jade jumped to her feet. 'What is he going to do?'

'It will be a lady doctor, Jade. Nothing to be frightened of,

I can assure you.' Anna smiled at her. She glanced at Jeff. 'Perhaps sooner rather than later?'

Jeff nodded. 'Now.' His face was tight with anger. 'To think we asked that ugly bastard into our house!'

Sharon had stood up too, followed by the two officers. 'If this is true, if Jeff doesn't kill him, I will.'

'What will happen to Zoë?' Jade hadn't budged. They all turned and looked down at her as she sat alone on the sofa. She looked up at her father.

'Zoë?' Jeff repeated, puzzled.

Jade nodded. She narrowed her eyes. 'She's Leo's lover. She hates me. She's jealous.'

'Who is Zoë?' Andy had taken out his notebook again. He glanced at Jeff.

'Another of our neighbours in Suffolk,' Jeff replied with a sigh. 'She and her husband moved in about four months ago.'

'And she has been having an affair with Mr Logan?'

Jeff looked at his wife. 'I'm always the last to know about anything like that.'

'She is,' Jade put in smugly. 'She is the one who should go to prison. She's touched me too.'

Sharon was studying her daughter's face. 'You are not making all this up, are you, Jade, to get back at Leo because he likes Zoë?'

'Hardly,' Jeff put in. 'Why would she do that?'

Sharon hadn't taken her eyes off her daughter's face. Jade dropped her gaze and studied her new shoes.

'I thought the police were going to drop this matter when I told them my son had made it up,' Sharon said suddenly. She looked at Andy. 'Why have they changed their minds?'

Andy consulted his notebook. 'A call from a mobile phone was made to the Woodbridge station repeating the accusation this morning. It was a man,' he added. 'And he withheld his number.' He looked at Jade and then at her mother. 'Could

that have been your son again, do you think, Mrs Watts?'
In his experience if parents started getting suspicious about
what their kids were up to, it paid to listen to them. Perhaps
they should follow up the mobile call. In spite of her despairing
shrug, Sharon struck him as being a shrewd woman, someone
who would never entrust her daughter to a bad apple. Still,
even shrewd individuals sometimes made mistakes of judgement. He turned to follow Anna, who was already ushering
Jade towards the door.

Steve was standing looking down at his wife as she lay in
the high dependency unit. She had been moved to a side
ward, and lay white and unmoving as the life-support systems
around the bed beeped and clicked around her.

Their daughter, Sarah, had come at last to see her mother
and had stood for a long time, staring down at Rosemary's
still, pale face. Watching her, Steve had tried to control his
anguish; it was years since he had given up pleading with
her to try to work out some kind of reconciliation with her
mother. He wasn't even sure what it was Rosemary had done
to drive her away so completely. He had kept in touch by
phone and postcard, and now and again, guiltily, by visits
which he had kept secret, but the implacable dislike Sarah
seemed to show towards her mother had left him numb and
bewildered. Now as she looked down, her face showed no
compassion at all. 'I suppose she was engaged in another of
her campaigns to ruin someone's life,' she said bitterly.

Steve flinched. 'She genuinely thinks she is in the right,
Sarah.'

'And she was in the right when she forced that footpath
across an old man's lawn, was she? When they put up the
fence to separate his little bungalow from the garden he loved
just on principle, when all the local people said they were
happy to walk past a different way. But not my mother. Oh,
no. He lived a hundred miles from her, it was none of her

business, but in she went, bustling with self-righteousness, and forced it all through the council and went to the enquiry, used every trick and legal loophole to get her way. He died, Dad!'

Steve moved uncomfortably in his chair. 'I know,' he said sadly. 'But he might have died anyway. He was an old man.'

'The local people said he died of a broken heart. No one ever walked that path, and Mother certainly didn't. She had done her bit. She smugly ticked another box on her list. She never went near it again. And here she is, up to her old tricks, and on her own bloody doorstep this time!'

Steve sighed. 'She believes she's doing the right thing, Sarah. So many people try and block footpaths. She believes passionately that someone has to fight to keep them open.'

'But this isn't a footpath, is it? There has never been one there.' Sarah hadn't moved. Her expression was still hard, her mother's face still impassive and, Steve thought, unbearably vulnerable. 'This time she's trying to desecrate an ancient earthwork and go against an entire community, and because of her this poor young man will probably go to prison.'

Steve gasped. 'Sarah, that is enough. That poor young man, as you call him, is a drunken yob who tried to murder your mother.'

'No he didn't. He tried to scare her away. I've read the papers.'

He looked up at her in despair. 'Aren't you the least bit sorry she's been hurt, Sarah?'

She opened her mouth to reply, then she shook her head, changing her mind about what she was going to say. 'Of course I am.'

'Then leave it alone, dear, please. She needs your love and your prayers, not a tirade of invective.'

Before she left she had bent and brushed her mother's forehead with her lips in a cold, angry kiss, then she gave her father a hug. 'Sorry, Dad. I can't help it. I hate what she does.'

He patted her arm. 'I know.'

'You hate it too, don't you?' she added. She sighed. 'No, don't answer that. I know how loyal you are.'

He stood still for a long time after Sarah had gone, watching Rosemary's face, wondering how much of what they had said she had heard.

'Come on, old thing. It's time we were at home,' he murmured at last. He reached over and touched the back of her hand gently. It twitched. His eyes automatically went to the nearest screen. The steady progression of pulses did not flicker.

A nurse put her head round the door and glanced at him. 'Everything all right in there?' The two other beds in the small side ward were empty, white sheets pulled tight. There was nowhere for him to sit but he was reluctant to perch on their pristine whiteness.

'How is she?' His voice came out cracked and husky.

She hesitated, and perhaps hearing his despair walked in to stand beside him, looking down at Rosemary's face. 'She's far away, bless her.'

Steve looked at her, surprised. He was used to the professional calm of the nursing staff. Compassion and gentleness, though he was sure they were there, were usually well hidden. 'Where do you think she is?' he murmured. He lifted the hand that was not tethered to drips and monitors and stroked it again.

'Somewhere where there is no pain. The doctors are thinking of waking her tomorrow.'

'Is that good?' He could feel himself pleading inside, but he didn't allow himself to let any hope register in his voice.

'They won't do it unless they think she is ready.' She smiled and touched his shoulder gently, then she had gone.

Hell was hot as she had always known it would be, and peopled with monsters. Steaming pools of volcanic lava bubbled at her feet as she tried to pull away, to hide, but the great black cliffs at her back held her trapped in the narrow confines of the valleys through which she roamed, trying, trying, trying to find a way out. Steve was there looking for her. For a moment she had thought she saw him, felt the touch of his hand, but he was gone and she was alone again in her torment. They knew she had moved the sword. She hadn't known it was protected by elves and fiends; it was guarded by the servants of Wayland the Smith God. Every way she turned she saw them, hunting her, furious, dangerous, out for her blood. If she could find it and return it, all would be well, but it wasn't there. She had left it on the ground under the hedge. Why? Why had she put it there? Why had she taken it? Why had she gone to the burial mound of the Lord Egbert? She didn't know. She was screaming in her dream but no sound came.

If Steve could hear her he would rescue her. He was there, so close by, but he was the other side of a glass so thick she would never break free. She saw the nurse come in and talk to him, touch his arm. She saw him bow his head and wipe tears from his eyes. The nurse came back with a chair and put it by the bed. He tried to smile at her and she patted his arm again, then she was gone and Steve was alone with her body. Was she dying then? Had they told him she was dying and they were going to switch off the life-support machine? Perhaps she was already dead and this was the hell from which there was no return.

Unless she could find the sword.

It wasn't there. Somehow she knew Zoë had found it and taken it to The old Forge. Zoë had showed it to Leo and he had picked it up and scrutinised it and looked at the blade and the hilt with a magnifying glass and copied down the runes which he saw there. He was excited by it; Zoë was frightened. It was Zoë who was the danger. Take it back, please take it back, she pleaded silently. Even if she had spoken out loud her cries would have been drowned by the bubbling of the lava pools at her feet and the roar of distant dragons.

They were leaving the forge. Where was the sword now? Did they have it with them? Zoë wanted to throw it in the river. She was afraid of the curse. She knew it was cursed. She didn't know the danger.

Help me!

Rosemary held out her hands, but they were trapped behind the glass wall. If they gave the sword to the gods of the river there would be no rescue, no respite, no mercy. She beat on the glass and now the only sound she could hear was the sound of her own screams.

Zoë stopped in her tracks and put her hands to her head. 'What is it?' Leo stopped beside her.

'Nothing.' Zoë hesitated. 'I thought I heard something. Someone calling.' They were only a hundred yards or so from the river, standing on the dew wet lawns, on their way down to the *Curlew*. Below them a thick cold mist was curdling round the trees. She shook her head again. 'It's gone. It's nothing. It was almost as though I could hear Rosemary.' She gave an uncomfortable laugh. 'I hope she's OK.' She turned and walked on. 'Come on. I'm imagining things.'

They headed for the trees and had just about reached them when she stopped again and turned to look back towards the forge. 'Did you hear that? There's a car coming.'

Leo stopped and swung round. 'Where?'

'It's going towards your house.'

'Take no notice. Whoever it is, we don't want to see them. We've got our mobiles, if it's anything important we'll hear about it soon enough.'

It had taken several trips to carry their supplies down to the *Curlew* and with each visit the mist had seemed lighter. All being well they planned to sail with the tide at midnight. 'Why wait?' Leo had said. 'I don't want to be here in the morning with Ken staring balefully over the hedge. Let's disappear for a bit, give ourselves a chance. We needn't go far yet. We can moor up somewhere and make final plans.'

He hadn't mentioned the fog and neither had she. Each time she glanced down towards the water it was clearer. Please God it would go soon. To her surprise she felt a clutch of excitement in her stomach as she listened to him. And as they made their way down the path for the last time with the final load of belongings she felt nothing but an almost childish sense of anticipation.

The dinghy was bobbing in the water at the end of the landing stage. Leo squatted down and gently pulled in the painter. 'Here, give me your things and I'll put them in.'

Zoë was too out of breath to speak. Letting him help her into the little boat, she packed the bags and boxes around her, ignoring the slight slop of ice-cold water on the bottom boards as she sat still in the bow. The dinghy was already heavily laden and they were low in the water, but the night was very still. There was almost no wind and the river was still very misty.

Zoë looked round apprehensively. 'You don't think the ghost ship is lurking out here, do you?' she whispered. 'I can feel something odd about the river.'

Leo paused as he pushed the last bag under the thwart and looked at her. Then he shook his head. 'The mist is clearing, Zoë. There is no ghost ship here. Not now.' He squinted into the distance at the burgee at the masthead of the *Curlew*. It hung limply; there was no trace of wind. 'And there certainly doesn't seem to be anyone else around at the moment,' he said half to himself. He gave her a reassuring smile. 'I'm sure we're fine. I don't think the ghosts are about. Not tonight.'

They drew alongside the *Curlew* almost soundlessly and

Zoë scrambled aboard. Standing for a moment in the cockpit she looked out across the water.

OK.' Leo climbed in behind her. 'We'll stow this stuff away and get ready. There's plenty of time. You don't want to change your mind?'

She looked at him and shook her head. 'No. This is what I want. Aboard the lugger.' If she was honest this was it; she didn't want to go back. She gave one last glance over her shoulder then she followed him down into the cabin.

Behind them the blue smoke from a distant bonfire drifted up into the air and carried the smell of sweet autumn-burning leaves into the slowly coiling wreathes of mist above the river.

21

The blue smoke drifted on the wind and carried with it the displeasure of the gods.

The sorcerer, the Christians called him, the priest of the old gods, the wizard, the maker of charms, the eater of sins. Augury and magic were his trade. He should have known the destiny of the village, should have foretold the arrival of the great longship from the northern lands, the escalation of the threat from the hungry Danes. But Anlaf had seen nothing. The wyrd sisters had not thought fit to warn him of what was to come. Now, as he walked slowly across the fields he could smell death on the wind, the foul reek of burning houses and charred flesh. He could see in the distance the pall of smoke still hanging over what had once been a village full of laughter and songs and love.

Leaning more heavily on his staff with each step he took, he approached what had once been the great hall and at last stood still, looking round. A man and a woman stood nearby; he could hear her sobbing weakly, all strength gone. Had they somehow escaped into the fields at the first sign of trouble, or were they from a neighbouring village which had so far missed the attentions of the invader? He stepped forward slowly, scanning the debris in what had been a fine proud building. The smouldering thatch of reeds lay in clumps. Nearby he could see the burned remains of a man. He felt nausea rise in his throat at the sight and he turned away. What could he, alone, do to bury so many? Already the carrion eaters were gathering. Crows and kites, magpies, buzzards, circling overhead. By dark the foxes and wolves would be creeping out of the woods and forests, drawn by the smell of death on the wind.

Abruptly he turned and walked to the place where the church had stood. Built of flint and stone, it had fared better than the hall, but the roof had gone. He stood where the door had once been and looked in. The altar had been defiled and pulled down, the gold cross and the candlesticks, the sacred book which lived on the altar, paid for by the Lady Hilda, were gone. What, he wondered, had happened to her? Had she fled into the woods or had the men from the sea taken her and raped and murdered her?

He heard a sound behind him and spun round, his heart thudding. At first he thought there was no one there, then he saw her, almost as though thinking about her had conjured the woman from the shadows. Her face was drawn and white, streaked with smoke, her gown torn, her hair no longer covered by a veil, tangled and loose on her shoulders. He saw she had threads of grey amongst the gold. He expected her to turn on him, the man who should have warned them what was to come, but she merely shook her head, leaning for a moment on the tumbled flints of the wall. Before, he reminded himself, they had been enemies, Christian and pagan, fighting for the soul of her husband. Now they were survivors, lost in a ruined world. He stepped forward and held out his hand. 'Are you alone, lady?'

She stared at him without recognition, her eyes unfocused, the horrors of what she had seen still there, lurking in their depths. He waited for several heartbeats before at last her vision cleared and he saw her spirit return from wherever it was that it had fled, and knew that she had recognised him. 'Your husband is three times blessed that he did not witness what we saw, Lady Hilda,' he said gently.

She nodded.

He hesitated, then asked, 'Your sons? Oswald?'

She shook her head. 'I don't know. Oswald dragged me away from the hall, he made me run to the woods with him and hide, then he left me. He said he was coming back to find the boys.' He saw her eyes swim with tears. 'I have been searching but there is no sign of them in there.' She pointed to the smoking ruins of what had been her home. She looked round again and he saw the shiver of fear run through her body. She was searching the ruins for a sign of the helmets and shields of their despoilers. 'Have they gone?' she whispered.

He nodded. 'They went back to the ship and sailed on the tide.'

'Why us?'

'We were unprotected.' He waited for a moment, searching for the words, then made himself say them. 'I failed to predict what was coming. I did not read the signs correctly. I failed you all.'

He too was near tears.

She reached out and touched his hand. It was a gesture of friendship, perhaps comfort. 'No one could have read the plans of such evil men.' She turned away from him and looked into the ruins of what had once been a beautiful little church. 'They have left nothing,' she murmured. 'Even the holy cross and the psalter have gone.'

'The holy cross was made of gold,' he replied bitterly. 'And no doubt they enjoyed burning your book of prayers.'

'Will you help me look for my sons?' she whispered after another pause.

They found Eric's body near the entrance to the hall. He

had died bravely; there were three enemy dead beside him, bearing the wounds of his sword. Hilda stood looking down at the body of her husband's sword maker and she made the sign of the cross over him. 'I'm not even sure he was a Christian,' she murmured sadly. 'But wherever he is, he deserves compassion. Hrotgar was an evil manipulative man and he murdered Eric's wife. Eric more than made up for any sins he committed by trying to protect our hall.'

She stooped suddenly, and tried to drag something from beneath his body. Destiny Maker lay there, its beauty and strength masked by mud and blood. 'The Vikings would have taken this if they had seen it.' She passed it to her companion. 'It is the most beautiful piece of workmanship. I don't know how it came to leave my husband's grave, but he would want it returned.'

Anlaf bowed and took it from her. He looked at it for a long time and nodded. 'We will rebury it before we go.'

'Go?' She looked at him shocked. 'I can't go. This is my home. My children are here somewhere.'

He gave her a grave smile. 'We have searched everywhere, Lady Hilda. We have found no trace of them. It is my belief that they escaped. I will take you to the ealdorman at Rendlesham, or, if you prefer, to the king, at Thetford. Your sons will find you if they have survived.'

She did not argue. Together they walked down the long field, the strips of land separated by balks of grass, through the burned village and towards the river and the sacred place which housed her husband's body. There she sat on the ground wrapped in her cloak while the man she regarded as a sorcerer, finding the spades, two intact, one broken, dug down into the tumulus.

Time passed as the man went on with his grisly task. The day grew dull and then at last it began to grow dark. He dug on, sweat pouring from him. She dozed off, worn out by the horrors and exhaustions of the day, and woke again only when it was full dark. She did not stand up when he came to the bodies of the two men buried there. He glanced round and he saw her shake her head, her eyes filled with tears. Gently he bent and laid the sword back at its master's side, still stained with their enemy's blood, then he began the back-breaking job of once more filling in the soil and making the graves safe from predators and thieves. Only when the task was complete did she stand up, in the moonlight, and walk towards the grave. He moved away knowing that she wished to pray. Now was not the time for him to rant and rave and shout his own prayers and charms to the gods. His gods had returned with the invaders and he had been left bewildered by their fury.

Sylvia led Ken into her front room and closed the door behind them. 'I've got something to show you,' she said.

She had thought about it long and hard since she had first seen the photos, wondering what to do, tossing her options into the air and waiting for them to fall around her ears.

She had seen them lying on her editor's desk several days before while she was waiting for him to return to his chair after spending what seemed like hours with one of the other freelancers at the table on the other side of the office. She had moved forward to get a better look at the top picture and then with a gasp of recognition had reached down and picked them up. They showed a man and a woman in various stages of undress, slowly subsiding onto the grass and in the last two wrapped round each other naked. One or two showed the woman's face and in the final one she looked at she saw the man and recognised him. It was Leo Logan. She shuffled back through the pictures. The woman was Zoë Lloyd, she was almost sure of it. She had only seen her that once, months ago at the sailing club.

'Ah,' the voice behind her made her jump. 'I don't suppose

you know who those two are?' Duncan Davies had returned to his desk without her noticing.

Wordlessly she nodded.

'And do they have names?'

She looked up at him, numb with shock. 'Where did you get them?'

'I am reliably informed that a tall, spotty youth with red hair stuck them through our letterbox before legging it down the road. He obviously meant them to be published, and assumed, rashly as it happens, that we would recognise them.'

'She,' Sylvia pointed with a less than steady finger, 'is my fella's wife.'

'Ah.' Duncan sucked his cheeks in thoughtfully. 'And the chap? Not your fella, I take it?'

'Leo Logan. I've met him a few times. He sails.'

'And are they famous? Celebrities? Worth being sued over?'

Sylvia shook her head. She needed to think about this. 'Absolutely not. And they would sue you, believe me.'

'I am not inclined to do anything with them. There was obviously malicious intent behind this. The kind donor has kept himself anonymous and we are a local paper, not a salacious red-top.'

He put his hand out for the pictures. 'Bin, I think. The cheeky bugger even suggested that I might like to pay him for some even more revealing shots. He was naive enough to include an email address but I don't suppose it's in his real name.'

Sylvia put her hand behind her back. 'Can I have them?'

He narrowed his eyes. 'Why?'

She gave him a complicit smile. 'Not sure yet, to be honest, but I think their judicious use might resolve a few problems. An unhappy couple and a pair of lonely singles might be able to sort things out with a bit of persuasion.'

Duncan had shrugged. 'As long as I don't see you take them,' he muttered, and turned away. When, moments later, he had retrieved a sheet of her copy from a file the photos had disappeared into her bag.

She looked at Ken now for several seconds, still uncertain. Supposing this went wrong? Supposing he was jealous and furious, and raced off home to retrieve his wife, his mind changed about leaving her? She had played this scene in her head a hundred times. 'I know your wife doesn't understand you. I know you said you would ask her for a divorce as soon as the moment is right.' All the usual baloney. Except he had never said it. He had talked about Zoë and their life together and she had gathered that things were not right between them. Obviously not or he would hardly have jumped into her bed. But he had never mentioned divorce as being an option; nor had he suggested for a single second that he wanted to make his relationship with her permanent. They had had fun. They had confided in each other. They got on well. Was she about to blow everything out of the water?

She realised suddenly that he was watching her, a quizzical expression on his face. She smiled at him and it dawned on her that she was drawing all the wrong conclusions. She would give them to him and let him decide.

'I saw some rather unfortunate pictures on my editor's desk. I persuaded him not to think about publishing them . . .' That was not quite true, but near enough. 'I wasn't sure whether I should show you, Ken, but I think maybe you had better have them.'

If this didn't seal the end of his relationship with his wife nothing would.

She handed him the envelope she had put them in and turned away to stare out of the window into her small back garden.

She turned back when the silence had drawn out just too long. He was standing, the pictures in his hand and his face was white. She couldn't tell if it was with shock or anger. 'I'm sorry,' she whispered. 'I shouldn't have shown them to you.'

He shook his head. 'No. You did the right thing. Thank you.'

He sat down abruptly and threw the photos down on the coffee table in front of him, then he put his head in his hands.

She sat down slowly in the chair by the fireplace and waited, leaning forward anxiously, watching him.

He looked up at last. 'Who took these?' he whispered.

'They were dropped off anonymously at the paper. Someone said it was a spotty youth with red hair.'

He gave a humourless grin. 'I'll lay money on that being our ne'er-do-well young neighbour, Jackson.'

'Jackson?' she repeated. 'Jackson Watts? The guy who nearly killed that woman with a tractor?'

He nodded slowly. 'He lives near us. An odious youth. It is the sort of thing he might do. He seems to have a grudge against most of the world, from what I've heard.' He touched the photo with a fingertip and she saw a moment of tenderness in his face. 'I've never seen Zoë look like that,' he said softly. 'We've been married ten years and I have never seen her look so happy.'

On the way to Sylvia's he had done one last thing for Zoë. He had taken the figure he had found under their bed and he had thrown it far out into the river. The ripples had spread in slow concentric circles until they had been lost in the flooding tide.

Sylvia chewed her lip, watching him. She said nothing, hardly daring to breathe.

Eventually she stood up. 'Shall we go sailing? she said brightly. At least it might distract him. 'The tide will be just right. We'll go in *Sally Sue*. She's all ready to leave. I was planning on taking her up the coast for the weekend.'

'And you have room for me?'

'I'll always have room for you, Ken.' She grinned happily.

There were other survivors of the raid, those who had not been in the village on that night. One by one as the days went by they crept back and stood surveying the still-smoking ruins, the slaughtered corpses, already defiled by kites and crows and foxes. They saw the ruined church where the bodies of Edith and Father Wulfric, shrouded and prepared for burial, had been lying in the nave. Instead of a Christian funeral mass they had disappeared in a pagan pyre which lit up the countryside for miles around. The ruins had cooled to reveal jagged remnants of its stone walls like ruined teeth amongst the blackened fallen beams of the roof.

The hall was almost all gone. Everyone who had attended the Lord Egbert's wake had gone with it. If any had escaped they had no means of telling. All that was left in the village were the mounds of blackened sedge and scorched wattle which had once been the cottages of the wheelwright, the carpenter, the potter, the men who worked the fields, and items that had been made of metal, things not worth stealing, pots and pans, bits of harness for the oxen and the horses. The animals had all been slaughtered or had scattered and disappeared. Eric's anvil and his tools were lying in the ruins of his forge. The iron figurine which had been used as the murder weapon and had so cruelly killed his wife was lost, buried in the ashes. Part of the forge cottage had failed to catch completely, had scorched and smouldered and gone out. One of the storehouses nearby had all but escaped the flames. The survivors shook their heads and wept and prayed, and where they could they buried what remained of the dead.

Away from the village the air was sharp with the smell of death and fire, and smoke still hung amongst the lofty pines. The burial mound was deserted. The Danish host had paused and skirted it and seen signs that it was recent; one or two had thought of the treasure that might be buried there, but they were fully aware of the curses which would fall on them if they disturbed the rest of the man within. This was no Christian burial site; this was the resting place of a man with a faith much like their own. They had cared nothing for the living

459

Christian inhabitants of the village, but the ghosts of those who had been laid to rest with proper ceremony were different. This place was to be respected and feared and left to the gods.

And those who returned left it alone as well. The family of the Lord Egbert had gone; his wife, his sons had fled or been slaughtered. There was no sign of anyone to tell them how it had happened. As they walked back to the top of the field and stared down at the river they saw the ship had gone.

The sad spectators wandered away one by one. The village would not be rebuilt for decades and when it was they did not restore the church. This part of the kingdom was in the Danelaw now; for the time being, the gods of the Vikings guarded the land.

The mist drifted up again on the tide and enfolded the place where the longship had lain at anchor and there the echoes of its passing would remain for ever, its deathly mission etched into the psyche of the land, its image imprinted in the mist and echoing in the wind.

Zoë found the sword wrapped in its newspaper in one of Leo's sail bags and pulled it out. 'You brought it with us.'

He glanced up from the chart he was studying. 'I couldn't bear to leave it. Sorry.'

She laid it, on its newspaper, on the chart table and suddenly she shuddered. 'No, Leo. We mustn't take it away from the grave. That would be unlucky. That's why Rosemary is in hospital. We have to get rid of it.'

She ran her finger gently over the hilt and the corroded blade. Flakes of rust came away on her skin and she shivered. Was it rust, or was it the remains of long-ago blood that stained the blade red? Once before, she knew in some distant part of herself, another woman had held this sword and wondered, just as she was, what to do with it. And the decision had been the same.

'You're not serious about throwing it overboard?' Leo was watching her face.

She shook her head. 'I still want to rebury it. We have to, Leo. To appease the gods and mitigate the curse. I don't want it on the boat a moment longer. I'm sorry. Let's do it before we go. Now.'

He stared at her. 'But the place is crawling with police and archaeologists.'

'There won't be anyone there in the dark. Why should there be?'

'Because looters and metal detectorists will swarm all over the site, that's why. You told me it had been in the papers. A mention of the word Anglo-Saxon in the press and the whole world will descend on that field.'

She closed her eyes unhappily. 'Then what shall we do? We can't keep it, Leo. I have the most awful feeling about it.' She was rewrapping it. 'Let's go back now. We can't sail with this on the boat, surely you see that? Supposing this is what the ghost ship is all about? Perhaps the guys in the ship are looking for the grave and the treasure that might be buried there. Either the dead man was a friend of theirs, or they were out to despoil the grave. We can't risk it. We can't!'

'OK.' He put a reassuring hand on her arm. 'You're right. That would be best. We'll do it now. Tonight.'

As he ducked out of the cabin his mobile rang. He pulled it out of his pocket and squinted at the screen. 'It's Bill Turtill. I'd better take it in case it's about the accident.' He put the phone to his ear.

Zoë climbed out into the cockpit and sat down staring out across the dark water. The *Lady Grace* was tugging gently at her buoy nearby. The chill off the river made her shiver. It was very quiet.

Huddling in her jacket she suddenly heard Leo's raised voice.

'He said what? I don't believe it. You have to be joking!' He scrambled out into the cockpit and stood near her, the phone clamped to his ear. 'No of course I haven't. The very idea. My God! Thanks for letting me know, Bill. I owe you one.' He switched off the phone and looked at her, his face a mask of anger. 'Jackson Watts rang Mike Turtill just now. Luckily Bill was in the room when he took the call and overheard it. Apparently Jackson is crowing; he and Jade have told the police that I molested her.'

'What?' Zoë felt her stomach clench with horror.

He shook his head. 'All I wanted was to help that child. I never touched her.' He looked at Zoë. 'You do believe me?'

'Of course I do.'

'I gather I can expect a visit from the police and social services.'

'Oh, Leo.' Zoë felt sick. 'Do you think that was the police – the car we heard?'

'Probably. I'll have to go back. We've got to sort this out.'

'You can't. They might arrest you!'

'Well, I can't stay down here and I'm not going to run away.'

'Why not? If we get away we can fight it from somewhere where you're safe.'

'Zoë, it will only make me look guilty if I run. I have to sort it out.' He shook his head in despair. 'I can't believe Sharon would think I could do such a thing.'

'I am afraid it might be my fault.' Zoë turned her back on him miserably. 'Jade warned me off. She more or less threatened that if I didn't back off and leave you to her she would make me regret it. And I didn't.' She reached over and squeezed his arm. 'I never ever suspected she would be capable of something like this.' She stopped abruptly. Manda had. Manda had warned her and she had taken no notice.

Behind them the little cabin looked warm and inviting and safe in the lamplight. She turned and climbed back down the companionway. Leo followed her and sat down opposite her. His face was pale and strained as he stared at her helplessly. 'Let's get one thing straight. This is not your fault. Not under

462

any circumstances.' He rubbed his cheeks wearily with his palms. 'What a mess.'

'It's the sword!' Zoë stared down at the newspaper parcel with a shudder. 'It's bringing bad luck to anyone who touches it. I told you we had to get rid of it. We shouldn't have brought it with us. It has to go back now. This minute. We have to go now.' Then she shook her head. 'No, you can't go. If the burial site is crawling with police – even if they have just left security guards there you might get arrested.' She ran her fingers through her hair in despair. 'Put it back in the bag. I'll go. You stay here and I will leave it somewhere near the site. If I can I'll bury it, if not I'll tuck it in somewhere nearby.'

'Zoë, wait.' Leo raised his hands. 'There is no need for all this. Whatever happens, I have to go and face them.'

'No.' She shook her head vehemently. 'What you need is a lawyer. Before you do anything else. Do you know anyone you can call?'

He nodded slowly. 'I do, as it happens. My friend Max. His firm acted for me in the separation from my wife. He's retired, but I would trust him with my life.'

'Ring him.'

He glanced at her, then pulled out his mobile again and she watched as he brought up his contacts list. The phone rang for a long time. 'No answer and no answer service,' he said at last. 'I suppose it is a bit late.' He put the phone down on the cabin table. 'And he might be away. He travels a lot. If there is still no reply in the morning, I'll ring his office.'

They looked at each other in silence for a moment. 'Do you think the police know about *Curlew*?' Zoë said softly. 'I wouldn't put it past that little cow to have told them.'

'She's not a little cow, Zoë,' he reprimanded gently. 'She's a confused kid.'

'Confused or not, she has dropped you in it and we have to get your name cleared.' Zoë stood up. 'Right, first things first. You can't risk dealing with this, but I can.' She didn't dare give herself time to think. 'Help me with this bag, then you can row me ashore.'

'You would do that for me?' He didn't move. 'Go off in the dark to a haunted, probably security-guarded burial ground in the middle of nowhere?'

She gave him a quick smile. 'Not such a middle-class housewife now, eh?'

'Oh, no.' He shook his head. 'Did I call you that? How wrong was I! I am breathless with admiration. You are the bravest person I have ever met. But I am not going to let you do it. Not alone.'

'So you are going to deprive me of the chance to prove my worth?' She zipped up her jacket. 'Leo, think! I know every inch of this place now. There is no danger. I will be very careful. No one will see me.'

She picked up the bag and began to edge along the bunk towards the door, then she sat down again. 'I'll be able to suss out the situation at home as well. I can see if the police have gone to The Old Forge and maybe,' her mind was racing ahead, 'I could go and see your friend Max first thing. Does he live locally?'

Leo was shaking his head, laughing. 'Zoë, Zoë, stop.' He reached over and took her hand. 'I don't know if you are right about me lying low but you have given me an idea. Yes, Max does live locally and the irony is, he lives down river from here. I could sail there.'

U

At the Hall, the stables were replenished with two new riding horses to accompany the squire's cob, though neither was strictly a lady's horse. A new blacksmith was appointed and moved into the cottage behind the forge with his wife and three children. He was competent and friendly and good with the horses, and soon made himself a part of the community. His black iron work was excellent and he turned his hand to some fancy decoration as well as the usual ironmongery of the estate.

In the servants' hall there was a conflict of opinion as to what had happened to Emily. Mrs Field and Mrs Davy, the cook, both thought she had run away, unable to bear her own guilt over Dan's death. The maids preferred a more melodramatic theory, that she had thrown herself in the river. Mayhew claimed there had been gypsies over the other side of the heath the day she had disappeared and reckoned they might have kidnapped her. If they had, he expounded one evening after dinner, licking his lips, she no doubt got a bit of the rough she had so obviously been lusting after. The frowns of Beaton and Mrs Field did nothing to quell his imagination and one of the maids became hysterical with fright at the thought of her mistress's fate.

Above stairs, Henry sat alone in his study as the evenings drew in and kept his counsel. If he had any theories as to the fate of his wife, no one knew what they were.

The farm workers were equally baffled as to what had happened to her. None of them had seen her, and she hadn't even bothered to send flowers to Susan's funeral, something which had been noted with extreme displeasure in the village. If George and Robert discussed it as they worked together in the fields, or supervised the repairs to the three great barns, no one heard them. Betsy and Jessie Turtill voiced the views of everyone for miles. 'Good riddance to bad rubbish,' they said. 'If she never comes back, it'll not be a moment too soon.'

Zoë stood in the dark on the edge of the landing stage watching Leo row away from her. He rested on his oars for a moment and raised a hand to wave. She waved back then resolutely she picked up the bag, as always surprised at how heavy the sword was, and headed up through the trees towards the lane. The second they had kissed goodbye and he had lowered himself back into the dinghy she had felt her courage deserting her. She wanted to call him back, she wanted to hurl the bag with its cursed contents into the river but she didn't allow herself to hesitate. There was too much at stake. Their happiness and maybe Rosemary's life depended on her taking this thing back to where it was found.

A breath of wind touched the back of her neck with cold fingers and she shuddered. She had Leo's torch in her pocket but she didn't want to use it, it would only draw attention to her if there was anyone in the fields. Her eyes were anyway rapidly getting used to the dark. She could make out the sky above the hedgeline now, the clouds swelling heavy and dull across the deeper black behind them. She was trying to walk quietly, glad of her rubber-soled sailing shoes. Somewhere nearby an owl hooted and she stopped in her tracks, her skin prickling with terror. 'Stupid!' she muttered. She took a deep breath and moved forward again, afraid now that she would miss the gap in the hedge that Rosemary had cut. Somewhere behind her Leo was quietly pulling up the sails, slipping the mooring and drifting silently out into the river. There was no going back now. If she failed he would be in danger not just from the police but from the sword and its curse. She tightened her grip on the bag handles, feeling her palms wet with sweat, and walked doggedly on.

She had almost passed the gap in the hedge when she saw it at last. She stopped and headed towards it, feeling her feet slip on the wet grass of the bank at the edge of the lane. Then she was in the field stumbling over the furrows, feeling the weight of the newly turned mud hanging from her shoes. There was no shelter, nowhere to hide as she made her way towards the centre, thankful there was no moon at least. She couldn't see the state of the site in the darkness; all she could make out was the silhouette of the small oak tree which stood out above the mound. Then suddenly she saw a light. She stopped dead, her heart pounding. There was someone there.

There was no point in turning back. Whoever was there might see her at any moment. She crept on, bending low, and realised as she drew slowly closer that the light came from a small tent which had been pitched at the edge of the copse. Almost as she recognised the faint outline she heard music and suddenly a muffled shout of laughter. Holding her breath she crept closer, aiming now for the far side of the copse furthest away from the tent. If the people in it were there on guard they weren't making a very good job of it; the entrance was firmly zipped up.

She felt better when she had reached the copse and crept into the shelter of the trees. The undergrowth had been cut back and the barbed wire had gone, but there were still a few small trees and shrubs which gave her enough cover in the darkness as she felt her way forward. Suddenly she noticed there was another tent, this one larger and square and in total darkness. It had been erected over the site of the excavations and appeared to be deserted. She paused, taking stock. She had reached the burial mound; whoever had taken the sword did not appear to have dug very far to find it. Surely the important thing had been to get it here. She didn't have to put it in the grave itself.

As she stood pondering what to do her eyes were caught by a movement in the distance. A shadow had moved in the tent and then as she watched the tent flap was unzipped from within and a figure stepped outside and stretched, yawning so loudly she could hear it from where she was crouching. She dropped to the ground and remained motionless. It was unlikely he could see her even if he turned round, but her heart was thudding like a hammer as she lay, her face pressed into the grass. He had flicked on a torch and she was aware of the powerful beam directed into the trees above her head and sweeping round the site.

'I can't think why they would assume anyone would come out to such a godforsaken spot with all that fog coming in!' The man's voice was clear as he spoke over his shoulder to someone in the tent. 'I'm going to take a slash then I'm for my bed.' She hardly dared breathe, held her breath praying he wouldn't come in her direction. He didn't. Minutes later he had ducked back inside the tent and the flap was zipped up once more. She waited several more minutes then cautiously she scrambled to her feet. She had to get rid of the sword, and quickly, and get away from here. She glanced over her shoulder back towards the river. It was growing misty and Leo was out there on the water alone.

Somehow she forced herself to take a step or two forward. Beneath her feet the ground was a tangle of grass and weeds. She couldn't dig a hole; stupidly she had brought nothing to dig with. Crouching down again she felt the ground round her in the darkness and found almost at once what appeared to be a rabbit hole. Her fingers touched bare earth and she felt the crumbly soil opening up beneath them. Moving as quietly as she could she put the bag down and drew back the zip. She pulled out the sword, cursing as the newspaper rustled in her hands. At last it was free of its wrapping. She shoved the paper back in the bag and carefully pushed the sword down into the hole. It met resistance almost at once, but she persevered, waggling it gently, not wanting to force it, feeling a strange sense of reverence now that she was returning it to the earth. As soon as it was level with the surface of the soil she stopped, looking down at it blindly in the darkness. Strangely she found she wanted to pray, but she didn't know what to say.

'I'm sorry. This shouldn't have been taken away. It belongs here,' she whispered. It seemed inadequate, but it was all that was needed. She bowed her head in silence, then slowly she began to fill in the earth over the rusty blade. Either it would remain there for ever or perhaps tomorrow, perhaps months hence, it would be rediscovered by the archaeologists and they would decide its fate.

It would be up to the gods of old what happened next.

* * *

Somewhere a bell was ringing. Footsteps echoed over the floor and a flurry of voices was speaking over her.

Rosemary frowned and for a moment her eyelids fluttered.

'She's waking up.' A male voice, deep and authoritative. 'Where is her husband?'

She heard that. Steve. Dear old Steve.

'He went home for a few hours. Have you got his phone number?'

She managed to open her eyes for a second, but the light was too bright and the effort was too much.

After picking up the buoy Leo climbed back into the *Curlew*'s cockpit and ducked down into the cabin. Carefully he drew the curtains across the portholes, then he lit the lamp, satisfied the light was unlikely to be seen unless someone was right down on the river bank. Sitting down, he let out a deep sigh.

Zoë was an amazing, gutsy woman and he had been astonished to find that he was deeply and genuinely besotted with her. The question was, did she feel the same about him? He rubbed his hands across his cheeks, feeling the ridges and irregularities of his scars. What did she see in him? He was a flawed man in so many senses, and now accused, on top of all the rest, of being a paedophile. He had no doubt she would do as she said and go and try to rebury the sword, but after that, would she come back? What had he to offer a woman like Zoë?

He bent and rummaged in one of his bags, pulling out a sketchbook. He opened it at his sketch of her and studied it, running his hand wistfully across her face, lingering over her eyes, her wildly blowing hair, the half-smile on her lips, then he glanced at the tide tables piled up on the end of the bunk. Should he wait for her at Max's as he had promised or would it be better for them both if he quietly slipped away and disappeared from her life for ever, leaving Max to clear his name.

Putting out the lamp he went up on deck and stared round.

The tide was almost high. It was time to leave. Once he reached Max's he would decide.

Quietly and methodically he began to ready *Curlew* for a voyage, raising the sail again, tidying the decks, tying the dinghy to the stern and at last casting off from the buoy. In total silence the boat moved slowly out into the middle of the river, drifting on the tide as Leo hauled in the mainsail and pushed the tiller over. He gave a wry smile as the curved brown sail hung above him in the dark. Ghostly was the only word he could think of to describe it.

Once he had drifted into the fairway there was wind. He sat at the tiller as the yacht drew steadily away, moving slowly but inexorably down, past the sleeping countryside, houses in darkness, fields deserted, the woods asleep as the moon sailed in and out of sight behind the clouds. The mist hung over the water in pale drifting threads; somewhere he heard a fish jump and at last the quiet bubble of the water beneath the forefoot as *Curlew* gained in speed.

A bird called from the saltings along the river's edge, eerily close in the darkness, and he heard a quick swirl in the water as another fish broke the surface. He could smell the mud as the tide began to fall.

He sailed on past Waldringfield sailing club, past The Maybush Inn with the blue umbrellas tightly furled against the damp night air, on past fields and woods, holding course with a single finger on the tiller. There were more wisps of mist round him now, rising off the water.

He would be there before long, and then he would make his decision.

The sword safely buried, Zoë wriggled backwards on her stomach for several metres then at last she climbed to her feet. There was no sound from the tent. The lights had been extinguished and with it the radio. She could hear nothing but silence and, as she reached the muddy field once more, the squelch and suck of her shoes as she stumbled across the furrows towards the hedge. If she had left footprints behind it was too bad. Nothing had been taken from the site so hopefully no one would look.

It seemed to take hours to make her way back towards The Old Barn but she reached it at last. She knew Ken wouldn't be there but even so she pushed open the door as quietly as she could. The house was in darkness and after kicking off her shoes she stood in the kitchen for several seconds listening intently. Nothing.

Still without turning on the lights she tiptoed across the great room in her socks and made for the stairs. She didn't turn on the lights until she had drawn the curtains of the bedroom tightly across the windows. Only then did she feel she could breathe again. Glancing at the bedside clock she saw it was just after three in the morning. Pulling off her muddy clothes at last she went and stood under the shower for several minutes and then it was all she could do to reach the bed before she collapsed into a deep exhausted sleep.

She was woken just after five by a frantic knocking on the door. Her heart in her mouth, she dragged on her dressing gown and ran downstairs, her brain befuddled with lack of sleep, expecting to see a policeman standing on the step, but it was Steve.

'Thank God you are here. Please, Zoë. My car won't start. The battery is dead. The hospital rang. She's waking up.'

With one glance at his shaking hands and his agitated face she knew she had to offer to drive him, tired as she was. Sitting him down in the kitchen with a cup of coffee she ran upstairs to dress. It took only minutes to find some fresh clothes and grab her car keys and ring Leo's mobile. It was switched off. She left a message then she ran back down the stairs and ushered Steve out into the cold of the early morning. She was, she realised, running on pure adrenaline.

She accompanied Steve up to the ward and stood behind

him as he looked down at Rosemary, lying unmoving on the hospital bed. She was still hooked up to the monitors. A nurse appeared. 'Mr Formby? Did they ring you? Rosemary showed some signs of waking up a couple of hours or so ago. She opened her eyes and moved a little.'

'Is that good?' Steve had stepped forward to take his wife's hand.

'It's hopeful.' The woman smiled. 'It happened at just after two a.m.'

It was just after two a.m. that Zoë had laid the sword back in the ground.

'I missed it.' Steve sounded completely defeated. 'I came as soon as you phoned.'

'She'll do it again.' The nurse moved a chair forward for him. 'I'll bring you both some tea.'

'Both?' Steve looked confused. He had forgotten Zoë was there.

'Is this another of your daughters?' The nurse looked at Zoë and smiled.

Steve looked even more puzzled for a moment, then he shook his head. 'We only have the one,' he said sadly. Sarah hadn't come back.

As the nurse disappeared he gave Zoë a wan smile. 'You are lucky you don't have children,' he said slowly. 'They can cause so much heartbreak.'

Zoë leaned across and gave his arm a little squeeze. 'I am so sorry.' She glanced helplessly round the ward and shook her head. 'I'll leave you to it, Steve,' she said. 'I have to go back, I'm sorry.' She bent over and touched Rosemary gently on the arm, then she kissed him lightly on the cheek and tiptoed towards the door. She didn't think Steve had even noticed that she was leaving.

22

'He never touched her, Jeff.' Sharon confronted her husband, hands on hips. 'The doctor said she is still a virgin and she admitted to the woman she made it all up. She was jealous of Zoë, the stupid little madam.'

Jeff shook his head and sighed. 'Why did we ever have kids, Sharon?'

'Gawd knows.'

'Where is she now?'

'Upstairs. She can't go back to school till she's out of quarantine for the bloody chicken pox. And she's not out of quarantine until the spots have healed, and she keeps on scratching them.'

'So what's going to happen about Leo?'

Sharon shook her head. 'They said someone else had made a complaint besides Jade, and I said, yes, it was my son and he would take back every word. I asked him, Jeff, and he admitted it. He said Jade blackmailed him. What is the matter with them? I am not having Leo hounded because of my frigging kids.'

Jeff gave a small wry grin, swiftly hidden behind his hand. 'Good for you. What are we going to do with them, Shal?'

There was a long silence. 'I won't be able to bear it if Jacko goes to prison,' she whispered at last. She sniffed and turned away. 'Are you going to take those dogs for a walk or what?'

Jeff nodded. 'Rosemary is holding her own,' he said gently. 'I rang the hospital. Normally they won't tell you unless you're a relative, so I said I was her brother.'

Sharon smiled. 'Please God she gets better. If he's charged with murder –'

'That policeman, Andy, said it would be manslaughter. He would go to prison, love. You have to accept it. He might anyway, for what he's done. The fact that she was trespassing doesn't make any difference.'

They stood for a moment in silence, looking at each other in despair, then at last Jeff turned away to look for the dogs' leads. 'We do have to sell the barn, don't we?' he said sadly as he picked them up off the sideboard and whistled.

Sharon nodded. 'We could never go back there, Jeff. We couldn't look them in the eye again, not any of them. Not after this.'

As the two dogs came running in from the garden he turned away from her so she couldn't see his face. 'You're right, I suppose,' he said. He couldn't believe it but suddenly he felt like crying.

Zoë parked outside the barn. The whole place was deserted now, each house empty, a feeling of loss permeating the air. She glanced across at The Old Forge and then forced herself to walk casually across the grass towards the gate. There was no sign of anyone having been there. The house was locked up. No one as far as she could see had forced their way in. If the police had called on Leo they had gone away again without leaving any sign.

Standing there outside his front door she was overwhelmed

with melancholy. Winter was on its way. She shivered, thinking of the ghosts and the cold grey sea heaving and breathing out beyond the river mouth like an animal, licking its lips, waiting for its next victim. Whatever happened Leo was not going to get her out there, over the bar. Her exotic shopping would be done no further away than Woodbridge.

She let herself into The Old Barn and ran up the stairs to the bedroom, glancing at her watch. She was going to drive to Max's house; that had been the agreement and she would meet Leo there. He had told her Max's address and how to find it, and jokingly she had said she wouldn't write it down in case she was searched by the police. Now she wished she had. It had sounded simple when she had repeated it back to him; now that seemed so long ago.

Leo hadn't returned her call and when she tried his number again his mobile was still switched off. She could feel panic building again. She could only pray he had got there safely and stashed the *Curlew* somewhere she couldn't be seen.

She still wasn't sure how long they would be away. Perhaps she ought to pack a proper bag now while she had the chance. There was so little room on the boat, but then again she could always leave it in the car if Leo looked at it askance. She pulled a holdall out of the cupboard on the landing and taking if into the bedroom she put it on the bed and turned to her chest of drawers. Nothing fancy, just trousers and sweaters for the cold nights on the river. She paused, thinking about the exotic clothes they were going to buy. Did he really see her in gypsy skirts and floaty scarves? If so, how was she going to manage on the boat? Her mind rejected the thought of setting out to sea, out of sight of land, across the ocean. That was not going to happen.

Pulling open one of the top drawers in search of warm socks, she stopped short. There was her passport. She picked it up and stared at it. If she took it she was implicitly accepting that they might find their way abroad. Unable to face the decision, she threw the passport on the bed. Something to think about at the last moment.

She was about to push the drawer shut when a box of tampons caught her eye. She froze, staring at them. She hadn't given the subject a thought when she was packing her stuff, but now in the silence of the empty house she found she was doing some unaccustomed calculations in her head.

She sat down on the edge of the bed at last and put her hand experimentally on her stomach. Steve's mournful statement about her lack of children must have hit a chord in some subconscious part of her brain. She wasn't on the pill; she and Leo had taken no precautions. It hadn't occurred to her, she was so used to the fact that Ken had had the snip. Was it possible?

She felt a flutter of excitement and then almost as quickly a moment of pure panic. Here, in this room, Ken had shown her that weird figure he had found under the bed. What had he called it? A grotesque fertility doll? Jade's curse. No. She shook her head violently. She stood up and looked round. What had Ken done with it? She had asked him to throw it in the river. Had he?

She swallowed hard and took a deep breath. If she was pregnant it was not because Jade had left that thing in here. It was because she had been careless. Or had she been deliberately tempting fate? And it was Leo's. It had to be. She and Ken had not had sex for weeks, if not months, and even if they had he was not capable of being a father. If he was, in spite of the op, they would have known about it years ago.

She glanced at her watch. There was plenty of time to drive into Woodbridge before she set off for Max's. Should she go and buy a pregnancy testing kit? Her brain was whirling. Perhaps it was better to pretend she hadn't thought about it, assume it was a false alarm and carry on as before with her plans to drive out to join Leo. What would he think

476

about a pirate baby? Her shoulders slumped. She doubted if it was part of his master plan to embark on fatherhood again at this stage in his life. Hadn't she mentioned it once in joking? Something about a wild child? He had not risen to the bait.

For a long time she sat there, deep in thought, then at last she stood up. Better if neither of them knew for sure at this point in the proceedings. She could be wrong. She probably was wrong. After all, stress can cause the same symptoms as early pregnancy, she had heard that time and again from worried friends. She was going to take Leo's advice, throw caution to the winds and wait to see what fate would hurl in their direction. She picked up the box of tampons again and looked at it, then with a shrug she threw it into the bottom of her bag just in case. On top of it she threw the passport.

She headed for the bedroom door, then she paused. She was still wearing her wedding ring. She pulled it off and stared at it for a long moment, then she opened the drawer again, tucked the ring into her little jewel box and closed the drawer with a bang.

It was late afternoon when she turned the car into the front gate of Leo's friend Max's cottage. It was a small thatched building at the end of a long single-tracked lane, nestling amongst willow trees very near the river. Below it there was a narrow creek and at the end of it a secluded boathouse which was where, she assumed, Leo had hidden the *Curlew*.

She got out of her car and looked round. The building was run down, the walls, originally a pale Suffolk pink, here and there stained green with lumps of plaster missing. She rang the doorbell experimentally. There was no reply.

There was a small garage beside the house. She went over to it and dragged the door open a foot or two. It was empty.

Making her way down the ill-defined track from the front

garden she scanned the river bank for the familiar mast. There was no sign. The whole place seemed to be deserted. She found the boathouse squatting amongst tall reeds and osiers and pulled open the side door. She stood staring down at the black water lapping against the pilings where surely the *Curlew* should be moored, and she felt her eyes fill with tears.

Leo wasn't there. He hadn't waited for her. Perhaps he thought she had lost her nerve; thought she had changed her mind. When he found Max wasn't there, had he decided to go as he had originally planned on the top of the tide and was already out to sea? Her trip to the hospital and then her decision to go back to The Old Barn had cost her several hours, hours during which he must have waited, wondering if she was going to come back and at last he must have given up. But she had phoned. She had left a message. She had explained.

She pulled her phone out of her pocket and looked at it. No signal. Perhaps he had never got her call. She slumped down miserably on the damp mossy boards and sat there, eyes closed, hugging her knees.

It was dark when she was woken some time later by the sound of the doors behind her opening. 'Leo?' Her heart leaped with hope and then plummeted again in a panic when she saw the silhouette of a stranger standing there. He had a torch in his hand and shone it into the boathouse, picking her up at once as she sat on the damp floor, too frightened to move.

'Zoë? Is that you?' He stepped inside. 'Sorry, did I give you a fright? I am Max, Leo's friend.'

Slowly she scrambled to her feet, trying to muster her thoughts. She could see him more clearly now in the reflected torchlight. He was tall and thin with grey hair, dressed in jeans and a Guernsey sweater. 'Come up to the cottage. You look frozen, my dear,' he went on. He held out his hand. 'Let's go and switch everything on, light a fire and have something to eat. Leo is no doubt in the pub at this moment and the first thing you can do is ring him from my phone indoors.'

Numbly she followed him up the path, through the front door and into a small low-ceilinged room. The house was cold and smelled of old wood fires and damp. 'I have only just got back,' he said over his shoulder. 'I flew back from Capetown last night.' He went straight to the fireplace and within minutes had collected firelighters and kindling and logs from the basket beside it. 'It won't take long to warm this place up.'

He turned and smiled at her. He was much older than she had at first thought, perhaps in his seventies and he had a kind smile. 'Leo rang me. Just as well. I arrived back to find a strange car outside my front door. I wondered if I had squatters!' He smiled again. His face was deeply lined and weather-beaten. 'When he arrived here he found there was no signal to phone anyone and I was clearly still away so he took *Curlew* on down the river. He tried to leave you a message but your phone was off. He left you a note, didn't you find it? He knew once you got here your phone wouldn't work either.' He paused, looking at her with concern. 'He has explained the situation, Zoë, and between us we have worked out a plan to deal with this wretched accusation if they persist with it, so, my dear, you needn't look so unhappy.'

Zoë felt herself blush. So far she had not uttered a word and she was suddenly aware of how she must look, crumpled by sleep, her face tear-stained, her clothes dirty from the floor of the boathouse.

'First we are going to ring Leo,' he went on, 'and tell him that his pirate's moll has turned up.' She blushed even deeper at the realisation that Leo must have told Max all about them. 'Then we'll eat, then tomorrow I am going to drive you down to Felixstowe Ferry where *Curlew* is moored.' He sighed. 'I wish he had waited here; we could have sorted all this out once and for all, but dear Leo, he does have a taste for the dramatic! I think he quite fancied the idea of being on the run and he couldn't contemplate being out of touch with the world. As far as I am concerned the lack of a phone signal here is bliss. But we always have the dear old landline.'

He pointed out the phone, black and Bakelite, in the corner.

'Leo?' Her hand was shaking on the heavy phone receiver. 'I thought you had gone without me!' Max had left her alone in his small study. The room smelled of damp.

'Would I!' The line was crackly and she could hear the sound of laughter in the distance. He was indeed in the pub. 'Didn't you find my note?'

'No. Where did you leave it?'

'In the boathouse. I thought you would go there to look for *Curlew*.'

'I did. But I didn't see a note. Never mind, I know where you are now. Max is going to drive me down to meet you tomorrow. I buried the sword, Leo, and Rosemary regained consciousness. That was why I was late. I had to drive Steve to the hospital. His car broke down.'

'So, the gods were pacified.' She could hear the smile in his voice. 'You are a brave woman, Zoë. Tell me all about it tomorrow. Max will look after you. He is a brick!'

The call ended, Zoë allowed herself to be shown up to a bedroom under the thatch; she was summoned down again almost at once for an improvised supper, as her host put it, quickly thrown together from some bits and pieces he had picked up at the village shop on the way home. Judging by the smell coming from his small kitchen it was improvised cordon bleu! She was handed a glass of wine, told to lay the table in the corner of the living room and in the course of the ensuing evening discovered that her host had known Leo for many years, had been the one to find Leo The Old Forge after the break-up of his marriage, that he himself was a widower, a passionate traveller and sailor, and that, as a retired

High Court judge, he would have no problem sorting out any repercussions reverberating from Jade and Jackson's wild accusations.

It was over coffee that he fixed her with a sudden gimlet gaze. 'You didn't drink your wine,' he said quietly.

She shook her head. 'I am sorry. I didn't feel like it. I could tell it was lovely.' She fell silent; the smell of the wine had made her feel nauseous. She looked up and met his eyes almost defiantly. He was, she had already realised, the kind of man in whom one could confide. 'I think I might be pregnant.'

'I see. And this was not, I take it, planned.' He did not seem shocked or even uncomfortable with her confidence.

'No.'

'Your husband's or Leo's?'

She didn't reply for several seconds. 'Leo's,' she said at last.

'Does he know?'

She shook her head. 'I've only just begun to suspect it myself.' She looked up at him. 'What do you think he would say if I am?'

She waited, watching his face.

'He misses his girls dreadfully,' he said at last. 'He was a good father. Is a good father,' he amended. 'She still rings him if there is a crisis and her current man fails her; she always expects Leo to drop everything, come to the rescue. And he does.'

'I would never try and come between them.'

'Nor could you.' He stood up, reached across the table, relieved her of her glass and began to sip it himself as he went over to the fire to throw on another log. 'Are you happy with the possibility of a baby?' he asked thoughtfully. He was standing looking down into the flames.

'Yes.' It was true, she realised. 'My husband never wanted children and had a vasectomy. I sort of went along with it without thinking it through very carefully. But lately –' She paused. She was remembering her dream. 'I suppose as I got older the time clock started to kick in. I realised that I had never made that decision for myself. I was regretting it enough to have dreams about it.' *When you have children, Zoë . . . your love for them must come first. Always.* Steve's voice echoed suddenly in her head. His words applied to Leo as much as her.

She came over and stood beside Max. 'I would never batten on Leo, Max. I am only just beginning to sense the possibility of freedom. If I am pregnant, and if I'm honest I hope I am, I want to cope on my own. I hope he will be there for me, but I would never want to do the little wifey thing again. I don't know if pirate molls can have small children in tow, but whatever I do, it will be on my terms.'

'He told me something very strange.' Max dropped into one of the two baggy old armchairs by the hearth. 'He thinks your destiny and his have been manipulated by the forces of Wyrd, the ancient spirits of fate and destiny. He was sitting watching the sun go down, he told me on the phone this afternoon, staring out at the river and he could feel them all around him. He said you had gone to bury a Saxon sword to appease an ancient curse. That sounds to me like his kind of woman.'

Zoë smiled. She was still staring down at the fire. 'You must think we are both dotty.'

'No. I've lived in Suffolk most of my life. From time to time we're all a bit duzzy, as we call it round here, but there's more out there than any of us will ever know for sure. If Leo believes it then he does so with good reason.'

'I'd like to think the spirits of Wyrd were with us.'

'And I'm sure they are, my dear. But be careful. They are powerful and not to be treated lightly.'

Next morning. Max greeted Zoë with a cup of tea and the news that he had spoken to the police in Woodbridge. 'The

482

accusation against Leo was withdrawn yesterday. You have nothing to worry about. It was made maliciously and the police are satisfied there is no truth to it. So, let us have breakfast, my dear, and then I am going to drive you into Woodbridge before we head down towards Felixstowe Ferry. 'We need to find out about the pregnancy. Better to know what we're dealing with, don't you agree?'

Putting off the moment for just a few more minutes she stood on the quayside watching the busy weekenders on their boats. She wasn't sure what drew her attention to the scarlet-hulled yacht motoring slowly down the freeway, but the sight of Ken at the wheel made sure she stayed staring at it. Almost at once she put a name to the stunning blonde standing at the mast, staring down-river ahead of them as they threaded their way between the moorings. 'Sylvia Sands,' she murmured. No wonder Ken had been so eager to be reasonable about their parting. 'Good luck, Ken,' she whispered. 'I hope she makes you happy.'

Shaking her head she turned towards the shops, leaving Max in the car. She was making for the chemist. Her purchase tucked into her handbag, she dived into the Ladies in the car park to do the test.

Returning to the car she closed the door and sat for a moment staring straight ahead through the windscreen. Max waited patiently, his hands relaxed on the wheel until she was ready to speak.

'It was positive,' she whispered.

'Are you pleased?'

'I think so.'

He turned and smiled at her. 'Good. Let's go and tell Leo.'

Just for a moment Rosemary had felt herself free. The fires had died and the gods were silent and she had found herself standing on a wild heath at the side of the burial mound. She could see the air all around her crisscrossed with gossamer

483

threads of light. Everything was linked. Everything had a pattern and a plan. She stared down at the earth of the grave and saw that the sword had been returned, but it was in the wrong place. It was in the wrong grave. It was where the murdered man and woman had lain. It wasn't in the hand of the warrior who owned it, who needed it.

She moved towards the mound, wanting to protest. Whoever had put it there had meant well but they had got it wrong. It had to go back in the right grave before it was found by the archaeologists and removed for ever. She reached out and saw the wavering light streaming from her fingertips. It was growing weaker. She was growing weaker. She could not move the sword.

Desperately she looked round. This was a place of magic, surrounded by spells, protected by charms and curses. She could see them now, the men and women who had gathered in this place and somehow she knew how they had died. He stood there, the tall man who had been the leader of his people, his illness shrugged off in death, his hand reaching out for the sword that lay on the ground out of his reach. There were those who had died at the hands of the Viking invaders, and a blonde young woman who carried her unborn child in her arms and at her side the swordsmith, the man who had made the sword Rosemary had pulled so carelessly from its sleeping place. There were generations of the dead; those who had died a natural death and those who had been murdered, a mother carrying her stillborn baby in her arms, men and women who had died in wars far afield and had been drawn back to the land of their birth and there, near her, stood the Anglo-Saxon sorcerer who had blessed and empowered this corner of a Suffolk field and forged from it an entry to the Otherworld.

The Christian priest Wulfric was beside him, as were generations of his successors, come to watch and to pray, and at last she understood. This was holy ground and she had wanted to defile it. She leaned forward in desperation and ran her fingers through the soil. It was light as dust. Her touch left no imprint at all.

She could see Steve, too, now, sitting at her bedside in the hospital as the alarms began to sound from the monitors and she watched in anguish as he began to cry. A nurse came and switched off the machines; she saw the woman put her hand gently on Steve's shoulder. Slowly the sound of his sobs began to fade into the distance as she felt herself drifting away.

Zoë told Leo about the baby as they stood on the beach looking out at the wild North Sea. The *Curlew* was moored round the corner in the river, sheltered from the sudden storm, and Max was waiting for them in the pub.

'It's a bit of a facer, isn't it?' she said at last, the wind whipping the words away. He hadn't spoken for several minutes, as they watched the waves crashing over the shingle banks.

He turned to look at her and she saw his face was wet, but whether from tears or from the veils of spume rearing up into the air and soaking the shingle she wasn't sure. He put his arm round her shoulders. 'It was your destiny to have a child,' he said. He was shouting against the roar of the wind and waves. 'That is what brought you to Suffolk. I am honoured that it is mine.'

She waited for him to say something else but he was staring out towards the horizon, watching the waves. So be it. She was content with that. She was a wild child now, independent and free, and her baby, whatever happened, was a pirate's child.

She realised suddenly that he had turned his back on the beach and was watching her. He grabbed her hand. 'Come on. Let's get to the pub and wet the baby's head. There can't be many children that have the Sisters of Wyrd as their godparents.'

* * *

Anlaf the sorcerer watched from the shadows as the archaeologists returned to the site of Lord Egbert's burial.

The curse went with the sword and the debt had been paid by the woman who had dragged it from the earth. An attempt had been made to put things right, to return the sword, even to bless the site. It was enough. He who had laid the curse, could lift it now.

This was a sacred place, it would always be a sacred place, a place of the ancestors, a place of dedication and of prayer.

He would mediate with the Sisters of Wyrd.

Out in the river the tide had turned. The mist was lying thick over the saltings. With heavy beating wings a formation of swans flew down the river towards the sea.

In Norse legend swans carried the restless Viking soul to the hall of the Valkyries. The ship would not return. The river was at peace.

Author's Note

There is no Timperton Hall or Hanley Heath and the events in this story are purely fictional. But . . . a ghostly ship does appear occasionally in the estuary of one of the Essex rivers. Maybe there is one on the Deben as well.

Sutton Hoo, is of course, real, as were the Viking raids along the eastern seaboard of these islands. AD 865 was the year that the *'micel hæðen here'* or great heathen army, led by Ivar the Boneless, headed for eastern England. As *The Anglo-Saxon Chronicle* puts it, somewhat laconically, 'And this same year came a great host to England and took winter quarters from the East Anglians . . . ' In the following years they were to travel north leaving 'immense slaughter' in their wake.

Thank you again to the team at HarperCollins, to Susan Opie and Lucy Ferguson, my brilliant editors, and to Carole Blake, my agent, as always my support and right-hand woman.

For further notes, photos and information about the book and its location please see my website www.barbara-erskine.com